Praise for Kate Thompson

'Inspiring tales of courage in the face of hardship'
Mail on Sunday

'A lively authentic social history . . . a hair-raising,
but always warmhearted tale'
My Weekly

'Astonishing'
Radio 5 Live

'Celebrates the lives of tough wartime matriarchs'
ITV News

'Crammed full of fascinating stories'
BBC2 Steve Wright

'Kate Thompson writes books that make you laugh
and make you cry, sometimes at the same time. You
cannot put them down. I advise you to read them all!'
Anita Dobson

Kate Thompson

Kate Thompson an award-winning journalist, ghost-writer and novelist who has spent the past two decades in the UK mass market and book publishing industry. Over the past eight years Kate has written nine fiction and non-fiction titles, three of which have made the *Sunday Times* top ten bestseller list. *Secrets of the Homefront Girls* is her tenth book.

KATE
THOMPSON

Secrets of the Homefront Girls

HODDER

First published in Great Britain in 2019 by Hodder & Stoughton
An Hachette UK company

5

Copyright © Kate Thompson 2019

A CIP catalogue record for this title is available from the British Library

Paperback ISBN 9781473698116
eBook ISBN 9781473698123

Typeset in Plantin Light 12/15.25 pt by
Palimpsest Book Production Limited, Falkirk, Stirlingshire

Printed and bound in Great Britain by Clays Ltd, Elcograf S.p.A.

Hodder & Stoughton policy is to use papers that are natural,
renewable and recyclable products and made from wood grown in sustainable
forests. The logging and manufacturing processes are expected to conform
to the environmental regulations of the country of origin.

Hodder & Stoughton Ltd
Carmelite House
50 Victoria Embankment
London EC4Y 0DZ

www.hodder.co.uk

I would like to dedicate this book to all the women of the East End who fill my head with stories and my heart with admiration

We cannot leave men to fight this war alone. Total war makes heavy demands ... The slightest hint of a drooping spirit yields a point to the enemy. Never must careless grooming reflect a 'don't care' attitude ... We must never forget that good looks and good morale are the closest of companions. Put your best face forward.

Yardley advert, 1942

PART ONE

Monday, 4th September 1939

Stratford, East London

I

Lily

Lily Gunn gripped her small attaché case, drew in a deep breath and turned into the Shoot. As she picked her way over the dung-smothered cobbles, she had the strangest sensation she was being watched by hundreds of pairs of eyes, peering out from behind Nottingham Lace curtains. She could almost hear the whispers lapping at the old brick walls.

She's back!

News of her return would doubtless be halfway round stinking Stratford come dinnertime.

Lily shivered and pulled her coat around her shoulders. The smoke-choked sky above her seemed to have shrunk to the size of a matchbox. She'd forgotten how claustrophobic her childhood neighbourhood was, especially now it was wrapped up in anti-blast tape and barricaded behind sandbags.

The narrow four-storey terraced houses, coated in centuries of industrial soot, bowed inwards into a central square. Lily shuddered as invisible fingers tightened against her throat. All the grime and filth of a hundred years seemed pressed into every crevice and brick. In the middle of the square stood a tiny 18th-century church, slumped in a pool of darkness, smothered in ivy and surrounded by a cluster of graves. There had been violent thunderstorms over London last night after Chamberlain's announcement, and the sodden graveyard almost seemed to be weeping.

War had been declared yesterday, but nothing had changed in this small grey corner in the furthest reaches of East London. Tucked away behind Angel Lane Market, this was the Shoot – a maze of alleys and narrow streets that could trap a stranger for a long time. No one strayed down the Shoot by accident.

Lily had often heard her childhood home referred to as one of the most notorious slums in Stratford: a place where, rumour had it, you'd come in through Cat's Alley, and your bootlaces would be missing by the time you came out the other end; an area known by the local constabulary as 'the bunk', such was its capacity to hide a villain or two.

To her knowledge, though, apart from the odd merchant navy man getting rolled when he came up from the docks, and the gambling pockets that popped up from time to time, crime here was non-existent. Law-abiding misfits were safe. Lily knew nothing happened in the Shoot without a certain woman's say-so.

A pale sun was struggling to penetrate the curdled sky, but the blackout blinds were already down and the mothers of the street were out, scrubbing their doorsteps as if their very lives depended on it.

Lily snorted as she sidestepped a pail of soapy water. Hitler might be trampling across borders, but God forbid you be branded the filthy cow of the Shoot. Give it half an hour and the lanes would be covered in a flannelly carbolic-scented heat as washday proper began.

The women of the square had high standards and Lily knew who set them. *Her.* Nell Gunn. The Shoot's chief female. The woman they respectfully called 'Auntie'.

But to Lily, Mother.

Lily's gaze swivelled to the graveyard and her heart knocked against her ribs. How can you love and fear a person all at once? Time had not dulled the red-hot mass of conflicting emotions churning her insides. Six years she had been away from this place. *Six!* So many times she had steeled herself to make the journey across London to see her family. Once, last Christmas, she'd even got as far as the bridge at Bow, clutching at brightly wrapped presents and false bravado, but her nerve had failed her when the smoking chimney stacks of Stratford hove into sight. So she had blamed her absence on work, throwing up excuse after excuse. Somehow, it had always seemed easier to stay away than to confront the turmoil of her past.

But now, this blasted war had forced her hand. The time for excuses was over.

'Come on, you silly chump,' she muttered to herself. 'You can do this.'

Lily's eyes roamed the tombstones until she spotted the familiar figure. She had imagined something would have changed in all these years, but sure enough, her mum was right where she had expected her to be. On her hands and knees, tugging weeds from the rank earth of the graveyard. Nell Gunn tended to that graveyard like it was a prize allotment.

Lily swore her mother had eyes in the back of her head because, in that moment, she rose up like a battered old sail and turned to face her, unblinking. Nothing about Stratford's mightiest matriarch had changed. Same deep-set penetrating green eyes, same coarse blonde curls scraped under a turban, the face underneath as hard as a hatchet. My God, she even had on the same starched pinny she'd worn the day Lily left, albeit a little more faded. Even soldiers got a new uniform every few years, didn't they?

'Coming in for a brew then, or what?' Nell sniffed, looking

her eldest daughter up and down as if she'd seen her only yesterday.

'Hello, Mum,' Lily said weakly, suddenly feeling like she had when Nell had caught her smoking aged thirteen, not a bit like the confident twenty-three-year-old woman she now was. 'You don't seem all that surprised to see me.'

Nell shrugged and pulled a Craven 'A' cigarette from under her turban. She lit up and inhaled deeply.

'When we heard the news on the wireless yesterday, I says to your father you'd be home.' She blew the smoke out on a sigh and picked a bit of lint off her apron. 'Fucking Hitler . . .'

Anger iced her voice. 'Give me a couple of bricks, a mallet and half an hour alone with that man.'

Lily winced at her mother's coarse tongue. Everything had changed, and yet, nothing had changed. She took in Nell's well-upholstered body, wrapped up in the ubiquitous pinny, her red, blistered hands and mouth as tight as a white-knuckle fist. Her mother had a fearsome reputation that was, for the most part, well-earned. No one wanted to stare down the barrel of an irate Nell Gunn.

'So how comes you're home? They lay you off?'

'Not exactly,' Lily replied cagily. 'They've had a reshuffle of staff, on account of the hostilities.'

Nell's sudden laugh was like a motorcar backfiring.

'Hostilities is it now?' she mocked. 'How la-di-da! They put a plum in your mouth down Bond Street?' Her gravelly voice dropped an octave. 'Let's call it what it is, shall we? War!'

'They're relocating me back to Carpenters Road,' Lily continued, ignoring her mother's acid aside, 'as a charge hand. An advancement they're calling it, but it doesn't feel that way. More like a step backwards.'

Lily thought of her job as a sales girl in Yardley's gleaming modern showroom and salon at 33 Old Bond Street, and of her small but comfortable lodgings in Hammersmith.

There had been a gentle rhythm to her life there under the tutelage of Miss Olive Carmen. Close her eyes and she could still see the frieze floral decoration, the queues that stretched round the block for their famous cosmetics. The scent of lavender, which drifted through the graceful salon, lingered in her imagination.

'Well, welcome back to the real world, girl,' said her mother, wiping out her memories like vanishing cream.

'I'd say you're bleedin' lucky to make charge hand at the factory. No one gets made up off the floor. Look at your sister, five years she's been there now and she's still on the belt in the lipstick room.'

Out of nowhere, hot tears burned Lily's eyes and angrily she dashed them away.

Nell's face softened, and she reached out.

'Come on, love, look on the bright side. Renee and Frankie'll be made up to have you home, as will your father. It ain't all bad.'

'I'm all right,' Lily murmured, recoiling from her mother's touch and plucking a handkerchief from her sleeve. 'I've just got grit in my eye. I'd forgotten how rotten the air is round here.'

Nell's expression remained impassive, obscured by the clouds of blue smoke that curled round her face.

'You still ain't forgiven me, have you?'

A rag and boner clattered by, the driver shifting the reins to one hand, so he could tip his cap to Nell.

'Morning, Auntie.'

Nell nodded back as she mashed her fag end out in the gutter.

'I did what I had to do, Lily,' she said softly, her eyes dark in the pallid grey light.

Lily stared bleakly out over the graveyard. 'I know, Mum, but it's hard being back. Surely you can understand why?'

But her mother had no chance to answer, for just then the steam hooter from the gasworks shrieked out. Six a.m. Another hour and all the Carpenters Road factories would be going off, wrenching the workers of Stratford from their beds.

'Right then,' said Nell briskly, clearly relieved at the interruption. Like most women of her generation, born in the shadows of the Victorian East End, emotions were not something Nell Gunn was comfortable discussing. 'The nippers'll be arriving soon. Frankie's up, Renee's out fetching the bread. I've still gotta make Snowball a cuppa and a bit of breakfast.'

'He still here?' Lily sniffed, staring over at the tatty bundle of rags that was slowly stirring into life. 'Why isn't he with the other tramps down Itchy Park?'

Bundled under a pile of coats in the church porch was Snowball, the local tramp. Life was fragile down the Shoot and for most, there was more week than money. Five services kept them going – goods on tick, the pawnshop, the tallyman, and a baker's on the Broadway that would sell Shoot families three loaves of bread and a lump of bread pudding out the back door for sixpence. The fifth service was Nell Gunn.

'Don't you look down your nose at him, madam,' Nell snapped. 'The only thing that separates you from him is the mud and blood of the trenches.'

'All right, Mum,' said Lily wearily, 'don't start.'

'You coming in then, or what?'

'I'm not stopping. I got a room in East Ham.'

'Suit yourself,' Nell replied. 'But make sure you come for your tea.'

'Maybe.'

Lily turned smartly and hurried off through the Shoot so her mother wouldn't see the tears that were now streaking down her cheeks. She had hoped that time away would've blunted her fear and shame, that somehow it wouldn't matter any more. But just being here again in the stench and grime of matriarchal Stratford had set off a wave of emotion that threatened to swamp her.

How could she set foot in that house again, so choked with memories? How could she ever undo what she had seen?

She shot a last look at the gravestones emerging from the tenebrous light.

Secrets. *Secrets*. Everywhere. Stinking Stratford was built on them.

2

Renee

Renee Gunn's breath came in gasps as she ran fast . . . faster still and with a sudden lunge, leapt up onto the back of the lorry that was trundling down Carpenters Road.

Gripping hard onto the tailboard, she whooped with all the bravado of a nineteen-year-old, laughing as her blonde curls whipped round her face. Only a chump would fork out on bus fares to the factory.

Carpenters Road at 7.45 a.m. was bedlam. Cranes loading and offloading barges from the canal next to the street, screeching and clashing, men shouting, factory girls in turbans streaming down the street, smoking and giggling. Horses and carts, milkmen, buses and, over it all, the incessant blasting of a dozen or so factory hooters . . .

This was Renee's kingdom, the noxious industrial backwater of Stratford, better known to all as Stink Bomb Alley. Bethnal Green had its blind beggar, Bow its bells and Whitechapel its Ripper, but Stinky Stratford made stuff. And of that, Renee was immensely proud. Her corner of East London might have been the poor relation of its famous neighbours, but its factories and firms kept generations of families in work, churning out goods for the whole country.

Factories flashed past in a blur as the lorry rattled under a low railway bridge, straight through the dirty puddle of stagnant water that always congealed there, showering a group of Clarnico sweet factory workers walking by.

'Time you took a shower, girls!' Renee hollered. 'But then, I always knew you was filthy!'

'Sod you, Renee Gunn!' screamed one of the girls, wringing out her sopping dress skirts.

'Charming!' Renee grinned back, flicking up her middle finger.

Renee Gunn was the blue-eyed, blonde-haired golden girl of Yardley's, cruising through life with a born insouciance and switchblade charm.

As the lorry picked up speed down the twisty-turny street, the stench of boiling animal carcasses from the abattoir mingled with the sickly scent from the marzipan factory.

The sound of the hooters began to fade away. Bugger it, that must mean it was nearly eight a.m. They'd be closing the gates any minute.

As they drew level with Yardley's neighbouring factory, Berger's, a chorus of wolf whistles filled the air.

'Aye-aye! Up the Lavender Girls!'

There he was, smoking his morning fag. Alfie Buckle, a so-called 'Berger's baby' who lived near the paint factory in one of the tied properties. Alfie was definitely the alpha-male of the factory – tall, blue-eyed, with a body honed in a boxing gym.

'Oi-oi, lads, here she is, Stratford's answer to Jean Harlow. Get down here and give us a kiss, Renee Gunn.'

'You wanna kiss? Come here and get it.'

'Very well,' he said with a reckless grin, grinding out his fag and sprinting after the lorry.

'You mad bugger!' Renee screamed as he leapt up beside her with ease and, gripping her tightly round her waist, kissed her firmly on the lips as a red bus flashed past them.

Renee drew back, her face breaking open into a wide smile.

'You stink of fags.'

'Just as well you smell so sweet then,' he grinned, running his hand dangerously low down the curve of her back before resting it on her bottom.

'I don't half fancy you, Renee Gunn. Come out with me tonight? They're showing *The Ice Follies* with Joan Crawford down the Gaff. That's a picture girls like, ain't it?'

'Maybe I will, maybe I won't,' Renee quipped back.

The lorry pulled over to the kerb.

'I know you're on the back, Renee Gunn, now clear off,' called the driver.

'Cheers, Fred,' she called, as she and Alfie jumped off.

'So . . . Tonight?' Alfie persisted.

'Very well,' she agreed, dazzling him with a smile she knew showed off her dimples.

'Smashing! Oh, and made sure you wear this.' He pulled a small package from his pocket.

'Alfie! Evening in Paris! It's my favourite. Wherever did you get it?'

'Boardman's, half a bleedin' week's wages, it was. But you're worth it. Eight p.m. Don't be late.'

He planted a final kiss on her lips, then turned and sprinted back up Carpenters Road.

Renee was still grinning as she pelted up to the factory gates.

Sandwiched between a fishmeal factory and a chemical works, Yardley and Co Ltd perfume and cosmetics manufacturer was a lavender-scented oasis in a cloud of stench.

The Victorian Factory Act had scarcely addressed the dizzying array of hazardous chemical processes most local factories employed. The area was built on the misery of older firms: poison gas, blinding acid spills and chemicals to crumble your bones and rinse your skin blue.

But rising up like a shining beacon out of a grim swamp of sweated labour was Yardley's. Renee felt a sense of pride she found hard to put into words that she worked for such a modern firm, one with space, a subsidised canteen and unheard-of staff welfare. They were also sticklers for punctuality amongst their workers, who were known locally as the Lavender Girls.

The elaborate wrought-iron gate slammed shut in Renee's face.

'Oh Bert, do a girl a favour?' she begged. 'I'll lose fifteen if you don't let us in now. Peerless'll have my guts for a laundry line!'

The old security guard, immaculate in his navy tunic, sighed extravagantly as he unlocked the heavy metal gate and swung it back open. 'Bleedin' hell, Renee Gunn, you'll do for me . . .'

'You're an angel,' she said, slipping a carton of cigarettes into his pocket. 'From Mum.'

Renee sprinted into the cobbled yard, past the teams of burly men standing on a raised level, open to the yard, rolling heavy wooden barrels onto great haulage lorries. She knew they'd be watching her and she didn't like to disappoint, so she hitched up her skirt a fraction as she ran.

'Another inch, Renee!' bellowed a voice.

'Not today, you saucy sod,' she grinned, blowing them a kiss as she slipped in through the factory door.

On account of her lateness, she'd missed the great rush towards the board on the entry wall, where clocking-in discs were located. Renee grabbed hers and clattered up the iron staircase, one floor up to the lipstick room cloakroom. With one hand she lit a fag, with the other she grabbed her deep burgundy overalls. Hastily buttoning them up, the cigarette clamped between her teeth, she pinned her blonde curls beneath a white turban, piling them up like cream on a trifle.

Remembering it was Nan's last day and therefore competition for Yardley's highest turban would be steep, she grabbed a scarf from her locker and bundled it under the turban, before turning to the mirror and polishing her teeth with her finger.

She took one last long drag on the cigarette, before mashing it out under the wooden bench and wafting her arm about to try to get rid of the smell.

'Oh sod it, if you're gonna be late . . .' she muttered. Turning back to the mirror, she fished out her Yardley lipstick in poppy red and slicked on a fresh coating. A quick touch-up with the Max Factor Pan-Cake she kept in her locker . . .

'Now I'm ready for work!' she announced to no one, snapping the compact shut and heading towards the belt, attempting to slip into her place unseen.

The hand on her shoulder was surprisingly heavy.

'That's fifteen minutes docked, Miss Gunn, and if I find you've been smoking in the cloakroom, I shall deduct a further fifteen. Now get on with your work,' ordered Miss Peerless, the lipstick room supervisor, whose age was uncertain, but the girls estimated her to be at least forty and therefore ancient.

'Miserable old cow,' Renee muttered under her breath as she slid into her place on the belt next to her best mate, Nan Rogers.

'And girls, one more thing before I start up the machines,' called the supervisor, clapping her hands together. 'After morning tea break, senior management require us all to be assembled upstairs in the canteen for an emergency meeting.'

'Do you think they're gonna lay off jobs 'cause of the war?' Renee asked worriedly as the machinery started up with a great groan and the conveyor belt shuddered into life.

'Search me,' shrugged Nan, covering her fingertips with little white paper thimbles to protect her skin. 'Don't much care anyhow. It's me last day, ain't that right, girls?'

The rest of the girls on the belt – Betty, Joanie, Joycie and

Mavis – didn't need any encouragement and soon their voices were drowning out the machinery.

Knees up Mother Brown, Knees up Mother Brown.
Under the table you must go. Ee-aye, Ee-aye, Ee-aye-oh
If I catch you bending –'

'– all right, all right,' laughed Nan. 'My wedding is more than a chance for you lot to get on the drink you know. Me and my Jimmy will be pledging our love and solemnizing our vows.'

Blank faces all round.

'But they'll be gin afterwards, right?' asked Betty.

Renee had to laugh. They might be a touch over enthusiastic, but the girls had done Nan proud. The whole belt was covered in streamers, balloons and gifts.

'You wait until tea break,' Renee winked.

Soon the lipsticks were flying down the belt and production was in full throttle, but the girls' incessant chatter didn't let up. They didn't need to stay silent in order to concentrate. They'd all worked their way up from service girls to the most coveted job in Yardley's, in the lipstick room. No one really knew why it had such status, beyond the fact that traditionally the girls in the lipstick department were the best lookers and, without doubt, had the highest turbans.

In a room packed full of smashing-looking girls, Renee and her childhood friend Nan were the belles of the lipstick room. When they had taken their burgundy overalls home and altered them so they skimmed every curve on their body, Joycie, Joanie and even little Irene, the fourteen-year-old service girl, had soon followed suit. When Nan and Renee had taken to filling out their turbans with smalls and socks to give them more height, soon everyone was doing it. When Nan started sending off to Hollywood studios for signed photographs of the stars, it triggered a craze that swept through all one thousand of the Yardley girls down Carpenters Road.

Every floor at Yardley's factory housed a different production unit. Powder and soap workers were on the ground floor, distinguished by their white overalls. Next door to lipstick on the first floor were creams and brilliantines, who wore a dreary brown. The only other department Renee, Nan and the girls envied was that of the perfume girls on the top floor, who wore emerald green and smelt permanently of the English Lavender Water they helped pack, unless they happened to be packing April Violets, in which case they got called 'Cat's Nats'.

It didn't really matter what floor you worked on, though, as all the girls of Yardley's were united by their three main preoccupations. Boys. Sex. Make-up. Most of the girls had begun working at fourteen, fresh from school, and their formidable education in the ways of the world had continued on the factory floor.

Renee snuck a sideways glance at her old pal Nan and felt sadness, and if she were honest, a twinge of envy. They had shared everything together, even starting at Yardley's on the same day when she was fourteen and Nan was sixteen. Now twenty-one, Nan was going off to marry her childhood sweetheart, Jimmy Connor, before he went into the Navy. As was custom, she would have to hand in her clocking-in card, as Yardley's wouldn't employ girls once they had married.

'Nan, what am I gonna do for fun when you're a respectable married lady?' Renee groaned. 'You'll come and see us for dinner, yeah? We'll still go for mie and pash?' she grinned, throwing in their secret silly language. 'Or chish and fips?'

'You're joking, ain't yer?' Nan exclaimed. 'I won't wanna be seen consorting with factory girls once I'm married.' She tapped her slender waistline. ''Sides I can't eat that food no more. My Jimmy don't want me getting fat.'

'Ooh, you stuck up cow,' Renee laughed, poking her in the ribs. 'Just 'cause you're moving to East Ham, don't be thinking you're a cut above.'

Nan's mum and stepdad had spent a small fortune renting them a flat in the more upmarket neighbourhood of East Ham. Despite being born in the Shoot, everyone knew Mrs Rogers had delusions of grandeur and, when it came to her little girl, only the best would do.

Nan shrieked with laughter and cocked her little finger up in the air. 'Too good for the likes of you.'

'You'll be sewing curtains round yer keyhole next,' Renee teased.

'Seriously, though, Renee sweetheart,' Nan said, her smile tailing off as she picked up the sterilising flame to level off the end of the lipstick she was holding.

'Don't expect to see too much of me. My Jimmy likes everything just so. We're getting the keys to our new place later, so I'll be tied up with making it lovely for him and being the perfect wife . . .' She batted her eyelashes and lowered her breathy voice.

'Jimmy leaves for sea the day after we marry and I ain't gonna let him leave the bedroom.' She winked. 'He wants me in the family way before he leaves.'

Pinned to her tunic was Jimmy's regimental Naval Crown badge, which, like so many others, Nan wore as a sweetheart brooch.

Renee felt deflated. She found Nan's departure far more unsettling than the announcement on the wireless yesterday morning that they were at war with Germany, as selfish as she knew that was. Anyhow, the talk down the Shoot was that it would all be over by Christmas. Renee's father himself had said so, so it was bound to be true. In fact, he'd even trotted off to place an illegal bet on it straight after the declaration. Mind you, he'd bet on two flies crawling up a wall. But still, for Renee the breaking apart of their tight-knit little friendship felt more catastrophic to her personally than a foreign dictator invading a country she'd never really heard of.

'Honestly, girls, I'm so happy I could burst,' Nan announced to the entire belt, similarly oblivious to the shadow of war. 'I really hope you all find the happiness that me and my Jimmy have.'

Joycie sighed.

'Oh Nan, what I wouldn't do to be you. Come back after the wedding and give us the lowdown, won't you?'

She lowered her voice as Miss Peerless walked past.

'I wanna known *everything*.'

'Leave off, you nosy cow,' Nan laughed breezily, but there was an edge to her voice that only Renee detected. Nerves, she supposed. For girls like them, who'd spent their whole lives having the fear of God drummed into them about getting 'in trouble', Renee wondered if Nan was scared at the prospect of actually doing 'it' and what went where. For all their cocky chat, she suspected Nan was as clueless as she.

'Least you won't have to prick your finger and pretend to have bled, like Daisy who works in brilliantine did after she got married,' whispered Joanie.

'She never?' gasped little Irene as she scurried past the belt on an errand.

Joanie nodded, eyes wide as pebbles. 'That's what Sandra in soap reckoned . . . Anyhow, we got our Nan to tell us what's what now, ain't we? How else are us girls gonna know how to get a fella's pecker up.'

She raised her little finger suggestively and the whole belt fell about.

'We could always ask *him*,' Joycie winked, as the poor hapless service boy from the stockroom came in wheeling a large wooden barrel of animal fat for the lipstick churn.

A chorus of whistles filled the room as eighteen-year-old Walter Smith, nicknamed Whiffy Smithy, walked past the belts.

'Show us your muscles,' called out a curvy girl by the name of Fat Lou on the lipstick-packing bench.

'Oi, Smithy, can you help out?' hollered Joanie. 'Only, now we're at war, us girls need to know how to keep a fella's morale up. Any suggestions?'

Smithy took one look at Renee, who everyone knew he was hopelessly in love with, and his cheeks scorched as red as beet. A great cackle of laughter rose up over the belt, with all the girls hooting like a pack of hyenas. Poor Smithy! He was shy at the best of times, but in Renee's presence he just couldn't seem to control the colour of his face.

'Why you asking me, girls?' he replied. 'How would I know?' His good nature was born out of an instinct for survival. Being one of the few lone males on the factory floor meant an acceptance that you would always be the butt of the joke.

'How comes you always answer a question with a question?' asked Joanie.

'Do I?' he joked, and the girls screeched even louder.

'Stop it,' Joycie protested. 'I'm gonna wet myself.'

Somewhere at the back of Renee's mind lurked the uneasy thought that perhaps the girls imagined that if they laughed loud enough, they could drown out the uncomfortable new reality they had awoken to that morning . . .

At 10.30 a.m. the machines shut down and a cantankerous tea lady with a penchant for snuff shuffled in wheeling her trolley.

'You girls,' she muttered. 'Everything's funny, even when another bloody war's been declared.'

Little Irene had been round earlier collecting everyone's tea break orders, so in no time, they were all polishing off mugs of strong tea and crusty white dripping-filled rolls.

'A toast, to our girl Nan,' declared Renee, holding up her tea mug. 'You're a bloody pain in the backside at times, but I ain't half gonna miss you.'

'To Nan,' came back a chorus of excited voices.

'Up the Yardley's,' Nan laughed, giggling as all thirty girls in the lipstick room descended, smothering her uniform with ribbons, bows and bright paper flowers. As was customary, every woman that left to get married could expect to be decorated like a tree at Christmas. They made merry hell at her, scoffing and tickling her ribs, until every available bit of her tunic was covered and Nan was helpless with laughter.

'I gotta get the bus later,' Nan protested, as Renee attached a bright silver balloon to the top of her turban.

And then, checking the supervisor's back was turned, Renee fetched the bottle of whisky she'd nicked from her dad's supply and set about topping up all the girls mugs.

'Hell's teeth,' said Nan, shuddering after she took a swig, 'no wonder they say as how it puts lead in your pencil.' And then, arching one pencilled brow: 'Not that I reckon my Jimmy'll need that.' A gale of filthy laughter echoed round the lipstick room.

'Come on then, knock it back,' urged Renee. She felt her duties as chief bridesmaid extended to getting the bride-to-be pissed on her last day in the firm. In the past, girls leaving to get married were made to down as much alcohol as humanly possible down the Carpenters Arms in the space of a tea break, but the forelady banned that after a bride-to-be called Patsy on the talcum machine drank so many port and lemons, she accidentally pressed the wrong button, sending an enormous cloud of English Lavender talcum powder billowing out of the chute instead of up. The clear-up had taken days.

''Ere,' said Fat Lou, wincing as she swallowed back her tea, 'who do you reckon our new charge hand'll be?'

'I still don't know why Sal decided to join the WAAF,' Joanie sniffed.

'Uniform most likely,' Nan replied. 'If I weren't getting married, I'd almost consider it myself.'

'Oh, let's not talk about the war,' Renee groaned, 'it's all anyone can bleedin' chat about, and like me dad said, it'll be done with by Christmas. Let's talk about where my Alfie's taking me tonight instead.'

'Behind the Regal,' Joanie quipped.

'Do you mind?' Renee said with mock offence. 'You know I don't let him go beyond the dotted line.'

'Rumour has it,' said Joycie, leaning in, 'that Elaine in the typing pool has gone *way* beyond the dotted line with Billy from dispatch.'

'That's office girls for you,' declared Fat Lou. 'All fur coat, no knickers.'

Miss Peerless glared over as they collapsed into yet more fits of helpless laughter.

Suddenly they were interrupted by a small cough.

A service girl, green as a gardener's thumb by the looks of her, stared up at Renee.

'I-I am sorry to interrupt,' she stammered. 'But could you possibly tell me where I can get a long weight from?'

She glanced down at her list. 'I'm also looking for a rubber mallet for the brilliantine machine. I'm in a bit of a hurry as I also need to go to the personnel office.'

The girls glanced at each other, before doubling over. The whisky was clearly beginning to take effect, as Nan laughed so hard she had to dribble her tea back in the mug.

'What is so funny?' the girl asked, her large liquid eyes reproachful.

'Oh sweetheart, is it your first day, by any chance?' Renee asked. 'You're a new Lavender Girl, are ya?'

'How do you know?'

'Come on, I think you've been tricked, darlin'.'

'Oh, I see,' she said, confused. 'The joke is on me.'

Renee took in the trim, slight figure, the solemn brown eyes and the sad little smile that hovered about the corners of her lips, and felt her usual chippiness melt. Despite her youth, there was something strangely old-fashioned about the girl. She may have been in the overalls of a service girl, but her eyes, the colour of smoked glass, belonged to an old woman.

'Tell you what, want me to show you where the office is?'

'Oh, thank you, yes please,' she said, relieved.

'You may take her to the office, Miss Gunn,' said Miss Peerless, looming up behind as the bell to signal end of tea break rang. 'But I warn you, if you're using this as a cigarette break, I shall know.'

Renee rolled her eyes as Miss Peerless walked off, and stuck out her hand.

'Don't mind the dragon. I'm Renee Gunn. Pleased to meet you. Looks like you're stuck with me then. What's your name, sweetheart?'

3

Esther

'E-Esther Orwell,' she stammered. What was wrong with her? When faced with such a vision of glamour, Esther couldn't seem to get her words out straight. Although, to be honest, since she and her mother had arrived in Stratford three days ago, after a long boat journey from Holland to Harwich, she didn't know if she was on her head or her heels.

Esther felt totally dazzled by this group of confident girls with their tight red tunics, jaunty turbans and loud, easy laughter.

But it was Renee who seemed to hold a hypnotic effect. She had the most perfect complexion Esther had ever seen, with a soft velvet bloom to her skin and cornflower blue eyes.

'You have eyelashes like feathers!' she blurted before she could stop herself.

'Yeah, she buys 'em off the market,' quipped a slightly glassy-eyed girl who, strangely enough, had a silver balloon stuck on her head.

'Ignore her,' Renee laughed, 'that's Nan, she's only sore 'cause she ain't allowed to eat pie and mash no more.'

'These are the girls on my belt: Betty, Joanie, Joycie and Mavis. Little Irene's a service girl, like you.'

And then she was off, sashaying across the floor, reeling off names as she passed by each belt. Esther had to scurry to keep up with her. In all her fifteen years, she had never seen anything like it.

One side of the room was filled with half-a-dozen heavy lumps of machinery, attached to a central dais. Next to each machine was a large, stainless-steel drum of constantly churning creamy liquid, in different shades from pink to red.

As they passed by, the pungent smell of the liquid hit Esther's nose.

'Pig's blood,' Renee remarked cheerfully. 'Stinks, don't it?'

'Don't worry, it's not really,' she added, seeing Esther's shocked face. 'That's the lipstick, it's what we call it before they add the perfume.'

The liquid ran through a pipe into the machine and came out the other end in shiny moulds, where teams of girls worked seamlessly to pack them, each lipstick checked for quality, before being passed on to the next girl, who levelled it off with a sterilising flame, before it trundled round to have a cute lid, complete with a red wax bumble-bee popped on top.

Dexterous fingers worked seamlessly as they darted to and fro over the machines and belts. Loud music blared out from a tannoy system. Those that weren't singing were chattering away ten to the dozen. No one seemed much concerned that war had just been announced. Or about the fierce heat either, Esther thought, plucking at her collar. The unseasonably warm September sunshine was beating through the strips of anti-blast tape on the factory windows, its broiling heat causing condensation to trickle down the walls.

The smell of warm animal fat and stale sweat, combined with whatever that unholy stench was blowing in from the open window, was making Esther feel unwell. This was not the vision of Yardley's her mum had promised her.

Her head was spinning by the time they reached the other side of the room, where long lines of girls sat at trestle tables, surrounded by ribbon, cellophane and labels.

'This is Fat Lou and her team, they're responsible for packing,' said Renee, pointing to a chubby, jolly-looking girl who was busy counting boxes and chalking them up on a board. 'May, Joan, Irene B, Kathleen, Rita, Gladys, Minnie and lastly, Irene C . . . Meet Esther.'

'All right, darlin'. Welcome to Stinking Stratford,' said Irene B.

Was it her, or did this factory seem to be staffed almost entirely by girls called Irene?

Esther was relieved when Renee swung open two double doors and they entered the cool of an iron stairwell.

'I'll take you up to the offices.' A bright smile broke open her face. 'But first, a quick fag.'

She pushed open the door to the brilliantine room cloakroom and tapped the side of her nose.

'I thought you worked in the lipstick room?' Esther puzzled.

'I do, but smoking in the cloakroom's strictly forbidden. Better they get the blame than us,' she winked, sitting down on a bench and sparking up a Craven 'A'.

'Want one?' she asked, shaking out the packet and thrusting one at her.

'I'm not allowed to smoke. My mother, a nurse, she says they are no good for your health.'

Renee shrugged and stuffed the packet back in her overalls pocket. 'She's got some funny notions.'

'Are you not worried?' Esther asked, shooting a nervous glance at the door, 'Miss Peerless said—'

'What Miss Peerless don't know, won't hurt her,' Renee insisted with a devil-may-care grin.

Esther could sense Renee scrutinising her as she blew out three smoke rings, her red mouth a perfect O.

'Where you from then? I mean, you don't sound as if you're from East London.'

'No. I am from Vienna.'

'Blimey. You're a long way from home. How comes?'

Esther gripped the edge of the slatted wooden bench.

'In a word. Hitler. He does not seem to be very fond of us Jews.'

'Aaah,' said Renee, for the first time looking uncertain of herself. 'Do you mind me asking?'

'No. My father, he is a laboratory assistant, and my mother, she is a nurse. They both worked at the Children's Clinic at the University of Vienna Hospital. In Vienna, one in five residents are Jewish, as were many of the faculty members who taught at the University.'

'You'll feel right at home in the East End then, lots of Jewish firms,' Renee remarked. 'Good as gold they are. "Make a friend with a Jew, and you've made a friend for life", my mum reckons.'

'I wish everyone shared your mother's beliefs,' Esther replied. 'At first, they stripped us of our rights of citizenship, our jobs and our homes, and then came Anschluss . . .'

'The joining of Austria and Germany,' she added, seeing the look of confusion on Renee's face.

'And life . . .' She broke off, picking the hem of her tunic. 'Life became unbearable.'

'So how . . . Why Stratford?' asked Renee intrigued.

'My mother has an uncle who runs a milliner's along Angel Lane. Benjamin Cohen. Maybe you know him?'

'Course I do, his hats are the business.'

'Well, he could provide proof of employment for my mother, but not so for my father.'

Esther closed her eyes and saw the swastika flags fluttering from balconies, the smoke, broken glass and leaping torches. The elderly Jewish man in her block of flats forced from his home in his nightclothes by a phalanx of stormtroopers and forced to scrub the pavement . . . The wild exodus from her beloved city as hundreds of Jewish families mobbed the emigration agency.

'We were lucky to find safe passage here and work.'

'And your father?' Renee asked. 'Where's he?'

'He was arrested at home, taken to a special collection point then transferred by train to a work camp to "perform detention". Whatever that means . . .'

Her voice tailed off.

'What's a work camp?' asked Renee.

'Time will tell. Until then, we have hope,' Esther said, forcing a smile and then, anxious to change the subject: 'Now tell me what I need to know so that I don't fall prey to any more of these tricks.'

'Well,' said Renee, shuffling up next to Esther and placing an arm round her. So close Esther could smell her English Lavender-scented face cream. 'I reckons you and me are gonna be firm pals from now on, so stick with me and you'll be fine.

'Watch out for the room supervisor, she's always the one in pink, and the charge hands, they're in orange. They can make life difficult if they think you're not pulling your weight. We work eight a.m. to six p.m. One hour for dinner, two tea breaks. Two toilet breaks, don't squander them. Avoid the soap and powder rooms like the plague.'

'Why?' Esther asked.

'They're on the ground floor, right next to the canal, ain't it? You wanna see the size of the dirty great rats that end up caught in the soap machines. Blood and hair everywhere.'

Esther grimaced.

'Powder room's not much better. That talc gets up every bleedin' orifice. You come out looking like a ghost.'

Esther's head was reeling as she tried to take it all in.

'Soon as the dinner bell goes, it's elbows out and first come, first served for the canteen scramble. Mr Lavender, he's not really called that, he's the big boss. He's a lovely gentleman, be sure to smile and look busy when he comes in.'

'Anything else?'

'Yeah, you're the gofer. Accept it. You're there to sweep up, get the tea break orders and run errands. But work hard and in six months to a year, you'll make the belt and then the chance of bonus work. Make the most of the perks of the job too. Once a month on a Friday there's a staff sale in the canteen, where you can buy items at cost price. Oh, and if you win the most productive belt or the good housekeeping award, you'll be sent up to Yardley Bond Street for a make-over. There's smashing perks at Yardley's.'

Renee stubbed out her cigarette under the bench and flicked the stub out the window towards the evil-smelling canal beneath.

'Lastly, if you see girls stealing, smoking or carrying on, don't, whatever you do, nark on them.'

'No, I shan't,' Esther replied, not really knowing what to nark was. She realised she was going to need a crash course in cockney.

'I'll give you a for-instance,' Renee went on. 'Ray on the brilliantine belt. She's been nicking lipsticks for years. Little cow. We all know about it. No one would ever dare steal in the lipstick room, more than our life's worth. Trust me, when you meet my mum, you'll understand why, but if you see Ray at it . . .'

'If you see Ray at what?' demanded a wiry-looking girl in brown overalls who had walked in unseen.

'Hello, Ray, how's your luck, darlin'?' Renee asked, completely unfazed to have been caught out.

'And what are you doing here? I thought I sent you on an errand?' she said to Esther.

'Oh, it was you what sent her for a long weight, was it?' Renee remarked. 'Well, you've had your fun, Ray, now hop it.'

Ray ignored her and took a step closer to Esther, a malevolent look on her thin face.

'You wanna know what my mum says? She says we're fighting your war.'

Esther froze. Her stomach made a slow crawling movement.

'And if you ask me . . .'

'Which no one did,' interrupted Renee.

But Ray ignored her, stepping another foot closer to Esther, her eyes glittering with a hatred that was sickeningly familiar.

'I reckon she's right.'

'Oh, shut your trap, Ray,' sighed Renee.

'No, I'm gonna have my say,' snapped Ray, pointing a long finger at Esther. 'It's your lot what brought the war to our doorstep. My mum says if you can't tell a Jew by the nose, you can recognise 'em by the smell of garlic.'

She poked Esther hard in the chest, her eyes cold as she sniffed the air like a bloodhound.

'Go back to where you came from . . . Yid!'

Renee cracked her knuckle and drew back her fist. Wham!

It happened so fast. A flash of red, then Ray was sprawled over the cloakroom floor, clutching her cheek.

'Your mother always did talk out her arse,' Renee smiled.

'You've had it now, Renee Gunn.'

In a flash, Ray was on her feet, then the two factory girls seemed welded to each other, rolling round the floor in a blur of hair and stocking tops.

Ray seemed to be winning, until Renee wrenched off her turban, sending lipsticks skidding over the floor.

No one seemed to notice the door to the cloakroom fly open.

'What in heaven's name?' Miss Peerless exclaimed.

'Please, miss, she attacked me when I accused her of smoking in our cloakroom,' blurted Ray, kicking a lipstick under the cubicle door out of sight.

Miss Peerless blew angrily out of both nostrils, her eyes thinning into narrow black pools.

'I've had it up to here with you, Renee Gunn. We're all due in the canteen now for a meeting, but afterwards you're to go and see personnel. Honestly, is it not enough that this country is at war?'

She held open the door and the girls filed out sheepishly.

'Why didn't you tell her about Ray, that she'd been stealing?' whispered Esther, as they filed up the metal staircase and into the canteen on the top floor of Yardley's.

'Told you,' Renee sniffed, rubbing the side of her temple, where Ray had wrenched out a fistful of hair. 'I ain't no nark.'

'Thank you, Renee, but you didn't have to stand up for me.'

'Course I did,' she replied. 'My mum raised me to stand up to bullies. She should leave you alone from now on.'

Esther looked at the larky cockney and thanked her lucky stars she had her as an ally. As they walked into the canteen, they were joined on all sides by turban-clad girls, spilling into the room in a great chattering, fragrant wave.

'What happened to you?' Nan asked, taking in Renee's ripped overalls as they joined her and the rest of the girls from the lipstick room.

'Don't ask. Look lively, girls, here comes Mr Lavender.'

Just then the stench of rotten meat, hot and marshy, blew in through the window nearest the canal. Esther looked around. No one batted an eyelid.

'What is that smell?' she grimaced.

'Didn'cha know?' Renee replied. 'Stratford has seven different types of air, 'pending on which way the air's blowing.'

'And right now,' grinned Joanie, 'I'd say Hunt's is boiling up the bones over the Cut.'

'Nah,' chipped in Fat Lou. 'That's Oxo down Waterden Road.'

'Sssh,' hissed Miss Peerless. 'The Managing Director is about to speak.'

A hush fell over the room as Mr Gardener, one of the bosses of the family-owned firm, affectionately nicknamed Mr Lavender, climbed a small makeshift stage covered with a Union Jack flag.

He cleared his throat into the microphone and the sound reverberated around the canteen.

'Thank you all for assembling here today. You do not need me to tell you of the grave news that greeted us yesterday morning.' A deep silence fell over the room.

'I have nothing but the utmost faith in you, our loyal workers and in this firm.

'In 1770, The House of Yardley was formed. In 1921, we received our first royal seal for soap. In 1932, Yardley stopped using a French perfumier, sourced its own lavender, planted it in England and now Norfolk's fields blaze with purple.'

He paused, gripping the edge of the lectern.

'I have no doubt that when we win this war, you Lavender Girls will still be working here, producing great British products . . .'

His speech was met with applause. He lifted both hands and the smile faded from his face.

'But until that time, I'm afraid changes must take place. We now have very little influence on the type or character of business we do. That unenviable task is now in the hands of government officials, who have the fearful responsibility of directing the country's production for the war effort.

'For some time, we have been searching for land that will not be directly on the route likely to be taken by hostile aircraft. We have acquired five acres on the Barnet bypass just outside Boreham Wood, where we shall with immediate effect be transferring raw goods. All production of talcum powders, brilliantines and perfumes will now happen at Boreham Wood, along with the immediate evacuation of all office staff.'

An enormous hubbub immediately rose up.

'It goes without saying,' he said, raising his voice over the swell, 'that we shall provide suitable billets for all workers, and anyone from the lipstick and soap departments remaining in Carpenters Road shall also be given the option of relocation to the safety zone should they wish.'

'Not bleedin' likely, pal,' muttered Renee under her breath. 'I ain't moving to Boreham Wood. Sounds like somewhere you'd go to die.'

And then, in a louder voice . . .

'Fanks, sir, that's ever so kind, but I shall be sticking here, if it's all the same to you.' Renee struck a jaunty music hall pose. 'I should miss the air too much.'

A titter of laughter ran over the room and the Managing Director couldn't help but smile.

'Thank you, Miss . . .'

'Renee, sir. Renee Gunn from the lipstick room,' she added proudly. 'Worked here since school, lavender water flowing through my veins, sir!'

'Well, Miss Gunn. I admire your spirit.'

'I should rather a pay rise than your admiration, sir! Especially if we're to be bombed while working.'

A stunned silence fell over the canteen and Miss Peerless looked like she had been slapped with a wet fish.

'Miss Gunn!' she spluttered.

'It's quite all right, Miss Peerless,' he replied, an amused smile tugging at his lips. 'I rather admire Miss Gunn's pluck. You are quite right, of course, and I shall be arranging an extra two shillings a week efficiency money for Carpenters Road staff.

'But regardless of wages, be under no illusions. There are

trying times ahead. We shall be converting the old powder department into an air-raid shelter, connected to the national telephone exchange, and we shall need plenty of volunteers for fire-watching and ARP duty.'

Renee's hand shot up.

'Thank you again, Miss Gunn. The men are disappearing from the factory, as you are doubtless aware, and in time, I'm sure they shall introduce conscription for women too. Those who do stay on need to be aware that I suspect the Board of Trade will requisition these premises, producing as we are luxury items, and find a greater purpose for your hands.

'Until then, we are a reduced but indomitable team. Something tells me Yardley will have an important role to play in this war as women cling to their femininity. The fairer sex shall have to put their best face forward and will have a duty to look their very best. Good looks and good morale are the closest of allies, after all. Yardley shall be at the very forefront of such a morale-boosting initiative.

'Let us return to our work, and remember our motto, girls, "Beauty from Order Springs".'

He shot one last curious look at Renee, then swept from the room, leaving a stunned air in his wake. The girls immediately huddled round Renee.

'Blimey, Renee,' breathed Joycie admiringly. 'I don't know where you get your nerve. But ta, that extra money'll come in handy, with my brothers gone. Mum'll be chuffed to bits with that.'

'Whatever next?' said Nan wryly. 'You going to start up a union, Renee?'

'The bosses would sooner shut this place down than start a union, you silly girls,' admonished Miss Peerless, who'd been listening in. 'Why else do you think you enjoy such wonderful advantages like the Social and Sports club, whist drives, film shows, subsidised canteen, the beanos and dinner dances . . .'

'All right, keep your wig on, everyone,' Renee replied. 'I ain't trying to cause trouble. I know Yardley's is a fair firm, but if I think something ain't right, I'm not one to keep quiet about it.'

Esther stared up at fighting glamour girl in awe, and wondered: where on earth had she got her strength from?

4

Lily

Lily finished unpacking her few belongings in her new lodgings, before casting an eye at the small clock on the mantel. Eleven a.m. The bosses at Yardley's had told her she wasn't needed until midday. On account of a staff meeting in which they were outlining the changes at the factory, it was felt easier if she made a clean start of it after dinner break, which gave her a little over an hour.

Guilt tugged. She'd been harsh on her mother earlier, when it was obvious she'd been trying, in her own way. Lily stood up quickly, smoothed down the rose-covered eiderdown and reached for her handbag before she could change her mind. If she hurried, she could nip back and tell her she would come round for tea after work. If she must be here, then surely it was better to make a clean slate of it all.

Heels clicking on the cobbles, she hurried back to the Shoot. She spotted her mother as soon as she turned into the square, swilling down her doorstep with a bucket of scalding hot water and carbolic. Nell glanced up through the steam and her face softened.

'Mum—'

'Lily—'

Nell laughed. 'You first.'

'I just wanted to say that . . .' But Lily's voice trailed off as a curious little face peeked out from behind her mother's dress skirts.

The breath stopped in her throat.

'Oh my . . .' she breathed.

Instinctively, she crouched down to the boy's eye level and met his serious gaze. She could feel her mother's presence looming over her, but she could not tear her gaze from her little brother's face.

'Hullo, you must be Frankie. I'm your big sister Lily.'

Frankie stared back at her, his pale face oddly impassive, before huddling in closer to his mother.

'She don't bite, Frankie,' Nell chided. 'Say hello.'

Suddenly both of their attention was drawn elsewhere as the heavy odour of Yardley's April Violets drifted over the doorstep.

'Watch out,' Nell muttered under her breath, gripping her bucket tightly. 'A bleedin' happy Harriet by the looks of her.'

'Mrs Gunn, I say, Mrs Gunn, a moment of your time.'

Lily straightened up and turned round to find herself face to face with the wearer of the oppressive perfume.

'Mrs Clatworthy, Director of Education and Head of the Evacuation Scheme in Stratford,' barked a middle-aged woman clothed nearly entirely in head-to-toe tweed.

'What can I do for you?' Nell asked suspiciously, placing a protective arm round Frankie's shoulder. Outsiders were neither welcomed, nor trusted round these parts.

'You may not be aware of this, Mrs Gunn, but the majority of schoolchildren in Stratford have now been evacuated to the safety zones.'

Nell stared back at her without blinking and Lily felt uncomfortable.

'Because of the expeditious manner of our evacuation plans, it has been possible to bring forward the evacuation of school-age children and the majority are now residing in billets in Woodbridge in Suffolk.'

'That's nice for them,' Nell replied smoothly.

'I-I don't think you're quite following my train of thought, dear . . .'

'Mrs Gunn to you.'

'The point is, your son Frankie needs to be evacuated for his own safety. There are also a number of children still living in this square that really ought not to be here.'

She glared over at a scruffy pack of kids, turning a giant barge rope over the cobbles and taking it in turns to skip.

'There is a final coach leaving outside the Town Hall in one hour. If you pack a bag for young Frankie, I can take him now.'

'No.'

'I beg your pardon?' she bristled.

'I said no,' Nell replied, taking her hand off Frankie's shoulder and taking a step closer to the official, the shadow of her turban swallowing her whole. 'I ain't packing my son off to live with God knows who in the countryside. Where I go, he goes.'

'Mum, perhaps you ought to hear—'

'Keep out of this, Lily,' Nell ordered.

'B-but that's preposterous,' Mrs Clatworthy spluttered. 'To say nothing of irresponsible. The schools are to close down. How is he to continue his education?'

'Listen, lady, last I heard, evacuation was voluntary,' Nell snapped, and then, making a stab at her clipboard. 'So you can rub his name right off your list.'

'Do you know I answer to the Ministry of Health?'

'I don't care if you answer to the ministry of silly fucks, love, as long as I've got a hole in my arse, he ain't going!' Lily closed her eyes. This was not going to end well.

Mrs Clatworthy stared hard at Nell Gunn, clearly weighing

up her options. Rummaging around in her handbag, she pulled out a copy of the *Daily Herald*.

'Listen to this, Mrs Gunn, in today's newspaper:

'*If I had been a little boy or girl, I would rather have enjoyed yesterday's evacuation,*' she quoted. '*Is there a child in the world who does not like (a) picnics, (b) train journeys, and (c) mysteries? Yesterday, a, b and c were all rolled together in an alphabet of excitement.* Doesn't that sound wonderful?'

'What a load of old flannel,' Nell snapped. 'Frankie's stopping here. That way if we die, we all die together!'

Mrs Clatworthy's face darkened.

'Very well then. Suffer the consequences.'

Nell tugged Frankie's hand and pushed him inside the passage as Mrs Clatworthy turned on her heel and stomped off across the square, bristling with anger.

Lily waited until she was out of earshot.

'But Mum, maybe she has a point? If London is on the direct path for enemy action, which the bosses at Yardley seem to think is going to be the case, then mightn't it be better if Frankie's out of harm's way? I'm just thinking of what's best for—'

'When it comes to Frankie, you leave the thinking to me. He's *my* son. Understood?'

Her green eyes flashed dangerously, darkening to the colour of lichen and a deep silence smothered the cobbles.

Lily sighed. 'Yes, Mum. I understand.'

Once more, she was reminded that this doorstep was her mother's domain. She and no one else ruled the roost round here.

'I better get going to work, I'll see you later,' she said.

Lily cast one last curious glance at Frankie, at the solemn little face now staring out from the other side of the sash window, before turning and hurrying in the direction of Yardley's.

Once at the factory, Lily waited nervously by the lipstick machine as the girls filed back into the room after their meeting in the canteen. She held the palm of her hand against her sternum and blew out slowly. First her mum and brother, now her sister. This morning's reunion was turning into a baptism of fire all right. Renee had been thirteen when she'd left home, a little tomboy with scabby knees who could outrun any boy down the Shoot.

And now! Lily felt choked at this visible reminder of all she had missed. Time was a mysterious thing, even more so than God. Six years had passed in the blink of an eye, and yet her sister was scarcely the same person. Her logical brain told her the woman walking across the factory floor towards her now, all curves and chutzpah, was her little sister, but her heart refused to believe it, conflicting feelings spinning through her helter-skelter. Somewhere in the distance, she heard the room supervisor introducing her.

'Welcome back, Miss Lily Gunn, Yardley's youngest ever charge hand, fresh from Bond Street, a Stratford success story.'

Lily locked eyes with Renee and, for a terrifying moment, she thought her little sister might slap her. She wouldn't have blamed Renee if she had, leaving home in the way she had, cutting herself off for so long. In her instinct for self-preservation, she had been thoughtless to the effect it would have on the rest of her family. Lily suddenly saw that now. But her fears were unfounded, for instead Renee hurled herself into her arms with a sob. She smelt faintly of whisky and lavender, and Lily felt an emotional punch deep inside as they clung to one another. Far away from the East End, she had told herself it was right, that cutting herself off from her family was the only way to deal with what had happened, with what she had been forced to give up. But now, here, she experienced a pain so raw it felt like grief. All those missed birthdays, all the lost years.

'Lil, why didn't you tell me you were coming home?' Renee whispered, eventually pulling back.

'I'm not coming home, Renee, I've got lodgings in East Ham.'

Lily heard her voice, so formal, and hated herself.

Renee looked crushed, her blue eyes swimming with tears.

'Lil. It's been six years. *Six years*. We ain't seen hide nor hair of you.'

'I know and I'm sorry . . . I've been busy,' was all she could manage.

'But . . . But why did you stay away so long?' Renee's voice faltered. 'I-I thought it was me, that you hated me.'

'Oh Renee, no . . . No, not ever,' she insisted, reaching for her hand. 'You're my little sister, how could I possibly hate you?'

Renee shook her head, looking for an explanation of sorts.

'I really have been frantic,' Lily ploughed on. 'Yardley's have me on training courses at their beauty school in Wales every weekend, then I'm working in the salon in the week, which keeps me terrifically busy.' That much at least was true.

'And also, it takes an age to get from West to East London.'

'It's at the end of the Number 25 bus route, Lil!' Renee protested. 'It ain't Timbuk-flaming-tu.'

Lily laughed in spite of herself. 'Still a lippy little cow.'

'No, Lil, I'm grown up now. I've got a boyfriend, Alfie,' Renee said proudly. 'I've turned into a woman. I'm a lipstick girl now.'

'I can see that.' Lily smiled sadly, tucking a stray blonde curl back under Renee's turban. 'You've grown into yourself. You're beautiful, but then I always knew you would be.'

She felt a slight snag in her breath.

'And what's Frankie like? I only saw him briefly earlier.'

'He was a baby when you left,' Renee replied awkwardly.

The silence stretched on, then curdled inside her.

'What, is he all right?'

'Six years is a long time, Lil. He's seven now, he's . . .' Renee stumbled on the words. 'He's complicated, is all.'

A story was etched on Renee's face that Lily couldn't read, but then out shone a look of pure love.

'Oh, but he's proper clever, right enough,' she grinned. 'Such a way with his words. You'd never know he's a Gunn. The Little Prof, Mum calls him.'

Lily laughed. 'I've got a lot of catching up to do, I can see.'

'So come tonight, for your tea? I'm meeting Alfie on the High Street at eight p.m. then he's taking me to the pictures, but please come and have some grub with us before.'

Lily hesitated, thinking of the strained scene on the doorstep earlier.

'Oh please,' Renee begged, holding together her hands imploringly. Lily looked down at her long soft fingers, tapered through hers.

In the corner of her vision, Lily could sense the room supervisor tapping her clipboard, chilly disapproval coming off her in waves.

'Very well,' she relented, smoothing down her orange overalls. 'But now, back to it. We don't want anyone questioning the validity of our work.'

Renee's smile was like a splash of sunshine in the shade.

'Right you are, boss. Cor, I can't believe I'm saying that! My big sis is my new charge hand!'

She turned to go, but paused, her impish grin stretching further. 'Oh, just one thing, Lil, sorry, boss! Where did you drop 'em?'

'Drop what, Renee?'

'All your ain'ts and yer fings? Also, you picked up a few aitches somewhere in Bond Street? Got yerself an edemucation now, is it?'

She winked to show Lily she was only joking.

'Hark at my big sister talking all proper now. Sounds like you've swallowed a dictionary.'

'In that case, let's look up W . . . for work!' Lily laughed.

'Touché,' Renee quipped as she sashayed back to the conveyor belt. And then, over her shoulder, 'See, you ain't the only one who knows big words.'

At six p.m. the steam hooter blasted out over the grimy rooftops of Stratford and the girls joined the sea of workers from Yardley's and Clarnico's who were clocking off. Some poor young lone male from Berger's was bravely running the gauntlet through the throng of jeering women in their red, white and blue overalls.

Lily smiled at the new girl, Esther's wide-eyed expression, as she took in the hundreds of chimneystacks, all pumping smoke into the soupy air as they made their way back up Carpenters Road to the High Street.

'How was your first day, Esther?' she asked the younger girl.

'To be honest, Miss Gunn . . .'

'Call me Lily outside work, please, I insist.'

Esther smiled. 'Very well, it wasn't the best of starts, Lily, but it's certainly taken a brighter turn after meeting you all,' she replied shyly, and Lily squeezed her shoulder. She instinctively liked this girl, who was so different from all the other cocksure girls at Yardley's. And something about her plight, being forced to up-sticks and leave her home, resonated with Lily.

'It's a touch you joining us in the lipstick room, Est,' said Renee, tugging off her turban and letting her blonde waves cascade down her back. 'And even better that scrawny little thief Ray's being shipped out to Boring Wood.'

'This is me,' said Nan, slowing at the bus stop.

'Come here, you,' said Renee, throwing her arms around her. 'I'll be around bright and early Saturday to help you get ready.'

'So, you're really marrying your Jimmy then?' Lily asked her younger sister's best friend.

Despite her best efforts to disguise it, there was a slight edge to her voice that Nan obviously picked up on.

'Of course,' she replied. 'Why wouldn't I?'

'No reason. I'm very happy for you.' She could have said more of course, so much more, but she hadn't come back to rock the boat.

'I wish you luck, Nan,' she said. *God knows she'll need it, marrying Jimmy Connor,* she thought to herself.

'Well, you're welcome to come to the wedding now that you're back,' Nan said appeased. 'Mum's hired a hall and a band, *and* we're having our photos taken at Boris's studio in Whitechapel,' she boasted. 'It's going to be perfect.'

The 208 bus slid to a stop next to them. It was dusk but already its headlamps were partially dimmed to comply with the blackout.

'You deserve it,' said Renee loyally, giving her pal a last hug before she boarded the bus. Lily watched them, a queer look etched on her face.

As the bus trundled off into the coal-scented gloom, Esther followed the Gunn sisters under the railway bridge, past the Carpenters Arms, where many a Yardley girl celebrated the week's end with gin and orange, and onto the High Street. Here Esther's gaze grew even wider and Lily tried to see it through a newcomer's eyes. The hustle and bustle certainly left the senses reeling.

Shops, pubs and picture houses jostled for space down the vibrant thoroughfare and branching off from the main street ran miles of soot-blackened terraced housing and tenements, all stewing in poverty. Threading its way through it all, like a thin grey snake, was a complicated network of waterways and canals emanating from the River Lea to transport waterborne cargo.

'Cooke's still going then, I see,' Lily smiled, as they passed an eel, pie and mash shop, the delicious scent of meat and parsley liquor drifting out through the door, mingling with the smell of asphalt, horse dung and chemicals drifting over from the nearby factories.

'Course. We'll have to go there for our dinner now you're back. That is unless you're too grand to eat in a place that has live eels out front,' Renee teased.

Lily took a playful swipe at her little sister.

'You're never too posh for pie and mash,' she bantered back.

'How are you finding life down the Lane then, Esther?' Lily asked as they turned off the High Street. 'It's very different to Vienna, yes?'

'You could say that,' Esther acknowledged as the street theatre that was Angel Lane stretched out before them in the gathering gloom.

Markets were a refuge for vagrants, villains and vagabonds, to say nothing of formidable housewives, and Angel Lane was the ripest of them all. Mist was steaming in lazy swirls from a pile of horse dung and Lily pulled Esther out of the way just before she trod in the pile of muck.

'That's the Broadway,' said Renee, pointing back in the direction from which they'd walked. 'That's where you get all your smarter department stores, like Boardman's. Nan'll have got a chit to spend down there as a wedding present from Yardley's. But down here,' she said, turning to face the lane with a proud smile, 'you can get anything from cat's meat to corsets. As long as you're prepared to haggle.'

Esther scurried to keep pace with Renee, who didn't so much walk as wiggle, treating the lane like her catwalk.

As darkness settled, the costermongers had begun extinguishing their coke braziers, sending ribbons of greasy smoke drifting up the narrow street. Blackouts were going up over the shopfronts.

'Harold Hitch's eel pie shop, Nellie Maud's dining rooms, Cohen's for your fish and chips,' said Renee pointing out her favourites. 'Betty Flaum costumier. She does the best schmutter and Ballito silk stockings, her and the hole in the wall. Just watch out for the schleppers trying to tout for business.'

As they walked, it felt like one long procession of odours: steaming beetroot, grated horseradish, wriggling eels in trays, skinned rabbits, spices and over-ripe vegetables from the barrows.

An earthy pong hung over their heads as the stallholders did their best to sell off the last of their produce. A babble of Yiddish, Romany and cockney jargon rose up into the brackish air.

'All alive-o,' hollered a winkle seller. Five yards from him, an Indian toffee man was hawking his wares: 'Indian toffee, good for the belly, ask your mummy for a penny.'

It was as if all the sounds of the metropolis had been squeezed into one narrow lane.

'All right, Snowball,' called Renee to the tramp, who was busy picking bruised fruit out of the gutters. He waved back with a toothless grin, trousers bound by frayed string, and Lily was once again reminded of the poverty of her childhood home.

'What is that man doing?' Esther asked. At the side of the market, with a small crowd gathered around him, stood a well-built man wearing only greasy, coarse trousers. An old ship's rope was tied around his neck, with two men on either side tugging on it for dear life.

'Oh, that's Billy Boyton, the strongman,' replied Renee,

unfazed at the sight of the man's veins bulging like thick red worms out his neck.

'But they will strangle him, no?' Esther said, gripping Lily's arm in alarm.

'He was doing this act when I left six years ago,' laughed Lily. 'So I very much doubt it.'

Yards from Billy, an old couple on a crockery stall were having a very loud and heated row, to the amusement of the onlookers.

'Don't worry, it's just a show for the crowd,' Lily reassured Esther, waving away a hawker who thrust a greasy paper bag filled with sliced pigs' ears under her nose.

Esther looked relieved when they reached her mother's uncle's milliner's shop.

'It doesn't even feel like there is a war on here,' she murmured out loud, as she pushed her key into the door by the side of the shop that led to the rooms above.

'See you tomorrow and thanks again, Renee, for what you did this morning,' she said, pausing on the doorstep.

'Think nothing of it, darling,' Renee said with a wink.

'What did you do for her?' Lily questioned as they walked on, heels tapping on the cobbles.

'Oh, nothing much, just helped her out is all. She was getting eaten alive by Ray and her pals,' Renee remarked as they slipped down Reeves Court into the Shoot.

'Turning into Mum, are you?' Lily asked, raising one eyebrow.

'There's nothing wrong with helping people out, Lily,' Renee said protectively.

Lily's gaze flickered to the graveyard and her eyes darkened.

'I'm not sure about coming . . .'

But it was too late to turn back. The door to number 10 flung open and there was their mother, showing out Old Ma Hitchin as she was known, a mother of twelve from the Shoot.

'Thanks, Auntie,' said the neighbour, gripping her string bag in one hand and Mrs Gunn's wrist in the other. 'You've got me out of a real scrape.' There was a feverish look on her face that made Lily instantly feel uneasy.

'Think nothing of it, dearie. Ta-ra,' Nell replied. 'Be lucky.'

Nell's eyes settled on her two daughters and lit up.

'Look who I found, Mum,' grinned Renee, leaning over to kiss her mother's plump cheek.

'You came,' Nell said to Lily, her voice softening.

'I said I would this morning,' she replied.

Showing Old Ma out, Nell flung open the door. The aroma of something meaty cut through with carbolic drifted from the dark passage.

'I've done oxtail stew and dumplings. Your father's back from work.'

Nell picked up a bucket and mop propped against the frame and shunted open the kitchen door with her rump.

Lily stepped into the kitchen and breathed the familiar scent of her childhood as she took in her father sitting at the table.

Pat Gunn was a man of few words. Small and wiry, not much further through than a coat hanger, with a broken nose and a finger in every pie. Pat did it all, from teaching boys of the Shoot to box down West Ham boxing club, to racing pigeons. Rumour had it, he even did the odd bit of enforcing for a local villain. Part of his left ear was missing, bitten off by Porky Reynolds of the Upton Park Mob, so local legend had it.

His day job was unloading coal and timber with a gang down Dagenham docks.

'Hello, Dad,' said Lily.

'Hello, girl,' he replied gruffly, rising and giving her a big hug. 'Don't stay away so long next time.'

Lily knew that's all that would be said on her six-year absence from Stratford.

'You've kept the place nice, Mum,' she remarked, looking down at the lino, so clean you could have eaten your dinner off it, and the bleached nets over the sash windows.

A coal fire crackled in the grate and a tray of Lily's favourite bread pudding was cooling in the scullery for afters. Even the rug that only got laid out when she had visitors was down, and Lily felt a scorch of shame. This was her mum's way of making peace.

'It all looks lovely,' she said, removing her gloves, unpinning her hat and hooking her coat on a nail by the door.

'A woman's judged by her curtains,' shrugged Nell, wiping her hands on her wrap-around apron. An unspoken truce of sorts had been reached.

'Now tea'll be a half-hour, girls. Why don't you go and get washed up?'

She glanced up at the clock over the mantel, surrounded by her beloved Toby jugs, and frowned.

'Where's Frankie? I sent him out to get some coke from the gasworks hours ago.'

'Probably got his head in a bleedin' book somewhere,' Pat muttered, without looking up from his copy of the *Daily Herald*.

'All right if I go to the flicks with Alfie this evening?' Renee asked, nicking a slice of bread from the table.

'Bit hard this,' she mumbled through her mouthful.

'Harder still when you ain't got none, girl,' Pat replied. 'Be back by ten p.m.'

Upstairs, Lily looked around the cluttered bedroom she used to share with Renee. Pots, jars, brushes and unguents jostled for space and copies of *Woman's Own* were strewn across the floor.

'Blimey, Renee, there's more make-up here than at Yardley's salon in Bond Street.'

'Girl's got to look her best,' Renee winked, sitting down in front of a tiny mirror to start her ablutions.

'Q . . . X . . .' she began, drawing the letters out emphatically. 'Q . . . X . . .'

'What on God's earth are you doing, you nitwit?' Lily laughed.

'My face exercises, *Woman's Own* reckons it does wonders for sagging contours. Touch me toes a hundred times a day too an' all, to stop rolls round me tummy.'

Lily took in her sister's velvety skin and svelte figure.

'Don't talk daft, you don't have any sagging contours. You're a kid.'

'Except I ain't a kid no more,' Renee said hotly and Lily cursed her lack of tact.

'You're right. I'm sorry. Look here, why don't I do your make-up for your date with Alfie tonight?'

'Oh, would you, Lil? That'd be smashing. I wanna find out all the beauty secrets of Bond Street!'

Impulsively, she reached over and kissed Lily's cheek.

'What was that for?' she asked, amused.

'I'm just so happy to have my big sister home,' Renee beamed back, her blue eyes shining with sincerity. Lily shifted uncomfortably. The sense of shame and guilt she imagined she had buried so deep, was lurking stealthily just below the surface after all. The realisation was a depressing one.

Distracting herself, Lily quickly rummaged around in her bag, pulled out her make-up kit and busily began making up her little sister's face, like she did for all the society ladies of Bond Street. Except not one of them could hold a candle to Renee's luminous beauty.

As she dotted skin cream on her sister's luscious lips, then applied lipstick with a fine camel-hair brush, before blotting then alternating with more cream, then more lipstick, it struck her as ironic. The wealthy West End ladies forked out a small fortune on the latest Yardley's Vanishing Cream, snowy English Complexion Cream and Sparkling Tonic Lotion, all promising glowing youthful loveliness. Yet here was a girl from the sulphurous slums of Stratford's Shoot with skin as dewy as a peach.

Lily thought back to Yardley's most recent advertising campaign. *There are no more old or ugly women!*

Yardley's was taking on the big boys of the American cosmetics world, like Max Factor, with glamorous products at affordable prices for all. Her bosses had cottoned on to the fact that ordinary working girls wanted to look like their favourite Hollywood idol to 'catch their man'.

Yardley's cherry red lipstick wasn't just coloured oil, fat and wax in a tube. It was escapism; a beautifully packaged dream. The gold art deco tube smothered in tiny stars held more than mere lipstick. It contained the promise of a better life. Wasn't that what they were all striving for?

Meanwhile, back in the real world, the damp walls leaked noise as the sound of Mrs Trunk at number 8 screaming at her husband drifted through the room, followed by a thud and the sound of breaking china.

'Flying plate night?' Lily asked as she slicked white Vaseline on Renee's eyebrows.

Renee nodded.

'Mum's round there most nights calming them all down and soothing the kids after one of their slap-up rows, then they go and do it all again the next night.'

Lily felt an ache in her guts. How she wanted more for her sister than life down the Shoot, falling into the fate that she was bred for. As nice as she was sure this Alfie Buckle was, odds on he'd want her sister chained to the sink, cobbling together a home on the never-never and churning out pramfuls of babies. Renee was too bright and spirited for that kind of life. It'd be like nailing a butterfly to the wall.

'Have you got a fella?' Renee questioned, watching Lily intently in the mirror.

Lily slicked a brush over a block of mascara and carefully began doing out her sister's feathery lashes.

'No. No interest in one either.'

'Why?'

'Miss Carmen – that's the supervisor at Bond Street – she's invested a lot of time in training me up. Sit still. One day, I hope to travel to Paris, or better yet, New York to learn all the latest beauty techniques.'

Lily smiled as she blew on a powder puff, before dusting a light coating of Yardley's featherlight Complexion Powder in peach over Renee's cheeks.

'I want another life. A life where women have options beyond the factory, the bedroom and the kitchen.'

'You must have the right needle to be back in the factory then.'

'It won't be for long. As soon as the war's over, I'll be returning to Bond Street. I'm seeing this as a small hiccup. There now . . .'

Gently, she turned her sister's head back to the mirror.

'Oh my days! I look like . . . like . . .'

'Jean Harlow,' Lily grinned triumphantly.

'What's that shade of lipstick?'

'Burnt Sugar. It's been especially created to go with the colour khaki.'

'Oh, don't let's ruin the evening by talking about the flamin' war,' Renee scolded.

Lily sat on the bed and watched as Renee changed into a pale green silk crêpe de Chine dress, pin-tucked with shoulder yokes and a pleated skirt she'd run up herself with some material she'd bought from a remnants half-price sale at Roberts Department Store.

'I wish I had boobs like yours,' Renee sighed, appraising her figure in the mirror.

'But you can,' said Lily, showing Renee how to fill out her bra with soft folds of tissue paper.

'You know all the dodges,' Renee said admiringly as Lily took a diamanté hair-slide from her bag and clipped it into her blonde wave. Renee was pleased now that she'd paid 12/6 for the new perm on Saturday. Nearly a whole week's wages, and she'd had to sit through three hours of agony being washed, baked and set. 'The latest from Paris,' the stylist had assured her. It bloody ought to be at that price, but it was worth it. Renee's platinum blonde hair fell in soft waves about her face.

'You're going to knock this Alfie's socks off,' Lily smiled.

Renee gazed back at her admiringly, and for a small moment, Lily was almost pleased she was home.

'Oh, nearly forgot,' Renee said, rummaging about in her bag, and pulling out a bottle of Evening in Paris. She gave herself a liberal drenching of the heavy musky scent, before dabbing some down her cleavage.

'Now I'm dressed!'

'That's not how you apply perfume,' Lily laughed, dabbing a little on her finger.

'You're supposed to lightly spray your skin *before* you dress, and here,' she said, smoothing the scent along the silk of Renee's eyebrows. 'You wear the perfume, not the other way around. That's how all the debs wear it.'

'This is where I've been going wrong all me life,' Renee said with a great hoot of laughter. 'I've never sprayed perfume on me knickers and eyebrows.'

'I'm serious,' Lily replied. 'Subtlety is key. You need to think about what you tell people about yourself through your scent. Evening in Paris . . . Well, it's heavy stuff. Their slogan is *She knew he couldn't resist,* after all! How might we mislead a man if we're drenched in the stuff?'

Renee stared at her blankly.

'Come on, let's go down for tea,' Lily smiled. 'See if Mum recognises you.'

5

Renee

'What on earth do you think you look like?'

Her mother had a face that could've stopped a funeral, and Renee began to wonder if she'd perhaps overdone it.

'Everyone's wearing make-up these days, Mum,' she protested. 'Shop girls, secretaries . . .'

'Actresses!' bellowed her father, gaping at her from over his *Daily Herald*.

He drew on his Woodbine and his nostrils flared angrily.

'And you smell like the bottom of a whore's handbag.'

'Have you anything to do with this?' Nell fumed, rounding on Lily.

'Don't blame her,' Renee protested. 'I'm nineteen now, Mum, it's time I went me own way.'

'The only way you're going now my girl is back up them stairs to get that muck off your face.'

'Thirty minutes alone with you and she comes down looking like a right gaytime hussy,' Nell thundered, pointing her wooden spoon at Lily.

'No bloody wonder the birth rate's rocketing when girls are dressing like that,' fumed Pat, returning to his paper.

'I knew this was a mistake,' Lily snapped, grabbing her coat and hat before storming out.

'Now look what you've done!' Renee protested.

'Mind how you talk to your mother,' Pat grunted.

'That's right. Any more of your sauce and I'll knock you into the middle of next week.'

'Least I won't have to go to church Sunday.'

Bang. Nell's beefy hand landed with a stinging clout right round the side of Renee's head, sending her new diamanté clip skidding over the lino.

Stifling a sob, Renee ran up the stairs and slammed her door shut. Inside her bedroom she threw herself on the bed and beat her fist against the cushion. Hang it all! What was bloody wrong with her mum? It was only a bit of make-up, weren't it? All the girls wore it these days, and yet her mum was behaving as if she'd come down dressed in nothing but nipple tassles! And Lily! She groaned. Her lovely big sister Lily, not even sat down for her tea and already driven out by a row. Mortifying! Tears of frustration streamed down Renee's cheeks as she kicked off her heels and collapsed back on the bed. How many times had she dreamt of Lily coming home to Stratford? Apart from the odd letter, they'd not set eyes on her for years, so to see her there, so smart and elegant, in the factory this morning was like every Christmas and birthday rolled into one. She couldn't have been more chuffed if Mae West herself had sashayed into Yardley's! Proud? Not many!

Renee's head spun as her eyes travelled up a faint patch of damp creeping up from the skirting board. What had gone wrong with their family? Lily's name hadn't exactly been banned this past six years, but Renee had known better than to mention her for fear of upsetting her mum. Mind you, it hadn't stopped Nell laying out an extra plate every Sunday dinner, just in case, and bragging to half the Shoot how her eldest daughter was doing ever such an important job up West. Renee adored her big sister, she was so proud of her for following her dreams and having a career. How many girls round these parts could say that? And now their mum was doing her damnedest to drive Lily away again, when they'd only just got her back. Why? It was as if there was an unspoken narrative being played out, and only Renee wasn't privy to it. There had to be more than they were both letting on. If she had to lay money on it, she'd say a man was behind it. They usually were. Renee didn't doubt Lily's story on following her career, but there was more to this story. And her mum certainly wasn't going to share it with her.

'Miserable old cow. When I'm a mum I'm gonna do a much better job,' Renee vowed under her breath, lighting up a cigarette in an act of rebellion. Her mum hated her smoking, even though she did herself – hypocrite. Renee threw the bedroom window open, though, just to be on the safe side.

Straight away she heard her mother's voice bouncing off the tenement walls. Wasn't hard, she was like a klaxon when she got going.

Curiosity piqued, Renee's misery was quickly forgotten as she poked her head out the window for a better look.

Below her, Nell was standing on the doorstep with a small crowd of women from the Shoot assembled around her.

'What's wrong?' her mother asked a worried-looking Elsie from number 16, who seemed to be the group's mouthpiece.

'There's some blokes here from the Town Hall, Auntie, they want a public meeting in the square,' Elsie replied, wringing her apron. 'It's an emergency, apparently.'

Renee rolled her eyes as she puffed a smoke ring out the window. It always was an emergency. She could never understand why her mum put herself out for the women of the Shoot, always becoming embroiled in the latest neighbourhood dispute, fighting their battles like some sort of cockney Boudicca.

Without another word, Nell gestured to Pat and the pair

of them marched over to the church, where two men in serge suits were surrounded by an angry, apron-clad crowd. As Nell and Pat Gunn approached, they parted like the Red Sea.

'What's the meaning of this?' her mum demanded, knuckles resting on her hips.

Sensing a fight was about to kick off, Renee quickly mashed out her cigarette on the window-ledge, slid on her shoes and bounced off the bed, scrambling down the stairs. No one wanted to miss a Shoot dust-up!

By the time Renee got down into the square, the atmosphere was electric, worry and fear etched onto the residents' faces.

'They want us to leave our homes, Auntie,' called a woman, clutching a small child in one hand and a dog straining at its leash with the other. 'They can't make us do that, can they?'

'Mrs Gunn,' piped up an oily-looking man with a comb-over and a clipboard. Renee weighed him up in an instant. All top show with his mascara-clad moustache.

'We are calling on residents in vulnerable areas to evacuate their children to the safety zones and to make themselves available to sleep in council-owned official shelters by night.'

'And why might that be?' Nell asked crisply.

'You are in an unfortunate area with a lack of shelter. Anyone earning less than £250 a year is entitled to a free Anderson shelter, but as far as I'm aware there are no back gardens in which to dig such a shelter, so we are requesting that residents retire to local shelters by night.'

'And where are these shelters?'

He consulted his clipboard.

'Your nearest is Carpenters Road school, or the public street shelters on Kerrison Road.'

'Let me get this straight, you want us to bed down on the floor of a school hall?'

Kate Thompson

'My dear lady, public policy dictates . . .'

'I'll tell you where you can shove your public policy,' Nell snapped. Watching from the edge of the crowd, Renee winced. She almost felt sorry for the fella. Nell Gunn was a powerful orator when she had the wind up her. Some said you could hear her all the way from the Whitechapel waste when she had a point to make.

'Years this war has been brewing, pal, and now we're facing the filthy terror again. You've had months in which to build decent underground shelters for the families of Stratford and the best you can come up with is a school hall? People are going to die!'

She turned to the crowd, knuckles on hips.

'Any of you feel safer sleeping on the floor of a school?'

The silence was deafening as she turned back to the council officials.

'While your lot was off shaking hands with Hitler, it was left to my lot to keep this country's coffers going. I remember when Mr Chamberlain came home waving his silly bit of paper, saying: "Peace for our time," 'cause Adolf had told him, so it must be true. Well, he made chumps of the lot of you, didn't he?'

The man moved his hands down the serge creases on his suit trousers, plucking at the threads.

'Mrs Gunn, I must protest . . .'

'Oh, I know about protests, pal. I was with the crowds at the Battle of Cable Street when we fought back the fascists three years ago. We all saw it coming.'

'Did you indeed?' he replied, a glimmer of a smirk twitching at his lips. 'Quite the subversive, anti-authoritarian spirit, aren't we, Mrs Gunn?'

A vein in Nell's temple pulsed dangerously and she stepped up the church steps next to him. At five foot nine in her turban, she towered over the smaller man.

'Don't you dare look down on me, young man,' she thundered. 'You might think I'm common and I dare say I am. But I got common sense and a heart twice the size of yours. The rich'll be safe in their country retreats, you can bet your life they will. When it comes to war, it's always the poor who suffer. So you go back to the powers that be and see if you can come up with something a little better than the floor of a school hall.'

Nell crossed her arms, pugnacious to the end.

'Until then, we're stopping here. We ain't just Londoners see. We're cockneys. And that means we'll fight to the end.'

'You tell him, Mum!' Renee hollered, before she could stop herself.

A newspaper photographer from the *Stratford Express*, lurking unseen, stepped forward and trained his lens on the scene. *Pop!* The flashbulb went and the dog straining at his leash finally sprang free and made a beeline for the official's ankles.

'Get this mutt off me!' he roared. 'It ought to be destroyed, as should any cats or pigeons you're keeping down here.'

The photographer captured the whole unfortunate scene.

'Stop taking photographs!' yelled the council official, flapping his trouser leg as the dog unravelled his hem.

'Are you off your nut, chump?' bellowed Pat, hauling the dog off him. 'The pets down here are like our family. What next? Shall we bring out our elderly, wring their necks an' all?'

'We have tried to help,' snapped the flustered official, picking up his briefcase from the ground. 'You are on your own then.'

'Except we ain't,' Nell replied. 'We got each other.'

Suddenly a bloodcurdling scream bounced off the tenement walls, and a lady ran hysterical from her home into the square.

'It's my Geoff! Someone help me! I-I think he's dead.'

A great wail erupted from her body, before she crumpled onto the cobbles in a heap.

All hell broke loose. Pat was first to leap into action, followed by more men, as Nell raced to comfort the woman.

'Get out of it!' she yelled at the council officials. 'There are going to be more deaths unless you sort us proper shelter.'

As Nell folded the desperate woman in her arms, every single woman there sensed the drama and tragedy unfolding before them. What none of them knew was how chillingly accurate Nell's prediction would prove to be.

In the chaos of that moment, Renee made a split-second decision. A decision she would later come to regret.

She glanced up at the rusting clock over the church door, heart hammering

Five minutes to eight. Anger and defiance pumped through her veins. Could she?

With her mother preoccupied, now was the perfect moment. *Better to seek forgiveness than ask permission*, she thought with a capricious smile. 'Sides, that old boy Geoff the fishmonger wouldn't be dead. Penny to a pound he'd been on the drink.

With that, she raced back upstairs to her bedroom, arranged her pillows to look like a body under the bedcovers, turned off the table lamp's dim 30-watt bulb and slipped from the house like a thief.

Alfie was waiting right where he'd said he would be, on the corner of the High Street and West Ham Lane, and her heart picked up speed. He was leaning nonchalantly against the wall, smoking a cigarette. Although his face was blurred by the darkness, he still looked achingly handsome under the shadows of his hat.

Renee had to hand it to him. Out of his work overalls, he

wasn't half a sharp dresser. He'd saved for months for a Max Cohen suit, cut just so, a quarter inch of brilliant-white cuff on show, blonde hair freshly slicked back with brilliantine.

As she drew close, his deep blue eyes, cut like gemstones, looked her up and down appreciatively.

He whistled under his breath as he pushed off the wall.

'You're late. Just as well you're worth the wait. You look the business, Renee.'

The scent of him filled her senses, woody and musky, his breath Euthymol-fresh, as he held out his arm.

'Don't we make a fine pair, Miss Gunn. Shall we step out?'

She giggled and took his arm.

'Silly bugger.'

At the pictures, Alfie rattled the door but it was firmly bolted.

The poster advertising Joan Crawford and James Stewart in *The Ice Follies of 1939* had a banner pasted over the top of it.

'All picture houses in Stratford are shut until further notice . . .' read Alfie.

'. . . by order of the Home Office,' finished Renee.

'I don't believe it!' she wailed.

Alfie sauntered round the side, peered through a round porthole window.

'We could always bunk in like I did when I was a nipper,' he joked. 'Wanna leg-up?'

'It's not funny, Alfie,' Renee protested. 'I've risked life and limb to sneak out and meet you. There'll be blood on the moon if my mum finds out!'

'We could go up Ilford, to the Palais? You like dancing,' Alfie suggested.

'Except that'll probably be shut an' all!'

'Well, we'll have to make our own entertainment,' he said with a wink.

'Do you mind?' she snapped, feeling her mood grow sour. 'I ain't that kind of girl.'

She yawned and shivered from the cold.

'May as well go home then.'

'Don't be like that, Renee,' Alfie coaxed, taking his coat off and draping it round her shoulders. 'Let's just go for a walk instead.'

Sighing, she relented and they made their way down to the Cut. Their walk took them down what was known locally as the Longy, a long path that ran past Nicholson's gin factory. The smell of mother's ruin oozed into the smoky sky and Renee's stomach churned. A lot of the girls at the factory were rather partial to gin, two stiff fingers sloshed in a beaker, sneaked into a dance hall, but it always just put her in the mood for a fight. Renee's thoughts strayed to her mum. Had she discovered she was missing yet? Were she and her father out looking for her? She felt even queasier.

'Got a smoke?' she asked, forcing the image of her mum's face out of her mind.

Reaching into his pocket, Alfie shook out two fags and lit them up.

Together they sat on the edge of the Cut, dangling their feet over the milky water. On the other side, a clattering of hooves broke open the still air. A barge horse was making a break for freedom, his battered hooves sparking against the cobbles.

'I know how you feel, pal,' said Alfie, blowing a long stream of blue smoke into the canal. 'I can't wait to get out of here either.'

'Oh, that's charming, that is.'

'You know I don't mean it like that, Renee,' he soothed, brushing his thumb up the inside of her wrist. 'But I wanna be out there beating the Boche with my big brother, not working in a flamin' paint factory. Where's the glory in that?'

Renee felt his shoulders tense in frustration.

'Our Billy's been in the Navy for three years, having adventures of a lifetime. Meanwhile, what am I doing? Mixing paint is what!'

He flicked his fag butt into the canal.

'I went down the Employment Exchange on my dinner break. They told me that come January I can register for military service, Navy, Army or Air Force.'

'What'll you choose?' she asked.

'You have to ask?' he said, lifting one eyebrow.

It was a silly question. Renee knew that Alfie came from a long line of sailors, most of the young men round here went into the merchant navy.

'Looks like you're stuck with me for another four months,' he said, turning to her, his eyes sparkling in the gloom.

The blackout had descended over Stratford like a velvet cloth and suddenly Renee realised they were all alone in the darkness. Her skin prickled as Alfie trailed his fingers up her arm and cupped the back of her neck.

'I'm gonna miss you, Renee,' he said throatily. 'I think I'm falling in love with you.'

'Shut up,' she laughed, embarrassed. 'You're only making out.'

Love. He'd actually said the L word. For all her chutzpah, Renee suddenly lost her front and her gaze slid to the inky water.

'I'm not, Renee, I swear it,' he said, taking her face in his hands and gently tilting her gaze back to his. They kissed, his warm lips brushing softly against hers, his thumb sliding down the nape of her neck, but Renee couldn't relax. Her mum's face kept hovering in and out the darkness. The smell of gin and rotten canal water grew more potent, turning her stomach. What was wrong with her? In public, she could put on a good show, act like a confident girl about town, but here, alone with Alfie, she was out of her depth. *Relax,* she told herself, forcing herself to calm down. It was only kissing. They'd kissed hundreds of time. But the declaration of war had added an urgency to Alfie's touch. She could almost feel the hot blood snaking through him, the adrenalin egging him on.

'Renee, you smell so good,' he groaned, kissing her neck as his hand crept further up her thigh and began tugging at her suspender belt.

What the . . . ? This was all too fast.

'You wearing that new perfume I bought you? It's driving me wild.'

Renee shifted uncomfortably and felt her stockings snag against the concrete path. In the factory, she could banter with the best of them, but nerves had stolen her voice.

Suddenly, before she knew where she was, his other hand was ambushing her bottom. Humiliation scorched through her. She had a notion that Alfie really cared for her, but in that moment, she felt as cheap as could be. All dressed up and for what? Laddered stockings after a quick fumble by the side of a grubby canal? The mucky sod!

'Do you mind, I ain't some tuppenny upright!' she yelled, finding her voice. Her hand landed with a stinging slap on his cheek and he fell back. Jumping to her feet, she stumbled down the path, his voice calling after her.

'Keep yer hair on, Renee. Come back . . . Come back!'

But Renee couldn't get away fast enough. Humiliated tears blurring her eyes, she stumbled further into the darkness.

The evening was as black as Newgate's knocker and Renee panicked as she suddenly realised she had no idea where she was. The dark had folded in so stealthily, it was like running through ink. This blackout was going to take some getting used to. She jumped as something warm and oily brushed her cheek.

Heart thumping, she picked her way gingerly along the Cut, tapping her foot in front of her until she felt the stairs. Finally back on Broadway, the moon emerged, throwing out a faint silver light.

She managed to orientate herself by the smells. The wet fish shop, the baker's, then the stench of beer told her she must be nearing the Two Puddings, her father's local at number 27 the Broadway, or as it was more commonly known, the Butcher's Shop, on account of the blood spilt regularly over its white-tiled walls. Its windows and familiar arched blue neon sign were all blacked out, but the rumble of deep cockney voices and laughter could not be disguised.

Clutching the bottle-green tiled frontage, Renee saw a faint torchlight swirling patterns on the pavement, casting half-illuminated shapes in the shadows. The light led up to a shapely ankle and then a low purring voice: 'Looking for some fun?'

'No thanks, darlin', but go down the Longy and you might find someone who is,' Renee snapped, pushing past.

She felt so stupid. Her sister had been right about that perfume all along. That's why Alfie had bought it – he thought he'd get something in return!

With a huge sigh of relief, Renee arrived home and, reaching in the letterbox, pulled out the key she knew would be attached to the end of a piece of string. What a night. What a fool she had been to think Alfie really cared for her. He was only ever trying to get into her knickers. Maybe her mum had been right about most men after all? At the thought of her mum, she felt a prickle of shame. She could hear her voice in her ear.

Tell the truth and shame the devil.

She'd just been so cross, though, at her mum's reaction to her makeover, at embarrassing her in front of Lily, that she behaved badly.

Renee moved with the agility of a tomcat, avoiding the floorboards she knew creaked. Her mum would have turned in long ago, but she didn't want to risk waking her.

She pushed open the parlour door with one finger and peeped in. The dying embers of a fire glowed softly in the grate. The smell in the room was moist and sharp. Carbolic and oxtail stew sweating on the heavily distempered scullery walls. If Nell Gunn were ever to be bottled as a scent, she would be Eau-de-Carbolic. Or even more apt, 'Eau-de-Distemper'. Absurdly, the thought made Renee giggle.

'You won't be laughing in a minute, my girl.'

Nell's pale face slid from the shadows. She'd been sitting in the easy chair under the fringed lampshade in the corner.

'Where have you been, you crafty little cow?'

Renee groped for an answer.

'Oh, never mind. I don't want to know. I'll deal with you later. Meantime, we got bigger problems. Frankie's gone missing. Oh and Geoff, our neighbour, remember the nice fella who taught you to ride a bike?'

Renee nodded slowly, a sense of horror slithering over her as her mum stood up and walked closer to her, so close she could see the tiny broken veins in her cheek.

'Turns out, he hanged himself.'

The carbolic air closed around her.

'*No*,' Renee sobbed, her hand flying to her mouth in shock.

'*Yes* actually, so you might well look upset, madam, but while you was sneaking out behind my back, all hell was breaking loose here.'

Renee began to weep, but Nell shook her roughly.

'Oh, save me the crocodile tears. Now you're home we need to get out and join the hunt for Frankie, so wipe that muck off your face and change into something more practical,' she ordered, glaring suspiciously at the ladder in Renee's stocking. Renee moved up the stairs as if in a dream. This morning she had been so blasé about the war, and already one day in, conflict had come to their doorstep by the bucket-load. Renee did not know it then, and later she would laugh at her naivety, but all their lives had shifted key. This was only the beginning.

6

Lily

Seven-year-old Frankie had officially been missing since noon on Monday and by Wednesday dinnertime, the Gunn family was going out of their minds.

Nell had been persuaded to stay put at home in case he showed up, but Pat was leading rotating search parties consisting of half the men from the market and docks. Even the local gang of boys, the Bricky Kids, and Snowball the tramp were out hunting for him. It was all anyone could talk of. Rumour was rife.

A strange man had been seen down the Shoot that morning. A sailor with a German accent was seen walking away with a boy Frankie's age. A boy matching his description had been seen boarding a train at Stratford.

But it was all wild conjecture. Renee, Lily, Esther and the girls sat in stony silence in the canteen at Yardley's on their dinner hour.

'It's my fault,' said Renee miserably, pushing away a plate of untouched meat pie and lighting up a cigarette.

'If I hadn't sneaked out like that to meet Alfie, none of it would have happened.'

'Don't talk daft,' soothed Lily. 'Frankie had already been gone eight hours by then, you had nothing to do with it.'

'She's right,' said Esther gently. 'Can you think of any

reason why he would just take off like that? Perhaps if you know *why* he ran away, it might make it easier to work out where he's gone?'

'That makes sense. Can you?' asked Lily.

'He ain't cut from the same cloth as other boys his age. He's sensitive, Lil, know what I mean?' Renee's face flared with anger. 'Well, actually, how would you? You don't know him on account of not coming near us for the past six years.'

Her sister's unflinching words slammed a guillotine between them, and Lily's hand drifted from her sister's shoulder.

'Oh Lil,' gasped Renee. 'I'm sorry. I didn't mean that. I'm just so tired I don't know what I'm saying. I've hardly slept.'

'It's all right,' Lily whispered miserably. 'You're right. I don't know him at all.'

Fat Lou placed a protective arm around Renee and glared at Lily for so long that despite her superior status, it was she who looked away, forced to stare instead at a glob of congealing gravy on the tabletop. Lily sensed – and not for the first time since her return – a divide. She was definitely the outsider here at Yardley's, not part of their tribe in the boisterous lipstick room, and not just because she was their supervisor. Lily knew why. She had dared to escape Stratford, and by taking a job at Bond Street she had rejected their insular world. She knew they thought she was a cut above and therefore was not to be trusted. If only they knew the real reason she had left, she thought with a snort, they wouldn't think her so high and mighty then. In fact, they would almost certainly have a few choice Anglo-Saxon expletives in their vocabulary for her. Irritated, Lily picked up a napkin and scrubbed the gravy off the tabletop as if it were memories and not leftover food she was trying to wipe away.

What was it about the East End? So suffocatingly parochial, heaven forbid you stepped out of line and dared to be different. She longed to share her ambitions with them, a future which included a career, rising through the ranks of Yardley's, continuing her training, earning enough money to never have to pay anything on the tally, nor rely on any man. She wanted wages, not housekeeping. Before the war, these dreams had been within reach. Olive Carmen had even hinted that one day she could help her oversee the opening of an overseas salon. God knows she had sacrificed enough for that privilege.

'Factory too grubby for you, is it?' Fat Lou said, cutting into her thoughts as Lily folded the gravy-stained napkin. Lily ignored the barb – she was trying to needle her and she wasn't going to take the bait.

'Not really,' she replied. 'Canteen's just the same at Bond Street.' Actually, it wasn't. She thought wistfully of the polished wooden floors and white linen tablecloths. The sugar was served in silver bowls there, not in a cup attached to the counter with string. Even the toilets were marked 'Ladies' and 'Gentlemen' not 'Male' and 'Female'. But what was the point in trying to explain her hopes and dreams to any of them, when it was Nan's life, all mapped out with Jimmy Connor – *Jimmy Connor, of all people* – that most of the girls here envied, not hers. She folded her arms. Better to stay a little aloof and professional. If she didn't get too involved, it would make her transition back to the West End all the smoother.

An awkward silence fell over the tabletop, broken only by a small voice.

'I think families need to pull together in times of trouble. You can only hope to find him by staying united.' Esther. Everyone turned in surprise, for most of them had forgotten she was even there.

Lily looked at the fifteen-year-old who had been forced to flee her country, and whose father had been missing a lot longer than Frankie and in far more dangerous circumstances. She felt her shame deepen.

'She's right,' sighed Renee, closing her hand over Lily's. 'I'm so pleased you're back. You're here now and that's what really counts.'

Renee picked up a copy of the *Stratford Express* that was sitting on top of the Formica canteen table. Three stories dominated the front page.

The suicide of Geoff Povey, the fishmonger from Angel Lane who, so distressed by national affairs, had hanged himself at his home down the Shoot. The disappearance of Frankie Gunn and a third headline: *Shock as Shoot tenants refuse to move*, over a photo of a strident Nell confronting the council officials.

'Listen to this,' spat Renee, as she read a quote in the article from Mrs Clatworthy, head of the evacuation scheme.

'*We are sorry to learn of this distressing news. I myself warned Mrs Gunn that her son should be sent to the safety zones in the first wave of evacuation. Cities are simply not a safe place for our children in wartime*. Sanctimonious old crone,' Renee muttered, pushing away the paper and bursting into tears.

Thinking with her charge-hand, rather than her big sister hat on, Lily took Renee's hand.

'Come on, we're going to see the welfare officer, I don't think you should be here.'

Renee allowed herself to be led to the only office personnel member left at Yardley's, Miss Rose Rayson.

With her warm brown eyes and gentle voice, Miss Rayson had been at Yardley's since well before the last war. She was a voice of reason and comfort, dispensing sanitary towels and aspirin to the hundreds of young girls who trooped through her doors weekly.

'Your sister was right to bring you here,' she said calmly to Renee. 'How can you possibly be expected to concentrate around machinery with your brother missing? I'm signing you both off on full pay until young Frankie returns home.'

'But I'm charge hand, I should be here,' protested Lily.

'No buts. I'm signing you both off. Now off you go home to your mother where you belong.'

Where I belong? Lily wanted to scream out. I don't belong with the Gunn family any more. Not after what happened. When a dream so precious had been wrenched from her it left her breathless. But she said none of this, of course.

'Thank you, Miss Rayson,' she replied instead, bowing her head politely.

They reached the door and her voice called after them.

'He'll come home when he's hungry enough.'

How Lily hoped she was right.

Renee needed to nip to the loo before they left, so both girls headed into the cubicle just as the bell sounded, which signalled the end of dinner break.

And so it was that both Renee and Lily overheard the lipstick girls as they piled into the lav for a last quick smoke.

'Poor Renee,' said Joycie, oblivious that she was in the cubicle five feet away. A pause, followed by an exhale of smoke, 'Wonder if Lily's return's got anything to do with Frankie doing a bunk?'

'Yeah, I mean, she's hardly the friendly type, is she?' piped up little Irene. 'Bit snooty, if you ask me. Chalk and cheese her and our Renee, ain't they.'

'Don't judge a book by its cover,' came Fat Lou's voice. Lily could picture the glint in her eye. 'She might come over like an ice queen, but I bet she's all burning up inside.'

Through a tiny crack by the door hinges, Lily could see Fat Lou running her hands up and down her voluptuous body in jest, her lips puckered and her eyes closed.

'Bet she left 'cause she was having a passionate and doomed love affair.'

'Ooh,' breathed little Irene, perched on the edge of the sink, swinging her skinny legs. 'Go on!'

'I heard she got a massive rise off Mr Lavender to return,' said Joanie.

'I heard she gave him a massive rise,' quipped Joycie. Ribald laughter bounced off the tiled walls and Lily bit her tongue in anger.

'What, you reckon she's having it off with the boss?' gasped little Irene, eyes out on stalks.

'You know what they say, the truth's always stranger than fiction,' laughed Fat Lou. 'Trust me, she's hiding something. Hang about, is that Peerless?'

The sizzle of four fag butts being hastily extinguished filled the air, followed by the banging of the toilet door. Silence.

Lily stepped outside and ran her wrists under the cold tap. She couldn't bring herself to meet Renee's gaze in the mirror as she came out.

'They're only messing,' Renee said eventually. 'It's just banter.'

'Trust me, it's forgotten already,' said Lily tersely.

'But it would really help, Lil, if I knew why you left so suddenly.'

'I told you already, I wanted a life beyond Stratford and when a position came up in Bond Street I went for it. Don't you get it, Renee? I want an inside toilet, a proper garden, hot running water and money left over at the end of the week. Sorry if it doesn't sound like one of your *Woman's Own* pot boilers, but there it is.'

She tugged down the roller towel and briskly dried her hands to disguise the tremble.

'Come on, let's clock off.'

Outside on Carpenters Road, leaning against the gates to Yardley, was Alfie.

Renee took one look at him and her mouth tightened. She gripped Lily's arm. 'Keep walking.'

'Renee,' he said, his face a picture of regret. 'I've been

trying to speak to you since Monday evening. I'm so sorry, I don't know what came over me. But you have to believe me when I tell you how much I care about you.'

'Go to hell, Alfie Buckle!' she yelled.

'Renee, you have to believe me,' he pleaded, jogging backwards to keep up with her as she strode off down the road. 'I heard about Frankie. Me and the boys from Berger's have been out looking all over for him. I won't rest until I've found him.'

'Stay away from my family, you hear me?' Renee cried, her voice quivering. 'Or I'll send me dad round.'

Alfie slowed and stared after them in despair, tugging his cap off and pushing his hand through his mop of blonde hair.

'I'll find him!' he called after them. 'I'll prove myself to you.' Renee didn't even look back. Lily glanced at her little sister in admiration. Perhaps when it came to matters of the heart, Renee had more gumption than she credited her with.

Back at the Shoot, Lily and Renee found their mother with her head in hands at the table, her eyes raw from weeping. With a jolt, Lily realised it was the first time she had ever seen her fierce matriarch of a mother cry.

She had not shed a single tear when her own beloved mum, Nanny Jess, had died, nor when Pat had been badly injured in an accident down the docks, nor when Lily had announced she was leaving. All this she had borne with a dry eye. Nell Gunn didn't believe in crying. Now, though, she looked hollowed out with pain and fear.

All around her, women from the neighbourhood were busying themselves with useful tasks: making tea, peeling potatoes, scrubbing steps . . . In the centre of this whirlwind of activity, Nell looked as vulnerable as her daughters had ever seen her.

'Any news, Mum?' Renee asked hopefully.

'I've raised ten bob doing a whip down the market for Mrs Povey. Insurance won't cover her husband on account of it being suicide and she's got five little 'uns want feeding.'

Her face puckered.

'The only respectable death in wartime is a wartime one,' she remarked sardonically.

'That's nice, Mum, but I meant about Frankie.'

She shook her head and Lily realised she was helpless in the face of a missing child. Supporting a widow, laying out the dead and birthing new life. All this Nell Gunn could do with ease. But making sense of this . . .

'Why?' Nell whispered, staring at the untouched cup of tea in front of her. 'Why would he just take off like that? He won't last five minutes out there alone. My Little Prof ain't cut out to be on his own. He's got no street smarts at all.'

More tears coursed down her weathered cheeks.

'Do you think your father's too hard on him?' she asked Renee.

Renee shrugged uncomfortably. 'You know Dad.' She turned to Lily.

'Dad's never got his head round Frankie preferring books to boxing. The East End way of trying to make a man of him – a belt and two cauliflower ears – ain't gone down well.'

Nell nodded.

'It's true. Our Frankie ain't one to run wild with the Bricky Kids. Your father gets well jibbed that he won't play knock down ginger, or any of the games we played growing up. He can't understand him.'

Lily longed to be able to contribute towards the conversation, offer some useful insight, but there was nothing she could say. The extent of her communication with Frankie had been one quick hello on the doorstep in six years . . .

'Has anyone checked the library?' Renee asked suddenly.

'It's been searched and the librarian knows to get in touch if she sees him,' Nell replied. 'Go and have a look in his room, girls, see if you can't see a clue that I ain't spotted.'

Lily trailed after Renee and found herself holding her breath as they walked into the small bedroom in the attic.

'Maybe you can see something I can't?' Renee suggested, waving her arms round his room despairingly. 'You know, fresh eyes and all that.'

Lily's large green eyes took in the rows of books, with their well-worn spines, neatly displayed alphabetically on the shelves. Emblazoned on the walls were incredibly intricate scale drawings of 17th-century sailing ships. Frankie's bed was as neatly made as any she had seen, with hospital corners.

'Blimey, where are the catapults and smelly socks?' Lily joked vainly.

'I told you, our Frankie's the studious kind,' Renee replied, sinking onto the bed.

'They must love him at school.'

'You'd think, wouldn't you?' said Renee. 'But – and here's the queer thing – he don't get on with his teachers at all. They're always threatening to expel him for being disruptive in class.'

Wearily, she rubbed her eyes. 'It's caused murders with Dad. He says Mum's not strict enough with him.'

Lily stared around in dismay. It was like she'd walked in on the closing scene of a play, without seeing any of the first half. A mystery with more questions than answers.

'And these?' she asked, picking up a box filled to bursting with hundreds of matchboxes, many with beautiful bright and delicate artwork on the cases.

A smile flashed over Renee's face.

'Oh gawd. Those. Frankie's fanatical about matchboxes, been collecting them since he was four. He loves 'em. He goes to Bow every weekend. He's on first-name terms with the gateman at Bryant & May. They give him a box of the latest fancy brand every Saturday. S'pect they'll stop doing all these now war's broken out.'

Her face fell and she lowered her voice.

'That's what really worries me, Lil. That he may actually have been taken. He would never leave home without those matchboxes.'

Lily felt a cold clammy fear inch up her spine. Please God, let nothing have happened to him. She couldn't stand it.

Suddenly there was a shout from the Shoot and both girls ran to the window.

'The police are down the Sewer Bank. They're pulling something out,' shouted a boy.

One by one, taped-over windows round the square flew open, and then they were running.

Panic, dark and electric, closed in as Lily, Renee and Nell reached the Sewer Bank first, so named as it was the deepest, darkest, filthiest spot by Stink House Bridge, a narrow channel responsible for carrying sewage to the treatment works at Barking Creek and to the outfall on the Thames.

A place where anything and everything washed up, from dead cats to old bikes.

A small crowd had assembled and were watching in horrified silence as a team of local constabulary waded out to the middle of the swirling waters and were attempting to extricate something. The surface was so covered in grease, oil and debris, they left tracks behind them.

Nell hurtled through the crowd.

'Mum, come back,' Renee pleaded but Nell seemed possessed of a superhuman strength and flung her youngest daughter back.

'Please, officer!' she roared, when she reached the edge, nearly toppling over herself. 'Is it him, is it my Frankie?'

The officer hauled a leaden mass of what looked like dark wet hair from the water. Renee screamed and buried herself in Lily's arms, but Lily forced herself to look, her heart punching through her chest.

Time seemed to still before his words came up to them.

'It's a dog,' he called and the crowd breathed as one.

Nell blew out slowly and muttered a prayer under her breath, before her knees buckled from under her.

'Come on, Mum,' said Lily gently, and together she and Renee heaved their mother off the ground.

'I don't know how much more of this I can take, girls,' she muttered, her face blanched of all colour.

'Why don't I fetch you a drop of brandy, then maybe later we visit the church and say a prayer, Mum?' said Renee shakily. 'That always makes you feel better.'

'Renee's right,' said Lily. 'You've had a terrible shock.'

Together the Gunn girls took their mother's arms and guided her back to the Shoot. For the first time since her return, Lily felt something approaching a sense of belonging. The circumstances were beyond terrible, but in its own strange way this hideous ordeal was drawing them all closer.

Later that afternoon, Lily followed her mother from the special evening service the vicar of the Shoot's church had organised so that the residents could pray for Frankie's safe return. Praying seemed about all they could do right now. Nell stood and thanked everyone for their help in the hunt for Frankie, now officially Stratford's biggest, as they filed out into the graveyard. People were running out of words and, at a loss as to what else to do, had started cooking. The kitchen at number 10 was covered in a small tidal wave of watery stew. The neighbourhood was showing its love and respect for Nell through cooking. But it would not bring Frankie home.

When the last person had left and the vicar was locking up, Lily realised she was at last alone with her mother.

After the chaos and cacophony of the Sewer Bank, the graveyard was a quiet enclave. Skeins of smoke drifted over the church, lit up a dazzling pink in the faded air. The gravestones were smothered in frosted spiderwebs, as delicate as lace.

She looked at the sign over the door:

And I am here in a place beyond desire and fear.

It seemed somehow to sum up the strange quality of this ancient patch of land.

Quite suddenly, Nell took her hand in hers, her face vulnerable in the gloaming. Lily could feel the calluses and gristled knuckles of hard labour. It was a worker's hand, huge as a beef bone and permanently bunched into a fist.

Behind her head rose a tomb, above it, a dirty angel covered in grime and lichen stared down at her reproachfully.

'Please come home, Lily, I can't lose any more children,' Nell said quietly. 'You'll have to share with Renee, but I need you home.'

Lily nodded. 'I will. But please, Mum, tell me this.' She glanced about, then lowered her voice.

'Is there any chance he could have seen you . . .' She stumbled on the words. 'You know . . .'

A muscle in her mother's jaw tightened and she dropped her hands.

'No!'

They walked back to the house in silence but at the door, Lily turned to her mother.

'I'm going to go and search again, Mum.'

'Let me get my coat and I'll come too. I can't stand to sit here no longer. I feel useless knowing my boy is out there.'

'No, Mum,' Lily insisted. 'If Frankie comes back, whose face is it he's going to want to see?'

It was a brave woman who said no to Nell Gunn, but at her daughter's words, she relented.

'Very well.'

Lily joined the teams of people out searching for the missing child in the oily depths of the blackout.

The problem was, Stratford was filled with no end of places to hide, from the miles of canals, locks and factories, to railway goods yards and markets. Instinctively, Lily headed to the Stratford works, the sprawling area where thousands of locomotives were built and serviced. On overcast days, the fire and smoke that billowed from the works gave Stratford the appearance of hell. Now there was only darkness as thick as treacle.

'Frankie!' she called, swinging about her covered torch. It threw out a slim band of light over the greasy rails. 'Frankie!'

Her voice sounded tinny, echoing off the sides of the giant goods sheds.

And suddenly the heavens opened. Lily tripped on a rail and fell, winded, at the side of the tracks.

'Damn it!' she cried as a thick slick of scarlet oozed from her knee. And then she began to weep, and once she started, she found she couldn't stop, tears and rain streaking down her cheeks in the darkness. She wasn't just crying for her missing brother. She was weeping from the burden of carrying so many secrets. Fat Lou had been right in her speculation earlier that day. She was hiding something, though nothing as obvious as an affair with the boss. Please! She only wished it were that simple. These were secrets she had locked inside for so many years. Secrets which, even now, were racing to the surface and threatening to suffocate her.

7

Lily

Saturday, 9th September, the day of Nan's nuptials, dawned sunny and clear, the weather entirely at daggers with the dark fear that had gripped the Gunn family.

'I can't go, Mum. It ain't right with Frankie still missing,' Renee said as she walked into the kitchen. Lily was already up, sitting at the kitchen table with her mum, nursing her second cup of tea.

Nell looked up wearily and lit a cigarette with a shaking hand. In the crisp morning light, Lily was stunned at how much weight her mother had lost in just one week.

'Mum, where are your Toby jugs?' Renee asked, suddenly noticing they were gone from their place on the mantel.

'I pawned 'em,' Nell replied. 'To give the money to Mrs Povey. That poor woman is struggling. God knows why, but the word "suicide" carries such shame.'

'But you loved them,' Renee protested.

'What does it matter? They're only silly jugs. The only thing that matters in life is my kids . . . and now . . .' She choked on a sob and tears streamed down her face. She made no effort to brush them away and they dripped silently onto the scrubbed tabletop.

'Mum, I'm worried about you,' said Renee softly, coming up behind her mother and draping her arms about her shoulders. 'That's why me and Lil can't go today. Nan'll understand, with Frankie still missing an' all.'

'Renee's right, Mum,' Lily agreed. 'We ought to be here with you.'

Nell heaved a huge sigh, the lines on her face deepening.

'Now, you listen here, girls,' she said, clamping her hands over Renee's and raising them to her lips to kiss. 'You'll both go and represent the Gunn family. Your father's got a massive team up from the docks today, and they are gonna leave no stone unturned. Look at this,' she said, suddenly turning her attentions to the local paper. 'Bloke fell to his death through an asbestos ceiling, putting up blackout blinds in a factory in Plaistow. The publican of the Maypole has become the first man in England to be prosecuted for insufficient blackout blinds and, to top it all, they're releasing men from prison so they can join the forces.'

Wearily, she passed a hand over her mouth.

'Innocent men being sent to prison and guilty men being freed. The world's gone to hell in a handcart! So, you go and see that pal of yours married, and you wish her well from me. God knows someone in Stratford should find a little happiness in this mess.'

She raised her eyes to the heavens.

'Actually Lord, if you're listening, show the Gunn family a little mercy, would you?'

Lily squeezed her mum's shoulder and took her cup of tea into the backyard. A flash of pink caught her eye.

'What the . . . ?' An enormous dead pig had sailed over the back fence and landed with a fleshy thud on the roof of the outdoor lav. Its insides had been gutted, but he eyed Lily mournfully as his head flopped over the side of the outhouse. Just when she thought things couldn't get any stranger!

Alerted by her cry, Nell and Renee came rushing into the yard. Unfazed, Nell rolled up her sleeves and hauled the gutted pig off the roof of the privy, as if a dead animal arriving over the back wall was a perfectly normal occurrence.

'Would you look at that?' she exclaimed, pulling out a sack from the belly of the pig. Chocolate, tea, stockings, sweets, tinned fruit and all manner of other goodies spilled from the bag.

'Your father brought home a lovely lascar seaman from the docks for a cup of tea late last night. He must've liberated a few items to say thanks. By the time we get this lovely boy butchered, he'll feed half the Shoot,' she grinned.

'Well you did ask Him for help,' Renee said, nudging her mother.

'Blimey, I must have a direct line,' she replied.

Lily stared gobsmacked as her mother began dividing up the stolen booty on the floor of the yard. In her years away, Lily had forgotten the East End's unique economy.

'Dear me. That would never have happened in Bond Street,' she murmured eventually.

Within moments, Renee and Nell were doubled up, helpless with laughter. It was infectious and Lily couldn't help but join in, wiping the tears from her eyes with the edge of her handkerchief. For one brief moment, it felt good to do nothing but laugh.

'Right, enough of all this,' Nell said, straightening up. 'You girls better go upstairs and get your glad rags on. You don't want to walk in late to church.'

When Lily came down one hour later, dressed in her best pale lavender suit, cinched in at the waist, with snowy white collars and cuffs, she found her mother out in the yard, deftly butchering the pig.

'I didn't know you knew butchering skills,' Lily remarked, wrinkling her nose.

'My first husband taught me,' Nell grunted as she heaved

the pig over. 'He was from a long line of butchers. About the only useful thing I got from the whole bleedin' marriage.'

'I thought he was a boxer,' Lily replied. Her mother's first short-lived marriage at the age of seventeen was not often discussed and she'd always been intrigued by it.

'He was that an' all.'

'Why did the marriage break up?' Lily asked. 'Only, you've never said.'

''Cause he kept bringing his boxing skills home with him.'

'What, he raised his fists to you?' she asked, aghast.

'And his boots, his belt, or whatever else he happened to have to hand.'

'Oh Mum, I didn't know . . .' Lily's voice trailed off.

'No, and don't be discussing it with our Renee neither,' Nell said sharply, wiping the blood from her hands on her apron before fixing Lily with a knowing gaze.

'So you see, Lily, you ain't the only one who's suffered, my girl, we've all made sacrifices in our life. It's called a woman's lot.'

Lily disagreed. Maybe in the 19th century, but here now in 1939, women deserved the right to live in peace and safety, and to pursue their hopes and dreams, no matter how hard that road might be to travel. But wasn't that the self-same argument that led her to leave the Shoot in the first place? She felt a lump in her throat. If only she hadn't been so weak.

'I'm ready, how do I look?' Renee's voice interrupted the tension hanging over the yard.

'Oh darlin', you look beautiful,' Nell sighed. Lily had to hand it to her little sister. In powder pink, her blonde waves shining and the faintest touch of make-up, she was a peach.

'Have a wonderful time. I'm sure Nan'll make a beautiful bride,' Nell said.

Lily hesitated.

'Do you know what, I don't think I should go, Renee. Nan only invited me out of politeness, I don't expect she really wants me there.'

'She does and so do I,' insisted Renee. 'Please, you have to come. We've got so much time to catch up on. Also, if you want the girls to think you're one of them and not Miss Snooty Knickers, today would be a good start.'

Lily looked at her sister's huge blue eyes and felt her resolve weaken.

'Very well.'

'Oh girls, do us a favour, will ya?' said Nell. 'And drop this bag round to Mrs Barnett. I'd go meself, only I want to be in if there's any news on Frankie.'

Clutching the bag of groceries, the girls made their way to the furthest part of the Shoot where Mrs Barnett lived at the end of a tiny court with no natural light.

Lily wrinkled her nose. It smelt of cats' wee and putrescent vegetables. Even by Stratford's standards, this stank.

The door flew open and immediately Lily was assailed by a fug of sour, oniony-smelling air, which made her breath catch in her throat.

'Oh, hello dearies,' Mrs Barnett grinned, revealing a rotten row of stumps. She could have been twenty-eight or fifty-eight. It was hard to tell past the poxed skin.

'Come on in, girls, and don't mind the mess,' she said, clutching her back. It was only then they could she see was carrying, a small bulge protruding from a grubby apron.

Renee smiled and stepped in, seemingly oblivious to the squalor of the place. Everywhere Lily looked, there were nippers, crawling across the floor, sucking on sugar teats, or looking up from behind tattered furniture with big solemn eyes. The smell of boiled potatoes and soiled babies' napkins hung in the air, sharp and savoury.

Mrs Barnett caught Lily staring.

'He's only gotta hang his trousers on the bedpost and I'm caught,' she joked feebly. 'Now another little 'un on the way for my sins. Who'd be a bloody woman?' She stared about her in a daze.

'Ten in the bed and one up the bleedin' chimney. So, Auntie send you, did she?'

'Yes,' said Lily, snapping out her of torpor and holding out the bag of shopping. 'This is from my mum.'

'Oh, bless her.' Tears sprang into her eyes as she rummaged through the bag of tinned meat, condensed milk and treats from the black-market pig.

'Kids, you've got tea tonight.'

She turned to the girls, rheumy eyes filled with gratitude.

'I expect I don't look none too pretty to you girls, do I? And here's you all dressed up looking like ladies and smelling so fine. Believe it or not, I looked like you once, before my Bill got his hands on me.'

Instinctively, her blistered fingers moved to her black eye and with a tremor, she traced over its angry purple contours. Lily found herself wondering what the rest of her body looked like. The brutality some women put up with was beyond words. She thought about her mother's revelation in the backyard earlier. If it could happen to someone as tough as her, what chance did this slight woman have of defending herself?

Lily looked about the place again. The signs she had missed before were suddenly evident. The splintered doorframe. The fist-shaped hole in the wall. The dented skirting board. Mr Barnett, it seemed, had broken most things, including his wife's spirit.

'Why don't you leave him?' Lily blurted.

Mrs Barnett smiled, no trace of offence, only pity for Lily's naivety.

'And where would I go with all these kids?'

'But what about the police, have you not called them?' she persisted.

Mrs Barnett looked at Lily as if she'd just dropped down from space.

'Dear girl, they drink with my husband down the Two Puddings!'

Lily blushed for a fool, before turning on her heel.

She hurried from the Shoot, through Cat's Alley and out onto Angel Lane with Renee scurrying after her. Only then, away from the fetid air, did she feel like she could breathe.

'This place!' she snapped. 'I don't know how you stick it, Renee.'

Renee shrugged. 'It's home, ain't it? Come on, buck up. Esther'll be waiting for us. We've got a wedding to go to.'

The sight of the Gunn girls all done up in their Sunday best turned heads the length and breadth of Angel Lane.

Sharp-booted boys working their stalls stopped to stare. As always, it was Renee's diamond-hard, blonde glamour and tight curves – poured into a powder-pink, ermine-trimmed number – which caught their eye.

'Renee Gunn. You're as sweet as lemon honey,' whistled a coster by the name of Jack, King of the Fruit Sellers in Stratford. Tossing some fruit into a brown paper bag, he twisted it round and tucked it in her handbag.

'Try my juicy cherries, Renee,' he winked. Lily rolled her eyes. He was virtually salivating.

'Never mind the cherries, you should be watching your cabbages,' she snapped. He turned back to find the Bricky Kids pilfering from his stall. 'Oi!' he bellowed, Renee forgotten as he gave chase.

The girls made their way through the babble of schleppers and the housewives bantering for a bargain. Saturday morning at the market was as raucous as a carnival.

Lily shook her head at the sight of it all. The shoppers,

mainly women and old men since the war had broken out, haggling as if their lives depended on it.

Through the middle of them all weaved a husk of a man from the Great War with an iron support on his left leg and a sandwich-board banner emblazoned with *The End is Nigh*. Lily half wondered if he wasn't right. Renee seemed oblivious. 'Oh look, there's Esther. Cooeee!' she called over the crush.

Esther was waiting patiently outside her mother's uncle's shop.

'Are you sure Nan won't mind my coming?' she asked, worriedly smoothing down a plain grey wool pencil skirt. 'I've only met her once and this is all I have to wear.'

With her deep toffee-brown eyes and milk-white skin, to Lily's mind, she was far and away the loveliest of them all. Without her white turban, her long, dark hair cascaded down her back, black and silky like a cat.

'Don't worry, you look lovely,' she smiled down at the young service girl.

'You really do,' Renee enthused. ''Sides, this is a cockney wedding, everyone's welcome.'

'What's in the package?' Lily asked.

'Oh, not much, just some Jewish cakes and biscuits my mother made. I'm afraid we couldn't really afford anything more.'

'That's so thoughtful,' Lily said. 'We've got a traditional cockney gift. Soap, so they can always stay clean – Yardley's English Lavender of course . . .'

'Coal for warmth and salt for food,' cut in Renee. 'Mind you, there ain't enough soap in Stratford for Nan's mum.'

She stuck her nose in the air and affected a posh accent.

'My Nanette's getting a maisonette.'

Lily laughed, a lovely rich sound.

'Oh, leave off, Renee.'

'Come on, Lil. She's a dreadful snob and she's got worse in the time you've been away.'

'East Ham first, then it'll be Dagenham next,' Lily conceded. 'And then where?'

'Buckingham,' Renee quipped. 'Palace, that is.'

She tucked her arm through Esther's with a wink as they weaved their way up to the Broadway to catch the bus.

'Listen to her accent and you'd never know she was born down the Shoot, same as us. All kippers and curtains, that one.'

In East Ham, Nan's mum might've had aspirations above her station, but even Lily had to hand it to Carol Rogers. She'd done a lovely job organising her only daughter's wedding.

Nan and Jimmy cut a dashing couple. He so handsome in his Naval uniform and Nan radiant in cream satin with a sweetheart neckline, a long veil in exquisite Belgian lace and a bouquet of orange blossom. Her gleaming chestnut waves shimmering in the September sunshine.

'Blimey, you'd never know there was a war on, would ya?' Renee whispered as they entered the hall Nan's mum had specially hired for the occasion.

Almost no one in Stratford had a hall for their wedding reception. Usual practice was a church ceremony with everyone piling back to the bride's parents for sausage rolls, pickled onions, a keg of beer and a piano rolled out onto the cobbles. Lily was impressed as she took in the white-draped hall, with a glitterball, band and buffet heaving with food.

'They must've saved for years for this,' she remarked, sipping on a lemonade.

'Will you look at that cake,' Esther murmured, eyeing up the iced and frosted creation groaning with marzipan.

'Soon as Mrs Rogers bagged that insurance clerk after Nan's real dad died, she's been paying into a wedding fund,'

Renee whispered, knocking back a port and lemon and grabbing another one from the drinks table.

'Steady on, Renee,' Lily warned under her breath.

'What for?' she demanded.

'You won't remember any of this lovely wedding.'

'I know,' she said, draining her second drink. 'I'm getting roasted to forget. Forget there's a war on and somewhere out there, our Frankie's alone or worse, and we're all here making out like everything's "simply marvellous".'

'That's enough, Renee,' Lily muttered.

Suddenly the rest of the girls from the lipstick room piled in.

'Oi-Oi, Fat Lou, over here!' Renee yelled, before putting both fingers in her lips and letting rip an ear-drum shredding whistle.

Betty, Joanie, Joycie, Mavis, little Irene and Fat Lou gathered round, high-pitched voices all gassing away ten to the dozen.

Lily tried her hardest to relax and smile, but it wasn't easy to know your past was the subject of gossip and a part of her was still smarting after overhearing the girls' conversation in the toilet. But she had to at least try, otherwise this day was going to be very long.

'I like your hair, Joycie,' she said. 'Did you have a new wave?'

'Oh fanks,' she said, proudly patting her head. 'Did it meself with a home perm.'

'That's how comes she smells like an egg sandwich,' quipped Joanie.

'Oi leave off,' Joycie giggled, poking her in the ribs.

'Here, Renee, where's your Alfie?' Fat Lou asked.

'Don't know, don't care,' Renee said, lifting her glass to her lips.

'I saw him earlier, he was chatting to some woman on a timber barge down the Cut,' remarked Betty.

'Probably trying to make a grab for her, the mucky sod,' Renee scowled, feeling the sharp twist of betrayal in her guts.

'Hors d'oeuvre, girls?' asked Mrs Rogers, coming up behind them brandishing a tray. She looked remarkable in a pale-blue suit draped with a silver fox fur stole and hat with two taxidermy doves welded to the side.

'What's that, then?' Joycie asked, trying not to stare at her hat.

'It's a ham sandwich, cut up into forty pieces,' joked Fat Lou, grabbing a handful off the tray.

'It's a beautiful wedding, Mrs Rogers. You've obviously worked very hard,' remarked Lily, tactfully changing the subject.

'One tries, dear,' Mrs Rogers gushed, plumping her hair. 'What do you think, Lilian? Would this pass muster in Bond Street?'

'Oh, absolutely,' Lily nodded, trying to ignore Fat Lou and Renee pulling faces behind her.

'Such a shame your mother couldn't make it.'

'Yes, well, we are having a bit of a trying time of it, Mrs Rogers. You heard about Frankie?'

'News did reach us in East Ham, yes dear. Rather rum of your mother not to have him evacuated. Poor thing's probably taken *himself* off to the countryside.' She laughed at her own joke.

Lily fixed her grin in place as Mrs Rogers moved off to another group, leaving behind a cloud of April Violets.

'Snooty cow,' Renee muttered. 'Who does she think she is?'

'Cat's Nats,' the girls all said in unison as the smell of her perfume lingered.

'Who's the Cat's Nats?' Nan asked as she and her new husband appeared, working the room. Lily felt the back of her neck tense as she looked at the groom. She could see he was rat-arsed already, his gaze lolling predictably on Renee's boobs, but Nan was as sparkling and radiant as any bride Lily had ever seen.

'Never mind. You did it, Nan!' screamed Renee, hugging her best friend tightly.

'Yes, I always said Jimmy was the man for me,' Nan remarked, looking pointedly over Renee's shoulder at Lily.

'I wish you all the luck in the world, Nan,' Lily replied quietly as Jimmy wrenched his gaze away from Renee's chest.

'A toast,' smiled Nan.

'To old friends.'

'To old friends,' chorused the lipstick girls.

'And new ones,' Renee added, pulling Esther into the centre of their group.

'And Renee,' added Joycie loyally. 'For bravely speaking up and getting us an extra two shillings a week.'

After the wedding breakfast had been devoured, it was time for the speeches. Breaking with tradition, Carol stood up in place of Nan's stepfather.

'To know the happiness that my husband and I have enjoyed is all I have ever wanted for my Nanette,' she crooned.

Lily watched as Renee gave Esther a drunken wink.

'You'd never know she was from the Shoot like the rest of us, would ya?' she slurred. 'Her accent changed when she moved address.'

'Renee, mind your mouth,' Lily hissed. She knew she should have stopped her when she moved from the port and lemon to the gin and oranges.

Carol went on, oblivious.

'From the moment James and Nanette began courting on her eighteenth birthday, we all knew it was a match made in heaven.'

''Cept they never,' whispered Renee, her gin breath soft in Esther's ear. 'They started seeing each other in secret when

Nan was fifteen, but don't let the truth get in the way of a good story.' Esther's brown eyes widened, and Lily nudged her garrulous younger sister, shooting her a furious stare.

'What?' Renee whispered. 'It's true. Mrs Rogers got wind of it and caused blue murder. Jimmy threw her over until she'd turned eighteen, not before he made her have a quick bunk-up down the C—'

'That's enough!' Lily snapped.

'Sorry,' Renee said sulkily. 'I'm losing my best pal, I'm allowed to feel a little sore.'

But even Renee's acid asides dried up when Nan and Jimmy took to the dance floor. The band struck up Vera Lynn's 'We'll Meet Again' and Jimmy gathered his bride up in his arms. As they glided round the dance floor and the raw and melancholy notes slid over the smoky room, not a single person could keep their eyes off them.

In amongst the mayhem and chaos of war, Nan Rogers had married her sweetheart. Lily watched them closely, impressed at the seeming ease with which they had whitewashed the past. She wished she could do the same. To unknowing eyes, they were the epitome of the perfect golden couple. Only she knew better. How Lily hoped they'd make a go of it, but with Jimmy's form, Nan was certainly going to have her work cut out. With the first dance over, the band struck up something more up-tempo and soon the rest of the wedding party spilled onto the dance floor to join them.

Lily preferred to watch from the sidelines, keeping a half eye on her by now very merry younger sister.

As the room got hotter, shirt collars were loosened, heels were kicked off and the East End did what it did best.

'Come and kick your heels up, sis!' bellowed Renee from the head of a conga line she was leading that consisted mainly of the lipstick department.

Lily shook her head and smiled.

'There's only room for one Gunn girl on that dance floor!' she called back with a laugh. If she was honest, as keen as she was to curry favour with the girls, she had to consider her new position as charge hand. It probably wasn't the done thing to be seen clinging to the back of the conga line if she was to gain the girls' respect. Renee had no such worries.

'Up the Yardley girls!' she hooted, weaving in and out of the throng shoeless, glass held aloft.

The band were terrific and when they started playing the first few bars of the 'Siegfried Line', a great roar of approval bellowed out. Even Mrs Rogers seemed to have relaxed. One of the doves had slid off the side of her hat and was perched precariously by the side of her head.

The Yardley girls belted out the lyrics, slamming their feet on the parquet floor to the rhythm, voices like cannons.

Lily had to admire her sister's vitality as she kicked her heels up higher and higher, scarlet lips parted in laughter.

When Fat Lou hoisted her up on her shoulder with a great whoop, a circle formed round them, hooting and bellowing.

'We're gonna hang out the washing on the Siegfried Line'

Renee's blonde curls bounced as Fat Lou aped around, pretending to march like a soldier. She had to hand it to them as they all sang along to the patriotic new song. The lipstick girls were a determined tribe, committed to wringing every last drop of fun from this wedding, war or no war.

Lily wished she had some of her little sister's joie de vivre. Instead, she felt a deep ache of tiredness behind her eyes. She'd forgotten how rowdy an East End wedding could get. The singing was loud, feverish almost, and the stench of cigarette smoke and pickled onions was making her feel queasy. The floor was sticky with spilt beer. A drunken aunt was minesweeping forgotten drinks and two of the pageboys were secretly tying shoelaces together under the tables. She longed for the fragranced calm and order of the Bond Street salon. The biggest drama there had been when Bunty Paige had lost her tweezers. It was a world away from Stratford. Reaching for her bag and gloves, she made a decision and it was the best one she'd made all day. It was time to go home and slip into bed with a cocoa.

As she weaved her way through the steamy crowds, Lily saw something that made her stop. Esther was pushing open the door to the cloakroom that led to the lavatories when Lily spotted Jimmy eyeing her beadily. Putting down his pint, he slipped in behind her.

By the time Lily made it in there, the groom had Esther backed up in the corner, one hand snaked round her waist.

'Go on, just one little kiss,' he slurred, his eyes slithering down to her cleavage. 'You're such a pretty little thing. I'm off to war tomorrow. Don'cha wanna make a sailor happy?'

Disgust boiled up inside Lily.

'Your new wife is on the other side of that door,' she said icily.

Jimmy released Esther and swung round.

'Esther, why don't you leave?' Lily said in her calmest voice. The service girl didn't need telling twice and bolted.

'She's fifteen and what about Nan? I can't believe she actually married you after everything. You haven't changed a bit.'

Rather than look chastised, Jimmy lit up a cigarette and grinned like a wolf.

'Well, well, well, if it ain't Lily Gunn back in Stratford,' he said. 'You ain't a looker like your Renee, but I'd settle for a kiss off you instead.' He blew a stream of smoke into the darkness of the confined cloakroom. 'How about it, Lil, for old time's sake?' Leering, he cupped his crotch with one hand and winked at her. 'I bet you've missed what a real man feels like.'

Before Lily had a chance to reply, the door crashed opened and Renee appeared, shrewdly sizing the situation up in a moment.

'Oh, this gets better and better,' Jimmy laughed, loud and ribald, flinging an arm drunkenly round Renee.

'Both Gunn girls at once. What I wouldn't give for an hour alone with you two.' Lily winced, from her sister's breath it seemed Renee had drunk enough gin tonight to sink a battleship.

'Oh, go fuck a barrel!' Renee screamed and with a drunken howl, landed a knockout blow on the bridegroom's chin. Lily could've sworn she heard his teeth rattle in his head, before he staggered back and landed with a clatter against a rail full of coats.

Just when Lily didn't think things could get any stranger, Fat Lou squeezed herself into the cloakroom. She didn't even see Jimmy, out cold under the coats.

'Girls, you'll never believe it,' she said breathlessly. 'I just heard. Your Frankie's come home.'

8

Renee

Renee sobered up instantly, and was out and pelting down the street with Lily in hot pursuit.

'Renee, wait!' she could hear Lily yelling. 'At least put on your shoes.'

But being shoeless in the blackout was of no consequence. Frankie was home and Renee wasn't there. The blood roared in her ears as she hitched her skirts up and ran faster, Lily's cries vanishing on the wind.

She barely noticed as a horse reared backwards, showing the whites of its eyes, hooves skittering on the cobbles as she tore across a busy thoroughfare.

'Watch it, girl! There's a blackout in case you ain't noticed!'

Renee ignored the protests of the rag and boner as she flashed like a dart over the Broadway.

She tore through the gloom of the Shoot, busting her toe open on a cobblestone. Ignoring the blinding scorch of pain, she burst through the door into the light of the kitchen at number 10.

Enveloped in his mother's arms, hugged tightly into her apron skirts was her brother Frankie. His scared little face peeked out.

'Frankie!' Renee sobbed. And then she was in her mother's arms too, kissing the top of her brother's head.

Lily hung back shyly at the doorstep.

'Come here,' ordered Nell.

The Gunn women formed a ring, all tangled limbs, clinging to one another. In the centre of the circle stood a frightened little boy.

'Don't ever scare me like that again, son,' said Nell gruffly. 'Now Renee, put the kettle on, this young man'll be in need of a hot cup of tea.'

Renee turned. In the emotion of the moment, she hadn't even seen Alfie sitting in silence at the kitchen table.

'What are you doing here?' she snapped.

'Don't you take that tone, madam,' Nell scolded, laying a protective hand on Alfie's shoulder. 'It was Alfie what brought our Frankie home.'

Alfie stood and took Renee's hand.

'I promised you I'd find him, Renee,' he said quietly. 'I meant what I said.'

'About what?' she whispered, shocked at the depth of emotion in his eyes.

'About finding him . . . And about loving you.'

Renee caught sight of herself in the reflection of the kettle. What a sight. Her mascara was streaked down her face and her blood-soaked stockings were ripped to shreds.

'Good knees-up at Nan's?' Alfie remarked with a wry smile.

'Never mind that,' she said. 'Where did you find him?'

He tapped his head.

'You want to find a kid, you gotta think like one. I recruited the Bricky Kids. We found him hidden under a tarpaulin in a pile of coal under one of the barges. Reckon he'd been there all week. Mark you, he hasn't said a word to me.'

'But why, Frankie?' she asked, turning to her brother. 'We've been going scatty here.'

He made a pitiful sight. Only the whites of his eyes showed in his filth-encrusted face. Rake-like at the best of times, now his shirt hung off him as he stared at the floor in a daze of cold and hunger.

'There's plenty of time for all that,' interrupted Nell, taking a towel she'd been warming by the hearth and draping it protectively round his shoulders. 'Let's get some warmth into the lad.'

The door opened and with it a blast of icy air. A shadow fell over them.

'Dad,' choked Renee. 'Look who's home. Alfie found him.'

Renee had never seen so many conflicting emotions pass over one man's face like clouds. Relief, confusion, love . . . But the one that crystallised was rage. His hand absent-mindedly went to the tip of his bitten-off ear.

'It's all right, boys, hunt's off. He's home,' Pat called back to the group of dockers huddled behind him in the darkness.

Pat kicked the door shut with his foot, and with his hands began to draw off his heavy docker's belt.

'Your vanishing act nearly killed your mother. We've had half of Stratford and the docks out looking for you, you little sod. Don't you know there's a war on?'

He whipped his belt off with a snap.

'Now get here.'

Frankie whimpered and scrabbled under the table, but he wasn't quick enough. Her father's hand reached out in a flash, caught him by the ankle and dragged him back out.

'Nowhere to run now, boy,' he growled.

A cold fist closed over Renee's heart. When her father was in one of these moods, he'd start a fight with King Kong.

'Dad, no!' she cried. She thought about putting herself between them but to her surprise, Lily beat her to it.

'This isn't the way, Dad,' she said, her voice wavering. 'He's only seven.'

'Keep out of it, Lily,' Pat thundered, pushing her to one

side, before he turned his icy glare back to his son cowering on the floorboards.

'No Dad, please,' Lily begged, frantically plucking at the sleeve of his donkey jacket, 'let's sit and talk, it doesn't have to be this way.'

'You got a death wish, girl?' her father said, his deep voice tremulous. 'You ain't been around for six years and now you're questioning my authority. I won't tell you again, keep out of it!'

Nell caught Lily's arm as her father rounded back on Frankie.

'Never mind running away, you ain't gonna be able to walk by the time I'm done with you,' he vowed, raising the heavy metal belt-buckle high above his head. 'I should've made a man of you a long time ago. That's half the problem, we've spoilt you.'

In a flash, he flipped Frankie over and brought the buckle crashing down on his backside with a crack. Frankie's slender body twitched and shuddered before going slack.

'Defend yourself,' Pat roared, bringing the buckle down again and again on his thigh with increasing ferocity. The only sound was the thwack of leather and the sharp inhale of breath.

Renee sobbed as Alfie drew her into his arms. How much could he take?

The sound of breaking glass sliced through the air and Renee's head snapped back up.

Her mother was walking slowly towards her husband, holding the broken end of a milk bottle outstretched before her.

'I'm warning you, Pat Gunn. Put that belt down now. If you don't . . .' Her green eyes flashed dangerously. 'Well, you can only stay awake so long.'

'You wouldn't dare,' scoffed Pat.

'Try me.'

The room held its breath as husband and wife stared at each other from across the chasm, raw adrenalin pulsing through their veins. In all her nineteen years, Renee had never seen her parents have a cross word. In many ways, theirs was the most equal relationship down the Shoot. Her dad wasn't like the Mr Barnetts of this world. He'd never once raised his hand to her mother and gave her his wage packet religiously each Friday, so she never went short on housekeeping. In turn, her mother treated him like a king, making sure his tea was always on the table when he got home and never questioning where his business took him at odd hours. It was a rare occasion when Nell Gunn challenged her husband on anything. But, Renee knew when her mum meant business. And when it came to her youngest, Nell would do serious damage to anyone who harmed so much as a hair on his head. Like most East End women, when it came to her kids, she was a lioness.

Pat knew it too. Perhaps, paradoxically, it was one of the reasons he loved his 'old Dutch' as he called her.

He put his belt back on and, without a backwards glance, stormed out of the house, slamming the door so hard, the whole building shuddered.

Renee suspected claret would spill on the sawdust of the Two Puddings tonight.

Her father might have crossed a line this evening, but backing down to her mother would be a bitter pill for him to swallow. According to him, compromise was a weakness. For as long as she could remember, he'd preached: *Never take a step back, otherwise the opposition'll swamp you. If you see an opening, you take it.*

What a shame Pat had had two headstrong daughters and one bookworm son and not the other way round, Renee thought, her heart still hammering in her chest.

It was Nell who broke the stunned silence.

'Let him go and find a fight down the Butcher's Shop, and if he can't pick a fight there, he can fight with himself, silly old fool,' she muttered, picking the chair up off the floor with a trembling hand.

'And you get off home, Alfie, there's a good lad. Thank you again for finding our Frankie. Oh and Alfie, be a good boy and keep this to yourself. What goes on in the home, stays in the home, know what I mean,' Nell ordered. 'Mr Gunn's a little wound up at the moment, what with the war and Frankie running away.'

'I understand. My dad would've given me a right hiding an' all,' Alfie grinned, putting his cap on. 'War's making us all act a bit barmy,' he said, shooting a meaningful glance at Renee.

'Will you be all right?' he asked softly, as Renee walked with him to the door.

'Yeah,' she replied, with a weak smile.

As Alfie made to leave, he leant over and whispered in her ear.

'I meant what I said earlier, I do love you. I'm such a nitwit for getting fresh with you. Forgive me?'

'We'll see,' she replied, shutting the door on him. Actually, after today, she'd already decided to forgive him, but it wouldn't do to let him off the hook quite so quickly.

As her mum began sweeping up broken glass, Renee traipsed out to wash the blood and sweat off her body.

Never mind the war in Europe, she thought casting her mind back over the night's hostilities.

Renee helped her mum get the place cleaned up, while Lily dragged the tin tub in from the yard and heated up warm water.

Nell bathed Frankie in front of the fire while the girls prepared bread and dripping. They ate in exhausted silence, the only sound the rain bashing the bricks outside.

The events of the evening had fully sobered Renee up and now she was left with a banging headache. She knew she shouldn't have started on the gin, it always did put her in the mood for a fight. Mind you, she'd have knocked Jimmy out anyway for the way he'd tried it on with her and Lily in the cloakroom. What a toe-rag! And on his wedding day of all days! She hadn't really registered it at the time, but what was Lily doing in the cloakroom with Jimmy anyhow?

She gazed blearily at her big sister. Lily was staring at Frankie with a queer look in her eyes. Renee supposed it must be odd for her. After all, when she'd left, he'd been a chubby little baby. Now he'd matured into a small, slim boy with chiselled cheekbones and mature-looking features, who wore a permanently grave expression as if prematurely aged.

'It's raining stair rods outside,' Renee said, in an attempt to lighten the tension of the evening.

Frankie stared up from his bread and drip, his eyebrows drawn together in a frown.

'Don't be absurd. Rain is liquid water in the form of droplets that have condensed from atmospheric water vapour.'

Lily stared at him in astonishment.

'See what I mean,' Renee grinned, affectionately ruffling Frankie's head. 'He's our Little Prof, ain't yer, Frankie?'

Nell got up slowly and placed another chunk of coal from the scuttle onto the dying fire, before covering it with a sheet of newspaper to draw it. She turned and in the weak firelight she looked as if she'd aged ten years.

'Lily, why don't you take your brother up to bed?' she said wearily. 'Renee can help you.'

'I'll do it!' Renee protested. 'I usually read to him every night.'

'Not tonight, Josephine. There's enough gin in your veins to kill a rat,' Nell snapped.

Renee glared at her mum, but seemed suitably chastened.

Frankie stood and scrubbed his exhausted face.

'Mum, what'll happen when Dad gets back?' he asked.

'Don't worry about your father. Leave him to me.'

Frankie turned and went to the stairs.

'Frankie,' Nell added. He paused, his eyes vast dark pools in his face. 'Don't ever scare me like that again.'

Up in Frankie's immaculately ordered bedroom, Renee flopped down onto his bed and yawned, while Lily once more looked around in surprise at such a neat boy's room.

'Renee tells me you're collecting matchboxes, Frankie.'

He nodded seriously as he changed into his pyjamas.

'I have six hundred and fifty-four boxes. My ultimate aim is to collect one thousand.'

'Goodness, that's quite a collection,' Lily remarked, smoothing down a stray hair from his head. He winced and shifted away from her. A look of hurt flashed over her face.

'Give him time,' Renee mouthed.

'What's your favourite?' Lily asked.

'Why Wax Vestas, of course,' he replied, grey eyes lighting up as he finished buttoning his pyjamas. 'One finds the safety match, so beloved of the housewife, is inadequate when faced with the superior striking power of a Wax Vesta.'

Frankie came alive as he pulled a crate of matchboxes from under his bed and started talking Lily through his favourites.

'Don't get him started on matchboxes,' Renee chuckled, but Lily wasn't listening. She was absolutely fixated on Frankie, staring at him as if she were drinking in the sight of him.

He weren't half a funny little bugger. Renee loved him with all her heart, but Frankie was like a character from the Gothic era, locked away in a room full of matchboxes and books. There was no trace of the tough little cockney kid his birthright demanded.

'Don't you like to play outside with the rest of the children down the Shoot?' Lily asked, pulling back the blackouts. Carts made from orange-boxes, skates and homemade toys were strewn helter-skelter across the cobbles of the square.

'Like we did you mean?' Renee chipped in. 'I always did thrash you at conkers.' Lily rolled her eyes.

Frankie shrugged. 'My peers are very good at games and won't let me take part. The character of children is such that they naturally select the stronger ones. Alas, this is the nature of the beast. Besides, they are noisy and disturb my thinking.'

Lily looked at Renee and raised her eyebrows in disbelief. There were so many emotions etched on her face, but the one Renee recognised most was regret. Lily had missed a lot of her brother's childhood and it was funny, Renee thought as she looked from her older sister, to her younger brother. Seeing them together side-by-side for the first time in years, she was struck by the similarity in them. Frankie had Lily's colouring and slow and considered manner. Neither had her blonde hair or hot head. Both were outcasts too, in their own way.

'Do you have any friends?' Lily asked hopefully.

Frankie cocked his head in thought.

'Bobby. The gatekeeper at Bryant & May. He's very old. About forty at least, I think.'

Lily smiled and pulled back his bedcovers.

'Well, I know I'm only an old and boring sister, but I should like to be your friend also, if you'll let me. Perhaps we could go to the library together next week?'

He thought through this proposition as he clambered into bed.

'It closes at five p.m. sharp, with one evening on Thursday allocated to late-night perusing.'

'Thursday it is then,' Lily smiled.

'Late-night perusing?' Renee laughed, hauling herself off the bed. 'Honestly, Frankie, you are a case. A proper dictionary swallower, like your big sister.' She winked at Lily. 'You got all the time in the world to get to know her, but now it's bedtime.'

He stared up at her, huge silver eyes haunted by what, she could not tell. The flickering gas lamp showed up the fragility of his cheekbones.

'Renee, will you sit with me until I go to sleep? I'm . . . I'm afraid Dad'll come back.'

'Is that why you ran away, Frankie?' she whispered, over the hiss of the gaslight. 'Because of Dad?'

'No,' he replied. 'Mum said that if we were to die, we would all die together. I heard her telling another woman on the doorstep. I . . . I don't want to die.'

'Oh Frankie, you're not going to die,' she gushed. 'Mum just doesn't want you evacuated, she didn't really mean it.'

'Then why would she say it?' he asked. Renee searched the darkness, eyes flickering over his bedroom, but as hard as she tried, she couldn't find a suitable answer.

'Because sometimes adults say things they don't mean, and do things they wish they hadn't,' Lily said softly behind her shoulder. Her voice was so laden with sadness, Renee turned.

'Renee, mightn't I sit with Frankie and read to him for a while until he goes to sleep?' Lily whispered.

'Course, as long as Frankie don't mind?'

He shook his head, so Renee crept from the room. She paused at the door. Lily was opening a book from Frankie's bedside and already they were both engrossed. She doubted they'd even realised she'd left the room.

Next door in their shared bedroom, Renee wearily wiped off her make-up and massaged in her Yardley's cleansing milk. Her gaze fell upon Lily's put-me-up bed, hastily erected on the other side of the room when Frankie had gone missing.

In her tiredness, Lily had flung her handbag onto the bed and the contents had strewn out across the faded candlewick counterpane.

Lipstick, kirby grips, a Yardley's Freesia cologne stick and a letter. Amongst Renee's many traits, discretion was not one. She listened. Through the walls she heard the muted murmur of Lily's voice.

'It's not as if I'm sneaking into her room to look at it. She's in my room,' Renee reasoned as she picked up the paper and began to read. The beautiful cursive script she recognised instantly as Lily's.

I'm so sorry, my love. I hope one day we can be a proper family together, away from here, when the time is right. That's my wish . . . I didn't leave because I wanted to, but because I had no choice. One day I'll explain everything.

'Poor little chap, he was asleep before I even finished the first p . . .' Lily's voice trailed off. 'What do you think you're doing?'

Renee dropped the letter as if it were dusted with arsenic. 'Lily, you nearly gave me a heart attack!'

'If we're going to share a room, I must have my privacy,' Lily snapped, picking the letter up from the floor and bundling it in her bag. 'You have no right to read my personal correspondence.'

A sudden thought threaded through Renee's mind and wound ahead of itself.

'You've been having an affair with a married man, ain't yer?' Renee announced dramatically as she leapt to her feet. 'I knew it! That's why you're back in Stratford. One of the suits in the office at Bond Street, is it?'

Her hand flew to her mouth.

'Or was Joycie right, were you having an affair with Mr Lavender?'

'Oh, for pity's sake, Renee, take the weight off your brains and sit down,' Lily said angrily. 'You've pickled your common sense with all that gin.' She sighed despairingly. 'I've said it before, and I'll say it again. Life isn't like one of your magazines. I wasn't lying. Yardley personnel have said I'm needed far more here as a charge hand now war's broken out, than at Bond Street. It's the truth.'

'I know you're keeping something from me is all,' said Renee sulkily as she got into bed and pulled the coverlet over her.

'Well, I am my mother's daughter,' Lily muttered as she kicked off her heels and sat down, exhausted, on her bed.

'What d'ya mean by that?' Renee demanded.

'Forget I said anything.' Lily turned off the gas lamp, plunging the room into darkness.

9

Esther

The next morning, a Sunday, dawned crisp and bright. The overnight rain had washed away the malodorous soot, rinsing the cobbles clean. With factory work suspended for the day, a briny smell drifted over from the Cut, the barrage balloons hovering in the blue sky above like giant bloated fish in the ocean.

The scent of roasting dinners and overcooked vegetables drifted out from doorways as smartly dressed families arrived home from church, mothers going to their stoves or to collect their joint from the bakehouse, fathers to their local for a swift half. The kids of Stratford were delighted to be free and were pelting into the streets in the dazzling morning light.

As Esther walked with her mother, Julia, her thoughts strayed painfully to Sunday mornings in Vienna. Her father listening to her playing the violin, followed by a trip to his favourite coffee shop for delicious pastries. Her heart squeezed.

Just as they turned into the Shoot, a young girl, no more than eight or so, came a cropper when the home-made cart she'd fashioned out of what looked like two old orange-boxes careered into the kerb and flew apart. She let rip with a howl of pain and Julia rushed to help her, when a door flew open and a man ran out. He scooped the girl off the cobbles and into his arms.

'Come here, little pickle, there there,' he soothed.

'I think she's cut her knee,' Julia said. 'I'm a nurse, would you like me to look at it?'

'That's very kind, but I think she'll live,' he chuckled, inspecting the grazed flesh. 'If we have to amputate, she's got another . . . Half a mo, what's this?' he asked, pulling out a sherbet lemon from behind the girl's ear.

'Daddy,' she declared, delighted, unwrapping the sweet and stuffing it in her mouth, her tears dried up.

'I keep a reserve of them behind the tea caddy,' he joked, picking his daughter up and cuddling her. 'Happens at least once a day. Say goodbye to the nice nurse,' he coaxed, but she clung to him for dear life.

'Daddy's girl,' he grinned by way of explanation, closing the door.

Julia smiled at Esther. 'You were just the same. Are,' she corrected quickly. 'You *are* still a daddy's girl, no matter how old you are.'

'Am I?' Esther replied. 'Because the awful thing is, Mama, I've started to forget his face.' She thought of the prayer they had said on Friday evening, by the light of the shabbat candles, the panic she felt when she closed her eyes and tried to summon up his face, but there was nothing but tiny flickering candles.

'It is sad we did not have time to take the photo albums,' agreed Julia. 'But you don't need a photographic image, because your father lives here,' she said, softly touching Esther's heart. 'Not in your head.'

'But I'm scared that the reason I cannot picture him is because he's not alive.'

'Oi vey, the drama,' said her mother, throwing her hands in the air. 'Of course he is, but let us play a little game.'

Esther looked at the kids in the middle of the square bundling on each other's backs in a high-voltage game of Hi Jimmy Knacker.

'Not that kind of game. Let's draw a mental map. Close your eyes.'

Esther did as she was told.

'Can you see his crooked smile? The left side was always higher,' Julia murmured.

'Yes, I see it.'

'Good, now remember when he was pleased about something, the way he used to rub his hands together . . .'

'. . . and slap his thigh,' Esther recalled.

It was as if a door had opened in her mind and memories were tumbling through.

'Now listen.'

A hush fell over them. All Esther could hear was footsteps, a barking dog and little cockney voices.

'What for?'

'Johann Strauss. Your father's favourite composer. How he played his music, every Sunday morning.'

And the remarkable thing was, Esther could. It poured from an open window and filled the square, notes dancing through the air like dust motes. It was her father at his piano, bringing his love of music to the whole neighbourhood, his infectious joy filling up everyone's lives.

'Why does Hitler hate Jewish people?' Esther asked quietly.

Her mother winced and was silent for some while.

'I do not know the answer to that, but I do know he has no love in his heart, only hate. But we must hold fast to love, for love never dies.'

Esther nodded, tears trickling down her cheeks, for the memories of her father were now so bright it was as if he was standing right beside her.

'We will see him again,' Julia promised, lifting Esther's chin so that their eyes met. 'But until we do; wherever you go, whoever you meet, whatever you do, remember, you are your father's daughter. Make him proud.'

Esther nodded. 'I will.'

'You coming in then, or what?' Renee's voice tore over the square. She was standing at the open door to number 10, as fresh as a daisy. No trace of a hangover from the previous day.

'You must be Esther's mum,' she said, sticking out her hand. 'I'm glad someone's visited today, me mum's been on her hands and knees all morning. Hate to see that step go to waste.'

Julia grinned broadly and Esther could tell in an instant her mum was as enchanted as she had been by Renee Gunn.

'It certainly is sparkling,' she agreed, looking down at the doorstep.

'You could eat your dinner off that. Leastwise, that's what Mum reckons – we've never actually tried it, mind.' Renee paused and cocked her head. 'Hmmm. Doorstep dining? Could take off in Stratford.'

'Stop your prattling, girl, and let our guests in,' blustered Nell, coming up the passage behind her.

Renee made the introductions.

'Mum, this is my new friend from work, Esther Orwell, and her mum, Julia. They're refugees from Vienna.'

'Welcome to my home and to Stratford,' Nell said, bustling about and taking their coats. 'Please God for a swift end to this war so you can get home. Until then, any friend of Renee's is a friend of mine. You will stay for dinner?' Esther quickly realised it was a rhetorical question.

'We would love to. I'm afraid we don't eat pork, Mrs Gunn,' Julia said, eyeing the huge piece of pork belly and trotters hanging in the scullery.

'Course not, I got a rib of beef from under the counter that'll spread to two more mouths.'

'In which case, I insist on running home and fetching some Jewish cakes for dessert.'

'I'd never say no to that,' replied Nell, and Esther could tell the women would be firm friends. 'Have a cuppa first, mind.'

'Mrs Gunn, I heard about your son Frankie returning,' Julia went on as Nell poured tea from an enormous brown teapot. 'I'm a registered nurse back in my home city. Would you like me to look over him?'

'Would you?' asked Nell in surprise. 'Save me the cost of a trip to the doctor.'

She sighed and wiped her hands on a tea towel.

'It's a worry, I don't mind admitting. Now his school's evacuated, he ain't got much to do, apart from run errands, and he does love his books. Between you and me, Mrs Orwell, my husband reckons he's feeble-minded. Given half a chance, he'd pack the boy off to some sort of naughty boys' home, especially after his latest escapade. But I ain't having that. A child's place is by their mother.'

'I could not agree more,' Julia replied, folding her hands on her lap. 'You are right, Mrs Gunn. Love and security is what a child needs, not institutions.'

'Mama, maybe you could teach Frankie a few mornings a week?' Esther suggested.

Julia's face lit up.

'But of course, I would be delighted to. My uncle's shop is very quiet in the mornings. I'm sure he wouldn't mind.'

Mrs Gunn grinned, an enormous smile, which lit up every crevice of her face.

'Well now, that would be a fine thing, and a great relief all round.' She looked pensieve.

'I probably should warn you, though. Our Frankie likes his routines. He got suspended for a week once when they swapped art, his favourite subject, for arithmetic. Upended a table he did, the little sod.'

'He's got his mother's temper, all right,' Renee teased.

'Don't worry, Mrs Gunn,' Julia replied. 'I'm sure your son is neither flawed nor feeble-minded. Children just need a teaching method suited to their individual style of learning. I'm sure it won't take us long to work out whether your Frankie is a future poet or painter, mathematician or pharmacist.'

Nell lifted her eyebrows.

'Try tell his father that. He's convinced he's gonna be a docker.'

Dinner with the Gunns was a success. Nell Gunn might have been described as the most formidable and fiery matriarch in Stratford, but Esther felt the reputation was a little over the top. She saw only kindness and warmth. Even Pat Gunn seemed on his best behaviour in front of their visitors. He was sporting a black eye, though, but it felt a little impolite to ask why. Julia had examined Frankie and, apart from being a little malnourished and dehydrated from hiding on the barge, and having a couple of sore-looking welts on his thighs, declared him to be in reasonable health. There was a palpable sense of relief in the air. Renee had confided that there had been a right old 'set-to' after Alfie had returned Frankie home, but clearly today was a new day in the Gunn household. Frankie was home, Lily was home and all Nell's children were under one roof.

After the delicious dinner of roast beef and piping-hot potatoes roasted in dripping and served with a good dollop of thick, glossy gravy, Pat invited some musical pals back from the Two Puddings and, within no time, the furniture had been pushed back and someone had whipped out an accordion and a trumpet. It wasn't the classical music they were used to listening to on a Sunday morning, but Esther didn't care. Their music was a little like the Gunn family themselves – loud, gutsy and vibrant. To be a part of a family again made her feel lighter than she had in months. As the music flowed, so too did the black and tans for the men, and port and lemons for the women. Esther, Lily and Renee had joined in the dancing, giggling as they partnered up.

Only Frankie hadn't joined in, preferring instead to sit quietly in the corner with a book.

The whole day had sped past in a comfortable blur of food, laughter and song. When a man selling seafood door to door on a barrow knocked, Nell insisted the Orwells stay for winkles and watercress.

'No, I don't wish to abuse your kindness,' Julia replied firmly, putting on her coat. 'Besides, I want to get home before the blackout.'

'You're the only woman who's said no to my wife and lived to tell the tale,' Pat chuckled.

As their mothers chatted on the doorstep, Lily drew Esther to one side.

'Are you all right after what happened yesterday at the wedding?' she asked quietly.

Esther felt heat rise up her cheeks.

'I didn't lead him on, I promise,' she whispered.

'Oh, I believe you, Esther,' Lily replied, 'That Jimmy is a nasty piece of work. You stay well away from him, you must promise me.'

'I promise,' Esther replied, feeling confused.

'Come on, Esther, time to go,' her mother called from the doorstep. Lily smiled at her. 'Good girl.'

Outside in the gathering gloom, Julia tucked her arm through her daughter's as they cut through Cat's Alley, emerging into a deserted Angel Lane.

Without the costers crying their pitch and the scrape of barrels, the place was as silent as the grave. Skeins of smoke hung over the empty street. Only Snowball was there, peeling the specks out of a discarded apple with an old penknife.

'Good evening, sir,' Julia smiled as they passed, taking a leftover slab of bread-and-butter pudding Nell had insisted on tucking in her handbag, and giving it to the homeless man. 'I'll bring you a cup of tea to go with that soon.'

'Bless you, madam,' he replied, looking up with watery eyes.

'There is such poverty here in the East End,' Julia mused when he was out of earshot. 'But such community and heart. What a lovely and interesting family the Gunns are. To them, neighbours are family, I feel.'

'Mama,' Esther said.

'You have a question on the tip of your tongue.'

'I do,' she admitted. 'Frankie Gunn. You know why he is different, don't you?'

Julia paused, her breath hanging like smoke in the queer twilight.

'Perhaps,' she replied. 'He is certainly a very intriguing child.'

10

Renee

By December, the picture houses and dance halls had reopened, and life had resumed a semblance of normality. The evacuated children were even returning from the countryside, and some schools were open again, albeit with fewer teachers. Life down the Shoot continued much as before, oblivious to the 'bore war', as folk were now calling it, with Mrs Trunk and her husband having their usual Friday night rows, Mrs Barnett giving birth to her ninth child and Pat Gunn losing his bet that the war would be over by now.

At Yardley's, though, it was all change. Girls were leaving the factory in droves, swapping tunics for khaki, and the powder room was now a fully kitted-out air-raid shelter. Only lipstick remained fully staffed and, thanks to a boom in orders, was working at full throttle.

'Blimey, we can't turn 'em out fast enough,' puffed Renee, brandishing her sterilising flame one Friday just before morning tea break.

'Reckon as how everyone wants to look like Rita Hayworth. Did I tell you I got a signed photo of her back from the studio?'

'Once or twice,' Joanie grinned from the other side of the belt. 'I'll trade you Lana Turner.'

'Leave off. I'm only letting her go for Marlene Dietrich.'

''Ere Renee, who you gonna marry when you go to Hollywood?' called Fat Lou from the packing bench.

'Oh, Errol Flynn I should say, I got a right pash on him. When we marry, I'm going to get Max to do my make-up, you know Max Factor. He does all the big stars at Paramount.'

'Ooh, just picture it, Renee,' smiled little Irene as she pushed past a barrel of animal fat for the churn. 'Your name up in lights alongside Betty Grable.'

'Not much,' said Renee, with a great shriek of laughter. 'Renee Gunn from the House of Yardley.'

'Don't forget it's the staff sale in the canteen at dinnertime,' remarked Joanie.

'Don't forget?' Renee exclaimed, blue eyes sparkling. 'I've been limbering up my elbows.' With a comic grin, she pretended to flex her muscles. 'I've run out of complexion powder, ain't no one getting past me.'

'Renee,' Lily tutted from her table at the end of the belt. 'Be careful, you nearly set fire to Esther's turban.'

'That's all right,' Esther said as she walked round with her pad, taking tea orders for morning break.

Lily smiled at the efficient young service girl. She was only fifteen, but Esther was unflappable. She was already thinking of promoting her onto the belt.

'Sorry, sis,' Renee said. 'I'm excited about Christmas is all. Only a week to go.'

'I told you, it's Miss Gunn at work,' Lily muttered.

Her big sister was a funny old stick, Renee mused. At work she was the image of professionalism and was gradually getting a reputation for being firm but fair. But at home she was as soft as butter. She could spend hours on her hands and knees in Frankie's bedroom, listening as he talked her through his endless matchbox collection. Renee hadn't dared sneak a look through her things again, much less bring up why Lily left Stratford in the first place. She'd got a right dressing down for that and Renee had to concede, Lily guarded her private life zealously.

But a girl had to have her fun. All work and no play gave Renee frown lines.

'Right you are, Sergeant Major Gunn,' she grinned, with a mock salute.

'You are incorrigible,' Lily sighed, but Renee could see she was trying not to smile.

'War hasn't dented your spirits one bit, has it?' Lily remarked.

'Can't let the buggers get you down, can you?' she shrugged.

The bell for tea break shrieked and the machines shut down with a shudder. As the girls gathered round, tucking into crusty dripping rolls and slurping from mugs of tea, the welfare officer, Rose Rayson came round the floor handing out brown paper packets.

'Hello, girls. The Managing Director would like me to pass on his sincere thanks for all your hard work. Lipstick orders are going through the roof, so your efforts are appreciated.'

'Always a pleasure, never a chore, Mrs Rayson,' Renee winked, popping her wage into her overall pocket. Out of the fourteen shillings she now earned, ten would go to her mum, leaving four for her to spend as she wished. 'And you say ta to Mr Lavender for the pay rise, should keep me in make-up. Nothing else to spend it on. Do you know Boardman's has only got blackout material on offer in the windows?' She sniffed in disdain. 'Where's the usual Christmas display?'

'On the subject of which, I'm afraid the annual Christmas dinner dance at the Town Hall won't be going ahead this year, as I'm sure you will all have guessed,' said Miss Rayson. A great chorus of groans went up around the floor.

'Thank you very much, Hitler, for putting the kibosh on Christmas,' Renee grumbled.

'Please, girls,' soothed the welfare officer, raising her hands.

'We *will* still celebrate at Yardley's, but on a more modest scale. On Christmas Eve, the Managing Director has said we can finish at dinnertime, and he would like to invite you and all your families for a drink, carol singing, mince pies and a beauty contest in the canteen. Any interested parties should—'

'Count me in!' said Renee perking up.

'That's more like it, Miss Gunn. There's one more thing,' Miss Rayson added.

'I am looking for volunteers for the new fire-watching rota I'm putting together and for factory Air Raid Precaution duties, helping to fill sandbags, learning the correct use of a stirrup pump and so forth.'

'Fire-watching? Where?' asked Joycie.

'Where d'ya think, you nitwit,' laughed Fat Lou, rubbing a playful knuckle over Joycie's head. 'Up my Aris? On the roof of course.'

Everyone stared out of the windows at the snowflakes spiralling down outside and settling on the greasy waters of the Cut.

'Sounds dangerous to me,' said Joycie.

'And cold,' Fat Lou shuddered.

'I'll do it,' piped up Esther.

'Well done,' beamed Miss Rayson. 'The first volunteer and she is the youngest staff member at Yardley's.'

'Count me in an' all,' said Renee hurriedly. 'Can't have Esther up there on her own. 'Sides, there ain't gonna be no bombs.'

Renee's offer had a strange effect. The entire lipstick room soon put their name down on the rota.

'Wonderful,' said Miss Rayson, tapping her clipboard in satisfaction. 'Let's hope there's no enemy action, but management would like us to be prepared.'

'I was born ready, Miss Rayson,' quipped Renee. 'In fact, I know a song about the ARP.

'Under the spreading chestnut tree, Neville Chamberlain
    said to me:
"If you want to get your gas mask free;
Join the blinking ARP."'

The laughter was music to Renee's ears, but her smile soon
slipped when Miss Rayson produced something from behind
her back.

'Talking of which, Renee, I found your gas mask on the
roof of the dispatch department.'

She handed it to her with a wry smile.

'I wonder how it got up there?'

'I can't think, miss,' said Renee weakly, taking the hateful
thing and shoving it under her workstation.

The welfare officer turned to leave but suddenly remembered something.

'Oh, I nearly forgot, we shall have a new girl on the lipstick
belt at dinnertime. She's just filling out her paperwork in my
office.'

'Ooh, anyone we know?' Renee asked.

'Nan!' the girls all shouted in unison as they walked into the
canteen to find her sitting there nursing a cup of tea at their
usual table by the window looking over the Cut.

'What are you doing back?' Renee cried.

'Surprise, are you pleased to see me?'

'Of course,' Renee said, giving her a hug. 'But how? Why?
I thought you couldn't wait to be a housewife.'

'Truth be told, girls, I was going out my mind. It's actually
quite boring being a housewife. With Jimmy away and all,
there's only so many times you can polish your sideboard,
know what I mean?'

'And have you tried reading *Home Companion*?' she went
on with a dramatic shudder. 'I'd rather gnaw me own leg off

than have another night in with that. And don't start me on
my mum, she's round every day inspecting my doorstep.'

She lit up a cigarette and exhaled angrily.

'Unless I'm bleedin' assaulting it with a hearthstone, she
says the neighbours will talk. Like I care? Busy as bees with
their tongues, those old fishwives are!'

She stuck her chin out stubbornly.

'I thought Yardley's didn't let you work here after you
married?' Renee queried.

'They bent the rules,' she shrugged. 'They're so short-
staffed at the moment. Course when my Jimmy gets leave,
I'll have to be excused.'

She smiled secretly as she gazed out the window.

'Bless him. He's missing me that much, writes the soppiest
letters all the time, saying how he can't wait to get home to
me.'

Renee and Lily exchanged a look. In all the drama of
Frankie's return, nothing had been said about his leching in
the cloakroom on his wedding night. Instinct told Renee it
might be better to keep quiet, but she had an uneasy feeling
when it came to Seaman Jimmy Connor. She also got the
distinct impression that Lily knew more about Jimmy than
she was letting on. What had they been talking about in the
cloakroom when she'd walked in and interrupted them?
Renee didn't dare ask, for fear of getting her head bitten off
again.

'Between you and me, girls,' Nan breathed, lowering her
voice and gazing round the tabletop. 'My monthly's late. I
could be expecting.'

'Blimey, you don't hang about,' said Fat Lou, munching
on a hot sausage roll.

'What's *it* like then?' Renee asked eagerly.

'I couldn't possibly say,' said Nan coyly. 'But let's just say
my Jimmy knows how . . .'

Nan's voice was drowned out when Blind Eric, who played the piano every dinnertime in the canteen, started up.

Renee went off to fetch her dinner, returning with half a grapefruit with a cherry on top and a small roll.

'How comes you always get the best?' said Nan, prodding her cherry.

''Cause I keep the canteen ladies sweet,' shrugged Renee, as she tucked in. And then with a wink: 'Anyways, what you grousing at? You had your cherry and now you lost it.'

'Ha ha, very funny,' said Nan sarcastically.

'So, what's happening with your Alfie? Have you forgiven him for trying it on?'

'Yeah. I had to really, after he found our Frankie, but I've told him he has to prove himself before I'll get back with him.'

'Talking of your Frankie,' said Nan, 'I saw him earlier walking into the library with some old Jewish woman.'

'Oh that's Julia. She's teaching him from home, now his school's closed down,' Renee replied, forking a segment of grapefruit into her mouth.

'Is that wise? I mean she's a different religion, an' all. Not sure I'd be happy if that were my little brother,' Nan said coldly, turning her sharp eyes on Renee. 'You hear about all them Polish Jews they arrested down the market last week? Here illegally. Who's to say she ain't?'

'For goodness' sake, Nan, don't be so ignorant,' Lily snapped. 'Julia's a lovely woman and Frankie's coming on leaps and bounds under her tuition. I really don't see what her being Jewish has to do with it?'

'All right, keep your wig on, Lily,' Nan replied hotly. 'I didn't it mean like that.'

'Nan, Julia is Esther's mum,' said Renee tactfully.

Esther stared down at her cup of tea and an awkward silence soured the air.

A shout from outside broke the atmosphere and Fat Lou hopped out of her chair and flung open the window.

'It's only your Alfie!' she exclaimed, taking a big bite out of her sausage roll.

Renee rushed to the window. Shivering in the yard of next door's paint factory, Alfie was clutching a bouquet of red roses.

'These are for you, Renee,' he hollered up from the yard. 'I thought they were safer than perfume. Come for tea at my mum's later? My brother's home on leave. I want to introduce them to the lady I love.'

'Who's that then?' she asked cheekily.

Alfie made a pantomime of clutching his chest.

'The lady wounds me . . . You, Renee Gunn. You.' He threw his arms wide open, snowflakes cascading down on his face.

'I want the whole world to know it. I'm in love with Renee Gunn.'

'Aaahhh,' came the chorus of sighs from behind Renee. Even Blind Eric entered into the spirit, changing his jaunty music hall tune to Moonlight Sonata.

'You ain't off the hook that easy, Alfie Buckle,' she shouted back, loving the attention.

'What have I gotta do to prove myself then?'

She gazed over at the snow-flecked Cut. The Bricky Kids were down there as usual, fishing an old bike out of its foul, poisonous depths. In the summer, they delighted in taking all their clothes off and jumping in stark naked to embarrass the Yardley girls.

'Take your clothes off and jump in the Cut!' she yelled.

'What?' he gaped. 'It's cold enough to freeze the balls off a brass monkey.'

'Very well,' she sighed, making to shut the canteen window.

'Oh, hang it all,' he sighed, putting down the roses and

starting to unbutton his factory overalls. 'It's canal water flowing through my veins anyhow.'

'I don't believe it!' screamed Fat Lou, her voice tearing through the whole canteen as she showered them in pastry crumbs. 'He's only stripping off!'

The floor shook to the sound of scraping chairs as a stampede of Yardley girls pelted to the window.

Renee could hardly look. He was down to his underpants, then he hooked a finger over the waistband . . . Two hundred or so turban-clad Yardley girls pressed their noses to the steamed-up glass.

In one fell swoop, Alfie streaked through the yard at Berger's and vaulted the wall that separated the factory from the canal.

'Geronimo!' he hollered, launching himself into the water with a deafening smack.

The factory held its breath as his head disappeared under the dark waters.

A second later, he emerged, swam to the side and hopped out, shaking water and droplets of oil from his head. His naked bottom glinted in the frozen air.

'You want a butcher's at the other side?' he joked, threatening to turn round.

'No thanks, you saucy sod. From what I heard it's none too pretty!' bellowed Fat Lou.

With chattering teeth, Alfie turned around and legged it back inside the warmth of the factory. The canteen thundered with applause and wolf whistles.

'Blimey, Renee,' murmured Fat Lou in astonishment. 'That's put me right off my sausage roll!'

Renee was still smiling as she clocked off later and made her way round to Alfie's for tea.

She'd barely put her hand on the knocker when the door was answered by Alfie.

'Glad to see you got some clothes on now,' she joked, taking in his smart suit. Alfie tightened the knot of his tie.

'I'm gonna do things properly this time, Renee,' he vowed. 'I mean it. I want to introduce you to my whole family. I want 'em to meet the girl I'm head over heels with.'

Renee smiled and took his hand as he led her into the passage.

'Come in. Me mum's letting us use the front parlour, usually saved—'

'I know, for best. My mum's the same.'

'Not sure if it's in honour of you or my big brother. I think it's probably you,' he grinned. 'They can't wait to meet you.'

He flung open the door and a sea of expectant faces stared back at her.

'Come in, duckie, make yourself at home,' said his mum, rushing forward. 'Get out of it, you lot,' she said, shooing off a load of kids from the chaise longue, which Renee suspected would usually be covered in a dust sheet.

A toothless old woman in an armchair got out a magnifying glass and squinted at Renee through it.

'Ooh, ain't she lovely, you done well there, son,' she said, nodding approvingly. 'She's like one of them film stars.'

'My great-nan, Martha,' he explained to Renee, before turning back to the elderly lady.

'You're not wrong there, Nanny Martha. Renee's entered into the Yardley beauty contest, she's a shoo-in.'

'Stop it, Alfie,' Renee laughed.

'Put that away, Nan,' scolded Alfie's mum, taking the magnifying glass. 'You'll make her feel like a specimen.'

What a clan the Buckle family were! There were so many aunts, uncles and cousins stuffed into the tiny room that Renee's head spun as Alfie introduced her to everyone. In no time at all the windows were steamed up from laughter and the beer was flowing, along with the stories. Renee immediately felt at ease within such a warm and rumbustious family and she was aware of Alfie's eyes on her the whole time.

The eldest Buckle son, Billy, was home on leave and held the whole family spellbound with thrilling tales as he arranged the salt and pepper pots on the table.

'This is us, this is the Jerries,' he grinned, grabbing a teaspoon to demonstrate how they had outmanoeuvred the Germans in battle.

'They fired a broadside, but we anticipated it and quickly swung across.' His green eyes gleamed. 'The shells burst and shrapnel dropped all over our turret. We could hear it, like stones dropping on a tin roof. They thought they had us, 'see.'

'Oh Bill, whatever did you do, son?' exclaimed Mrs Buckle, raising her hand to her chest.

'The battle went on for an hour, but we must have hit her oil or summit, 'cause we saw the flames go up. We all come up on deck, everyone cheering. Oh Mum, it really was tremendous, I only wish you could've seen it.'

'And is it true, son, what they're saying in the paper?' said his father, taking out a copy of the *Stratford Express* and reading out loud.

'*Fair-haired and good-looking, Seaman Buckle is a stalwart example of a typical British seaman. In his three years' experience he has crowded an amazing series of adventures. Seaman Buckle, in fact, can claim to have helped fire the first naval shot of the war. Just four hours after war was declared, his ship sank a big German Merchantman in the South Atlantic.*'

Billy shrugged. 'I don't know about that, Dad, but reckon as how we got the Huns on the run all right.'

'Oh love, we're all so proud of you,' gushed Mrs Buckle, throwing her arms around her son.

'Three cheers for our Billy,' declared an elderly uncle, who had been quietly puffing on a pipe in the corner.

As the room filled with cheers, Mrs Buckle cranked up the wireless and Mr Buckle set about busily refilling glasses.

As handsome and heroic as he obviously was, Renee hadn't been looking at Billy. Instead, she'd been studying Alfie's face. For the first time since her arrival he had stopped gazing at her and was now listening in awe to his big brother, and there and then, she knew she'd lost him, just as she had truly won him.

Alfie spied her face and drew her out of the room and into the darkened passage.

'When are you going?' she whispered, breathing in the soft soapy scent of him.

'I can register for military service in January.'

'But that's only a month away,' Renee protested, staring down at the floor.

Gently he tilted her chin up and kissed her softly on the mouth.

'I've got to go soon, Renee, otherwise I may never get the chance for active service. Our Billy reckons the war'll be over soon and I'll never forgive myself if I don't fight.'

Two of Alfie's younger cousins who'd been spying on them in the darkness suddenly burst out giggling and ran upstairs.

'Alfie loves Renee,' one taunted, hanging over the bannister.

'Shove off, you little tyke,' Alfie teased affectionately.

But then under his breath, 'I do though, love you that is, and when I come back, made a man of myself, I'm going to marry you, Renee Gunn. I don't care what it takes, I'll throw myself in a hundred evil-smelling canals if I have to.'

He slid his fingers round the back of her neck and brought his lips to hers again.

'I'm going to look after you, for the rest of my life.'

Renee silenced him with a bittersweet kiss, for there was nothing left to be said.

I I

Lily

With Renee over at Alfie's having tea, Frankie having extra arithmetic tuition at Julia's and her father down the Two Puddings, Lily found herself alone with her mother. Stretching her feet in front of the fire, she yawned and wiped her hands over her face.

'Tired?' Nell asked.

'Just a bit.'

'It's a lot to get your head round being in charge of others,' Nell said. 'And learning a new job.'

'You're not wrong there, Mum,' Lily agreed. 'I feel like my entire time's spent not on ensuring the smooth running of the belt, but in containing the energy of those girls. Do you know Renee nearly set fire to Esther's turban earlier!'

Nell's body heaved with laughter.

'They're a handful all right them girls, but they've all got good hearts.'

'I'm not sure I've got their respect, though,' said Lily, frowning. The memory of them gossiping about her in the toilets still stung all these weeks on.

'Be fair, but firm and you'll soon win them over,' Nell said as she untied her pinny and shrugged on her coat.

'Going somewhere?' Lily asked.

'I hope you don't mind, love, but I've got to nip out for

an hour or two. There's mashed potato and a nice bit of gammon keeping warm in the range.'

'Course not, Mum. Anywhere nice?' Lily asked.

Her mother didn't answer as she rifled through her big black handbag.

'Sorry, love, what'd you say?' she asked, looking distracted as she took off her turban and pinned on a big black hat.

'Nothing, Mum, you get on. I'll be fine.'

'Ta-ra, love,' said Nell, planting a kiss on her daughter's head.

The door slammed shut and Lily was left alone with only her thoughts and the ticking of the old clock on the mantel. The sound of Mr and Mrs Trunk warming up for a row drifted through the paper walls. Lily turned up the wireless, but Mrs Trunk had a voice like a klaxon when she got going.

She picked up a well-thumbed copy of Renee's *Woman's Own* and idly flicked through it, trying hard to focus on an article in the beauty pages.

Some of us are anxious, some lonely and tired, but isn't that just one more reason why you and I should include our faces in the scheme of decoration and cheer up ourselves and others? Isn't it worth that extra five minutes in the morning to be a cheerful sight?

Try telling Mrs Trunk that, Lily thought with a grimace. She nibbled pensively on her lower lip, then, before she could stop herself, threw down the magazine and was up and buttoning up her coat and pinning on her hat. Opening the door, she slipped out just in time to see her mum scurrying up the furthest end of the Shoot.

She didn't really have the faintest idea why she felt compelled to follow her, other than a fermenting suspicion based on past experience. If she was right, and Lily hoped to God she wasn't, then her mum was playing a very dangerous game indeed and now war had started, the stakes were even higher . . .

Nell Gunn moved quickly for a large lady, and Lily nearly lost her a few times as she was swallowed by the shadows of the blackout. Fortunately, the moon was high in the sky, surrounded by an aureole of mist that faintly illuminated the tall black feather sticking up from the brim of Nell's hat.

Deeper and deeper she plunged into the guts of the grimy tenement, vanishing into the mist of an alleyway like a bird in flight. Lily would have lost her altogether had it not been for the feather.

Nell paused outside the rattiest basement flat. Lily recognised it instantly. Mrs Barnett's. Suddenly, Nell turned and Lily dodged into a pool of darkness under a fire escape.

Her heart thumped. Had she seen her? Her mum stared up and down the deserted court, as if she were watching out for something, or someone. In her hiding place, Lily hardly dared to breathe as Nell remained motionless by the door. Finally, she knocked softly. Almost immediately the door opened a fraction and her mother hurried in clutching her bag.

Lily checked her wristwatch. 9.05 p.m. Maybe her mum was helping with the baby or the kids, but surely they'd all be asleep by now? She waited, hiding in the frozen shadows of the fire escape. And waited, until her fingers were stiffer than a corpse and her feet were solid blocks of ice.

Finally, after what must have been more than an hour, the door opened and a pale slither of light fell out, cutting a shard across the icy cobbles. Her mother and Mrs Barnett were huddled together, deep in conversation. She couldn't make out their voices, but her mother seemed to be comforting Mrs Barnett. She was agitated, her voice rising and falling. Lily strained to hear . . .

I can't go into double digits, Auntie . . .

Lily couldn't make out her mother's response, but she

quickly fished into her purse and pulled out a note, which she tucked into Mrs Barnett's apron pocket.

Just then a figure swelled up through the darkness towards them. Mr Barnett!

One look told her he'd been on the drink as he bounced off a wall and staggered on, his heavy boots crunching on the icy ground. Lily had seen what that man was capable of. The memory of that visit back in September when they'd dropped off groceries to Mrs Barnett before Nan's wedding trailed uncomfortably through her mind. The splintered door-frame, the ugly bruises. Lily froze in fear. Should she call out? Warn her mother?

It was too late. He was at the doorway. The voices were muffled to begin with, then raised in anger . . .

'Keep out of what don't concern you, Auntie!'

Her mother was trying to placate him, Lily could see that, but he was in her face, his eyeballs inches from hers, trying to intimidate her like the drunken bully he was.

'Get off my fucking step!' he thundered, finally losing his rag.

Nell's fists rested on her hips. Usually a sign she was going nowhere.

For a drunk, he could certainly move. With lightning speed, he turned and, with a great grunting lunge, grabbed Mrs Barnett by the throat and pinned her against the greasy wall. Her head hit the masonry with a crack.

Lily's heart lodged painfully in her throat as she wondered what to do. Should she scream out? Call for a policeman? But to her great shame, she did neither of those things. Fear had left her oddly mute.

Instead, she watched in horror, as Mr Barnett's fingers formed a vice round his wife's neck. She looked like one of the chickens that hung from the front of the butcher's, speared and helpless.

'Let her go,' her mother warned in a low voice. 'You're hurting her.'

'I couldn't give the shiniest shit.'

'I said, let her go . . .'

'Or what?' he taunted, as blood seeped down the wall and dripped onto the ground.

He gripped his wife's chin, yanked her terrified face in the direction of Nell's so that their eyes met.

'Tell her to go, you.'

Y*ou?* He couldn't even be bothered to call his wife by her name.

'This is my last warning,' Nell replied, rage threaded through every syllable. 'Get. Your. Hands. Off. Her.'

He laughed in Nell's face, before stamping hard on his wife's slippered foot. She slithered into the bloody gutter in a broken heap.

Lily choked back a sob, fear exploding in her chest.

But then her mother did something she would not have believed had she not seen it with her own eyes.

'I warned you,' she said as she slid the pin from her hat. The jet bead on the end glinted in the pearlescent moonlight. A flash of metal and she plunged it fast and deep into his privates. The howl of pain told her that it had hit its bullseye. He hit the cobbles like a sack of spuds.

Nell stood over him and calmly slid her hatpin back into place.

'If I hear you've touched her one more time, I'll be back to finish the job off. Understood?'

Mr Barnett whimpered, saliva spooling from the sides of his mouth as he clutched himself in agony.

Nell turned and gently helped Mrs Barnett off the ground, but Lily wasn't sticking around to watch any more.

Turning, in a blind panic, she ran straight into the fire escape, getting her buttons tangled in the wrought-iron step.

'Who goes there?' called out her mother's voice in the darkness. With a desperate wrench, Lily yanked her coat free and ran as fast as she could all the way back to the Shoot.

She slowed by the church and seemed to stumble straight through into the graveyard itself. She hadn't noticed earlier, but the old black railings that circled it were gone, taken by the council to be melted down for the war effort. Without them, the graves seemed to spill into the street so there was no way of seeing where the graveyard ended and the Shoot began.

The dead were among them. Lily paused by a gravestone, clutching the lichen-covered edge as her ragged breath returned to normal. Skeins of mist floated through the still night air; a feeling of melancholy soaked deep beneath the rank earth.

Why had she come back to these sooty, closed-in streets? What made her think that anything would have changed?

A rustle interrupted the still of the night. The bushes at the furthest, darkest corner of the graveyard trembled as if at any moment, something might burst from their fetid roots. Dead winter branches reached out from behind the moss-bitten gravestones, like long spiny fingers.

'Snowball!' she cried. 'Is that you?'

A restless wind moaned and creaked in answer. Above, a wild white moon rode high, veiling the churchyard in a ghostly curtain of light and shade. Below, only bodies.

Lily wasn't hanging around to see what it was. Instead she fled from the graveyard back to the safety of number 10.

Grabbing her tea from the black leaded range, she breathed out slowly, trying to quell her wildly pounding heart. The mashed potato sat like lumps of wet concrete in her mouth as she forced herself to eat the meal her mother had left out. She was still forcing it down thirty minutes later when her mother walked in the door, bringing the smell of cold smoky night air with her on fronds of mist. *Why had she taken so long to come home, what had she been doing?*

Nell stopped at the doorway and stared at her for what felt like a very long time, her feathered hat casting a long shadow over the distempered wall.

'All right?' she said eventually, her eyes black holes in the glow of the gas lamp.

Lily nodded and forced down another mouthful.

'Yeah, all quiet here,' she mumbled. 'Nice tea, Mum.'

Her mother's face was bone white from cold, her face rigid as she slowly slid the pin from her hat.

'I'll make us a cocoa,' she muttered, turning her back to Lily. Lily didn't know what was most frightening. The look of quiet rage on her mother's face, or the earth under her finger nails. A deep silence folded over the room, smothering Stratford and its secrets.

The next morning, a Saturday, Lily sleepily pulled the blackout blinds back to find the soot-caked slate rooftops of Stratford sparkling white. The graves that had last night looked so ominous now seemed like something from a Disney cartoon. Lily scolded herself. She had let her imagination get the better of her. But the memory of her mother's violent visit to Mrs Barnett's, now that was harder to sanitise.

'Look, Renee, there must be four inches of snow out there,' she remarked. 'We better leave a bit earlier so we're not late for our shift. It'll be slippy as anything out there.'

'Eurghh,' groaned a voice from under the candlewick counterpane.

Lily pulled back the sheet and laughed out loud.

'Is this the look you're planning for the beauty contest next week?'

Lily had already been asleep by the time Renee got back from Alfie's. Her face was caked two inches thick with cold cream, she had a pink satin eye mask on, and her blonde hair was woven round pipe cleaners and covered with a slumber helmet. Even the hair net had an impudent bow on the top.

'What?' she groaned loudly, pulling her mask off and squinting.

'I said,' Lily laughed, pulling the ear-plugs out of Renee's ears, 'is this the look you'll be modelling at the beauty contest next week?'

'Oh, leave off,' Renee said, yawning and stretching her hands above her head.

'Be an angel, Lil, and fetch us a cup of tea while I do my exercises.'

Lily shook her head as Renee sprang out of bed in her powder-blue cami-knickers and began her morning ritual of bending down to touch her toes.

'Gotta look my best if I'm gonna beat Nan for the Miss Homefront crown.'

'Is she entering?' Lily asked. 'I didn't think married women were allowed.'

'They ain't usually,' Renee puffed, flinging out her arms. 'But this war's sent everything topsy-turvy.'

'I shouldn't think her new husband'll be too happy if he hears of his wife parading about in a one-piece in the canteen.'

'That mucky sod,' Renee snapped. 'More arms than an octopus, that one.'

'Oughtn't you to tell Nan what happened?'

Renee's blue eyes widened.

'You're joking, ain't yer? I ain't getting involved in that, thank you very much. When it comes to her Jimmy, she thinks the sun shines out of his every orifice.'

Renee sat down on the velvet-upholstered stool in front of her kidney-shaped dressing table and began her facial exercise.

'Q. R. S . . . Here Lil, what comes after S?'

'T?'

'Ooh, don't mind if I do, ta Lil,' she winked. 'Nice and strong with one.'

Lily picked up her sister's turban, rolled it up and lobbed it at her head with a grin.

'You're a caution, you are!' Lily groaned. 'And it's Lily, not Lil. You make me sound like an old char.'

'You still love me, though, don't yer, Lil?' Renee smiled.

She did, Lily reflected as she walked down the creaky staircase into a kitchen so cold, there was ice on in the inside of the panes. Renee Gunn was an infuriating and saucy cow, but she loved her little sister with all her heart.

Her mother had been up for hours, as usual, and had already cleared the snow off the street and made a huge pot of porridge. Frankie was at the table trying to pick the lumps out of his with a spoon.

'Ooh, you're getting right up my bugle, you are,' Nell said, giving him a clip round the ear. 'Just eat it!'

She turned to Lily, rolling her eyes. 'The Little Prof won't eat nothing with lumps in. I ask you, everything's gotta be the same bleedin' texture. Well you won't be so fussy if they bring rationing in like everyone reckons they will.'

Frankie remained oblivious, studiously picking every last lump out of his bowl.

'Oh, for pity's sake, go and give this to Snowball,' Nell scolded, her patience finally snapping. She took away the bowl and passed Frankie an enormous slab of bread and jam. 'And tell him to come in and have a cup of tea and a warm by the fire.'

Once Frankie had left, her mother sighed and looked suddenly very weary.

'You all right, Mum?' Lily asked. 'You look tired. You were out late last night. Why don't you sit down and have a cup of tea?'

'Sit down?' Nell exclaimed. 'I got half-a-dozen napkins what want washing before Mrs Trunk and Mrs Barnett drop the nippers off, and I gotta scrub the stairs and get a stew on.'

'Oh Lord,' she clamped her hands to her head. 'I forgot Mrs Povey's leaving her three with me 'an all.'

'The fishmonger's wife?' Lily queried.

'Yeah, I'm looking after hers while she takes over the running of the shop after her husband, well, you know, passed on.'

'He didn't pass on, Mum,' Lily said, pouring two cups of tea from the pot on the table. 'He hanged himself, leaving his poor wife to deal with the war, three kids and a business. Selfish, if you ask me.'

Nell narrowed her eyes as she replaced the tea cosy on the pot.

'Everything's so black and white to you, ain't it, Miss Judgmental? One day, you'll understand.'

'Where were you last night, Mum?' Lily asked quietly, observing her mother's reaction through the steam.

Nell opened her mouth, but an icy blast shot through the house as Frankie came in with Snowball the tramp. The man looked close to death, his lips chilled to a strange bluish hue and the cardboard which patched his boots a wet, pulpy mush.

'Come on now,' Nell said, hurrying over and gently prising the boots off his feet, while guiding him to an easy chair by the fireside.

'I . . . I can't stay, Mrs Gunn,' Snowball murmured, rocking back and forth and looking about uneasily.

'You can stay for the time it takes me to make you a bit of brekker and a couple of cups of Rosie Lee,' she insisted. 'Fried bread dipped in egg and chips do you? I'll send Pat out later and see if we can't find you a new pair of boots.'

He opened his mouth, then closed it again.

'Egg and chips, in a few jiffs,' she grinned, kissing a dazed Snowball on the head.

As she busied herself over the hearth, Lily drained her tea and turned to take Renee's up to her.

'Why do you put yourself out for everyone down the Shoot?' she asked, wondering whether her mother was the only person to permanently have a bowl of peeled potatoes sitting in salted water in a pan, just in case anyone popped in that needed feeding.

''Cause if I don't, who will? Look at that man.' She gestured to Snowball, warming his hands by the fire.

'He has nothing to live for except what is past. Served in the Great War and now he's nothing but debris. No place to lay his head. No hot food to eat. It's a disgrace. *Someone* has to care.'

Her eyes narrowed.

'Down the Shoot, everyone is somebody. We *all* count.'

Lily turned to go, but her mother's hand pulled her back. Her smile slipped.

'Think you forgot this.'

In her hand was Lily's coat button. It must've been yanked off as she fled from behind the fire escape last night.

Lily felt her stomach slip down into her boots.

'I . . . Er . . . I . . . Um . . .'

Nell slipped the button into Lily's pocket. Her voice was the same low warning tone she had used on Mr Barnett last night.

'What goes on inside the Shoot, stays inside the Shoot. Understood? Keep your trap shut.'

Lily said nothing. On her walk to work she considered the extraordinary paradox that was her mother. Capable of stabbing a man with a hatpin one moment, then scooping up a homeless man the next. How could any woman be so

violent and yet so tender? So beholden to the Lord, yet a
law-breaker? Lily lacked the vocabulary to understand the
complexity of her mother's life. But she did know this,
Nell's respectability down the Shoot had been hard won.
She was the neighbourhood's chief female, driven by a
strong sense of female solidarity, but, Lily wondered, at
what price?

By the time Lily clocked in at Yardley's, all the talk was of
the Christmas drinks and beauty show in eight days' time.

Those that didn't want to enter the beauty show could
perform a song or a little skit to entertain.

In the past, Yardley socials had been legendary in Stratford
and a reason for most girls to seek employment there. Thanks
to the Yardley Club, workers enjoyed black-tie dinner dances
with a coach laid on and the Yardley Follies, a dance troupe,
performed annually at the Theatre Royal. The theatre had
closed at the outbreak of war and was yet to reopen, and war
had put paid to lavish dinner and dancing. But a bash in the
canteen was not to be sneezed at.

'Will there be free booze?' Fat Lou asked Lily, as they took
a breather for morning tea break.

'Yes, Lou, food and beverages will be laid on,' Lily smiled.
'And there will be a prize for the overall winner of the talent
and beauty show. A free makeover at the Bond Street store.
Mr Lavender's calling the competition Miss Homefront this
year.'

'Yes!' screamed Renee, punching the air. 'I'm going up
West, girls.'

Renee cocked her little finger and did a fake catwalk over
the factory floor, swanking it up.

'All them girls, done up like a dog's dinner,' she sang out,
taking a turn around the belt, 'but we all know, there's only
one winner.'

She winked dramatically, and the lipstick girls fell about.

'Don't be so sure of that,' remarked Nan, slyly patting her turban, which was even higher than usual. 'You ain't got it in the bag yet, Renee Gunn.'

'Wot'cha got under there, Nan?' grinned Renee, making a grab for Nan's turban. 'You been nicking drawers off the line again?'

It was well known that the battle for Yardley's highest turban was usually helped with a few strategically placed socks and bras stuffed underneath.

'Leave off,' Nan said, batting her hand away, but Renee made a playful lunge for her.

'I said get off, Renee!' Nan snapped, pushing her back so hard that Renee nearly toppled into the lipstick churn.

'All right, what's biting you?'

'I'm missing Jimmy is all,' Nan replied, blinking back tears. 'It's all right for you. You've got your Alfie still here, but you wait and see.'

Renee's face softened.

'Sorry, Nan. I was only yanking yer chain.'

Lily watched the exchange between Renee and Nan carefully, wondering at what point she should step in. If Renee thought having her big sister as charge hand meant she would have an easy ride of it, she was wrong. Lily was determined to stamp her authority down so that she couldn't be accused of playing favourites with her spirited little sister.

Three months into the job, Lily was learning how to deal with the upper echelons of management, when to let something go and when to stamp down. Her mother's advice to be fair but firm was good and she was determined to tread this path. Since her appointment, the lipstick belt had increased productivity and Lily was proud of this fact.

'Right, enough of all this. Pull out and let's get back on the belt, girls,' she ordered. 'And Renee, stop goading Nan.'

'A quick word, if I may?' Lily felt a tap on her shoulder and turned to find Miss Peerless looming over her. 'In Miss Rayson's office.'

Two floors up, in the smarter offices and face to face with her two superiors, Lily refused to feel intimidated.

'Is something wrong?' she asked.

'We're very happy with your work,' Miss Rayson said smoothly. 'Production has increased since your arrival. But it's come to our attention that there have been some discrepancies in stock. The numbers counted don't match the final tally. Mistakes happen, we expect that, once or even twice. But on three separate checks now, the numbers don't add up. Lipsticks are going missing.'

'Are you saying we have a thief?' Lily asked cautiously.

'No one's saying any such thing, but I am asking you to stay alert, Miss Gunn. Security will be upping their regular checks at clocking-out, so if there is a thief, she will quickly be flushed out.'

'Of course, I'll be watching closely,' Lily replied.

Miss Peerless cleared her throat.

'I'm not telling you how to do your job, Miss Gunn, but if I were you, I'd have my eye trained on that new service girl.'

'Esther?'

'Yes, the Jewish girl,' Miss Peerless said coldly.

'But she's such a hard worker, so conscientious,' Lily protested, fighting down the urge to ask what her faith had to do with it. 'As a matter of fact, I was going to recommend she be promoted onto the belt when her twelve months as a service girl are up.'

Miss Peerless's mouth tightened into a thin line. 'What do we really know about her, other than a reference from her mother's uncle?'

'What are you saying exactly?'

'Most new starters have two people to speak for them, a

teacher and a relative. I mean, she's not one of our local girls, is she?' Miss Peerless's voice lingered on the word 'local'.

'Meaning?' Lily demanded.

'Meaning she might have family at home she needs to send money to. And she is alone with the stock when she takes it down to dispatch. War can make people do desperate things.'

Lily felt her blood rush to her head. 'She is a guest in our country working hard to prove herself,' she protested. 'Her father's detained in a work camp, for goodness' sake. What Esther needs is compassion, not condemnation.'

'I think we all need to calm down,' said Miss Rayson, glaring at Miss Peerless. 'No one is pointing the finger at anyone. It's probably just a simple mistake. We are living through trying times. Now, can we talk over the plans for the fire-watching rota?'

Miss Rayson may have navigated them into safer waters, but Lily desperately fought down the urge to slap Miss Peerless across her smug face.

As she clattered down the iron staircases clutching the new fire-watching rota, the welfare officer's plea to *stay alert* ricocheted around her brain. How long could they all remain on alert before something happened? All of Stratford was stuck in a dreadful state of limbo. Watching. Waiting. Hoping.

12

Esther

Christmas Eve blew through Stratford on the back of a bitter snowstorm, the coldest winter in a century, freezing lead pipes and turning the Cut into a solid sheet of ice. The Mayor appealed for calm as snow piled up and the desperate demand for coal grew. Nell made Renee, Lily and Frankie take round extra bags to all the grateful residents of the Shoot, and they knew better than to ask where it had come from.

Esther, meanwhile, had taken to accompanying her mother as she visited the elderly of the neighbourhood, dressing their ulcers and tending to them for free to save them the cost of a trip to the doctor's. It was these small acts of kindness that made such a big difference in a place like the Shoot.

The Bricky Kids seemed to be the only ones unfazed. It was the crack of dawn but they were already out, turning the Shoot into a glittering blizzard as snowballs and excitable shouts tore back and forth over the square. Despite the war and the cold, the magic of Christmas had infected everyone.

Julia wanted to pop in on Mrs Trunk, who had a nasty case of bronchitis, and had plans to teach Frankie in the morning. As it was still early, Esther came too so she could knock for the girls and all walk to work together. They found the Shoot a hive of activity. Steps were scrubbed. Rag rugs beaten. Coppers were gently heating. The Shoot's chief female had been up and at it since four a.m., pulling lavatory chains and running taps to prevent the pipes freezing up. Most of the women in the square had followed her lead and were out in force, their lively voices lapping at the old brick walls.

'Cooee,' called Esther, sticking her head in the kitchen, her breath so cold it hung like steam.

'Come in and warm up,' called Nell. 'Tea in the pot, help yourselves, the others won't be long.'

Pat scarfed down his tea as Nell fussed round her husband, making sure he had his sandwiches and flask of Camp coffee.

'Now, be sure to be back for Yardley's social at dinnertime,' she ordered. 'One only down the Two Puddings. Our Renee's in the beautification competition, the Gunns gotta be there in force.'

'Beauty contest, Mum,' Lily corrected, shooting Esther an amused look as she walked in.

'That's what I said, weren't it?' Nell tutted.

'Don'cha worry, my old Dutch,' Pat grinned, wrapping his wiry arms around his wife's voluptuous, apron-clad body. 'I'll be there to support our Renee. Go and see Jack the Butcher down the Lane later. He's keeping us a decent joint under the counter.'

Esther watched as Pat slipped a bundle of notes into her apron pocket. Nell's eyes shone dizzy with love as she kissed him firmly on the mouth.

'Be lucky,' she whispered.

'You might be later,' he winked, squeezing her ample bottom.

Lily rolled her eyes and looked away in disgust, but Esther felt a pang deep inside. What she wouldn't do to have her father here, see him kiss her mother once more.

Determined to be brave, she glanced over at Frankie methodically counting some spilt grains of salt on the tabletop. Just seven, yet he moved through the world like a monk in a contemplative order. He didn't seem to share any characteristics with the rest of the Gunns.

'Go on, son, why don'cha get out there with the Bricky Kids, have a snowball fight, get yer hands dirty?' Pat urged Frankie now, full of festive cheer. 'When I was your age, I was earning a bundle running errands in the snow. Go and knock the neighbours and see who wants something running down the pawnshop.'

Frankie said nothing, just carried on counting, but Esther noticed the slight tremor in his hands.

'Dozy sod,' Pat tutted, jamming his cap on. 'You're coming carol singing with me and the Bricky Kids later, like it or not. Ain't you better be on your way, Lil and Esther?'

'Waiting for Renee,' Lily replied.

'She'd be late for her own flamin' funeral, that one,' Pat muttered before heading out into the snow. At the far sight of the Shoot, a forlorn figure was gingerly hobbling across the cobbles.

'Morning, Mr Barnett, I'd hate to see the other fella,' Pat called out jokingly.

His face jerked up and immediately paled. Nell joined her husband on the step, folding her arms over her apron.

He took his cap off and nodded at Nell without making eye contact.

'I had a few too many, managed to dance with a lamppost,' he replied in a colourless voice.

Pat roared with laughter and tapped his head.

'Up here for thinking, my son, down there for dancing.'

Mr Barnett laughed lamely.

'I'll remember that Pat, ta.'

'Make sure you do,' Nell called after him. Pat kissed her goodbye and left.

'Sorry about that,' Nell said, turning back to Julia and Esther. 'It's like Piccadilly Circus round here this morning.'

'It's Christmas Eve,' Julia shrugged. 'What do you expect?'

'Which is why I feel like I'm taking a liberty asking you to teach the Little Prof.'

'If he would like a lesson this morning, then I'm more than happy to teach him. I just need to pop in and check on Mrs Trunk first.'

At the mention of a lesson with her mother, Frankie's face lit up and he flung himself into Julia's arms.

'There's your answer,' Nell chuckled. 'Careful, Frankie, you'll be doing Mrs Orwell a damage.'

'It's all right,' smiled Julia, hugging him back. 'Frankie and I have just come to a very interesting part in the book we are reading on 17th-century spice routes, have we not? Frankie is teaching me so much.'

'Gracious,' he exclaimed, drawing his brows in a curious fashion. 'One does what one can.'

Nell roared with laugher as she picked up the teapot.

'Where did you come from, Frankie Gunn?'

'You have one very clever young man here.' Julia smiled down warmly, and Esther could see the bond between them was strong in just three months. She felt no trace of jealousy, only gratitude, as she knew helping Frankie was keeping her mother's mind off her husband, particularly while Esther was at work.

'All right, Est, Mrs O,' grinned Renee, as she clattered down the stairs, fizzing over with a natural ebullience.

'You ain't going out like that?' Nell gasped, setting down the teapot with a thump.

Renee's hair was done out in curlers, so her turban sat a mile high on her head, and her bare legs were stained with gravy browning.

'It's the beauty contest later, ain't it? No one ever said being beautiful come easy.'

She grabbed a piece of bread and marge from the table,

clamped it between her teeth, before picking up her gas mask and clocking-in cards.

'Have you been borrowing my mascara?' Lily asked, suspiciously.

'No, I ain't,' Renee replied. 'It's a *Woman's Own* beauty dodge. Burn down a cork and use the ash to blacken your lashes out.' She fluttered her lashes at Esther. 'Works a treat, don't it, Est? Now come on, look lively. Can't have you lot making me late. Age before beauty,' she winked, letting Lily step out into the snow first.

'Cor,' Renee shivered as Esther followed her out the door. 'It's colder than a polar bear's cock out here.'

Despite the cold, Esther felt her face heat up.

'Language,' Lily scolded, lifting her eyes to the heavens. Renee looked nonplussed, swanking her way across the square like an actress.

Lily and Esther followed, but Lily slowed down, her attention caught by something.

'Wait up, Renee.'

'What's wrong?'

Lily gestured to the Trunks' doorstep. The door stood wide open, banging in the icy wind. What looked like wheel marks led away from the door in the snow.

'Odd's on they've done a flit!' Renee announced. 'Mum,' she yelled, 'you better get out here.'

Esther looked at Lily puzzled. 'What's a flit?'

'It means moonlight flit, Esther,' Lily explained. 'It's what people do when they're behind on the rent. Load up their life on the back of a barrow and run under the cover of darkness.'

Nell and Julia emerged into the square and Nell immediately disappeared inside the Trunks' house. She emerged a minute later, looking grim.

'Empty! I told her I'd speak with the rent man and sort it.

Flitting and on Christmas Eve of all days. It's no life. What kind of Christmas them kiddies gonna have now?'

'Not much of one, and I'm concerned about her too,' Julia worried. 'She has a rattling chest.'

'Should we get word to Dad, see if he can't find 'em?' Renee asked.

'No point, love,' Nell replied. The breath left her body in one big sigh. 'They'll be long gone by now.'

'You really do see the women of this neighbourhood as your responsibility, don't you?' Julia said softly.

'Down the Shoot, neighbours are as close as family,' she replied in a tone that brooked no argument. 'Solidarity. It's the only way to survive, see?'

She turned to Esther and her two daughters.

'If you remember only one thing, girls, it's this. Out there the partriarchy rule. In here down the Shoot, it's the matri-archy.'

She drew herself up right and turned to Julia.

'Well, no sense in those empty rooms going to waste. Why don't you and Esther move in?'

'Move in?' Julia exclaimed.

'Yeah. Think about it. You said yourself the rooms are tiny above the shop and there's no privacy for Esther. And it'd be easier for our Frankie to come to you for lessons.'

'Oh please, Mama,' Esther begged, clutching her sleeve.

As nice as her mother's uncle was, he wasn't half as much fun as Lily and Renee Gunn.

'But they won't give that whole house to us, surely?' Julia replied.

'I'll send my Pat round to have a word with the landlord. Trust me, love, it'll be yours. I'll drop the keys round later.'

Esther couldn't contain her excitement and kissed Mrs Gunn on the cheek.

'Oh thank you, thank you.'

'You're as daft in the head as our Renee,' Nell chuckled. 'Now hurry up, or else you'll be late clocking in.'

'That's a touch, ain't it,' Renee beamed, slipping her arm through Esther's as they set off. 'We're neighbours.'

At the factory, Esther was so busy running errands that the morning flew by in a haze of work and song. She was surprised when the conveyor belts shut down.

'It's Christmas!' whooped Renee, ripping off her turban and slinging her arm round Esther's neck.

'You can come with me to the khazi. There's work to be done.'

'But I'm not entering Miss Homefront,' Esther replied, alarmed.

'No, but I am and unless you got two hot spoons, I need someone to help me into my bathers.'

'Right you are,' Esther laughed.

'Is there anything more you need me to do, Lily?' she asked.

'No, you go off and help Renee and I'll see you in the canteen in a bit. Good luck!'

Following Renee into the toilets, Esther was surprised to see the place had already been transformed into a steamy boudoir.

Little Irene, Joycie, Betty, Joanie, Mavis and a dozen other girls were frantically painting on lipstick, slapping on Pan-Cake, fluffing up hair and changing into one-pieces ready for the beauty show. Only Fat Lou was missing. It was hard to tell where the cigarette smoke began and the hair lacquer ended as the girls craned for every inch of mirror space.

Esther spotted Nan sitting on her own in a toilet cubicle, desolately smoking a cigarette.

'I thought you were entering, Nan?' she asked. 'Are you all right?'

Renee was hopping about on one leg as she attempted to pull up the tightest bathing suit Esther had ever seen.

'Yeah, what's wrong with you? You look like a tit in a trance. Get ready sharpish and paint on a smile while you're at it!'

Nan burst into tears.

'I can't!' she snapped. 'I got the curse.'

'But I thought you was . . . You know . . .' Renee whispered, pulling up her bathing costume and letting her hands hover over her belly.

'So did I,' Nan said miserably. 'I had two missed bleeds, only now I'm bleedin' something rotten. It ain't taken, has it?'

'Oh Nan,' said Renee, crouching down beside her in the tiny cubicle. 'It don't sound like it, no.'

'I'm never gonna have a baby. What if I'm barren?' Nan blurted, fresh tears misting her beautiful pale eyes.

'Don't talk daft,' Renee admonished. 'Of course you'll have a baby. Bleedin' hell, within a couple of years, you'll have a whole clutch of 'em hanging off your tit and, trust me, then you'll look back to this conversation and wish you was right. Ain't that so, Est?'

They both glanced up at Esther.

'Erm, I'm sure you're right,' she blustered, backing out of the cubicle.

She'd been warned by locals that Yardley's would offer her a formidable education in the ways of the world. She was beginning to see what they meant, but at times like this she felt well out of her depth. Worse still, like she was intruding between two old friends.

'I'll help Renee get ready,' said Nan icily, kicking the door closed in her face.

The canteen was a far safer space. Esther looked around, marvelling at its transformation. The trestle tables had been pushed back and a makeshift stage erected at the far end. A curtain of dazzling stars trembled over the stage and a glitterball cast fragments of dancing light over the lino floor.

Gay paper garlands made from cut-up strips of old copies of the *Yardley News* were strung from the ceiling and in the corner stood a Christmas tree, surrounded by gifts donated by employees for the Children's Ward of Queen Mary's Hospital in Stratford.

Blind Eric was playing a lovely dancehall number, his hands tinkling over the ivories.

'It's beautiful,' she marvelled.

'Shame they can't do anything about the smell,' Blind Eric sniffed. The canteen had boiled up a mutton stew for dinner earlier and that, combined with the stench of offal from the fishmeal firm over the Cut, had brewed up a particularly earthy pong.

Esther and those girls not entering the beauty contest took their places at the table, alongside her mother, Lily and Nell Gunn. The place was rammed solid with Yardley workers and their families. Esther noticed Miss Peerless staring at her in a peculiar way, so she smiled across the table at her. The lipstick room supervisor looked as if she were about to say something but took one look at Nell and seemed to think better of it.

Nell Gunn was the most extraordinary woman Esther had ever come across.

Nail hard, yet there was nothing but warmth in her heart. She watched, intrigued, as woman after woman came up to the table to say hello to Nell. Renee and Lily's mum was certainly treated with deference in the neighbourhood.

She was wearing a striking hat, which Esther couldn't take her eyes off, a huge velvet number with a long, black feather perched defiantly on top. Coupled with a sweeping jet-black gown and button-down boots, she cut an intimidating figure. Esther silently thanked her lucky stars that Stratford's matriarch had taken a shine to her mother.

Nell caught her staring.

'You like it?' she asked. Esther nodded.

'This hat's as old as time.'

She ran her fingers over the sweeping rim, a secret smile playing over her mouth, before leaning over to whisper: 'If this hat could talk, it'd have tales to tell that'd make your toes curl.'

Esther's eyes stretched wide as she waited expectantly for the rest of the story, but instead, Nell brought out an old pocket watch from the voluminous folds of her dress skirts.

'Where's Pat and Frankie?' Nell tutted, irritated. 'I told them to be here by now.'

'He'll be here, Mum,' Lily soothed. 'It's Lou I'm worried about, I haven't seen her since we clocked off.'

Suddenly a hush descended over the canteen as the Managing Director took to the stage and began a speech thanking the loyal workers of Yardley. First up were the Yardley Follies, who high-kicked their way over the stage in perfect rhythm then performed a lightning-fast tap-dancing routine.

Esther watched the whole performance in wonder. It may have been a canteen in the backwaters of East London, but there was such pride and infectious joy rippling through the room. And such smashing-looking girls! To Esther, each and every one was a beauty queen. She'd been in Stratford long enough now to know that looking good was a badge of honour. No one had much in the way of money but with a little imagination and a bucket-load of swagger, you could always look the part.

Next up were Mickey and Johnny from dispatch, though she barely recognised them under the teetering heels, thick make-up and enormous ginger wigs.

If anyone in the room seemed perturbed to find the two burly men, who were usually seen shifting enormous pallets round the yard, dressed up as a couple of pantomime dames, they didn't show it. Instead, the crowd roared with laughter, rocking in their chairs at their madcap antics.

Pat Gunn slipped in, obviously the worse off for drink.

'Sorry I'm late, I took the Bricky Kids carolling.'

'What, down the pub?' Nell muttered. She looked ready to give him a proper mouthful, but she was interrupted . . .

'And now,' said the compere as Mickey teetered off stage left. 'The moment you've all been waiting for, Miss Homefront 1939! Let's give the girls a warm hand,' he winked.

The crowd sat up eagerly, and thunderous applause swept over the canteen as the girls sashayed out onto the stage to a chorus of wolf whistles. Pat put his fingers in his mouth and whistled so loud, Esther could feel her eardrums vibrating.

'Who will take the coveted sash and crown and make it onto the cover of the *Yardley News*?'

Renee was hamming it up for all her worth. When it came to her turn in the spotlight, she paused dramatically, hand on hip. In nothing but a white one-piece, heels, red lipstick and wavy blonde hair, she looked at least as beautiful as Greta Garbo or Betty Grable. So luscious was she in all her treacly loveliness, Esther could not keep her eyes off her. But Renee only had eyes for one man.

With a lascivious wink, she blew a kiss down to Alfie, who looked like he might expire at any moment.

'You have composed a little ditty, I understand, Miss Gunn?' said the compere.

'That's right,' she said, clearing her throat. 'Here goes . . .

'Are you a Carpenters Roader? Do you flinch at the odour?
Export and invoice all day?
Do you polish and pack? How's your aching back?
Is the lipstick belt turning you grey?
Do you box or inspect? Pass and reject?

Are you East End or West End?
Are you wrestling with soap, or struggling to cope,
With all the demands war does send?
Whether you sell it when out on the road, Or massage the
client's fair cheek ...
Forget it my friends, and throw off your load –
IT'S CHRISTMAS AT YARDLEY'S THIS WEEK!'

Renee did a sassy little bow and the canteen erupted.

'So shy and retiring, my little sister,' Lily remarked wryly.

Esther giggled. 'She is not short on chutzpah, as my mother would say.'

Suddenly, there came an enormous thud from the side of the stage and the crowd fell into silence as a pantomime horse skidded onto the stage, right in front of the beauty contest entrants.

Esther couldn't believe her eyes as it capered this way and that with the compere in hot pursuit, scattering the swim-suit-clad beauties. At last he got a hold of its tail and yanked it off, to reveal Fat Lou.

'Me mother always said I looked like the back end of a horse, so here I am,' said Lou with a toothy grin. 'Have I won then, or what?'

Lou's spectacle brought the house down and people were wiping tears of laughter from their eyes.

'That girl's a caution!' hooted Pat. Only Renee looked slightly put out to have to share the limelight. But her smile returned when she was declared the winner, sticking her chest out and shaking back her blonde hair as the compere slipped the sash over her head.

'I've been robbed,' hollered Fat Lou, clutching a horse's backside under her arm.

'Oh shut up and come here, you big, sexy woman,' chirped Renee, silencing her with a big kiss.

The evening was declared a success all round and was just winding up, when the sound of children's singing drifted up from the yard outside.

> *'O little town of Bethlehem*
> *How still we see thee lie*
> *Above thy deep and dreamless sleep . . .'*

'Let's have a look,' suggested Pat, getting to his feet and cautiously lifting one blackout blind.

'Dim the lights,' he suggested.

The compere did as he said, and soon the whole crowd was clustered round the windows looking out.

From out of the velvet darkness emerged a sight that would melt even the hardest of dockers.

A dozen or so of the Bricky Kids were huddled by the side of the frozen Cut, shivering in patched-up pullovers and boots stuffed with cardboard to keep out the leaks. Fat snowflakes spiralled down over their faces as they sang their hearts out. Esther spotted little Frankie at the back of the group.

> *'. . . The silent stars go by*
> *Yet in thy dark streets shineth*
> *The everlasting Light*
> *The hopes and fears of all the years*
> *Are met in thee tonight'*

Pat touched his hankie to his eye. 'Hark at them poor nippers, singing their hearts out for a few coppers. Look, they're so cold, their kneecaps are running up and down their legs!'

'Oh bless 'em,' said a lady.

'Let's have a whip-round, shall we?' Pat suggested, whipping off his cap and handing it round the crowd.

The sound of chinking coins filled the canteen as the workers of Yardley's, whose generosity was well oiled by the free booze, dug deep.

As the crowds dispersed, Esther overheard Nell muttering to her husband.

'So that's why you're so pie-eyed.'

He nodded. 'We've done most of the pubs in Stratford on this one. I had to have a pint in each mind, to make it look legit.'

Rolling her eyes, Nell wrenched the cap out of his hands. With a rustle, she produced a small pouch from under her stiff petticoats and in one swift move, deposited the takings in it.

'Every single ha'penny in here and the rest of your earnings on this little scam is going on Christmas presents for the Shoot and Bricky Kids. You still got time to get down Boardman's.'

'Of course, my love,' he replied. Seeing Esther staring openmouthed, he gave her a little wink

'Charity begins in the Shoot, know what I mean?'

The next day, Esther gazed out of her new bedroom window at the snow-flecked square beneath. Dozens of kids were already out, trying out their new toys. Whip-and-tops, jacks, footballs and scooters were being eagerly put to use and shared amongst the crowd of kids for whom this Christmas Day was now officially the best, as well as the coldest, on record. Esther and her mother had only a few possessions, so moving had taken all of two hours when they'd got back from the show last night, but already her mother was hard at work, turning the empty rooms into a home and hanging up their clothes.

Being Jewish, she and her mother did not celebrate Christmas, but the Gunns had still insisted they take time off from unpacking to join them for dinner, eager for them not to be alone during the festivities. Esther didn't mind admitting how much she was looking forward to it. In fact, it was all nearly perfect. This house, her job at Yardley's, her new friends, safety . . . The acceptance and warmth they had found in this small, vibrant corner of East London was giving her a sense of purpose she found hard to put into words. Her heart gave a painful twist in her chest. If only her father were here to share in this welcome.

Next door, she heard the sounds of the Gunn family waking up to Christmas morning. The scrape of Pat's shovel clearing snow from the step, Renee singing a Judy Garland number and from somewhere deep in the heart of the house, Nell's rich throaty laugh.

Esther blew on the taped-up window. Her hot breath misted over the pane. Between the gaps of the criss-crossed tape, she wrote four words.

I love you, Papa.

She rested her forehead against the cool glass.

'Stay safe, wherever you are . . .'

13

Renee

As 1939 folded into 1940, January came in with biting winds and days so short it was barely worth getting light.

A leprosy outbreak in Leyton and a new round of military registration under the Royal Proclamation of 1st January had neighbourhood nerves stretched to breaking point. According to an article in the *Stratford Express,* 1,081 of the district's finest young men, who had reached the age of twenty, registered at the Employment Exchange for military service – including Alfie Buckle and most of his pals in the factory.

'There ain't gonna be any flamin' men left in Stratford at this rate,' groaned Joycie, reading the article over dinner break in the canteen.

'Or food,' sighed Fat Lou, poking a finger at another front-page article, which gloomily told of the new food restrictions the government had brought in. Bacon, butter and sugar rationed, with more food schemes believed to be imminent.

'Men are on ration, food's on ration . . . Whatever next?' sighed Nan.

'You can't ration love, though, girls,' sighed Renee, gazing through the icy windows to where she could see the Berger boys loading up pallets in the yard, their breath hanging like smoke in the freezing air.

'You're in love with Alfie?' said Lily, looking up in shock from a watery bowl of soup. 'Only felt like yesterday you were telling him never to talk to you again.'

'That was before he found Frankie and oh, I don't know, girls, he's changed is all. He seems really serious about me and him having a future together.'

Renee thought of his large and lively family party before Christmas, of their stolen kisses in the passage. Unlike their doomed date the day after war had broken out, everything about this new Alfie felt right. Being introduced to his family had to mean something, surely? She'd be lying if she didn't admit to having tried out her name with his. Renee Buckle. Mrs Renee Buckle. Had a lovely ring to it.

'Why are you grinning like a Cheshire cat?' asked Fat Lou.

'Me to know, you to find out?' she taunted.

'You haven't . . . ?' gasped little Irene.

'Get your mind out the gutter, Irene Battersby,' Renee laughed. 'I'm in love is all.'

'Well I think it's lovely, Renee,' said Esther shyly. 'Or should I call you Miss Homefront 1939? You make a dashing couple.'

'Thanks, darlin',' Renee laughed. 'You're a sweetheart. Talking of Miss Homefront, I'm going for my makeover at Yardley Bond Street later as part of my competition win.'

'Ooh, la-di-da,' teased Joycie.

'I'm probably too famous to hang about with the likes of you actually,' joked Renee with a wink.

'Has anyone seen the new *Yardley News*?' questioned Nan. 'We should've had it by now.'

'Oh yes, about that . . .' said Lily. 'I'm afraid I heard from the bosses, it's not going to come out while the war's still ongoing. Can't spare paper now it's . . .'

'On the ration!' chorused the entire table.

'Never mind,' sniffed Renee. 'I'm gonna look like Betty

Grable by the time I've had my makeover, and then my Alfie's promised to take me up the Lyceum.'

'Penny to a pound that's not the only place he wants to take you,' flashed Nan crudely. 'Probably after a quick knee trembler. Remember, he's got form.'

'Not all men are like . . .' Renee snapped back before stopping herself.

'Like who?' Nan demanded.

'Nothing, forget I said anything,' Renee said hurriedly.

Renee cursed her big mouth and, thankfully, Lily changed the subject. While the girls dissected which of the remaining Berger boys they'd have a quick fumble with and which they'd marry, Renee's thoughts drifted back once more to Alfie. Something between them really had changed. A new kind of intensity had threaded its way through their relationship.

The thought of his imminent departure, the uniform that awaited his entry into the Royal Navy, had cast an unreal air over the short time they had left. As the day inched ever closer, they grew together, like two trees bending in the wind. They had barely been aware of their intensifying closeness, but images of Alfie now cartwheeled through her every waking thought. So much so that on that afternoon's shift, she accidentally fused the machinery that operated the lipstick conveyor belt.

'Wake up, please, Renee,' Lily muttered under her breath as she summoned an engineer. 'I've covered for you twice today, but Miss Peerless is already watching this belt like a hawk.'

'Sorry, Lil,' she apologised, her blue eyes sparkling under her turban. 'I'm just excited about my makeover is all.'

As is the way when you are looking forward to something, the afternoon seemed to take an eternity, so much so that by the time Renee and Lily clocked off, she virtually ran to the bus stop.

'Whoah, slow down, you got ants in your pants?' laughed

Lily breathlessly as she jumped onto the back of the Number 25 bus after Renee.

'Now please, Renee, remember no larking about when we reach the salon,' Lily begged as they sat down on the wooden slatted seat, her gas mask perched on her lap.

'Where's your gas mask, Renee, you haven't lost it again, have you?' she chided.

'Oh look, conductor's coming,' said Renee, hastily changing the subject. 'Have your ticket ready to punch.'

'Lavender Girls?' he enquired, letting his eyes linger a fraction too long on Renee's slender ankles.

'That's right. How d'ya know?' beamed Renee.

'I can always tell when your lot get on, makes the whole bus smell of roses and lavender.'

'Aaah, ain't that lovely?' she said, winking at the delighted conductor.

'And that's another thing. Talk proper,' said Lily, lowering her voice. 'None of your ain'ts and fings.'

Renee rolled her eyes, pulled out her compact and began dabbing at her nose with a papier poudre.

Lily got out her copy of fashion bible *Vogue* and tried to read, but Renee was far too excited to sit in silence and read out loud an article entitled *Neat Heads* about actress Deborah Kerr, who had cropped her hair into a bob.

'*War work, whether in services or factories, has brought a wave of shorter hair – for neatness, easy cleanliness and good looks*,' Renee read.

'Sod that,' expostulated Renee loudly. 'My Alfie would do his nut if I cut all my hair off. Honestly, you can't tell the "he"s from the "she"s 'cause of this flamin' war. Whatever next, women in slacks?'

'For pity's sake,' Lily snapped. 'Must you sound so common, Renee?'

Renee's face crumpled.

'Don't get a cob on!'

'Sorry, sis,' said Lily, immediately remorseful, 'I didn't mean that. But really, you're going to have to start facing up to a few uncomfortable truths. So far, this war hasn't touched you, but things will change and it won't just be hairstyles. Mark my words.'

Renee sat in sulky silence as the conductor walked up the aisle pulling down the blackout blinds at the windows.

Her mood was quite forgotten as, thirty-five minutes later, they stepped off the bus near Claridge's.

'Oh Lil, will you look at that!' Renee exclaimed. 'Even the sandbags look posh!'

The majestic hotel appeared gleaming out of the fog. Smart liveried doormen welcomed in a stream of uniformed officers and fabulous-looking women, who may or may not have been their wives. An RAF officer and his date spilled out in a cloud of smoke and laughter, before vanishing arm-in-arm into the blackout.

'War don't half make people randy,' Renee remarked enviously, watching them and wondering whether she and Alfie cut such a dash.

'Come on, you,' sighed Lily, rolling her eyes.

Taking her sister's arm, she directed her past the enormous stuccoed Mayfair townhouses to Yardley's salon at 33 Old Bond Street.

Renee felt like a star of the silver screen as a uniformed concierge swung open the door and ushered them into the fragranced white showroom.

'You must be Miss Homefront? Welcome,' smiled an elegantly dressed young woman with the most perfect teeth Renee had ever seen.

'Olive,' said Lily, hugging the woman warmly before turning to Renee. 'Allow me to introduce Miss Olive Carmen. She's in charge of beauty products here.'

'Sorry I look somewhat dishevelled,' she apologised. 'It's been frightfully busy here today, rumour went round we had new stock in and we've had queues round the block.'

'Renee Gunn, the younger,' Renee beamed, sticking out her hand.

Miss Carmen's eyes widened in surprise.

'You are a secretive thing, Lily. You never said you had a sister.'

'Didn't I?' she replied, looking flustered. Renee stared at her curiously. Why on earth would she not have told her she had a sister? Unless . . . ?

Discreetly changing the subject, Olive gently took Renee's arm and guided her across the showroom through a white archway, to the adjoining salon, where two perfectly made-up assistants in crisp white coats and glossy red lips were waiting.

'Now girls, Miss Gunn here from our Stratford factory is to be thoroughly spoilt. They work them very hard over there in Carpenters Road, and it's thanks to Renee we are able to meet the demand for lipstick.'

'Lie back and relax, dear,' smiled one. 'What look would you like?'

'The one that means I get to try as many products as possible,' she quipped.

Renee reclined in the plush white leather chair and surrendered to the cool touch of their fingers, removing her grimy East End make-up with Liquefying Cleansing Cream, while massaging in a rich lavender-scented hand cream.

Before her eyes flickered shut, she caught sight of Lily and Olive huddled together by the partially open door.

If there was one thing factory girls were good at, it was lip-reading – with all that noisy machinery you had to be – which is why she was able to tell exactly what it was Miss Olive Carmen mouthed to Lily under her breath.

Have you seen him?

Lily looked panicked. *Not here*, she mouthed back.

It was the briefest of moments, but that look on Lily's face was a picture. Usually so composed, whoever 'he' was, he'd certainly got her sister in a flap. Renee pushed down her hurt that Lily refused to confide in her, but it nagged away inside. *She doesn't trust me enough to share her love life. She refuses to tell her posh work mates about me.*

By the time her makeover was finished and they stepped outside, Renee had worked herself into a lather.

'You look every inch the beauty queen you are,' Lily smiled.

'Admit it, you're ashamed of me!' Renee rounded on her accusingly.

Lily's smile vanished.

'What? Why would you think that?'

'I may be blonde, but I ain't thick. What you said earlier on the bus, about my accent. The fact that you've never breathed a word about me to your pals here.'

'I promise you, Renee, I'm not ashamed of you. It's just that, well, my life here and my life in Stratford belong to two different worlds.'

Her words were resolute, but her eyes flickered briefly downwards, a gesture almost imperceptible. Renee stared hard at her sister, and knew then with a certainty that this secret Lily was keeping from her involved a forbidden relationship. But whenever Renee tried to get near, encourage her to open up, she became as impenetrable as a blackout blind. Renee sighed. She might only be nineteen, but she was a woman now. When she was Mrs Renee Buckle they'd have to take her seriously.

'Oh, do cheer up, Renee,' Lily urged. 'Why don't we go shopping while we're here?'

Renee's eyes instantly lit up. No sense ruining a trip up West.

'Oh, go on then, twist me arm! Sorry, twist one's arm.'

Lily gave her a playful punch then dragged her through

the pebble-grey fog in the direction of the Tube. Despite the tension of earlier, the Gunn girls had a lovely evening, tracking down *Vogue*'s bargain frock of the month – a natty little crepe polka-dot number – to Marshall & Snelgrove, and Renee made a hasty pencil sketch of a gay little navy wool Jaeger swagger suit she liked the look of, but couldn't afford, so that she might run it up herself.

They even had time to pop into a new company Olive had told Lily about, a hat hospital off Bond Street, who promised to breathe new life into a battered old felt hat of hers. Renee marvelled at the ingenuity. A hat hospital, whatever next? Wait until she told the girls. Shopping done, they celebrated their stylish thriftiness by popping into Lyons Corner House on Regent Street for coffee with a dash.

By the time they jumped off the Number 25 at the Broadway and returned to the Shoot, the fog had cleared and a sharp sickle moon had risen over the jumble of roof-tops. A dark figure was crumpled on the doorstep. One of her mum's charity cases, Renee reckoned.

But then the outline shifted, a pale and haunted face gazed up at her and the breath froze in her lungs.

'Alfie! I thought we was meeting on the High Street?' Renee murmured, putting down her bags. 'Alfie? Whatever's wrong? You're scaring me.'

'It's my brother, Rene . . . He's . . . He's . . .' Emotion shattered the words in his throat.

'Oh, Alfie, no!' Renee choked back a sob, and slid to her knees beside him on the frozen doorstep. Lily tactfully slid past to give the couple some privacy, squeezing Alfie's shoulder.

'I'll fetch you a drop of Dad's whisky,' she whispered, before gently shutting the door behind her.

Alfie looked at Renee, a broken man, barely registering Lily's offer.

'When?' Renee asked.

'This afternoon. We got a telegram. His ship was torpedoed. All souls lost.'

'I . . . I . . . I don't know what to say, Alfie,' she wept, sliding her hand through his. 'It don't feel real.' She thought back to the strong, larger-than-life man they had last seen just weeks before, so dashing and full of daring tales.

'I'm worried about Mum,' Alfie went on, lighting a cigarette with a trembling hand. 'She ain't said a word since the telegram's come. Just sits there staring out the window, like. Doctor's come and given her a sleeping draught but she's in another world.'

'It's the shock,' Renee replied.

'You wanna hear the laugh of it?' he said with a brittle snort. 'We was supposed to be hosting a party for my great-nan Martha this afternoon, remember her? A hundred and one today, born 1839. She's taken to her bed and refusing to come out since the news. "How am I still alive when my great-grandson is dead?" is all she says.'

Renee shook her head, speechless, for there was no answer to that. Leastwise, not one that made sense.

Alfie looked at her and his features softened. He traced his finger down her cheek.

'I'm sorry, Rene. Here you are looking like such a knockout and I've brought you down. If you don't mind, I don't feel like dancing tonight.'

He rested his head on her shoulder.

'Of course not,' she soothed, stroking his head. 'Why don't we go for a walk?'

'I'd like that,' he replied. 'Especially as tonight is my last night.'

'Oh, Alfie, no!' she gasped. 'You can't mean that? Surely you're not still leaving tomorrow? After everything that's happened?'

'I've got no say in it, Rene,' he said, straightening up. 'Even if I wanted to stay, I can't. I've joined up. I'm in the Navy now. Train leaves at the crack.'

Renee shook her head despairingly. 'But how can you . . .' The words she wanted to say thickened and refused to spill. Somewhere in the Shoot, an old gramophone record was turning, the raw and melancholy notes of 'Blue Moon' sliding through the mist. The languid voice gripped Renee's heart and squeezed it tight.

'How can I what, Rene? Go to war with my brother still floating about at the bottom of the ocean? Do you think that the war takes into account the death of Billy Buckle? There are a hundred Billy Buckles dying every minute. We don't all have a right to three score years and ten. Breath stops.'

He stubbed his cigarette out in the snow with a sharp fizz and stood up, smoothing down the creases in his trousers.

'I'm going tomorrow, Rene. If anything, it's made me more determined. I'm going out there to fight the Germans. For our Billy.'

Tears spilled down his cheeks and Renee found the sight of her man crying deeply unsettling.

'I-I'm sorry,' he said gruffly, wiping his eyes with the back of his sleeve. 'Probably best I'm on me own . . . I'll only bring you down.'

He wheeled and stumbled from the Shoot.

'Oh no you don't, Alfie Buckle,' she said, running after him and catching him by the arm.

'Don't you dare shut me out, especially if . . .' Her voice faltered. 'If we're to spend the rest of our lives together.'

He took in her beautiful blue eyes, huge and luminous in the moonlight.

'You're right, Rene. Sorry, come on, let's walk.'

★

By the time Lily returned with the whisky, the couple had already left, their walk taking them through the dark silent streets of the Shoot and down to the Cut.

Renee felt as if she were walking a path of no return, their footsteps echoing eerily over the frozen waters of the canal. The moon was mocking them, looking for all the world like the Grim Reaper's scythe, slicing through the inky darkness. The glamour and gaiety of the West End already felt like a world away.

They wandered in silence down a backwater canal, lined with cavernous slaughterhouses, tanners and a whalebone factory, their hulking brick walls hiding unsavoury truths. The stench of something unspeakable oozed into the crisp January air. Death was everywhere.

Alfie slipped his hand into hers, both their hearts thudding like fists.

They wandered past the Bricky Kids, booting an old leather ball about on a patch of dirt-and-cinder scrub land, and Renee could see Alfie was itching to jump in and hammer the ball past the scrunched-up coats that passed as goal posts.

'No footie today, pal,' she laughed, holding onto his arm tightly. 'Tonight, you're all mine.'

'Me and Billy was just the same at their age,' Alfie said with a sad smile, giving the boys the thumbs-up. 'Thought we'd end up playing for West Ham. It's all we dreamt of, in fact.'

'And what about now?' she questioned, as they dodged past a line of Local Defence Volunteers and cut down Peggy Leggy stairs, past the railway lines at the bottom of Abbey Lane. A goods train thundered past, belching great clouds of steam and coal smoke into the sidings.

'Joining the Royal Navy,' he replied. 'Avenging my brother's death'

Renee felt the crushing disappointment like a blow and

stopped to lean against the high wall that ran down the alleyway at the back of the Adam and Eve pub.

'Hold up, Rene. Are you crying?'

'I'm sorry, I know I'm being selfish,' she said, furiously blinking back tears.

But it was too late, her tears were falling freely, washing runnels in her perfectly made-up face.

'Now my mascara's run,' she sobbed, taking a playful swipe at him.

'Hey,' he laughed, dodging her hand and taking her in his arms instead. 'What's the matter? I don't want to remember my Rene like this.'

'Oh, I'm sorry, Alfie,' she cried, plucking her handkerchief from her blouse and dabbing at her eyes.

'I . . . I had the fancy I might feature somewhere in your future. Ignore me, I'm being daft . . .'

She hesitated. Oh, hang it all, life was fragile. The spectre of loss was round every corner. There was only the here and now.

'I . . . I just love you is all.'

Her words quivered in the air between them.

Alfie stared down at her, his eyes impossibly blue in the frosty night sky. A dense winter stillness draped the air. And then his lips were on hers, soft and warm, his hands encircling her waist. As his tongue probed hers, warm fingers brushing down the back of her neck, she felt aware of nothing but the heat from his skin, the contours of his body against hers.

He broke off and tenderly cupped her face in his hands. In that moment, Renee had never loved him more.

'You will wait for me, won't you, Rene? When I'm out there, I . . . I need to know I've something worth fighting for at home.'

'Oh Alfie, don't be such a daft sod,' she said, pushing back a mop of blonde hair that had fallen over one eye. 'You're all I want.'

His smile broke her heart in a thousand different ways, and she pulled his mouth back to hers.

This time his kisses were different, more urgent, brushing down her neck, exploring the warm space between her collarbones, turning her tummy to liquid honey. Warm scents of woody soap came in drifts from under his collar. Her senses were full of him. She sighed gently and Alfie seemed to take this as a sign, letting his hands brush up her leg, past her stocking top to the warm flesh of her thigh. They both knew he had crossed an invisible line, but neither had the willpower to stop it.

Billy's death had lent an urgency to everything. To live, to fight, to love . . .

Recklessly, her hips arched up to meet his and she let her hands stroke up and under his shirt, trailing her fingers down the flesh of his spine. She explored his body, sliding her hands up his neck and into his hair. Instantly, he tensed, his skin prickling beneath her fingertips.

The moon dipped behind a cloud. His voice came huskily out of the dark.

'Renee Gunn, what are you doing to me?' he moaned, resting his forehead on the brick wall above hers. 'I can't go to war without knowing what . . .' He hesitated, his eyes flickering back to hers. 'What it feels like. You know, Rene, properly.'

'W-What if someone sees?' she whispered, suddenly feeling scared. Her heart was beating unfathomably fast.

Alfie gazed along the length of the deserted alleyway, at the backs of the terraces and the pub with their blacked-out windows.

'No one can see us, Rene.' He brushed her lips softly with his thumb. 'It's just you and me.'

Their breath hung like steam in the coal-scented night. Somewhere over their heads, a searchlight swooped through the star-spangled vault, the sky the colour of deepest navy velvet. Laughter and the strains of an old music hall number echoed over the wall.

But here, now, they were alone. And in the morning, Alfie would be gone. Renee stood up on tiptoe, eyes smouldering, and her warm mouth found his. Their bodies fused and melted into the darkness of the blackout. The sickle moon came out from its hiding place.

PART TWO

Friday, 24th May 1940

14

Esther

The sun was beating against the flyblown windowpanes, heating the lipstick room up like a furnace.

'Esther, be a sweetheart and fetch us a glass of water, will ya?' called out Renee from the conveyor belt, quickly rolling a stick of Yardley's Freesia cologne over her forehead and wrists to cool her down, a little trick all the girls swore by.

'I'm sweating buckets here.'

'Coming up, Renee.'

The room was louder than she had ever heard it. The girls were belting out 'Bless 'Em All' by George Formby, but with the word 'bless' replaced with a word her mother would be shocked by. If Esther was honest, she too had been a little taken aback at the fruity language when she started at the factory, but eight months on, she was used to it now.

In fact, there wasn't a single day she didn't look forward to coming to work. She might only be the gofer, running errands, making up boxes and taking the tea break orders, but she loved her job. Lily had even hinted that when she'd served her twelve months as a service girl, she'd promote her onto the belt if she carried on working hard, with the promise of piece work on top.

Output in the factory had been cut to 25 per cent of pre-war figures, but here in the lipstick room, they were churning them out like bullets, supplying the beleaguered public with an accessible treat – bright-red lips being an easy way to create a flash of glamour – leastwise, that's what Lily reckoned. But more importantly for Esther, it was helping to keep her mind off her father. There was still no word as to his precise whereabouts, despite repeated letters to the Red Cross.

'Permission to use the khazi,' said Renee, putting her hand up, when Esther reached her with her water.

'That's the second time in an hour,' frowned Lily from her table at the end of the belt.

'Toilet breaks rationed now an' all?' Renee snapped.

'Five minutes,' Lily replied, calling a replacement over from the packing bench. As Renee rose, her face blanched of colour and she gripped the edge of the belt.

'Renee, are you all right?' Esther whispered, gently holding her elbow.

'Right as rain, sweetheart,' she said, taking a big breath in. 'Just a bit dizzy is all. It's this flaming heat.'

'Esther, run down to dispatch and fetch us a barrel of oil, the churn's running low,' said Lily handing her a slip.

'Coming right up, Miss Gunn,' Esther smiled.

Clattering down the stairs, Esther crossed the yard and into a dark and dusty warehouse.

She handed the slip to a young male worker, one of the few left at Yardley's, and he squinted down at it.

'Vegetable oil,' she said helpfully.

'Thanks. Bloomin' eyes. Useless,' he said apologetically. 'Bit like the rest of me. That's how comes I'm stuck here while most of the rest of warehouse are beating the Boche.'

Esther gazed at him in the gloom. He had a face that could best be described as average: red hair, a smattering of freckles and a huge gap between his front teeth. But put together, it was a warm and familiar face. Suddenly, she recognised him as the poor lad who always blushed beet when he had to deliver anything up to their floor.

'You're Whiffy, aren't you?' she smiled. 'I'm Esther. Don't worry, I'm not really where I should be either. That's the war for you.'

'Actually, it's Walter Smith,' he said. 'Couple of misfits together, eh? Here let me wheel this over to the lift for you.'

He loaded the barrel up onto a trolley and began pushing it across the yard, immediately tripping over a slightly raised cobblestone and stumbling.

His cheeks reddened into two bright triangles.

'Useless clot, I am. My dad reckons I could fall over in an empty room.'

'I don't think you're useless,' Esther replied softly. 'Look at how you're holding together the warehouse.'

'That's not true, but it's kind of you to say,' he grinned, pulling open the wide service lift door. 'I'm joining the Local Defence Volunteers on Monday, gotta to do something to play my part. My mum's on the nerve pills already. Now Belgium and Holland have been invaded, she's convinced we're next. But it ain't gonna happen, especially now we got that troublesome old adventurer Churchill in charge. No Jerry's gonna goosestep up my street.'

'That's what so many people in my country thought, you have no idea . . .' She broke off, ashamed to find that her hands were trembling.

'Esther, I'm sorry,' Walter murmured, mortified.

'Please think nothing of it,' she said and then, totally on impulse, or perhaps to ease his embarrassment, 'Listen, it's my birthday today, would you like to come over for tea later? My mum's putting on a little spread, nothing much, but it would be nice to have you there.'

'Really?'

'Really,' she replied.

Hastily, he whipped off his flat cap and turned it nervously between his fingers. 'In that case, I should like it very much indeed.'

She blurted the address just as the lift door began to close.

'Hang about,' said Walter, jamming his hand in the door. 'How old are you?'

'Sixteen,' she replied shyly.

'Smashing, I know a song about that . . .' Esther watched in astonishment as he began to sing an old ballad.

A wide smile blossomed over her face as he serenaded her in the service lift. A huge, daft grin lit up his, transforming his ordinary features into something quite extraordinary.

'Whiffy Smiffy, my old son, what you playing at, yer soppy chump?'

Bill Bradley from dispatch loomed up behind him and clumped Walter round the back of the head so hard, his cap fell from his fingers.

The lift door closed but not before Esther saw his cheeks scorch red.

As the lift travelled up two floors, she pondered on why she hadn't mentioned her birthday to any of the girls, but had just invited a perfect stranger round for tea. Esther couldn't really answer that, other than he made her laugh.

As she passed the lipstick room toilet, she was distracted from her thoughts by the muffled sound of sobbing. Parking up the barrel, she pushed open the door. Smoke curled over the top of a cubicle and, gingerly, Esther prodded the door. It swung open. Renee was perched on the toilet lid, a fag burning in one hand, tears streaming down her face. She had bitten her lip so much, her usually immaculate cherry red lipstick was smudged clean off. She jumped in alarm when she spotted Esther.

'Renee. Whatever's the matter?'

'Oh, thank God it's you. For a minute, I thought it was

old Peerless. She still ain't forgiven me for that punch-up with Ray. I just nipped in as I thought I'd started the curse. It ain't come yet but it must be on its way as I'm crying something rotten over everything.'

'You must be missing Alfie terribly,' Esther said. 'He's been gone now what, three months? Any word?'

'You've no idea, Est,' Renee replied, grinding her fag out on the floor and wiping her eye with the back of her sleeve. 'It's been four months and one poxy letter. It's to be expected, I s'pose. He can't tell me where he is, but I know he's working ever so hard.'

Renee paused, and Esther could tell there was more.

'I'm a good listener, Renee,' she coaxed.

Renee opened her mouth, but suddenly a blast of air swept through the cubicle and before either could make the slightest move, Miss Peerless was over them. She scooped the fag butt off the floor and held it between her fingers like it was a grenade.

'Right, Renee Gunn, you've had your last warning over this. Personnel department. Now.'

'It was me, Miss Peerless,' Esther blurted. 'I'm really sorry.'

The room supervisor's eyes narrowed as a look of triumph flashed over her face.

'Leaving Yardley property unattended. Smoking on company time. This really is lamentable behaviour, Miss Orwell. I don't know how people behave in your country, but here in England, this sort of thing won't do at all. No, no, no. You do remember our motto, do you not? "Beauty From Order Springs"! I was half considering Miss Gunn's request to move you up on the belt when your probation is up, but I think you know what my answer will be to that now. Pull your socks up, Miss Orwell. There are plenty of young *local* girls who would love this job. Report to personnel on your dinner break.'

She swept out of the room like a dark tornado and if she'd had a cloak, Esther felt sure she would have swirled it behind her.

'Rotten old cow,' Renee mouthed as the door slammed shut.

'Why did you do it, Esther?' Lily asked, disappointment written all over her face as they walked back to the lipstick room. They'd just come from a meeting with Miss Rayson and Miss Peerless in the offices upstairs and Esther had been given a royal dressing down for smoking in the toilet on company time. She'd been warned in no uncertain terms: one more misdemeanour and she'd be out.

'I had to fight really hard for you not to hand in your card there and then,' Lily went on. 'Don't ask me why, but Miss Peerless seems to really have it in for you.'

Esther had a sneaking suspicion she knew why, but she kept quiet. She was already in enough trouble.

'I'd expect that from Renee,' Lily continued, 'but not you, Esther?'

Esther knew it was wrong to lie to Lily, but she'd made the split-second decision to cover for her friend and now she had to stick by it, or she'd lose Renee's trust forever. 'Never nark,' wasn't that what Renee had said on her first day? And she hadn't hesitated to jump to her defence then. Loyalty was a virtue her father prized and Esther had a feeling he would approve.

'I'm sorry, Lily. I won't let you down again,' she promised.

'Make sure you don't, you've only got four months until I can officially promote you, if I can get it past Miss Peerless that is. Keep your nose clean.'

'Oh, I will.'

They reached the door of the lipstick room and Lily swung it open.

'Oh, and give up the smokes, Esther,' she remarked. 'I really don't think it suits you.'

The rest of Esther's sixteenth birthday went by mercifully quickly and by the time a dozen steam hooters went off the length and breadth of Carpenters Road, the sense of euphoria was palpable. Friday evening and the whole floor was demob happy as they clattered down the stairs and took it in turns to clock out.

'Who's coming down the Carpenter's for a gin and orange?' asked Fat Lou, knuckling the top of little Irene's head. 'My brother's home on leave. Mark you, he's so tight, he can peel an orange in his pocket with one hand, so don't expect him to get a round in.'

'Nah, I'm going to leg it down Angel Lane,' said Joycie. 'Rumour has it, they've got some new silk stockings in down the Hole in the Wall.'

'I'll join you, Lou,' said Nan. 'Saves sitting in on me own again.'

'That's the spirit, Nan. It's Empire Day tomorrow, we should be celebrating while we still got one,' joked Fat Lou.

'I gotta go fetch the pie and mash and run it home, otherwise I'd have joined you,' chirped little Irene. 'Thank God that's off the ration, else Mum would've flipped her lid.'

Esther listened as the girls bantered back and forth about how to spend their precious free time. Only Renee didn't join in and seemed lost in her own world. Since Alfie had left, it was like a light inside her had dimmed.

Outside, Walter was crossing the cobbles. He took one look at Fat Lou and broke into a run.

'Oh no, not again, Lou. I gotta be somewhere important.'

'Come on, girls, gis a hand,' Fat Lou hollered, putting down her bag and pelting after him. Esther watched in astonishment as most of the girls in the lipstick department cornered Walter and got him into an empty barrel. Before long, the hapless man was being rolled about over the cobbles of the yard by a gang of about twenty shrieking Lavender Girls, all killing themselves with laughter. Even more amazingly, Walter was laughing along too as he was bounced about. The English did seem to have a very strange sense of humour at times. A bit eccentric, but very lovable, Esther thought with a grin.

She glanced to her left. Renee was standing back and watching, a sad little smile on her face. Usually if there was any tomfoolery to be found, she was in the thick of it.

'Thanks for earlier, Est,' she said, squeezing her arm. Even looking pale and fragile, she was still disarmingly beautiful. Her mascara was smudged a little and her lips looked naked without their usual slick of red. 'You're a real pal.'

'It was the least I could do,' Esther said truthfully. 'You saved me before, remember, on my first day.'

Renee said nothing, just gazed in the direction of Berger's factory.

'He'll be home safe before you know it,' Esther continued, squeezing her hand.

'Your lips to God's ears,' Renee replied with a faint smile.

A shrill whistle shrieked over the yard.

'Silence please. Everyone, open your bags on the way out,' yelled Bert, the older security guard. 'Spot checks.'

'Bleedin' cheek,' seemed to be the general consensus amongst the, by now, mainly female workforce of Yardley's as they formed a disgruntled queue.

As they drew nearer to the front, and Esther saw the two uniformed guards frisking women and searching bags, she felt her heart knock against her chest. Ugly memories of life under the Nazi regime flooded through her.

'Now you get to experience what a real woman feels like,' Fat Lou joked as she reached the front of the queue, holding her arms out and eyeballing Bert. Once she was done, it was Nan's turn.

She stared witheringly at Bert as he patted down her body and scrutinised the contents of her bag.

'You wanna hope my Jimmy doesn't hear about this,' she sniffed, snapping her bag shut as he waved her on.

'You, turban and shoes off,' said Bert, singling out Esther. 'Empty the contents of your bag on the table.'

'Come on, Bert, that ain't fair,' Renee protested. 'No one else has had to do that.'

'Sorry, Renee', he apologised. 'Just carrying out orders from on high.'

Esther stepped forward and felt her the blood in her veins turn to ice.

Humiliation coursed through her as she slowly unwound her turban and stepped out of her shoes.

She bit down hard on her lip, dug her stockinged feet into the tiny stones on the cobbled yard, anything to detract from the tears that were threatening. Was this the lot of her people, destined forever to be the scapegoat? Was persecution to be expected, even in a democracy like this? Everywhere Esther looked, it felt as if a thousand accusing eyes were boring into her, and yet, she'd done nothing wrong. Concentrating hard, she drew on the mental map her mother had drawn in her mind of her father's face. For she felt sure that a bag search, however humiliating, was nothing to what he was going through. The whole yard fell silent as Bert frisked her down, even running his fingers roughly through her hair to check for stolen goods.

From the corner of her eye she saw Walter marching towards them, anger emblazoned on his usually placid features.

'That's enough, Bert,' he yelled. 'She sixteen for pity's sake, you can see she ain't got no stolen goods on her.'

Suddenly a cry went up from behind them. A wiry young

canteen worker by the name of Annie Gibbons, who Esther had seen cleaning tables, was struggling with a security guard.

'Get'cha hands off me,' Annie demanded. 'Cook said I could take home leftover stale bread. Ask her, if you don't believe me.'

'Yeah, but it's what's inside it that troubles me,' said Bert, strolling over. Pulling out an old loaf of bread, Esther could see it had been hollowed out. Bert turned it upside down and five or so lipsticks clattered onto the floor.

'Ten out of ten for using your loaf, girl,' he laughed. 'Come on, upstairs with you,' he ordered, gripping the struggling girl's arm and dragging her across the yard.

Immediately, a great hubbub went up among the assembled crowds, but Esther wasn't hanging around to hear the gossip.

Thrusting her feet into her shoes, she grabbed her bag and ran out of the gates.

Esther ran fast. So fast that the sounds of shrieking hooters and crashing cranes merged into one mighty roar in her head.

Tears of humiliation blurred her vision so that she didn't see anyone following her until she felt an arm on her shoulder.

'Whoa, slow down there.'

Reluctantly Esther turned around, wiping her face roughly with her sleeve. When faced with a sobbing girl, most boys his age would run a mile. Not Walter Smith.

'Better out than in. Leastwise, that's what my mum says,' he remarked, rummaging around and producing a dirty handkerchief.

Esther couldn't help but laugh through her tears.

'Your mum says a lot of things.'

'Cor, not many,' he laughed. 'She's the only person I know who can go on holiday and come back with a sunburnt tongue. Why use one word when twelve'll do?'

Esther laughed and blew her nose.

'That's better. Wanna tell me what happened back there?'

'I'm sorry, Walter. To be suspected of being a thief, well, I cannot tell you how that makes me feel. I was raised to tell the truth always. To think that I could steal from the very company I have so much gratitude for . . .' She broke off. 'I . . . I try to tell myself it is ignorance, the snide remarks, the suspicion. Just because I am Jewish.'

'It's only a couple. Please don't think we're all like that,' Walter pleaded. 'By and large, us cockneys are a tolerant lot. We have to be, because the way I sees it, we're all the same deep down, ain't we?'

'Except it's me that has an alien registration book in my bag,' she replied quietly.

'I-I . . .' Walter stumbled for something appropriate to say, but gave up, reaching out instead and cupping her hands in his. The warmth of his skin against hers was soothing and just like that, her anger dissipated. In that moment, there was a tangible shift in the space between them, a quickening, a connection. Esther felt it in the tightening of his fingers, saw it in the dilation of his pupils.

'Do you have pie and mash in Vienna?' he asked suddenly.

She shook her head.

'No, I've never tried this pie and mash. The girls seem to talk about it a lot, though.'

'Oh, well you are in for a treat, Esther,' he grinned, taking her bag from her to carry. 'Because we're gonna go right from here to Cooke's and I'm going to treat you to the food of the gods for your birthday.'

Half an hour later, the pair ran giggling through Cat's Alley clutching piping hot cartons of pie and mash, parsley liquor spilling from an old Oxo tin and running over their knuckles.

'Mama!' called Esther, as she walked through the passage, licking the delicious liquid from her hands. 'I hope you don't mind but I've brought home a friend from work . . .'

Her voice tailed off. Her mother was sitting in the kitchen.

The table had been laid for her birthday tea and it looked a treat. A small Victoria sponge with real jam, pickled herrings, gala pie, potato salad and a pot of tea covered in a knitted cosy against which were propped two letters. A perfect scene, except it felt as if all the oxygen had been sucked from the room.

A fire flickered in the grate, but her mother's face cut a ghastly tableau.

'Mama?'

She shook her head slowly.

'My darling . . . I have just received a letter from your uncle in Vienna. The news is the very worst.'

Esther watched as the colour drained from Walter's cheeks. Slowly, deliberately, she put down the pie and mash and crumpled into a seat.

'H-How?'

'Tuberculosis . . . Apparently he was imprisoned in a ghetto in Poland whilst waiting transportation to a camp. The conditions in the ghetto . . .' Her voice broke off. Her hand flew to her mouth, as if to contain the horror.

Esther replayed in her mind the thoughts of how she would react if faced with this news. And now the worst had happened, she felt strangely calm. She heard the creak of floorboards as Walter walked behind her, felt his hands upon her shoulders, but she felt as if her body were somewhere up on the flaking ceiling.

'What's this?' she asked, picking up the second letter.

'Your uncle had in his possession a letter your father wrote, to be given to you.' Julia closed a hand gently over her daughter's fist, but Esther pulled away and picked up the letter instead.

My beloved dear Esther. Always hold together in love and faithfulness, and God will bless you. God bless us all for a speedy reunion.

On her sixteenth birthday, the secret hope she had carried for so long in her heart died. Devastation. Shock. Agony. And a hot, bright anger that sliced through Esther, erupting in a ferocious outburst. She slid from her chair to the floor and beat her fists against the wooden boards until she felt hollow. When at last her mother calmed her, they clung to each other, sobbing. Discreetly, Walter pulled the blackout blinds halfway down and slipped from the house.

15

Renee

It had been a long and punishing day for Renee. Not because of the spot check at the factory at clocking off. Annie Gibbons might be in hot water, but it was small fry compared to the problems she was facing. Usually, the first thing Renee did when she got home was to sit in front of the mirror and fix her face, but now she collapsed on the bed.

Renee closed her eyes and concentrated on stopping the room from spinning. In the darkness, she heard the scrape of metal in the yard as her father dragged the mangle back, the hoiking up of phlegm, followed by the wet splat of spit hitting concrete. A communist family over the other side of the Shoot were having a noisy meeting.

A muffled cry tore through the thin wall that separated her bedroom from Esther's and Renee flinched. Was it crying, or laughing? It was so hard to tell when even the washing flapping on the line outside sounded like roaring. Noises flew at her in the darkness. Why did she feel like she was so sensitive to everything?

Oh, who was she kidding? She knew why. Renee's blue eyes snapped open as she stared down at her ever-so-slightly bulging tummy.

Three – or was it four? – missed bleeds. The bone-sapping

weariness. The repugnant smells that made her want to retch despite being raised in the stench of Stratford. It all added up to an uncomfortable truth. Somewhere deep inside she knew the pregnancy had taken, was as much a part of her now as the nose on her face. She felt her abdomen thicken, her emotions rage. This was no longer a collection of cells, but a baby, growing limbs and finger-nails and hair.

She longed to confide in Lily, but when she played it back in her mind it all just sounded so, well, sordid. She could imagine the conversation.

Lily – 'Where did you do it?'

Renee – 'Behind the Adam and Eve'

Lily – 'Did you use protection?'

Renee – 'I crossed my fingers, does that count?'

Renee's head slumped into her hands. Oh God, it sounded worse than sordid. Lily would call her an irresponsible fool and she'd be right. She had allowed herself to be ruled by her emotions, not her head, and now she was in trouble. Deep trouble. She hadn't just crossed the infamous dotted line. She'd smashed through it. In sleeping with Alfie before he put that ring on her finger, she'd broken every unwritten rule in the book. No matter that half the girls in the factory had probably done the same, it didn't matter. They didn't have Nell Gunn for a mum. Oh God, her mum . . .

Panic, dark and electric, prickled up her spine.

'It's gonna be all right, Renee Gunn, you just have to hold your nerve,' she murmured.

She pulled Alfie's letter from its hiding place under the floorboard. She had written to him straight after she had missed her first period. His response, soon after, from mili-tary training camp, had filled her with relief.

My darling Renee,

You've made me the happiest sailor in the British Navy. I know the timing's not ideal, but knowing you could possibly be carrying my baby makes me so happy. I know you say you're not certain, but I expect by the time you receive this letter you will be.

But look, whatever happens, it'll be all right, you'll see.

You just have to hold tight, my beautiful girl. As soon as I get my next leave, we can get married. It'll have to be a quickie down West Ham Registry Office and our kid'll be a six-month baby, but that don't matter to me. I love the bones off you. Look after yourself, that's my child you're carrying after all. Make sure you're eating well. I know that won't be easy now rationing's come in, but I'm sure your mum has her ways. Sorry if that sounds like I'm lecturing you, I'm not, but well, I can't write the words. I want to tell you just how proud you've made me.

We're being shipped out to ---------- in ------- in the next couple of days but we're due leave. We really have got the Huns on the run, so don't you worry yourself, it can't be much longer. Stay calm, be patient, I'll be home and I can't wait to make you Mrs Buckle. Until then, Miss Homefront, my girl, I love you with all my heart and more besides.

Your Alfie xxx
PS – your letter smelt of Yardley's Lavender, it reminded me of home.

Renee squeezed her eyes closed as a tear slid down her cheek. His censored letter also left a residual smell, not sweet like lavender but something darker, of cigarette smoke and damp khaki. She stroked the creases of the paper, as if by touching his words, she could summon him up into this tiny bedroom. 'You ain't got no flaming genie, Renee Gunn,' she scolded herself, angrily dashing away the tear. 'Ain't no one gonna grant you a wish at your command.'

'Why you talking to yourself?' The figure of her mother looming at the doorway made her jump. Quickly, she stuffed the letter under her candlewick counterpane.

'Come and give us a hand folding the washing and then it's tea. The butcher looked after me earlier so it's boiled bacon and pease pudding.'

'Course, Mum,' Renee smiled, sucking in her tummy and standing up.

'You all right, darlin'?' Nell enquired, holding her hand to her forehead. 'You're looking peaky. They working you too hard at the factory? Want me to go and have a word with the forelady? You need to get a union going there, I've long said it.'

Renee's head spun. Her mum was like a terrier when she got going.

'No, no, please don't do that, Mum. I don't want to end up crammed in some sweatshop.'

Renee gazed at her mother's chest, wrapped up in a faded pinny, the washday hands hooked over her apron straps, the sheer comforting carbolic-scented mass of her. In that moment, she longed to rest her head on her chest, feel those hands tightly knitted round her body, holding her close, like when she was a nipper and had grazed her knee. She needed to wrap her mother's strength around her like a soft blanket.

'M-Mum, can we talk?' she ventured. A voice in her head sounded. *Do it now. Tell her.*

Nell sat down heavily on the bed and patted the space next to her.

'Come on then . . .'

The door downstairs thudded, a reedy voice called up the stairs.

'Cooee, Auntie, can you come downstairs and check on Julia? She got a letter and now her blinds are down.'

Nell's face fell and she crossed herself.

'Please God, not that. I have to go. We'll talk later.'

'Mum,' Renee blurted, gripping her mother's wrist. 'Please stay.'

'Renee, love,' sighed Nell, gently unhooking her daughter's grasp. 'I can't do that. Apart from her uncle, Julia's all alone here. I'm responsible for her and Esther now. She needs me.'

I need you, Renee thought sadly.

Nell kissed Renee on the forehead with surprising tenderness. She had reached the top of the stairs when Renee called over.

'Mum, I love you all the money in the world and two bob.'

'Where did I get you from, Renee Gunn?' she laughed. 'We'll talk later, darlin'.'

Deflated, Renee ducked out of the house as her mother went off to solve yet another Shoot crisis. She had to get outside, try and assemble her fractured thoughts.

As she emerged from the gloom of the alley and out into the bustle of Angel Lane, Renee marvelled at the scarcity of produce on the stalls, the lengthening queues. She had a hunch some women joined the back of one without even knowing what it was they were queuing for.

Where was the colour and joy, the small comforts of life? No bath salts, no street lamps, cream-filled cakes, no perms or cosmetics. Hardly a bleedin' kirby grip to be had in the whole of Stratford.

Like a magpie, she found herself drawn to the glittering window display of H. Samuel, and rested the palms of her hands flat against the cool glass.

Let a lucky wedding band be your token of happiness, read the signage.

Her head spun as if she were on a tightrope, the finest of lines between domesticity and disgrace. All that stood between her and respectability was a slender silver band. To have a baby out of wedlock? A little bastard? Why, wasn't that what all girls knew to be the ultimate disgrace, a shame upon your house? An uncomfortable image of sixteen-year-old Betty Maguire, an old friend of hers from the lipstick room, slid through her mind. She could still almost smell the fear when Betty had confided to her she was expecting. The father, a spotty young oaf who worked in dispatch had denied responsibility and when Betty's own father had found out . . . Renee closed her eyes and shuddered. Poor Betty. He'd thrown her out on the street in full view of the neighbours, called a tart and disowned her. Actually disowned her! Last Renee heard, Betty had gone to a mother-and-baby home in Kent where her son had been adopted, then she'd moved up North to take a job in domestic service. Renee still saw Betty's mother occasionally down the market. She was a broken woman. Just like that, Betty had been expunged from her family tree.

A hot, foul fear gripped Renee. Now *she* was Betty, the fallen woman.

'Oh God, come home, Alfie,' she whispered, her breath misting over the window. 'Just make it home soon.'

Sighing, she turned back and bumped straight into a news-paper hawker.

'Watch it, miss.' And then, thrusting that day's edition of the *Stratford Express* at her, he called out, his voice high and shrill. And from the mouth of a child spilled news that was to drop a grenade into her personal crisis.

'Read all about it. Troops in retreat.'

Renee took the paper, her hands trembling so much she could scarcely read the words. Her fate rested on such a maelstrom of chaos she could not even begin to guess. All that stood between her and salvation was the German Army . . .

On Sunday, the vicar of the Shoot's church held a special service to tie into a national day of prayer, a far smaller version of the services taking place at St Paul's Cathedral and Westminster Abbey. There was scarcely a family in the Shoot who did not have a son trapped on the beaches of Dunkirk, and the tiny church was packed. The news had stunned them all, but none more so than Renee. She clasped her gloved hands together and dipped her head, her skin as pale as death. She had barely slept since news broke of the ongoing evacuation of British troops two days ago. The 'phony war' as it had been dubbed had come to an abrupt end. Never had the threat of invasion felt so real, nor the stakes so high. The Shoot had awoken from its slumber.

Just before church, she'd had had to pretend to Lily she had forgotten to brush her teeth so she could rush back upstairs and in private, bind her stomach in bandages she had bought from Gertrude's Pharmacy. She had wrapped them so tight, the skin on either side puckered and now they were digging in uncomfortably. Guilt tore through her as she thought of the little life unfurling inside her. The life that, despite being conceived in love, bore the deepest shame.

'We are called to take our place in a mighty conflict between right and wrong,' declared the vicar, dramatically raising his robed arms aloft. The very action sent a fresh wave of dizziness spiralling through Renee. Mrs Barnett was on the same pew and the pungent smell of mothballs emanating from her coat was doing strange things to Renee's tummy.

Oh God, she was going to be sick, she could feel saliva flooding her mouth.

'Our mettle is being tested like never before, but in these turbulent times we can all lean on His broad shoulders.'

Renee stared up at the figure of Christ, nailed to the cross. It felt like he was staring mournfully straight down at her tummy.

Renee shot up, clutching her mouth and, bumping prayer books out of hands, fled from the pew.

Ignoring her mother's furious glare and the open mouths of the congregation, she ran from the church. The hot sooty air hit the back of her throat and she clung to a gravestone, dry retching and swallowing back bile.

'Drink this, hot tea's just the thing when you feel sick,' came a soft voice.

'Snowball,' she murmured, wiping her mouth with her sleeve. 'How long have you . . .'

'Long enough to know a girl in trouble when I see one.'

She stared long and hard at him. *How could he know?*

There was no malice, or threat in his expression. Just compassion.

'Must have been something I ate,' she muttered.

'I expect so, miss,' he said, pouring stewed brown tea from his flask into a cup and pressing it into her hand.

'I can't take this from you,' she protested.

'Please, miss. Let me do something for the Gunn family for a change.'

Renee drank gratefully and the sweet, creosote-strong tea seemed to revive her.

She looked Snowball up and down as if seeing him for the first time. The tramp was such a permanent fixture in the churchyard, like an ivy-covered grave or an old relic, she almost ceased to see him any longer.

All day long he shuffled round in clothes that were more hole than cloth, inspecting every gutter in the market for specks. To her enormous regret, Renee realised she didn't really ever see him as part of the community. What had driven him onto the streets in the first place? A bad debt, no work, an unsympathetic landlord perhaps? Or just a simple mistake?

Everyone could make one of those. Maybe they were not so different, she and he, after all.

'Renee Gunn, over here now.' Her mother was standing in the church vestibule with a face like thunder, as a fearful congregation spilled into the graveyard.

'Thanks for the tea,' she said, handing Snowball back the flask and bracing herself for a dressing down.

'You're welcome,' he replied, before seemingly vanishing among the gravestones.

'What's wrong with you, girl?' Nell demanded.

'Showing us up like that by running out,' Pat muttered, put out because he'd far rather have been at the Two Puddings for his Sunday morning pint.

'I'm worried about Alfie is all,' she protested weakly.

'Oh love, you don't even know if he's in the Channel,' said Nell. 'Most of the women in this neighbourhood have got problems bigger than yours, darlin', believe you me. Take a look at poor Julia and Esther. They've lost a husband and a father.'

Renee hung her head.

'A quick word, if I may, Mrs Gunn, about young Frankie,' interrupted the vicar to Renee's relief.

Until now nobody had paid much attention to the youngest Gunn, who was trailing along behind.

'There is no peace unless one abides by His presence.'

'Sorry, I'm not following?' said Nell.

'Young Frankie has missed the last four Sunday school lessons.' The vicar turned to Frankie. 'Is everything quite well with you, young man?'

All eyes swivelled to Frankie, who looked up at them, face impassive.

His reply was so astonishing, that despite her misery Renee almost laughed out loud at the gaping mouths in the church porch.

'Perfectly,' he replied.

'So may I ask why religion no longer features in your Sundays?'

'I wouldn't say I'm unreligious, I just have no proof of a higher being. Until I do, it would be a waste of my time and yours for me to attend Sunday school.'

It seemed to take an age before Nell's jaw scraped off the floor. Renee had never seen her mum look so flustered.

'I'm ever so sorry, Vicar,' Nell stuttered. 'He'll be back at Sunday school next week. You can count on it.'

Pat gripped Frankie's ear.

'You. Home. Now.'

The congregation scattered as Pat dragged young Frankie across the square by his ear with Nell, Renee and Lily running behind.

Once inside, he slammed the door so hard, the sash windows rattled.

'What's your game?' he bellowed, unbuckling his belt.

'Where have you been going on a Sunday, boy?' Nell demanded.

'The museum in Bethnal Green, or sometimes I take a book and read in Vicky Park,' he replied truthfully.

'You know whose influence this is, don'cha?' Pat blazed. 'It's that Julia putting ideas in his head. She's got more education than sense, if you ask me.'

'Who is sense?' Frankie asked, bewildered.

'That's enough of your sauce,' Nell yelled, clipping him round the ear.

'What's that for?' he replied, rubbing his ear.

'Everyone calm down,' said Lily, but their father's temper was rising like smoke up a bottle as he lashed off his belt.

'I've had a gutful of you, boy. As from tomorrow, you start back at school for proper lessons. Enough of this bleedin' nonsense.'

'No!' Frankie screamed, slamming his hand down on the table. 'You can't make me go back there. I hate that school.'

Pat's eyes widened.

'How dare you answer me back! You're gonna get the hiding of a lifetime now.'

'No,' screamed Lily.

He moved towards Frankie, the belt pulled taut, but Nell flung herself between them.

'You have to stop mothering the boy, Nell,' Pat growled. 'Now step out the way.'

Voices grew louder in the square and suddenly they became aware of a group of burly men at the door. Pat's gang from the docks.

'There you are, Pat!' said one, who had a nose even flatter than Pat's and ears like cauliflowers.

'What's up, Tommy? I'm busy.'

'I know, Pat, but the skipper's asked us to take the tugs over to Dunkirk. Churchill's asked anyone with small boats to get over there and help rescue some of our boys. You in or what? We're leaving now.'

Pat glanced from his stricken family, back to his other family, the gang he had worked alongside at Samuel Williams and Sons Ltd for over a decade.

'What'cha reckon?' he said, quickly threading his belt back on. 'I've been dying to have a go at the Germans. Let's go.'

He reached over and kissed Nell on the cheek.

'Who knows when I'll be back, love, stay safe.' He grabbed his wallet and cap. 'And cut the apron strings. Or I will . . .'

And then he and his resilient band of tough river men were gone, raw adrenalin pulsing in their wake.

16

Esther

The next morning, a Monday, Esther came into the kitchen dressed for work.

Her mother looked up, red-eyed with grief. She, like most members of the Shoot had barely laid her head in rest these past two days.

'My darling, you're going to work?' she exclaimed. 'Lily said you could take a few days compassionate leave.'

'I know, but what will I do with myself if I stay here?' Esther replied, placing her hands softly on her mother's shoulders and gently massaging the knots in her neck.

Julia's eyes flickered closed and she sighed. Her weariness seemed to reach to her very bones.

'I have to keep busy, Mama. I'm needed at the factory.' She didn't dare tell her that if she stopped, for even a moment, the silent scream that had been building in her since news of her father's death would erupt, and then, she might never stop crying.

Julia took both her daughter's hands in hers and inhaled the soft scent of the lavender hand cream Renee had given her for Christmas.

'You're right, it's what your father would wish.'

'But will you be all right, Mama?' Esther asked.

'Yes, I'm teaching Frankie today, at least until his father

returns home. It seems Mr Gunn is not so keen on me tutoring his son any longer.'

Outside, a tall lanky figure was waiting under a gas lamp. When Walter saw Esther he straightened up and ran over to her.

'Walter? What—?'

'Esther, please hear me out. You've had such a rotten time of it, the trouble at the factory, your dad, and well, that is to say, I can't imagine what you're going through and well, I um, I . . .' He ripped off his cap. 'Oh damn it, Walter, stop being such a blithering idiot.'

'Are you talking to yourself?' Esther asked, with a smile.

'What I'm trying to say, in my usual cack-handed way, is I know how sad you must be and how frightening the road ahead must look, but I'll walk that path with you. If you'll allow me, that is?'

Esther looked at the deep stain of red spreading over his cheeks.

'But you've only just met me, you scarcely know me,' she replied.

He shrugged. 'When you know, you know.'

And the queerest thing was, she did too. Despite only having met Walter a few days ago, she had never felt so comfortable with anyone.

'Thank you, for caring,' she smiled.

Carefully, he took her bag and gas mask and together they set off, Walter making sure to always walk nearest the traffic in a gesture that made Esther feel protected. As they weaved their way through the market stalls, Walter chattered about his plans to go and sign up for the Local Defence Volunteers that morning, and Esther was grateful for the distraction. As the factory gates came into sight, she paused, remembering her humiliation at the bag search. Walter placed a gentle hand on her back. 'You can do it,' he coaxed, 'it's them who should feel ashamed, not you.'

To his credit, Bert the old security guard came straight over to her.

'I'm sorry about Friday, love, you do know I was only acting on orders.'

'I know, Bert,' she smiled back. 'No hard feelings.' Life was tough enough as it was without holding grudges.

'That's good of you, not sure I'd be so forgiving,' Walter remarked, handing her back her bag.

'The ability to forgive is one of the most powerful things you can do, my father swore by it.'

'Reckon he'd be ever so proud of you now, in that case.' Out of the corner of her eye Esther saw Lily approach.

'I better go,' said Walter. 'I'll come find you in dinner break. I've got a surprise for you.'

Before she had a chance to ask what, Lily was by her side.

'Esther, what are you doing here?' Lily murmured. 'I'm sure I told you you're entitled to some compassionate leave.'

They hung back as a stream of chattering girls clocked in.

'I know,' Esther replied. 'And I appreciate it, but I need to be here. We're so busy—'

'Never mind that—'

'Please, Lily,' Esther begged. 'Don't be kind to me, or I'll cry. I need to be here.'

'Very well,' said Lily, understanding.

'And please tell me, is there any word from Renee's Alfie? I know how worried she is.'

'No,' sighed Lily. 'And she's in bits.'

On the factory floor, the girls were quieter than usual. For the first time since war had broken out, the grave situation facing them all had finally hit home. The enemy was just across the Channel, no more than twenty-odd miles away. To many, it wasn't a case of *if*, but *when* they were invaded.

'What will we do,' worried little Irene, 'when they get here?'

'My mum reckons she'd top herself rather than live under German rule,' said Joycie.

'Ain't gonna happen,' yelled Fat Lou over the noise of the machines, from her packing station. 'Over my dead body. I'll go down to the beaches and fight 'em meself with two broken bottles and my fists, if I have to.'

'And I'll be by your side,' cheered Joanie.

'And what if they come out the sky?' asked Nan archly.

'Then I'll be waiting with a bloody big stick.'

Suddenly all the girls were cheering and whooping.

'Fucking Germans,' Fat Lou cried, rising up, 'they ain't coming in my manor.'

The change in mood was like the flick of a switch. As a sense of anarchic chaos overran the factory floor, only Renee and Esther remained quiet, each lost in their own thoughts. For Esther, the sudden realisation that if the Germans did reach Stratford, she, along with all other Jews would be immediately rounded up and sent where? A deep visceral fear overtook her. How long could they all keep running, and how far, before the Nazis took over every civilisation?

'Please, everyone pipe down and get on with your work,' urged Lily, clapping her hands over the din. 'I understand your fears, but we must keep calm and carry on.'

But the Lavender Girls couldn't be suppressed for long. When Walter walked in, a chorus of wolf whistles blazed over the floor.

'Morning, ladies. You're looking at the newest recruit for the Local Defence Volunteers, K Division,' he announced.

Esther couldn't help but smile. He looked so proud.

'We're to be the eyes and ears of the country. A quarter of a million of us signed up, so they're saying.'

'That's smashing!' Esther enthused. 'Will you be given a rifle?'

'Not exactly, they can't spare 'em. But you can do a fair

bit of damage with a broom handle. Rest assured. When Jerry lands on open spaces, I'll be waiting.'

'Sure they'll be quaking in their jackboots at the sight of you, Whiffy, with a broom on the Wanstead Flats,' Nan said crushingly. 'I've got a feather duster you can borrow an' all.'

Walter's face fell.

'Pay her no attention,' Esther whispered. 'I think it's terrific. I, for one, feel much safer knowing that we have people like you to protect us.'

The bell for dinner break sounded, and Walter took her arm.

'Follow me.'

'I can't,' said Esther. 'I put my name down for fire-watching duty on the roof.'

'I know, I'm coming with you.'

Up on the roof, Esther buckled up her tin helmet as Walter rummaged in his bag.

'Close your eyes,' he ordered.

'Pardon?'

'Please, Esther. Humour me.'

She heard rustling and then – 'Now you can open them.' Esther opened her eyes.

'Ta da, surprise, happy birthday.'

Walter had somehow hoisted an old orange-box up to the roof and covered it with one of his mum's best tablecloths and a daisy in a jam jar.

'Please be seated, miss,' he grinned, patting his hand on a Yardley's packing case.

'Welcome to Stratford's finest restaurant, the views are . . .' He squinted out against the thick layer of yellow smoke that coated the factories of Carpenters Road, 'not great actually.' He pulled out a flask of tea and some meat-paste sandwiches, along with a couple of slices of his mum's seed cake.

'Afraid the menu choice is limited, but management are working on that.'

'Oh Walter,' she laughed, shaking her head. 'What's all this for? It's not even my birthday.'

'I know that, but well, your actual birthday weren't really one to write home about, and you deserve to be made a fuss of.'

'You are so thoughtful,' she murmured.

'And no birthday's complete without presents,' he said, pulling something from inside his coat.

Esther put down her tea and took the gift.

'Sorry, no wrapping paper.'

It was a record. Esther read out loud the label. 'Johann Strauss – *The Blue Danube.*'

She stared up, her brown eyes filled with emotion.

'B-but this is my father's favourite composer, how on earth did you know?'

'I asked your mum. Fella I know what runs the record stall down Angel Lane got me a copy. And before you say, I know you don't have anything to listen to it on. My grandad's got a gramophone player he says you can have.' He grinned. 'He's mutton, so it ain't much use to him no more.'

'Mutton?'

'Yeah, you know, Mutton Jeff. Deaf.'

Esther was speechless.

'I wanted you to have something to help you feel closer to your dad.'

The tears she had worked so hard to stem now came, and Walter placed a gentle arm around her.

'I didn't mean to make you cry, but, the world is such a dark place right now, I wanted you to have something beautiful and uplifting to drown out all the noise.'

'I don't know what to say, or how I can thank you,' she said, turning the record over and over in her hands like it was a precious gem.

'Just allow me to have the first dance with you when we get the gramophone all set up.'

Esther leaned over and kissed his cheek.

'I'd be delighted.'

'D-does this mean you're my girl?'

'What do you think?' she replied, smiling.

'Yes!' said Walter, punching the air.

The rest of the afternoon passed by in a peaceable blur, the girls' earlier hysteria having been calmed somewhat by the arrival of Mr Lavender for a routine inspection. Back at the Shoot after work, Esther was eager to get home and see how her mother was. She worried for her, being on her own all day with nothing but her grief.

'Mama,' she called, pushing open the door and calling up the passage. 'You'll never believe what Walter gave me.'

Her voice trailed off. She found her mother in the parlour, surrounded by dozens of drawings.

'Look at these, my dear,' she said.

Esther hung up her gas mask and coat and picked up the nearest one.

It was London from a panoramic bird's eye view. The beating heart of the British Empire was expertly sketched out in all its sprawling, smoking glory. St Paul's shining dome rose up above the cluster of snaking streets, and on the majestic shining curve of the River Thames, a flotilla of small ships was steaming up the river. Heading where? Dunkirk? Every landmark had been accurately recreated in the finest pencil lines.

'This is very impressive. Who drew this?'

'Frankie. He showed them to me earlier,' said Julia. 'Look, there's more.'

Esther felt her jaw grow slack as she leafed through page after page of the most beautiful pencil drawings of streetscapes and buildings, factories, dockyards and shopping arcades.

'Look at this one,' Julia said, her excitement palpable.

At first glance, it could almost have been a photograph, but on closer inspection, it was the most astonishingly intricate scale drawing of Fenchurch Street Station. Somehow, little Frankie had captured every arch, girder and puff of steam in the most minute detail. There was a couple embracing on platform eleven. He'd even drawn the soldier's regiment number, chevrons and the stitching on his kit bag.

'Did he copy this from a photograph in the newspaper?' Esther asked and Julia shook her head.

'He says he recalled it from visits to the cathedral.'

'He did this from memory?' Esther asked, incredulous. The assured draftsmanship, the complex masterful perspective was recreated from memory alone!

Esther looked up at her mother.

'But he's seven years old!'

'I know. The boy has a prodigious talent . . .'

Her voice trailed off.

'What's troubling you, Mama?'

'He showed these to me today, but he refuses to show them to his mother or father. I think he fears what they will say or do.' She raised one eyebrow. 'Pat Gunn has plans for his son. I don't think any of them include honing his artistic talent.'

'But these aren't just any old pictures,' Esther protested. 'He has a rare gift.'

Julia nodded, her eyes brimming over with emotion. She leant forward in her chair. 'I know, and the more time I spend with him, the more I'm convinced he's like the students from back home . . .'

'Do you think?'

'I'm sure of it,' Julia replied. She picked up the picture of St Paul's cathedral. 'I plan on sending this one to Hans in

Vienna, not that I have much faith in it reaching him without being intercepted, but I have to try, for Frankie's sake.'

Julia traced her fingers softly over the pencil lines.

'I remember one of the last things Hans told me, before we were forced to flee. *"Not everything that steps out of line is thus abnormal or must necessarily be inferior."* For Frankie's future, these pictures *must* be seen.'

Esther and Julia fell into silent contemplation, both of them thinking the same thoughts. With the Nazis smashing down borders all over Europe and destroying everything in their path, was it already too late? And for Frankie, was the greatest enemy his own father?

17

Lily

By the Friday of that week, Pat and his gang from the docks were still missing and the news coming out from France was beyond anything Lily could've imagined.

It was a sombre group of girls who huddled over their usual table in the Yardley canteen. The only food on offer was a tureen of watery soup and a rather flaccid-looking piece of tongue served with boiled marrow, not that anyone had much of an appetite.

'Guess you could say that's the end of the bore war then,' said Fat Lou bluntly, tossing a copy of the *Daily Mirror* down on the tabletop. 'So much for having the Hun on the run. Hitler's having a great big smash-up, ain't he?'

Photographs showed streets littered with wreckage and bodies, smoke roiling into the horizon.

'We made a trip clean into hell,' the skipper of a small boat was quoted as saying.

'I can't bear to think of my Jimmy there,' wept Nan, burying her face in her hands. 'Please God, spare him, we've only been married five minutes.'

The girls sat in silence as her sobs echoed around the canteen, with no one sure what – if anything – they could say to alleviate her suffering.

'And what of your Alfie?' Esther asked Renee. 'Any news?'

Renee shook her head, her face a mask of misery.

Lily could've wept for her. Her little sister was scarcely recognisable from the bombastic young woman she'd first met on her return to Yardley's. The life seemed to have bleached out of her. Her skin had a sickly pallor and underneath the tabletop, Lily could see she had clenched her fists so tight, her fingernails were cutting crescents into the flesh on her palms.

'Count your blessings you ain't married, Renee,' Nan remarked. 'At least you ain't looking at life as a widow!'

Uncharacteristically, Renee said nothing, just nodded and traced a complicated pattern through some grains of salt on the tabletop.

'Nan,' said Lily tactfully. 'I don't think anyone can hold a monopoly on grief in these dark days. Look at Esther here. She's just lost her father.'

'To TB in a ghetto,' Nan snapped, dabbing her eye with a hankie. 'It's not as if he died in action.'

A collective inhale went round the table as everyone stared at Esther. She stood slowly, picking up her plate and mug.

'Excuse me,' she whispered, before making a dignified exit from the canteen.

'How could you say such a thing, Nan?' Lily blazed, once Esther was out of earshot. 'That girl will never see her father again. Her family and her homeland have been torn apart.'

'Oh, I know I shouldn't have said that,' Nan sighed. 'I'll apologise. I'm not sleeping at the moment.'

'You know what we need,' Fat Lou remarked, sparking up a Craven 'A'. 'We need a night out, cheer ourselves up.'

'There's a wartime knitting demonstration by Miss Muriel Grantham at Roberts this evening. It might be fun . . .' said Betty.

Fat Lou shot her a withering look.

'I said cheer us up, not bleedin' finish us off. No, I was

thinking about a beauty party. I've been reading about all these beauty dodges. Why don't we all meet tonight after work, try 'em out? I've got half a bottle of gin I found at the back of Mum's cupboard, she won't notice it's gone missing. Let's have a little beauty session over a couple of Gin and Its. What do you say?'

'Ooh, yeah, not much,' crooned Joanie. 'Come on, girls.'

'I've got a load of lipstick ends we could melt down,' chipped in Betty. 'Save us having to get the black-market lipstick they're flogging down the market.'

'Yeah, you know it's got lead in it,' warned Nan.

Sensing a good opportunity to show the girls that she wasn't a complete snob, and to cheer Renee up, Lily decided to get behind it.

'I think it's a splendid idea,' she said. 'I've got some of that new stockingless cream we could try out?' She turned to Renee. 'Why don't we see if we can't hold it at ours? Sure Mum won't mind, will she, Renee? Renee?'

Renee's head snapped up.

'Sorry, what?'

'Wake up, you dozy nitwit! Our *Beauty is a Duty* party tonight . . .' Fat Lou prompted.

'Yeah, why not,' she replied. And with every ounce of Gunn spirit she could muster: 'Let's show 'em our flag's still flying!'

Lily smiled, relieved. 'That's the Renee we know and love.'

Lily's eyes settled on an advert for Gala lipstick in the *Daily Mirror. A touch of brightness and hope for tomorrow.* A sign? Perhaps things could work out for the best.

By clocking-off time all the girls raced home with orders to meet at the Gunns' at seven p.m. Lily hung around until the factory floor was empty, checking the blackout blinds were securely fastened. The floor was deserted and as Lily settled herself behind her desk at the end of the lipstick conveyor belt, the silence was deafening. Being here all on her own was a little unsettling and she shivered as the sounds of the evening descended. The slap of the cleaner's mop as she washed the corridors outside. The rattle and sigh of the pipework, like an old lady sinking into a chair. The rustle of a tiny mouse scampering under the packing bench.

Lily pulled the letter out of her bag and started to read.

'Planning on burning the midnight oil, Miss Gunn?' Lily jumped. Miss Rayson stood at the doorway.

'No, no, just going to have a final check, then I'll be on my way.'

'You're the most devoted charge hand we've ever had,' she remarked. 'Please don't stay too late.'

'I won't, Miss Rayson,' she promised.

'Good girl, cheerio.' Lily waited until the clattering of her feet on the iron stairwell faded away, before she picked up the letter and began again.

Please don't think my leaving Stratford when I did means that I had no feeling for you. It is precisely the over-powering strength of those feelings that forced me to leave, for I knew there was no room for both her and me in your life. How I wish I'd had the strength to fight for you when I had the chance. You will think me weak. But know this, my love: I loved you then, I love you now, and I will go to the grave loving you.

Your devoted Lily xxx

Lily kissed the letter, folded it carefully and slipped it into her bag with the others. *Would she ever send them? To what purpose?* She didn't know, but writing these thoughts and feelings down was the only way to banish some of the pain from her heart. It was therapy, she supposed.

Out on Carpenters Road she slipped into the shadows of Stratford's looming blackout and wondered how many other people were concealing their true feelings.

By the time she got home, she found most of the lipstick girls already there. Her mother was in her element, bustling around serving up hot sausage rolls and mixing gin and orange so poky, one glug and you'd forget your own name. The ashtray was already spilling over with cigarette butts stained scarlet from lipstick. Heat and laughter spilled through the tiny terrace. The Tommy Dorsey Orchestra blared out through the hemp mesh on the wireless as the Yardley girls did their level best to paint over their troubles. Julia had agreed to take in Frankie for the evening, which was just as well as it was a strictly female domain at number 10 the Shoot.

'Come on in then, Lily, don't hang about like a bad smell on the landing,' her mother gestured, pressing a drink into her hand.

Lily took a sip and decided for that evening to forget her secrets. Domineering mothers, volatile younger sisters . . . In these matters she floundered, but beauty. Beauty she could do.

'Who wants some lovely lashes?' she asked, reaching for a candle from under the sink.

'Sorry, I'm late,' breezed Joanie as she came in and unpinned her hat. 'I started my ps and I can't find a sanitary towel for love nor money. Renee, you got one I can pinch?'

'Sorry no, sweetheart,' said Renee from the hearth where she was heating up her tongs and curling Esther's long silky hair into waves.

'I got one upstairs, help yourself,' Lily said, as she began welding blobs of melted wax onto the ends of Betty's lashes.

The Board of Trade Limitation of Supplies Order might have made cosmetics and scent as rare as hen's teeth, but the Yardley girls were nothing if not resourceful.

Fat Lou was chiselling out lipstick ends with a knife and handing them to Nan, who was melting them down with almond oil before decanting them into eggcups.

Lily had long discovered that powdered starch made a perfectly adequate replacement when her Pan-Cake had finished. Borwick's bicarbonate of soda under the arms did a nifty job of counteracting perspiration, and Pat's boot polish was a passable mascara.

'Just as well your father ain't here,' laughed Nell, when she saw her painting it onto Betty's eyelash extensions.

'Don't worry, Mum,' she grinned, 'a burnt cork works just as well.'

'You girls,' chuckled Nell, flopping down into an easy chair by the fire, covered with her favourite lace antimacassar, and resting her feet on an old pouffe. Her lisle stockings had rolled down to her ankles, not that she cared. 'Don't be thinking you're blazing a trail with your beetroot-stained lips and your gravy browning legs. You lot forget that my generation have already been through one war. I know every dodge there is to know.'

She folded her arms over her voluminous chest.

'Wanna know the real trick to having a complexion like Mae West?'

'Ooh, not many,' said little Irene, trying not to move her lips too much on account of the homemade face mask she was wearing. 'I'm not convinced this Fuller's Earth is working!'

'Maiden's first water,' nodded Nell knowingly.

'What's that, Mrs Gunn?' asked Joanie.

'Oh, don't start her,' groaned Renee, taking an extra-large slug of gin.

'Baby's first wee. Get the napkin on your mush and trust me, your skin'll come up lovely.'

'Mum, that's an old wives' tale,' laughed Lily.

'Wot'cha expect?' said Renee, winking at their mother. 'She's an old wife.'

'Ooh, you wicked cow!' shrieked her mother. 'You're not too old to put over my knee.'

'Sorry, Mum, you know I love you really,' said Renee, throwing her arms around her and kissing her cheek flamboyantly. Lily sneaked a glance at her younger sister. There was a feverishness about her behaviour this evening that struck her as odd. Her eyes were glassy with gin. The smile looked like it had been nailed on.

'My mum always puts mutton fat on her face,' confided little Irene. 'Swears by it.'

'Your mother's not wrong,' nodded Nell. 'The old ways are always best. Dripping's much better than cold cream, brings make-up off lovely an' all. I got some in the scullery. Anyone want me to fetch it?'

'No!' came the chorus of horrified squeals.

'Do you use it then, Mrs Gunn?' asked Betty. 'Only you've barely a wrinkle on your face.'

'That's cause I'm sitting on 'em, love,' Nell quipped.

'Mum!' chastised Lily as everyone fell about.

'What?' Nell shrugged with a mischievous gleam in her eye. 'At my age you choose your face or your figure.'

The air was thick with stories and scents, mainly down to a particularly noxious home perm Betty had insisted bringing over which stank of rotten eggs, but for two precious hours the girls shut out the privations of the war. Until the nine o'clock pips sounded and a BBC news flash crackled over the wireless.

The horrors on the blood-drenched beaches came crashing straight into the Gunns' kitchen.

'Through an inferno of bombs and shells the British Expeditionary Forces are crossing the Channel from Dunkirk in the strangest armada of ships,' came the tinny, detached voice through the hemp mesh. Lily sneaked a look at Renee's face. Her smile slipped as the BBC newsreader continued with his report.

'The Admiralty have confirmed the loss of three naval destroyers.'

'Oh no,' shrieked Nan, reaching for her coat. 'I gotta get home, in case there's word.'

At the same time, Renee set down her drink with a thud and raced upstairs. The party ended abruptly.

Once she'd finished helping her mother clear up, Lily made Renee a cup of tea and took it upstairs to her on a tray along with an aspirin. She pushed open the door to their shared bedroom. The lights were off and Renee's silent form lay under the coverlet, but Lily knew she wasn't really asleep.

Lily gently set down the tray on Renee's dressing table and padded around in silence in the darkness, getting ready for bed and then slipped between the covers. Sleep was impossible.

'Renee, I know you're awake,' she whispered eventually. 'Are you all right? I wondered if you wanted to talk about the news, earlier . . .'

'I'm fine,' came a hollow voice.

'Only tonight you . . .'

'Quiet,' Renee hissed, sitting bolt upright.

Downstairs she heard the scrape of the doorframe, the creak of warped floorboards.

'It's Dad! He's home.'

Pulling housecoats about them, the girls stole softly down the stairs, and listened at the kitchen door.

'Renee, I . . .' Lily whispered.

'Sssh,' Renee raised a finger to her lips, the whites of her eyes shining in the dim light of the passage.

The hiss of the gas lamp, the scrape of tea leaves spooned into the pot, then their father's voice, but not as they recognised it.

'I ain't never seen anything like it . . .' he moaned, his voice thick with exhaustion.

'Shh,' hushed Nell. 'You'll wake the girls.'

'Sorry, it's the guns, they've deafened me.'

Lily could smell her father from the other side of the door. Usually he smelt, well not dirty exactly, but of leather and coffee grounds. Today, he stank of wet boots and blood. His deep voice was louder than usual, so the girls could make out every word.

'We worked round the clock, running the tug almost up onto the beach to transfer soldiers to the Navy destroyers. The entire beach was black from sand dune to waterline with tens of thousands of men . . .'

He stumbled on.

'The sights on them beaches, Nell. Ambulances on fire, boats on fire, men on fire . . . We was getting bombed, shelled and torpedoed. Jerry was having us above, below and sideways. Chaos!'

Silence. Then the strike and crackle of a flaring match. Cigarette smoke drifted through the crack in the door.

'One lad, oh Nell, I'll never forget it. He'd been caught by shrapnel. It had pierced through his helmet, driving the steel clean into his skull. His brain was leaking all over the hull. "Leave me. I'm done," he said, but alls I could think was, *That could be one of the lads from the Shoot.*'

'So we made for the nearest destroyer. Out of nowhere, six Stukas. Bastards started dive-bombing us like a flock of seagulls. The scream of them sirens as they come at you. Oh Nell, I swear it got so close, I could actually see the pilot, his head strained back against the gravity, his mouth wide open. Bastard was laughing!'

'Oh Pat,' Nell breathed. 'Did you get the lad on safe?'

Lily realised she was holding her breath.

'We never got a chance. It got torpedoed, cleaved in half and went down right in front of us. Can't see as how there could've been any survivors. And Nell . . . That ain't the worst of it.'

Renee pressed her ear closer to the doorframe.

'When I got back to Dover I had a word with my mate in the Admiralty, he pulled some strings and I had five minutes alone with the list of crew on board.'

'Anyone we know?'

In the silence her father must've nodded.

'Able Seaman Alfie Buckle. But don't for God's sake tell Renee yet.'

There was an awful few moments of silence from Renee, as the two sisters stood frozen in the shadows.

'Oh Lil,' came a strangled voice in the darkness of the passage. 'What am I going to do?'

Three days later, Lily still didn't have the answer to that question. Dunkirk had changed everything. Being a community with a history of seafaring, close to the docks, Stratford bore heavy losses on those godforsaken beaches.

Not just twelve good sons down the Shoot, nor Miss Rayson, the welfare officer's brother, nor Alfie Buckle, but Nan's new husband Jimmy, too. All gone.

Lily glanced over at Nan, a black armband over her red tunic, hard at work, and felt her heart go out to her. It was true, she had found Jimmy's behaviour despicable, but no one deserved to lose their husband just eight months after they married him.

She thought back to their smart wedding do, the confidence with which the girls had all sung, 'We're gonna hang out the washing on the Siegfried Line'.

How darkly ironic that felt now that the Germans had trampled over it and the groom was dead.

Nan had taken a day off, but was now back on the lipstick belt and putting on a brave face. It was Renee she really worried about. She wore no armband, but Lily knew inwardly the loss of Alfie cut deep and with his body somewhere at the bottom of the English Channel, there would be no funeral to help blunt the horror of her grief.

It was now Tuesday and she had barely said a word since they had accidentally found out about his death in the early hours of Saturday. No amount of coaxing from their mum had encouraged her to eat.

To make matters worse, tomorrow, a public funeral procession had been planned along the High Street to a cemetery in West Ham for Jimmy and those other casualties whose bodies had been retrieved. The bosses at Yardley had kindly agreed to give any workers who wanted to attend time off, provided they came straight back.

A fear as thick as cat guts had stitched its way through Stratford, with people casting their eyes to the heavens as if they half expected Nazi paratroopers to come sailing through the blue June skies. Church bells had been silenced, only to be rung in the event of invasion, and in the countryside, street signs had been removed.

'Miss Gunn, a word.' The tap on her shoulder made her jump out of her seat.

'Sorry, Miss Rayson, you startled me.'

In her office, Lily cleared her throat nervously.

'I'm so sorry for your loss.'

Miss Rayson stared hard at her desk, gave a tight little click in the back of her throat. 'Thank you. Now, to business . . . Things are about to change. We have to give the old perfume rooms over to the manufacture of aircraft components and seawater purification tablets. Government orders. And now, alongside lipsticks, we shall also be producing and packing camouflage cream for the troops as well as other war work for Crookes Laboratories.

'All metals used in packaging will be vastly reduced and the majority of goods will now be packed in wax containers.

'I shall be extending the shifts and I'm afraid we'll all be required to work longer hours and take shorter dinner breaks.'

'Of course,' Lily replied. 'I don't think you will meet much objection from the girls. They are all extremely keen to do their bit.'

'That's the spirit. The whole country is pulling together and here at Yardley's, we must echo the national effort. We cannot let them win . . .'

Her voice wobbled but she quickly got it back under control.

'Of course. By the way, where is Miss Peerless?'

'Aah, yes I'm glad you mentioned that. She's left.'

'Left?'

'Yes. Signed off with her nerves. She's moved out to the countryside to stay with her aunt. I'm promoting you to room supervisor and Nan will be taking your place as charge hand.'

'Oh . . . Thank you,' said Lily, taken aback.

'May I ask whether there will be any advancement for Renee? She's been in the same position for a while.'

Miss Rayson looked thoughtful.

'Please don't take this the wrong way. I know she's your sister, but Renee's not exactly been shining at work lately. She seems to have gone, well, how can I put it? Off the boil recently.'

Lily sighed and stared out of Miss Rayson's office to the gates of Berger's paint factory next door. Except it was no longer Berger's, where young blood Alfie had last been seen haring naked through the yard. It had been requisitioned as British Feeding Meals Factory.

'Rest assured, I'll have a word with her,' said Lily. 'In her defence, she has lost a sweetheart.'

'I know,' said Miss Rayson. 'But right now, a lot of people are mourning. Hard work is the best cure for grief.'

'One more thing, Miss Rayson,' said Lily. 'Do I have permission to promote Esther Orwell onto the belt? She's worked extremely hard for nine months now as a service girl. I know we usually wait a year, but well, we could do with an extra pair of hands on the belt and she's more than capable.'

Miss Rayson smiled, a rare thing which hijacked the corners of her mouth and took years off her.

'I knew you would ask that. My answer is yes.'

Back in the lipstick room, Lily walked over to where a pale Renee was working in subdued silence. She touched her shoulder and Renee shuddered.

'Renee, you don't look at all well.'

'No, I don't feel it, to be honest. Would you mind if I left early, only there's someone I urgently need to see.'

Ordinarily, Lily would have said it was out of the question, but these times were anything but ordinary.

'Where are you going?' she asked.

'To see Alfie's parents.'

'Aah,' she said cautiously, lowering her voice. 'Very well, I'll cover for you this once, but please make up the time, Renee. You're already being watched by Miss Rayson.'

Her sister shot out of her seat and rushed for the door, so tightly wound up Lily doubted she'd even heard her.

18

Renee

Renee clocked off in a daze and took the long way to Alfie's parents' in order to summon up some courage. Since news of Alfie's death three days ago, she had turned this idea over and over in her shattered head until she thought she was going mad, but from where she was sitting, it was the only option left open to her. She walked with purpose, past Stratford railway station, which was awash with khaki, dodging the exhausted soldiers returning from Dunkirk. The troops tumbled out of trains, their uniforms torn and dirty, their boots cracked and worn. The Women's Voluntary Services were out in force in their vans, handing out strong tea, sandwiches and cigarettes to the returning troops. Renee couldn't bear to look at any of them, for she knew whose face she would be searching for. *Alfie Buckle. The father of her unborn child.*

She passed the picture house where they had met for their date and she remembered how handsome Alfie had looked that night, so vital and full of life. Now, he didn't exist, not in this world at any rate. She would never look upon his face again.

'Oh God,' she cried, pressing her hand over her mouth and stumbling on, the heavy hand of grief almost pressing her down into the pavement.

Outside her favourite Italian café, which served the best lemon ices, the pavement glittered with shards of broken glass. Since Italy had joined forces with the Germans, tensions were running high and anti-Italian riots had broken out. Italian traders whose own sons were serving with the British Expeditionary Forces had had their shop fronts trashed.

Renee composed herself and carried on her walk. When she reached Alfie's parents' turning, she hesitated, fear and adrenalin pumping in her chest. This was her last hope. Perhaps if she could explain her predicament to them, that a piece of their son lived on in her, they might take her in, support her. She was, after all, carrying their grandson or granddaughter. They had a right to know. She had Alfie's letter safely tucked in her handbag to prove his intention to marry her.

Her eyes were snagged by a poster on a community notice board. A beautiful woman with a knotted turban and scarlet lips seemed to look mockingly down at her as if she knew she was wearing patched-up stockings and her mother's bigger knickers.

Beauty is your Duty was emblazoned beneath in pink, along with all the things Renee could do, such as wear a touch of rouge, put her hair in a silk scarf or try stockingless cream. Six months ago, Renee would have agreed, lapped up the advice like a cat greedy for milk. But now, she was soiled goods.

All the same, she took out her Yardley lipstick in poppy red, a pre-war gold tube smothered in tiny stars and art deco swirls with a miniature red bee on the lid. Nan had given it to her just before Dunkirk as a gift. Popping open her compact, Renee slicked on a rich coating and instantly she felt a bit bolder. Pressing her lips together, she approached the Buckles' door and knocked.

The woman who answered was not the same woman Renee

had met that cosy December night, when the whole Buckle clan had gathered in the front parlour.

'I . . . I hope you don't mind me coming, Mrs Buckle. I wondered if we could talk?' Renee began.

Mrs Buckle looked vacantly at Renee and then, very slowly, she slid down the doorframe. A strange animalistic wail came from deep inside her as she hit the lino floor.

'Mrs Buckle!' Renee cried in alarm.

Suddenly she heard footsteps pounding up the passage.

Alfie's father gently helped his wife off the doorstep and ushered her inside like a child.

'Come on now, love, what did the doctor say about getting excited. Let me fetch you your pills.'

He turned back to her, his eyes haunted.

'I'm sorry, Renee love, but you shouldn't have come. Just seeing you reminds her of Alfie.' He scrubbed despairingly at his face. 'We've lost both our sons and we've got a one-hundred-and-one-year-old woman upstairs refusing to eat. It's just too much to bear. I . . . I hope you understand.'

And then the door closed between them, slicing their grief in half. Renee hurried away as twilight folded in around her. She had stumbled crassly into their pain with her painted lips.

Fear and shame slid down the back of her throat like oil. The pain was savage, a sense of emptiness gnawed deep inside. What had she expected, that they would welcome her in with open arms? She paused for breath. Leaning against the crumbling brick wall of a terraced house, she cradled her tummy as tears scored down her cheeks. Resting the back of her head against the wall, Renee felt the whole tangled mess of her life throb and hiss inside her skull.

The door to the house was partially open to let in the breeze. She heard the distant strains of the wireless and, with a jolt, realised that every house in the street must be tuned in to the BBC. From the shadowy homes, the Prime Minister's gravelly disembodied voice floated up the road.

'We shall fight on the seas and oceans. We shall fight with growing confidence and growing strength in the air. We shall defend our island, whatever the cost may be. We shall fight on the beaches. We shall fight on the landing grounds. We shall fight in the fields and in the streets. We shall fight in the hills. We shall never surrender . . .'

Fighting talk. But maybe that's what the country needed right now. Maybe it was what she needed too. And there and then, in the dark maelstrom of her grief, one thing shone out pure and clear. She was keeping this baby.

The next morning broke, a greasy grey streak in the congealing sky. It was the day of Jimmy's funeral. Renee had agreed to accompany Nan in following the funeral carriage from the house to his final resting place.

She had taken extra care to dress, taking out the seams on her black dress. Thank God black covered a multitude of sins, she thought as she and Nan got ready to leave. To deepen the gloom, the heavens opened, sheeting Stratford in tears. Somehow, Nan had spun her raw grief into something rather beautiful.

She looked as delicate as a china doll in an exceptionally well-cut black silk dress and black veil, satin gloves covering her slender wrists. A slick of Tangee lipstick had gone on orange, but stained to a deep theatrical red, the only colour in her milk-white face. She was quite the most striking widow Renee had ever seen.

'You ready?' she asked as two beautiful gleaming black horses, harnessed in black leather and silver livery, pulled a black carriage containing Jimmy's coffin right outside her home.

Nan held her head up high and nodded.

The slow procession began. The route was lined with locals who had come out to pay their respects; shops shut while they passed, blackout blinds pulled halfway down as a mark of mourning. Even the Bricky Kids had been scrubbed up and lined up on the pavement, caps in hands and eyes downcast, the stillest Renee had ever seen them.

Jimmy was a local boy, and his death on the beach had struck a chord. *NEVER SURRENDER* blazed from every newspaper hoarding in reference to Churchill's momentous speech the evening before.

Jimmy was clearly held in high esteem by the Royal Navy too. A Union Jack flag draped his coffin and the family group was followed by twenty sailors, West Ham Local Defence Volunteers and the British Legion.

There was total silence in the streets, save for the crackle and hiss of the funeral carriage's wheels on the wet tarmac.

At the church, after a short but moving service, 'Abide With Me' was sung and then the congregation spilled out in the graveyard.

Raindrops dripped from yew trees as Jimmy's body was lowered into the ground. Nan had been holding up fairly well until that point, but after she had placed a copy of their wedding portrait onto his coffin, she broke down in Renee's arms.

'How am I supposed to go on without him?' she sobbed.

Renee cradled her and stared at the scrawls of dirty black cloud scudding across the sky. What about her loss? Quickly, she squashed the nasty thought before it took hold. She had to remember her grief was not exclusive, no heavier than Nan's. She had every right to sob, more so, in fact, for she had at least done the respectable thing and married.

As the mourners drifted away, the rain came down harder, pinging off the gravestones, but Nan seemed reluctant to leave.

'Shall we get going back to yours?' Renee gently coaxed. 'This rain is brutal.'

As her gaze roamed about, she spotted her little brother, sitting under a yew tree, sketching the whole scene furiously into a notepad.

'Frankie!' she called, but he took one look at her and scrabbled like a frightened rabbit over the wall at the back the churchyard.

The sudden move caught Nan's eye and they both stared across to the furthest reach of the graveyard.

Huddled behind a bush, not thirty yards from where Frankie had been sketching, was a woman, holding the hands of two small children. Nothing so unusual in that. But it was the look on her face that stopped them both in their tracks.

Fear. Grief. And something Renee could've sworn looked like guilt.

'Why's that woman looking at me like that?' said Nan slowly. 'Who is she?'

Renee's flesh prickled hot and then cold. The two small boys huddled into their mother were the image of the man they had just seen slide into the soil.

'Wait! You there!' Nan called. Then she was running in the direction of the woman. When she reached the bush, they were gone. Vanished. All that was left was three pairs of footsteps in the sodden earth.

Back at home after the funeral, Renee found her brother in his bedroom. Frankie looked up, his face full of alarm as she pushed open the door.

'I ain't cross, little bruv,' said Renee, taking off her still damp coat and sitting down on the bed next to him. 'I'm just curious to know why you was at the funeral earlier.'

He looked up at her cautiously, as if weighing up whether

to trust her or not, and Renee regretted that she had not spent as much time with him of late. But what with her troubles . . .

They'd always had a close relationship, especially when Lily had been working away, and she adored her younger brother.

'Just drawing,' he said eventually.

'Is that your sketchbook?' she asked, nodding to the pristine notebook.

He nodded.

'Where you get it?'

'Julia bought it for me, only don't tell Mum or Dad,' he whispered.

'Brownie's honour,' she winked, holding up three fingers.

'But you're not a brownie, Renee?' he puzzled.

'It's a joke, Frankie . . . Oh, never mind. May I look?'

He pushed it slowly towards her.

'Blimey, Frankie, these are smashing,' she grinned, ruffling the top of his head. 'You can draw all right, you clever little thing.'

Her blue eyes widened as she flicked through page after page.

'No lie, some of these look like photographs.'

She came to one of their father. Frankie had drawn a grotesque caricature of him with boxing gloves instead of hands, his nostrils flared in anger in a colossal head, but his body that of a tiny ass.

Renee couldn't help but laugh out loud.

'I definitely won't be showing this to Dad.'

Then she found the one she was looking for. Frankie had captured every detail of the burial perfectly. It was astonishing. Every tiny last leaf on the yew tree, a spiderweb trembling precariously between two gravestones, Nan's face shrouded behind her veil and, hidden in the shadows, the mystery woman and her two children.

He had been closer to them and from that angle, they appeared to be in hiding, hovering behind an acanthus plant.

Seen closer up, the children looked even more like Jimmy than she had thought. They had his high forehead, jet-black hair and slightly pointed chin. She bit down on her lower lip.

What to do?

'Frankie, do you mind if I borrow this?'

Crouched outside the woman's flat after work two days later, Renee couldn't help but think she had set off the most dreadful chain of events. She had enough troubles of her own to sort out without opening another can of worms, but Nan was not a woman who would take no for an answer. As soon as Renee had showed her the sketch, Nan had taken it up and down Angel Lane Market on her dinner break. It had taken all of about ten minutes to identify the subject as Laura Cresswell, a young mother-of-two who worked at Clarnico's sweet factory and lived, ironically, not far from Yardley's on Carpenters Road.

'Where's her husband?' hissed Nan as she pushed open a side gate to the small residential building sandwiched between a can factory and a timber yard.

'Dead apparently, she's all on her own with the kids . . . Nan, I don't think we should be going round here. Why don't we knock on the door? Nan?'

'I just wanna know who she is and why she was at my husband's funeral,' Nan replied as she pushed open the back door, which led into a tiny scullery.

'Hullo?' she called out. 'Anyone in?' Her voice seemed to echo up the through the still of the ground-floor rooms.

Nan took one step, then two, and then disappeared into the room beyond.

In the concentrated silence, Renee was aware of the beating of her heart. Dread balled in her stomach. She knew Nan was grieving, that she had always been a little capricious, but this was all wrong.

'Come in here, quickly!' Nan's voice, full of alarm, drifted back to her.

Renee wanted to turn tail and get the hell out of there. What if the woman came back and caught them prowling through her home? If she worked at Clarnico, she'd be clocking off soon. And where were her children?

'Renee, you've got to come in here, now. You won't believe what I've found.'

'Nan, you can't go through her things,' Renee said as she tiptoed along the creaky passage. 'We have to leave, come back when she's . . .' Renee's voice trailed off.

Nan stood inside the tiny front room, her face as white as bone. In her hand was a framed portrait. She shoved it at Renee.

'I found it hidden in this drawer,' Nan blurted.

It took a while for Renee's brain to register what her eyes were seeing, her thoughts spinning and colliding. The woman they had seen in the graveyard was sitting in a photographer's portrait studio. In front of her, were two immaculately dressed little boys in sailor suits. Beside her, a handsome man in naval uniform, his arm draped about the woman. It was the perfect family shot taken before the man went off to war. The sort you saw in every portrait photographer's window display. Except the man in it was Jimmy, Nan's husband.

Nan's face was so pale, even her lips had lost their colour.

'How could he?' she whispered. 'How . . . how!'

The portrait slithered from her hand. It hit the floor and the glass shattered into hundreds of tiny pieces.

'Nan, please we *have* to leave,' Renee begged, hearing the Clarnico's hooter sound outside.

'How could he do this to me?' Nan repeated, not hearing Renee. 'That rotten bastard.'

Her voice grew louder, suffused with the anger that was building up a head of steam inside her.

'After all I sacrificed for him. Look at them nippers! They must've been carrying on for years!'

Renee suddenly felt very afraid. Nan was boiling over, out of her mind with anger and grief. Her eyes flashed dangerously, her pupils as dark as apple pips.

'After everything I went through for him. He knew how desperate I was to have a baby, and all along he had two with her.'

'Nan, I'm gonna find something to clean up this glass with.'

Shaking, Renee ran into the next room and found a broom, but when she came back, Nan had pulled the photo from the frame and was holding a match to it.

'Nan! No!' Renee screamed.

'That fucking cheating swine,' she ranted. 'Worse of all, he ain't even here to have a row with about it.'

Between them the photo smouldered then burst into flames.

'Don't you understand? He owed me a child, Renee,' Nan wept, her eyes glazed in the light from the flames. 'He owed me.'

The flames licked higher and higher, until finally Nan winced in pain and dropped the burning picture. It landed on a small rag rug. It took hold almost instantly.

'Bleedin' hell, Nan! Look what you've done,' Renee cried as the fire travelled along the rug like a living breathing object with an insatiable appetite.

'I tell you what, Renee, he's lucky he's dead. 'Cause if he was standing in front of me now, I'd flaming kill him myself.'

Renee looked about, frantically searching for anything she could find to extinguish the flames, but the smoke was growing denser and darker by the moment. Yanking off her cardigan with the intention of running it under a tap, she never got the chance because in that moment, the fire caught the blackout blinds.

'Oh Nan!' she breathed, as it devoured the dry material.

The speed of it all was terrifying, the acrid smoke catching at the back of her throat, making her cough; and all the while, at the back of her mind, all Renee could think of was the baby inside her.

'We gotta get out, Nan,' she choked, covering her mouth with her cardigan.

But Nan stood in front of the fire she had created, fixated. What Renee saw in her eyes, an ancient pain that seeped as dark as treacle, terrified her.

'Nan, please! Come now,' she begged, tugging on her sleeve. And then they were running, stumbling through the back door they'd arrived through, slipping unnoticed into the teeming crowds of clocking-off workers.

They were halfway back up the road, drawing level with Yardley's when the shout went up.

'FIRE!'

The crowds stilled and as one their eyes travelled to the great plumes of smoke hanging over Carpenters Road. Tinder-dry conditions and a warm breeze briskly fanned the flames and before long they could make out orange flames licking the roof of the wood yard next door.

'It's coming from the wood yard,' yelled a voice. 'Call the fire brigade.'

Dread balled in Renee's stomach.

'What've you done?' she whispered to Nan.

Nan turned on her, her voice no more than a hiss. The fingers gripping Renee's arm were surprisingly strong.

'Shut. Your. Trap.'

Her voice dripped pure venom.

'I mean it, Renee. You breathe so much as one word.'

Renee nodded, dumbstruck.

Her acquiescence seemed to mollify Nan. A sly smile tugged at the corner of her mouth. She pulled out a cigarette and lit it.

'Silly bitch,' she muttered, blowing out a long stream of smoke. 'Wreck my home and marriage, would ya? Now see how you like it.'

The clanging of fire brigade bells grew louder.

Renee stared at her. Who was this woman?

'Girls, what are you doing?' Renee looked up and saw Lily and Esther, who had been putting in a late shift at Yardley's. 'Come away and stop staring,' Lily demanded. 'The fire brigade are on their way and we must stay back. Nan for pity's sake put that cigarette out.'

Together, the girls assembled in the factory yard behind a hastily erected cordon and watched as three engines screeched to a halt in a flash of red further up the road.

'Look at the timber yard,' Esther exclaimed.

They all watched transfixed as the fire leapt and billowed from the roof of Gliksten and Son, sending a shimmering haze up Carpenters Road.

'Looks like it's already spread to the house next door,' Lily said, spellbound by the ferocity of the blaze.

Along the road, it was all hands to the pump. Three fire floats, motor pumps and auxiliary pumps battled a raging furnace.

'Be careful, Walter,' Esther cried as he headed up a human chain of Defence Volunteers passing up buckets of water from the Cut. Even the Bricky Kids were getting involved, pelting from the canal with wheelbarrows of water, for all the good it did. The fire was a solid wall, glowing white at its core.

Renee watched in a state of helpless stupefaction, unable to believe with her own eyes what was unfolding. It was as if Nan's anger was feeding the fire. It bellowed and roared, twisting solid metal girders until they glowed white and bent. Hundreds of gallons of water were pumped into it, and when supplies started running low, firemen fed the hoses into the Cut.

A high wind suddenly showered the onlookers with sparks.

'Everyone, to the other side of the Cut!' Lily yelled.

They ran over the canal bridge and through a shimmering haze of heat, then watched in horror from the other side of the water. At times, it looked as if the sheer force of the fire would overwhelm the firemen, but the extra water from the canal at last seemed to help bring it slowly back under control.

All the girls watched in horrified silence as the level of the Cut sunk gradually lower, as if someone had pulled out a giant plug. All manner of detritus was revealed, from rusting old bikes and prams to a sunken barge.

It was Esther who spotted the tiny body first, her blood-curdling screams so loud, they pierced even the roar of the pumps.

Walter was by her side in moments, shielding her from the heart-stopping sight.

'Don't look!' he cried. 'Everyone just look away.'

19

Renee

All of Carpenters Road had been sealed off for the past forty-eight hours while the police dealt with the grisly discovery and the fire was brought back under control, so Monday dinnertime was the first opportunity the girls had to discuss the shocking events of Friday evening.

'How could anyone do such a despicable thing?' Nan asked. Renee had to hold herself back from actually laughing. The front of her! How was she in any position to sit in judgment after what she'd done?

'My uncle, he's in the force, he reckons as how they've got orders from on high to start clamping down on abortionists,' said Joanie knowingly. 'It's getting more common since war started, apparently, and they ain't gonna look the other way no more. Bad for morale, ain't it?'

'I'm not condoning it,' said Lily, her voice wavering. 'But I think we should try not to judge. Goodness knows how desperate a woman must feel to get rid of a baby.'

'Desperation don't come into it,' Nan spat with vitriol. 'She was probably pushed into it. It ain't the mother I blame, it's the bloody abortionists. Them evil cows want hanging.'

A stunned silence fell over the tabletop.

'Nan,' warned Lily, desperate to be the voice of reason. 'I don't think it's quite that simple.'

Nan said nothing, just glared at Lily and speared a piece of apple with her fork.

'And what about the fire?' asked Esther. 'Does anyone know how that started?'

Until now, Renee had been listening in a state of abject misery, trailing her spoon through a bowl of apple crumble and custard and wishing Nan would pipe down. But at the mention of the fire, her head snapped up.

'Spark from a passing railway engine at the back of the timber yard, according to the local rag,' said Fat Lou. 'Word on the street is it caught some dried grass and then spread to a stack of timber in the yard. Did anyone see it on their way in this morning?'

'It's a great big smouldering wasteland,' nodded Betty. 'The buildings either side copped it too. Some poor Clarnico worker lost everything apparently.'

Renee felt like she couldn't breathe.

'A-Are she and her kids all right?' she managed.

'How d'ya know she's got nippers?' asked Fat Lou.

'Someone was talking about it clocking in earlier,' she said quickly.

'Miss Rayson assured me there were no fatalities or injuries,' said Lily. 'Nothing short of a miracle, if you ask me.'

In silence, the group gazed out of the canteen windows. A great pall of greasy smoke was still settled over Carpenters Road, staining the sky a bilious yellow. Even the clouds looked bruised. Betty was right. The timber yard further up the road was nothing but a mass of charred ruins, with the odd twisted skeleton of a metal crane emerging from the debris.

'Well, look on the bright side,' said Fat Lou cheerfully as she slurped back her tea. 'If Hitler does invade, he'll get to Stratford and think he's already done the job.'

The end of dinner break bell sounded.

Renee was about to follow the rest of the girls back downstairs, when Nan hung back, shooting her a pointed look.

'Looks like we got away with it,' she hissed, once the rest of the girls were out of earshot. 'I asked about. Apparently she's flown the coop, moved out to live with an aunt in Essex, taking those two little bastards with her. Good thing too, if you ask me, 'cause if she ever crossed my path . . . Seducing my Jimmy. I swear to God I'd . . .'

Renee stared, dumbstruck, across the table at her old friend. Where was the girl who she used to talk in silly riddles with and gossip about boys? Her behaviour was so volatile, she scarcely recognised Nan these days.

'What do you mean *we*?' she whispered eventually. 'I don't remember starting any fires.'

'You know what I mean, Renee,' Nan snapped. 'Point is, we're in the clear. They think it started accidentally. They can all claim on insurance, no harm done.'

'No harm done?' Renee gasped.

She wanted to argue back, articulate her horror that Nan could do such an impetuous, crazy thing, could ruin a man's livelihood, to say nothing of how wrong it was to lay all the blame for Jimmy's affair at the other woman's door.

'How do you know it wasn't Jimmy who seduced her?' Renee pointed out weakly. 'I doubt she took much pleasure being the other woman. She certainly didn't look like a seductress to me when we saw her in the graveyard.'

'How can you say that?' Nan seethed. 'What kind of cheap tart turns up at the graveside of her married lover? Look here, my Jimmy was a handsome man, a good provider too, she saw him as a meal ticket. It's her fault. All her fault.'

Tears suddenly filled Nan's eyes.

'Anyhow, I don't want to talk about it no more. What's done is done. None of us can change the past. Both of us just need to keep our traps shut.'

Renee nodded bleakly and Nan's tears seemed at once to evaporate.

'Oh, and by the way, I'm saying this as a friend and I know you'd do the same for me. But I can't help but notice you've really let yourself go since Alfie died. I'd lay off the crumble, if I was you.'

She smiled pertly. 'An ounce of cabbage is worth an inch of lipstick.'

Nan tapped her scarlet-painted fingernail down twice on the tabletop before sweeping from the canteen in a perfumed cloud. A terrible feeling of foreboding and fear unravelled inside Renee and, without even thinking, she gently laced her fingers together and rested them on her tummy.

Suddenly a dreadful realisation came to her.

The letter!

Alfie's last letter, in which he promised to marry her, the one she planned on showing to their unborn child one day to explain who his or her heroic father had been. It was missing! It had been in her cardigan pocket when they were in the house, right when she had taken it off to try and put out the fire . . .

She closed her eyes. There and then, she knew it was ashes, along with the rest of the charred ruins. Sorrow and pain scorched through her. *Enough.*

The fire had set in place a dreadful chain of events, like peeling off the skin of an apple only to find it rotten to the core. Maybe she was overreacting from a sleepless night, but a sense of impending doom seemed to coat everything.

She had to tell her mum, confide in her about the whole sorry mess before things spiralled even further out of control. Tonight. Straight after work.

The rest of the afternoon crawled by, and when the final bell sounded, Renee leapt from her seat and drew in a deep breath.

Having made the decision to talk to her mum, it was as if an invisible load had been lifted from her shoulders.

'You look a bit better today,' said Lily, rubbing Renee's arm. 'How you feeling?'

'All right,' she said slowly. 'At least, I hope I will be.'

'I know it's not easy losing someone you love,' said Lily. Her voice ached with loss, and Renee longed to reach into her sister's heart, pull her secrets from their hiding place.

'Come on,' said Lily, 'let's go home and see what Mum's made for tea.'

Back at the Shoot, they turned the corner into the square and a deep sense of warmth and love rippled through Renee. There was her mum, on her usual spot of a summer evening.

Nell and the rest of the women of the Shoot sat outside their doors in straight-backed chairs, jawing about this, that and the other, but generally enjoying the feel of warm syrupy sunshine on their faces while they peeled their veg.

Their voices were light in the soft air. Mrs Barnett's and Mrs Povey's kids were under Nell's watchful gaze as they turned a skipping rope over the dusty cobbles, their chants echoing off the walls. In the distance, Joe Loss and his orchestra crackled from a wireless. The net curtains behind Nell's head danced lazily in the breeze.

Renee smiled at the comforting sight of her mum on the doorstep. Nell Gunn was so solid, so immovable, like Stonehenge or Tower Bridge. Civilisations could fall, countries could topple, but Nell Gunn would still be found shelling peas into her apron lap. After the turmoil of the past week, Renee drank in the reassuring vision.

They reached the group and Renee threw down her bag and threaded her arms around her mum, squeezing her tightly in a hug.

'What's that for?' Nell chuckled.

'I'm allowed to hug my lovely mum, ain't I?'

Nell turned to the group. 'Where'd I get her from?'

Just then, the sound of a motor vehicle slamming its door sounded sharply at the far end of the Shoot. A dog barked a warning, raising its hackles and growling at the black-uniformed men marching through the square. Nell glanced up.

'Hello, Billy,' said Nell with a smile of recognition as they drew closer. 'How's your mum, she getting over that ulcer? Did she try that remedy I made for her?'

PC Billy Broadbent looked uncomfortable.

'I'm afraid we're here on a police matter, Nell.'

'Oh yes, what can I help you with, son?'

The sight of a Black Maria prompted windows and doors to open. The wireless snapped off. An unsettling silence cloaked the square.

The copper glanced at Renee and Lily.

'We can do this inside, Nell . . .'

'Anything you have to say to me, you can say in front of my family and friends,' she interrupted.

'So be it,' said an older officer, stepping forward and flipping open a leather-bound notebook.

'Mrs Eleanor Gunn. You are being charged under the Offences against the Person Act, 1861, with use of an instrument to procure miscarriage. We have reason to believe you have been carrying on an extensive abortion practice in this neighbourhood for many years. Anything you do say . . .'

Bedlam erupted as the women of the square rose up as one. A saucepan crashed onto the cobbles, sending potatoes and peas bouncing into the gutter. Angry shouts tore through the air.

'You can't do this! Get out of it!'

Only Nell remained seated, stock still in the chaos.

'I never had nothing to do with that baby in the Cut,' she murmured, 'I'd never do that.'

'We know that, Nell,' said PC Billy Broadbent gently. 'That woman has already been arrested. But we have reason to believe you have been burying foetuses in the churchyard.'

His gaze flickered to the graveyard beyond, the one Nell tended to so lovingly, and Nell's face paled.

'Mum!' yelled Renee. 'What's he talking about?'

Renee started to tremble as her mother stood slowly and extended her wrists.

Burying foetuses? Abortion practice? And why was she giving herself up without a fight?

'I can explain, love,' Nell replied, before turning to the police constable whom she had looked after as a child.

'Can I have ten minutes alone with my kids, Billy? Please?'

He shook his head, his face expressionless as he snapped on the handcuffs.

'I'm sorry, Nell. I'm under orders to take you down the station for questioning immediately.'

'No!' Renee screamed in disbelief, pulling her mother's apron as they led her towards the waiting van. 'You don't understand, you can't take my mum.'

Alerted by the commotion, Julia's door flew open. Frankie, clutching a notepad, peeked out from behind her.

'Please, Julia, get all the kids inside,' Nell urged, 'look after them for me, especially Frankie, until I'm out.'

'Renee, you have to let her go,' begged Lily, as she held a furiously struggling Renee in both arms. Fierce tears splashed down Renee's cheeks as she struggled and twisted.

'What's bloody wrong with you?' she screamed at Lily, finally wrenching herself free from her grip. 'You don't even look that shocked. W-we can't let them take Mum without a fight!'

Lily and Nell exchanged a look that Renee could not fathom, but it terrified her.

'Mum!' Renee sobbed. 'I don't believe it, none of it.'

'I'm afraid it's true,' Nell said, pausing as she reached the Black Maria. 'But please, child, do not look black upon me.'

And then she was gone. The doors slammed shut and the van sped off in a belch of petrol fumes.

20

Lily

In the same week that Nell Gunn was arrested in a borough-wide crackdown on abortionists, France fell and the swastika flew from the Eiffel tower. Somewhat incongruously to Lily's mind, both items sat side by side on the front page of the *Stratford Express*, which had been pushed through the letterbox that morning, along with a government pamphlet entitled *If the Invader Comes*.

But it was the revelation that her mum was a childminder by day, abortionist by night, rather than cataclysmic world events, which had shaken the foundations of her little sister's world. Seven days on, Renee seemed no closer to wrapping her head around the news and spent every waking moment when she wasn't working, lying on her bed staring at the ceiling. Since Alfie's death and their mother's arrest, Renee had totally lost interest in the world around her and her own appearance. She no longer bothered with make-up and increasingly swaddled her frame in baggy, shapeless clothes. And this from a girl who used to touch her toes a hundred times a day and needed a suitcase just for her make-up!

With their mother behind bars and bail denied until her trial in nine weeks' time, Lily knew the responsibility for holding the family together now fell to her. With their father working double shifts down the docks, it felt like they were all ships that passed in the night. Thank goodness for Julia, who ensured that at least the place was clean, that they all had a hot evening meal and that Frankie got to school, on his father's orders, and Sunday school.

In a strange way, though, the disclosure had come as a relief to Lily. It was at least one less secret to dismantle. From the moment she had followed her mum that night to Mrs Barnett's she had known in her heart of hearts that nothing had changed, that her mother was still 'helping' the women of the neighbourhood. This was the moment she had dreaded, and now the worst had happened.

Lily swallowed down her fear. She had to stay strong, for Renee and Frankie's sake if nothing else.

'Come on, sis, eat up,' she said, placing down a bowl of stew in front of Renee. 'Julia made it, it's delicious.'

'Not hungry,' she said flatly, pushing the bowl away.

'Renee, you have to eat,' Lily insisted. 'We've got an evening shift in two hours and you need the energy. Besides, you barely touched your soup at dinner break.'

'How could she, Lily?' Renee demanded, drumming her fork on the tabletop.

'Why don't you ask her yourself?' Lily suggested, ignoring the irritating tapping as she ate her stew. 'I'm going to visit her again on Saturday afternoon with Julia. She asked when you're coming in.'

Renee shook her head fiercely, her rumpled halo of blonde curls tumbling about her face.

'I'm sorry Lily. I . . . I can't. What she does, or rather what she did. It's unforgivable.'

As one, the two girls found their gaze drifting out the kitchen window, to the churchyard beyond. A soft twilight veiled the lichen-covered gravestones.

'It turns my stomach to look at that place now,' Renee spat.

'Renee, what you have to under—'

'No! I'll never understand,' Renee yelled, throwing her fork down with an angry clatter.

'It ain't right, Lil. I could never resort to . . . to that. I hate her for it.' She hugged her arms about herself defensively and began to cry.

'I won't forgive Mum. Not ever!'

Lily sighed and placed down her fork. *It was time*. She took a shaky sip of water.

'I used to disapprove of what she did as well,' Lily replied carefully, 'but since coming back, I think I understand. Mum gives women a choice.'

'You knew?' Renee gasped, pushing back from the table and staring agog at her sister.

Lily spread her hands out evenly on the tabletop and searched for the right words to explain.

'Hang on a minute,' Renee breathed, feeling as if a trapdoor had just opened up in her mind. 'That's the real reason you vanished, ain't it? You found out about what Mum does.'

To Renee's astonishment, Lily nodded.

Renee slapped her hand to her forehead and looked at her big sister aghast.

'All this time I've been searching for scandals on you when there weren't any! You left home because you discovered the truth about Mum.'

'You got one of your gaspers?' Lily asked.

'But you don't smoke!' Renee exclaimed.

'I suddenly feel like I need one.'

Renee fetched a packet of her mother's Craven 'A' cigarettes from the dresser and tossed them to Lily along with a packet of Swan Vestas.

Lily lit one up, drawing the smoke deep into her lungs. She caught a glimpse of herself reflected in the windowpane. She was shocked at how similar to her mother she looked in that moment.

There was no easy way to explain this, the truth was ugly however you dressed it up, so she plunged right in.

'Mum told me to take you and our Frankie out to Vicky Park one afternoon. You were twelve or maybe thirteen, I was sixteen, and Frankie was just a bubba in his pram. Halfway there, I realised I'd forgotten our jam sarnies, so I ran back, barged my way into the house . . .' Her voice trailed off and she blew a long stream of blue smoke at the ceiling.

'What did you see?' Renee whispered, afraid to hear the answer.

'A girl of my age, a bit younger, actually, and her mother sitting by the fire. The girl was sobbing her eyes out. Mum was out in the yard washing a Higginson's syringe with carbolic. I don't think I would've even guessed had the mother not more or less leapt to her feet and told me to keep quiet.

'Mum came through, tried to explain to me that the girl was in trouble, that she had helped her out. Then she said, and I'll never forget it . . .' Lily laughed, a brittle, hollow noise. 'She said: "What goes on in the house, stays in the house."'

'What did you do?'

'What could I do?' Lily shrugged. 'When the job came up at Yardley's Bond Street, I went for it and when I got it, I moved out. I wanted out of Stratford, away from this house, the Shoot, all of it. The memory of what I'd seen stained everything. I was sickened by it all . . .'

Her voice trailed off, her heart pumping. She had to stop right here, right now, before she revealed the whole story. Lily pressed her fingers against her mouth, desperate to tell the truth, but terrified of the consequences. Tears filled her eyes, which Renee misconstrued.

'It's all right, Lil,' she soothed. 'I'm not surprised you're upset, seeing all that. Keeping Mum's secrets all these years. It must have been awful, no wonder you stayed away.'

Lily nodded numbly.

'Then war broke out and you had no choice but to come home,' Renee went on.

'When they posted me back to Carpenters Road, I was dreading it. But you know the funny thing, Renee?' Lily sighed, massaging her temples slowly as if trying to arrange her thoughts.

'I'm not saying I condone it, but since I've been back and I see how Mum helps the women of the neighbourhood, the way she got behind Mrs Povey, the fishmonger's wife, how she continually comes to the support of Mrs Barnett when her old man treats her like a punchbag, I see she doesn't end life because she doesn't care, but rather because she does. She's giving women . . .' Lily paused, before reaching her hands out to Renee, entreating her to understand, '. . . alternatives.'

Renee raised one pencilled brow. 'You can't really mean that, Lily!' she scoffed.

'Honestly, Renee. I can't believe I'm actually defending her, but since I've been back, I see things differently now.'

Lily gestured to the window.

'Mum knows every single woman in this neighbourhood and their problems. Hidden bruises, moonlight flits, the slow grinding death of women like Mrs Barnett . . .' Her voice trailed off.

'Out there in the Shoot. That's the real war. The war on the Homefront.'

Renee shook her head.

'Well, I still think it's disgusting. She lied to me. To all of us.'

'No, she just kept a part of her identity hidden. There's a difference.'

'Not to me,' Renee snapped, jutting her chin out defiantly. Outside, the light was fading – silvery, tarnished. Inside, the kitchen felt strangely echoey. With Nell gone, the heart and soul had been wrenched from it.

Lily sighed and gathered up their dishes to take out to the scullery. 'You should never judge a woman until you've walked in her shoes, Renee. Thank goodness you've never needed a woman like Mum or found yourself in a predicament like that girl. Now come on, we best get back to work.'

Lily watched despairingly as her little sister buttoned up her summer coat and wondered, if she was this harsh now, however would she feel if she knew the whole unpalatable truth? Not about their mother, but about what she, Lily had done . . .

21

Renee

Summer rolled through Stratford, smothering the streets in an oppressive blanket of heat, the stenches so ripe, Renee half wondered if she couldn't scoop the smells up with her hands.

Nine weeks since her mother's arrest, and with her trial just three days away, she was stuck in a stagnant torpor, unable to forgive her mother, unable to confront the dreadful inevitability of her own situation.

Neither could Renee shake her sister's revelation. How could Lily have known about their mother's true identity all those years and not breathed a word?

Nothing felt normal any more, whatever the hell normal was. Her mum was an abortionist. Her best mate was an arsonist. And she was carrying her dead lover's baby . . . Renee stared down and got a jolt when she saw a stream of camouflage cream and not lipstick sail past her fingertips.

A chorus of wolf whistles rose over the clank of the machinery.

'Ain't no Jerry landing on the roof of Yardley's now I've been up there,' announced Walter proudly as he walked through the lipstick room.

'Why's that then?' Renee asked dully. Time was the fella

couldn't even speak to her without flaming red, but now his attentions seemed to have been diverted elsewhere.

'Is it safe for you to be up there?' asked Esther from the other side of the conveyor belt. Since Esther had been promoted, she had blossomed. Despite the loss of her father, she was knuckling down and growing in strength. Though Renee had a sneaking suspicion that had a lot to do with Walter's devotion towards her. He scarcely seemed to leave Esther's side these days and the pair were inseparable.

A lopsided grin spread over his cheeks as he gazed at her.

'Course. I had to get up there. Bosses asked me to erect some anti-invasion poles.'

Fat Lou cast a wink as she walked past before giving poor Walter a wedgie. 'I'm sure the sight of your erection on the roof'll be enough to send any Jerry running for the hills.'

The room fell about, with fifty or more women hooting with laughter at Lou's ribald joke. Good-natured as ever, Walter had the sense to laugh at himself.

'It's part of my duties now I'm in the LDV,' he said.

'What's that stand for then? Look, duck and vanish?' said Nan crisply.

'Actually, Nan,' Walter said defensively, 'Churchill's planning on renaming it the Home Guard.'

'Like I care,' she snapped. 'Anyway, enough of all this jawing, can we all focus on the job, please?'

'Ooh, Nan's got the needle,' joked Betty.

'Get on with your work, Betty,' she barked and Renee winced. She didn't mind admitting that Nan now scared her. Charming one moment, stunningly rude the next. Her mercurial moods were beginning to dominate the lipstick room and Renee got the uneasy feeling that after the fire, Nan was capable of anything.

Fat Lou raised her eyebrows behind Nan's head.

'Hark at Hitler,' she mouthed silently.

Nan certainly hadn't shied from throwing herself into her new role as charge hand, thought Renee. In fact, her turban had got even higher since her new promotion, towering positively pagoda-like on her head.

'Nan's right,' said Miss Rayson, who had loomed up behind them unannounced. She cast a quick glance at her watch.

'It's three thirty. *Workers' Playtime.* You are permitted to sing along.'

'Ooh, ta, Miss R,' said Betty as the jaunty new half-hour music programme came on. The BBC had scheduled it with the aim of reviving flagging spirits in the workplace. The only positive to have come out of Dunkirk seemed to be that the government was trying to keep the nation's morale up with new music programmes and even free milk for children.

'But please, Miss Burrows, no more stopping to write down the lyrics.'

She turned to Renee. 'A quick word, Miss Gunn. Nan, take over.'

As they walked up the steps to her office, Renee was aware of the furtive glances and whispers from passing Yardley workers. The East End jungle drums had had a good bashing since her mother's arrest, or had they guessed?

'Is this about my mum?' she asked, as soon as Miss Rayson softly closed her office door. ''Cause I knew nothing about it, I swear, and I won't need time off to go to the court on Monday 'cause I ain't going.'

'No,' Miss Rayson replied. 'Her activities do not concern me or Yardley's and I've granted your sister time off next week to attend the trial.'

She took her spectacles off the top of her head and balanced them on the end of her nose.

'No. I've asked you here because it's *you* I'm concerned about. Is there anything you'd like to share with me, Renee?' she asked.

Renee felt her stomach turn to a ball of ice.

'N-No. About what?'

'About your . . . How can I put this delicately? Your condition.'

'My condition, miss?' Renee replied, feeling her palms sweat.

Miss Rayson sighed heavily.

'I respect my staff, but you must respect me in return by telling me the truth, Renee. You've not been yourself for some while. Where is the girl who fought for a pay rise at the outbreak of the war? Your spirits seem . . . dimmed.'

'Please, miss, I've had a lot on my mind. Alfie's death, now my mum.'

'And I appreciate that, but this matter I feel is of a more physical nature.'

A voice screamed in Renee's head.

Tell her now!

'You can tell me anything, Renee,' Miss Rayson went on softly. 'In eighteen years here, I've seen it all before and I promise, I don't judge. My guess is you are what, six, possibly six and half months gone? I can make . . .' Her voice dropped as she leant forward in her chair, '. . . certain arrangements. Yardley own a convalescent home in Bexhill-on-Sea. A dear friend of mine runs a mother and baby home nearby. Don't you see?'

Renee shook her head, her eyes stretched wide. Outside, she could hear the cry of a gull circling the fish factory. Inside, the silence was excruciating. Miss Rayson was first to break it.

'When the time comes, I can send you in a company car and on company time to deal with your . . .' and here she inverted her fingers into speech marks, 'your "personal troubles".'

Renee stared, gobsmacked, at the welfare officer.

Was this a trick? To get her to admit she was expecting an illegitimate baby, before she had her frog-marched from the building without a reference?

Panic built stealthily inside her, like fingers closing round her neck.

'There ain't nothing wrong with me,' she blurted, scraping back her chair abruptly. 'I promise I'll work harder.'

Renee fled from the office, straight down the stairs, across the yard to the alley that led down to the Cut. It was only once she had lit a fag and taken a big trembling drag did she start to feel her breathing return to normal.

The August sunshine was blisteringly hot. Weeds pushed through the cracks and a verdant evergreen spread like a blanket up the factory walls. The stagnant air over the Cut was green with flies and the ripe smell of horseshit gusted over from a nearby forge.

She stared down into the greasy water. How had Miss Rayson guessed and so accurately? Oh, who was she kidding? There was only so long bandages and letting out seams could conceal her secret. Despite the chaos unfurling around her, this baby – Alfie's and her baby – continued to grow, a fresh new life oblivious to the world at war. She placed a protective hand on her tummy and wanted to weep for this little life that they had created.

Remembering her promise to Miss Rayson to work harder, she flicked her fag into the canal and trooped back inside.

At the end of the day, the girls spilled relieved into the yard and raised their faces to soak up the mellow rays of the late afternoon sunshine.

'Girls,' said Lily, clapping her hands. 'Before you all go. I just want to take a moment to say how very proud I am of all your hard work. I know every week it feels like we lose someone to the WAAF or the Land Army—'

'The backs-to-the-land army, you mean,' joked Fat Lou and everyone laughed at her smutty innuendo.

'Yes, thank you, Lou,' Lily groaned.

'I'm also aware that most of you, on top of putting in extra hours—'

'Do you mean double shifts, shorter dinner breaks and being seconded to make boring aircraft components?' Joanie piped up.

'Let Lily finish,' Esther ordered. Everyone stared in surprise at the usually mild-mannered girl.

'Thank you, Esther,' smiled Lily. 'I was trying to say that yes, on top of the extra work, I know many of you are also volunteering for the Auxiliary Fire Service or the Women's Voluntary Services. To a woman you do it without complaint, even though I know you're exhausted.

'I read an article in a magazine recently about sleep and courage – how to cope without it, and how to find it. Well, I think the writer ought to have spent a week watching you girls . . . 'Cause you're all bleedin' marvellous.'

Lily finished her little speech and everyone cheered.

'Can we go home now?' asked Fat Lou. 'Only at this rate it'll be time to come back for my evening shift.'

'Go on,' she grinned.

'Blimey, Lil,' Renee murmured. 'You're finally turning into a cockney.'

'I think I am, aren't I,' she replied with a grin.

'Right. I've got to head up to the roof for my fire-watching shift,' said Esther, buckling on her helmet.

'No topless sunbathing up there, Esther,' Fat Lou teased, wiping a film of sweat from her forehead.

They walked out of the gates and Betty turned to Renee. 'How's your mum holding up?' she asked.

Renee shrugged. 'How would I know?'

'You know Mum,' Lily chipped in. 'Says the women are nice enough, but complains that the tea's nothing but hot brown water and they don't clean the cells to her standard.'

Fat Lou chuckled.

'I bet she's running the show in there. I overheard some beaks asking questions about her down Angel Lane Market last weekend, by the way.'

'Bastards,' sniffed Betty.

'They're only doing their job,' Renee replied huffily, and Lily shot her a surprised look.

'If only they worked as hard to lock up the real criminals,' Fat Lou scoffed. 'Family next door to mine had their house looted after they evacuated.'

'Or the arsonist what fired up the timber yard,' added Joanie.

'I thought that was an accident?' said Renee, feeling her heart immediately start to race.

'My uncle reckons not. It was started on purpose, insurance most likely,' said Joanie. 'Leastwise, that's what the detective on the case now thinks.'

'Will you both go to the trial?' asked Betty.

'Yes.'

'No.'

Lily and Renee spoke at the same time.

'You have to be there!' Lily protested as they turned onto the High Street.

'Says who?' Renee replied angrily.

'Because she's our mum and it will break her heart!'

'Girls, you gotta come now,' urged a familiar voice.

Renee, still rattled from talk of the fire whirled round.

'Snowball? What you doing here?'

'I heard them, they're coming to dig up my home,' he babbled. 'They've just gone to get more shovels and men.'

'Who?' she replied, confused. She had rarely seen Snowball the tramp out of the graveyard or the market, so to see him here, on the High Street, made her feel discombobulated.

'The men in black. They're coming to dig up the graveyard.'

Adrenalin shredded her lungs as Renee followed Lily and the girls as they tore down Angel Lane Market, dodging stalls and barrows.

By the time they made it through Cat's Alley, her father and the vicar were already out remonstrating with a team of constables.

'But you can't do this. This is consecrated ground,' protested the vicar.

'We shan't disturb any graves,' remarked the detective, an older man with a moustache that looked like a dead rodent. 'It's the area at the back of the graveyard we want to search in connection to the activities of Mrs Gunn. Now, please step aside.'

'I beg of you, Inspector, please stop,' the vicar urged. 'You have no right.'

'This permit says I do!' he snapped, brandishing a piece of paper.

Renee felt the whole square tilt and nausea rise up sharply, as the police officers retired to the back of a Black Maria and started pulling out shovels, bags and protective gloves.

'Make them stop, Lily,' she wept, gripping her sister's sleeve. But Lily was as powerless and terrified as she.

And then, an extraordinary thing happened.

One by one, doors around the square opened. Mrs Povey, the fishmonger's wife, marched across the cobbles and took up position on the perimeter of the graveyard, in the shallow trench where the iron railings had once stood.

She tightened the strings on her apron and placed her hands on her hips as if she were digging in for the duration.

'Auntie saved me from destitution after my Geoff took his life. I'll not allow her to be persecuted.'

Her voice, loud and challenging, hung in the hazy heat of the square.

'Who'll join me?'

'I will,' said Mrs Mahoney, crossing the cobbles. 'I lost my husband and son recently, it's only her what treated me with any compassion.'

She linked arms with Mrs Povey.

'When my husband beat ten bells out of me every payday and the police looked the other way, she didn't,' said Mrs Barnett, struggling to keep her tears under control as she took her place beside Mrs Mahoney. 'I'm only alive 'cause of her.'

Julia's door flew open.

'I'm a Jewish refugee. To the authorities, an alien. To Nell Gunn, I am a human being.'

She took her place alongside the others.

Renee and Lily watched, flabbergasted, as an apron-clad army formed a human chain around the graveyard. Woman after woman, each with a story to tell, linked arms and formed a ring of female solidarity.

Soon, a solid wall of women circled the entire perimeter of the churchyard. One solitary man, Snowball, joined hands too.

'I'm a somebody to Nell Gunn, not a nobody,' he explained to the speechless detective.

Renee felt overwhelmed. Had her mother really touched all these lives?

'This is absurd, do you think we mean to be frightened away by a group of housewives and a tramp?' scoffed the detective when at last he found his voice.

Just then, a window scraped open above their heads. It was

an elderly woman with barely a tooth in her mouth, who hadn't been out since the first war.

'Maybe you'll take notice of a ninety-year-old,' she jeered. 'Come on, girls, what you waiting for? Let's run these bastards out of town.'

With that, she emptied the marshy-smelling contents of her chamber pot straight over the head of the detective inspector, followed by some old kitchen slops and tea leaves.

'How dare you pick on defenceless women!' she remarked with a winsome grin, the picture of exuberance despite her years.

For a split second, stunned silence. Then utter pandemonium.

'Get out of it!' yelled Mrs Barnett, hurling a rock-hard loaf of bread at the nearest policeman. 'This'll learn you to look the other way when my husband takes his fists to me.'

It landed with a soft thud between his legs. The look of surprise on his face before he crashed to his knees on the cobbles was priceless. The tension that had been simmering had been allowed its release.

Rotten fruit and veg from the market, stale bread and vegetable peelings, all were used as weapons as the hapless constables were pelted from every angle. Howls and screams filled the air. Months of pent-up frustration, anger and rage at the arrogance and neglect of the authorities spilled over into violence.

Fists shook. Boots pummelled the side of the Black Maria. A chant went up.

Shame on you! Shame on you!

Even the Bricky Kids were getting involved, pelting the constables with catapults of mud.

Renee and Lily stood back, open-mouthed, and watched their mother's loyal supporters in action. The vicar appealed for calm, but his pleas were drowned out.

At first the noise was barely audible over the rumpus, but it grew louder and louder still, like a speedway motorbike, boring through Renee's brain. The bushes in the graveyard began to tremble. A slate tile on the church roof slid off, smashing onto the cobbles. The vicar crossed himself and mouthed a silent prayer.

'What is that noise?' Renee cried.

As one, the crowd looked to the blue skies above, craning their necks and squinting against the sun.

'Cor! Dogfight!' yelled a thrilled Bricky Kid, dropping his catapult.

Within seconds, the battle of the Shoot was clean forgotten as everyone remained rooted to the spot, unsure whether to dive for cover, or continue watching.

A Spitfire and a Messerschmitt engaged in a deadly game of cat and mouse, soaring and swooping through the skies, cutting vapour trails through the blue.

Renee knew the Germans had been bombing RAF airfields and ports, but this was too close for comfort.

'Go on, get the bastards!' yelled Pat Gunn.

The Spitfire poured a deadly lead stream into the raider and it spiralled down, smoke pouring from its tail. The Spitfire rolled victoriously, and the women of the Shoot cheered madly.

'Look!' Lily yelled as a white puff blossomed against the brilliant blue. 'The Jerry's bailing out.'

'And he's coming down over Carpenters Road!' yelled a Bricky Kid, who'd climbed up to the church roof and was clinging precariously to some lead piping. 'Looks like he's gonna land on the roof of Yardley's.'

Renee and Lily looked at each other and had but one thought.

'Esther!'

And then the frenzied crowd was on the move . . .

22

Esther

Sitting on the factory roof half a mile away, Esther had a bird's eye view of the entire battle. She genuinely felt no fear, the worst, after all, had already happened in her life. So it was with fascination and a strange detachment that she watched as the plane wings broke apart and the burning fuselage hurtled from the sky, landing in the burnt-out remains of the timber yard.

A hollow boom ricocheted up the street, followed by a choking cloud of dust and smoke. The crash deafened Esther as she flung herself to the floor and, for a moment, there was nothing but perfect silence, the factory roof coated in grey mist . . . After a few seconds, everything came to life. The clanging of bells and screams snapped Esther out of her stupor.

Call it a sixth sense, but she already knew what she would see, and sure enough, when the smoke cleared, she spotted him. The German airman. The poor man was dangling mid-air, his parachute entangled on the anti-invasion pole Walter had just installed. He looked so helpless, his face wet with a smear of red.

In shock, his eyes bulged and when he caught sight of Esther, he began to mutter, kicking his legs wildly.

'*Nicht sorgen*,' said Esther softly, holding her hands out to him. '*Ich werde Ihnen helfen.*'

She moved slowly towards him, keeping her voice calm, saying over and over in German.

I will help you.

With a trembling hand, she reached up to him. If she could rip the parachute, he might slowly come down to the roof floor. The German airman looked at her suspiciously, but quickly realising a sixteen-year-old factory girl in a tin hat posed little threat, he reached out his fingers to her. Their fingertips were nearly touching when . . .

'What on earth do you think you're doing, Esther?'

The voice, shrill and high, speared the air, breaking the dreamlike moment and Esther turned in alarm.

'Nan,' she sighed, relieved, as she turned to find Nan and a handful of other Yardley workers who had climbed up the metal fire escape and onto the rooftop.

'Please, alert the military police, and someone help me get this man down.'

But instead of moving, Nan remained rooted to the spot, a look of utter vitriol etched on her face.

'Help you?' she spat. 'You must be loopy if you think I'm going help you free this . . .' and here she started to shake, '. . . this monster.'

Black-eyed and red-lipped, she pulled a shovel from behind her back.

'Go on, Nan, make saveloys out o' his brains,' urged an older woman behind her.

Nan raised the shovel and smiled, readying her body to make the first blow.

'This is for my Jimmy.'

Esther flung herself between Nan and the German.

'Please, Nan,' she implored. 'This isn't the way.'

Nan's dark eyes widened in surprise, before narrowing again. 'Get out my way, Yid!'

Esther's mind scrambled to find a way to reach out to Nan, make her see sense.

Her mind immediately went to her father, as it so often did these days. What would he say or do to calm Nan's terrible rage?

'You're better than this, Nan,' she implored. 'Please don't do this. I know you have lost the man you love, so have I, but we are not Germany, stripped of our souls, of our compassion . . .'

'Oh, please,' Nan laughed, her face as sharp as a hatchet. 'Save your breath. His kind killed my husband. I don't owe him any compassion.' She spoke through gritted teeth. 'Now. Step. Aside.'

'One day, people will learn of this war and be aghast at the wickedness of these times,' pleaded Esther. 'We will all be judged by our behaviour. Please, where is our humanity?'

'Where's my husband?' Nan yelled.

'My father is dead too, not in conflict, as you yourself said,' Esther said, struggling to control the tremor in her voice. 'He never got the chance to defend himself. He died slowly and painfully instead, at the hands of the SS, but killing this boy won't bring him back. He's not our enemy, Nan, don't you see?'

Somewhere beneath, Esther became aware that a small crowd had gathered in the factory yard, her friends Lily and Renee, and Walter, dear Walter, gaping up at them in abject horror.

'Nan!' Renee screamed. 'Come down.'

But Nan didn't even blink. Her mouth was wide open, a black empty maw spilling venom, her eyes blank hollows.

Esther had stopped listening. Her pulse was beating so loudly in her ears, she could no longer hear the savagery of Nan's words, she just knew she was not moving.

Four words pierced her reverie.

'He's got a gun!'

She whirled round. The German had pulled a revolver from his pocket. His hands were shaking violently, but the barrel of the gun was pointed straight at her head.

Esther didn't flinch. Her father's last written words danced before her eyes.

Always hold together in love and faithfulness, and God will bless you.

A strange sense of certainty washed over her and Esther felt her father by her side, invisible but almost certainly there.

'*Gib mir den revolver*,' she said gently, treacle-dark eyes focussed on his.

All of Yardley's held its breath. Somewhere in the distance, she heard sobbing, the German's heavy rasping breath, the pounding of heavy boots on concrete . . .

And then he slumped, the revolver clattering to the floor beside her.

The spell was broken. The military police broke through onto the rooftop and Esther was pulled back. And then she was in someone's arms. Walter's concerned face gazed down and one emotion shone through.

'Oh Esther, I thought I was going to lose you and I . . . I couldn't bear it because . . .'

And then his lips were on hers, kissing her with infinite tenderness.

Finally, he let her up for air.

'I love you, you see. You have no idea how long I've waited to say that. I think I knew I loved you the moment I set eyes on you.'

A shy smile spread over his face.

'You're the bravest girl I've ever met, Esther Orwell.'

Esther said nothing, just smiled and turned. Nan had already been taken down and was furiously storming along

Carpenters Road. The German airman had been cut down and was in handcuffs, about to be led from the rooftop by two military policemen.

'Please. Just one question,' he asked in halting English. 'How do you speak such good German?'

'I grew up in Vienna,' she replied. 'I am a Jewish refugee.'

'B-But you look just like them,' he stammered, pointing to Lily and Renee who had made their way up onto the rooftop.

'What did you expect?' she shrugged. 'That I would have horns and a tail?'

And then he was gone, led away and, in his wake, a cloud of disbelief.

Lily shook her head in awe.

'You could've grabbed that gun, shot him. No one would have blamed you, Esther, after your father . . .' The words died in her mouth as Esther shook her head vehemently.

'No!' she said fiercely. 'Because then I would be a barbarian like the Nazis.' And then, more gently. 'Don't you see, Lily? I could kill a hundred German boys like him, but what would that do, except fill me with as much hatred as them? It wouldn't bring my father back.'

The rest of the Yardley girls were waiting in the yard as Walter helped Lily, Renee and Esther down from the roof, and a spontaneous burst of applause rang out.

'Blimey, Esther, you've got guts!' gushed Betty.

'Yes,' Miss Rayson agreed. 'That was astonishingly brave. I'll be informing the Yardley family about this, of course, and the Town Hall. You deserve some sort of award.'

'I can think of something better!' winked Fat Lou, clambering up the ladder to the roof. Fifteen minutes later she was back with a bundle of parachute silk under her arm.

'Think you've earned this,' she smiled, handing it to Esther.

Esther let the silky white material slide through her fingers.

'Think of the beautiful dresses you can run up with that . . .' said Joanie, looking longingly at the coveted silk material.

'And blouses,' said Joycie.

'Knickers,' blurted little Irene. 'Knickers. That's what I'd make.'

And suddenly, they were all laughing, the tension of earlier released.

The thought of luxurious silk cami-knickers and blouses was a tempting one, but Esther already knew exactly what she was going to do with the material.

'I think we should let these two lovebirds have some time alone,' winked Lily, ushering the girls away discreetly.

Walter walked Esther home and once her mother had grilled her on the event and checked her over, she fetched them both cups of hot lemon tea.

'You would make your father so very proud,' Julia said, kissing the top of her head.

Esther smiled and smothered a yawn with the back of her hand.

'Don't stay too late, Walter. She's tired.'

'I promise, Mrs Orwell,' he replied.

Esther waited until she was sure her mother was back in the kitchen before turning to Walter.

'Did you mean what you said earlier?' she asked, cradling her cup.

He gazed at her through the steam.

'Every word, I promise.'

His eyes rested on his grandad's old gramophone, which he'd set up in the corner of the parlour.

'Here, let's have a dance to that record I bought.' He pulled the record from the sleeve and gently blew on it before placing it on the turntable and lowering the needle.

'What, now?' she laughed as classical music filled the tiny room.

'Good a time as any,' he replied, and taking Esther's cup and putting it on the sideboard, he gathered her in his arms.

As the melody slid over them, they moved together around the room, their steps perfectly in time. The music was sublime and somehow seemed to speak to her soul.

'Thank you for looking after me since my father died,' Esther said, searching his face. 'You make me very happy.'

'And you make me deliriously happy,' he replied. 'Tomorrow after your shift, I'm taking you to my favourite chop house for dinner.'

She shook her head and placed her fingers on his lips.

'No, tomorrow it's my turn to show you something of my world, the Jewish East End. I've been doing some investigating you see.'

'Proper little Agatha Christie, ain't yer?'

'I took a walk through the Jewish quarter the other day.'

'Petticoat Lane?'

She nodded, her face lit up with excitement.

'Oh Walter, it's nothing like the Jewish quarter of Vienna,' she breathed, brown eyes glowing.

'Not as fancy I'll wager,' he grinned.

'No, but . . . but it's . . . I don't know . . . alive! I bought pickled herrings and wallies from a barrel, wrapped in newspaper, *beigels* from a little old lady in a hessian apron down Brick Lane. Smoked salmon and hot latkes from Marks on Wentworth Street.'

Walter laughed at her enthusiasm, her words tumbling out.

'I saw old bearded men chatting outside the Turkish vapour baths. And the most fabulously beautiful girls with flashing dark eyes, so full of life.'

'I can't wait to see it with you,' he smiled, pulling her tighter into his embrace.

'Maybe we could move there together one day?' he ventured. 'It's only the other side of the Stink House Bridge after all, though to most round these parts, it'd be like emigrating.'

She looked up surprised and stopped, just as the record finished.

'What . . . you mean?' Her body stilled as the final chord quivered on the air.

Here his face grew serious, the trademark grin vanished, in its place a look of undiluted love.

'Esther, I want to marry you one day, and I know there's only one way that I could make that happen.'

'You'd convert?' she exclaimed.

'Of course.'

'But that could take years! Besides, I'm only sixteen.'

'Gives me plenty of time to learn Hebrew then,' he shrugged.

'But what'll your mum say when you tell her you want to marry a Jewish girl?'

'Plenty, knowing Mother,' he laughed. 'But you're missing the point, Esther. I don't care what she says. I don't care what anyone says, for that matter. All that matters is love. The way you act, your forgiveness towards that German earlier, you're showing me what truly matters.'

He slid his fingers through her long hair.

'You're the most remarkable person I've ever met.'

Esther went to reply, but was silenced when Walter bent down and planted the softest of kisses on her lips. When his mouth left hers, Esther rested her head against his chest and her eyes closed. A sense of peace washed over her.

All that matters is love.

Words she could almost hear her father saying.

The light in the bulb above flickered and the record crackled into life again.

23

Renee

The summer afternoon was fading away, the edge of the lonely sky tinged with the gold flush of a looming sunset.

Renee reflected on the strangest day she had ever experienced. After the dogfight and the German pilot bailing out, the police had abandoned their search of the graveyard, though Renee had a sneaking suspicion the crash had given them a welcome diversion.

She thought wistfully of Walter's public declaration of love towards Esther on the factory rooftop and despite the bitterness of her loss, felt nothing but happiness for her young friend. Esther was far too sensible and wise to make the mistakes she had. Though Renee could still never bring herself to think of any child of Alfie's as a mistake. She rested her hand on her tummy and gazed out over the smoking rooftops of East London as the sun bent to the horizon. Esther was safe in Walter's arms and no one deserved to be loved and cherished more than she.

Nan had gone home and Renee shivered at the memory of her face in those frenzied moments. She would have killed that German had it not been for Esther, of that Renee was certain. She had tried to find some semblance of the old Nan she once knew, but this woman was now a stranger to her. That ugly contorted look on her face when she lifted the shovel above her head. Crazed with grief and incandescent with rage . . . It was the same one Renee had seen when she had lifted the flame to the photograph.

And yet, despite all he had done, Nan had made a martyr of her cheating husband. Her heart had spread over with a thick leathery crust. Had she always been like that, or had Jimmy's death been the tipping point?

The moment of understanding pierced her with shattering clarity. If she continued on this path of anger towards her mother, refusing to forgive her and harbouring hatred, she would end up bitter, just like Nan. Or, she could forgive and find peace, like Esther. It was still hard to reconcile her mother as an abortionist, perhaps it always would be, but Renee knew she had to focus on the many other sides of Nell Gunn. Lily had told her she was motivated by a sense of female solidarity and Renee in her ignorance had scoffed at that. But what did those astonishing scenes in the square earlier prove? That her mum was respected and loved by all the women of the neighbourhood. She cared for them, *really cared*, and they in turn adored her for it. Nell might well have kept the more unsavoury details of her role in the Shoot private, but hadn't Renee herself lied to her mother, wasn't she indeed lying to her now? The epiphany was as sudden as it was profound.

'Oh God, what a bloody idiot I've been,' she murmured out loud, stuffing her knuckles into her eyes in frustration. Hopefully, it was not too late. There was only one place she needed to be. One person she needed to see . . .

Renee had to wait another day, until Saturday, to visit her mother at Holloway Prison and she was eaten up with nerves as she placed her handbag onto a table to be searched.

In the large and echoey visitors' room she scanned the tables, trying not to think what offences the women were in for. Nervously twisting the Woolworths ring she had placed on her wedding-ring finger, she finally spotted her mother at the far end of the room.

It struck her as ironic as she sat down on the small metal chair opposite her, that as she had been putting on weight, her mother had been losing it. Nell Gunn had always been a well-padded woman, but for the first time ever, Renee saw cheekbones. Without her turban and apron, clad only in a blue prison-regulation uniform, she looked small and vulnerable, the battle-grey walls bleaching her face of colour.

It had been nine weeks since she had seen her mother bundled into the back of the police van and in that time, there had been many changes. A faint brown line that stretched vertically from her tummy button to her pubic bone, a swelling of her breasts. Renee had sneaked a look at her ripe naked body that morning as she dressed and wondered with a smile what Alfie would have made of it all.

Deliberately, she had made no effort to bind down her bulging tummy. No more lies. It was time for the truth.

Her mother's smile on seeing her froze as Renee placed her hands protectively over the bulge.

'Hello, Mum! Pleased to see us?'

'Well, I tell you what, girl, you picked the right place to tell me. It's not as if I can throttle you in here!'

And then to Renee's absolute astonishment, she burst into tears.

'Alfie's, I presume?' she cried, wiping the corner of her eye.

Renee nodded. 'It happened the night before he left.'

'That's one hell of a going-away present!' Nell quipped through her tears.

And then they were both laughing, laughing and crying at the same time, as their fingers found each other's over the tabletop.

'You're not cross?' Renee wept.

'Oh, what good would it do now?' Nell replied. 'I'm upset you felt you couldn't tell me.'

'I tried, Mum, remember in my bedroom, just before . . .'

'Julia got the letter about her husband,' she groaned. 'I remember.'

She shook her head despairingly, her fingers tightening round Renee's.

'No touching,' barked a passing prison guard. Nell put her hands in her lap and sighed.

'I've been so bloody busy looking after the women of the Shoot, I neglected to look after the needs of my own children. I see that now,' she whispered. 'I've had a lot of thinking time in here.'

'No, Mum,' Renee implored. 'This ain't your fault. I see clearly now too, what you do for the women in our neighbourhood . . .' her voice trailed off uncomfortably.

'Lily helped me to understand.'

Nell raised her eyebrows.

'Well there's a turn-up.'

She swallowed hard.

'So, what you gonna do? Have you been in touch with a mother and . . .'

'Don't, Mum,' she interrupted. 'I want to keep this baby. Be a proper mum. It's all I've got left of Alfie. I'll be a good mum, I swear it . . .'

Renee thought she'd done all the crying that could be done in the privacy of her bedroom, but it seemed that her tears were an illimitable reservoir, as yet more flooded her cheeks.

Nell's face softened.

'Oh, my darlin' girl, do you have any idea how society will treat you? You'll be an outcast, nothing but a cheap tart. Remember Betty Maguire, disowned by her father? You'll be turned out of rooms, kicked out of jobs when people discover the truth. Trust me. It's no life for a little 'un.'

'I'm not daft, Mum, I know that. But I'll do whatever it takes, move away, start over with a story, I don't care, but please . . . Please help me find a way.' She gazed across the crowded prison room at her mother, her cornflower blue eyes begging her.

'Help me to keep my baby.'

The irony of her words was not lost on either of them.

Nell exhaled deeply, a sound that seemed to reach her bones.

'Very well. I can't make no promises, but I'll try. Since Dunkirk, things have changed. There may be some sympathy for your predicament if you can prove you were to wed.'

Her words gave Renee a small feather of hope.

'Really?'

'Like I say, I can't make no promises, but when I get out of here, we'll try to find a way out of this mess. Together!'

The hooter sounded, chairs scraped back and impulsively Renee grabbed both her mother's hands, held them to her lips and kissed them.

'I love you so much, Mum.'

Renee left feeling happier and lighter than she had done in months. Outside, she leant against the high prison gate, trailed her fingers down her tummy and smiled.

'I won't let you down, my little one. I know you ain't got a daddy, but I've got enough love for us both. You'll see.'

24

Lily

Ten a.m. Monday, 19th August 1940. The Old Bailey.

Lily nervously plucked at the hem of her skirt as she gazed round the heaving public gallery. It felt like all of Stratford and beyond had piled in to witness her mother's case. A simmering tension rose up from the long wooden benches, as people shuffled and cleared throats.

Only her father – at work, and Frankie – at school – were missing, thank goodness. There was no way Frankie should have to witness any of this. The story they'd told him was that Nell was away visiting a sick relative in Suffolk. Lily hated lying to him, but he was too young to understand.

Lily had dressed as smartly as she could in a bid to make the Gunns look respectable, teaming a crisp white shirt with a pussy-cat bow at the neck with a tailored waistcoat and skirt, topping the look off with a neat little angora pillbox hat. She glanced at Renee sitting to her left, bundled up in a coat despite the heat, anxiously picking at a flap of skin by her thumbnail.

'Don't worry, Renee,' she whispered. 'We have to remember what Mum's solicitor said, a prison sentence is highly unlikely.'

'But what if they came back to the graveyard when we weren't there?' Renee muttered. 'What if they've found evidence? That would be enough to put Mum away for a long time surely?'

Lily lowered her voice. 'Look, I had a chat with Billy on Saturday, when you were visiting Mum, strictly off the record as I think he felt bad for arresting her. Anyway, he told me that there are no more plans to search the grave-yard. I think it was more a show of strength on the police's part to deter any more women from doing the same. Besides, they didn't come out of it very well, did they? Added to which, Mum's pleading guilty so it's not really worth the manpower.'

Renee lapsed into silence and stared down at the dock.

Lily knew it was important to stay calm. It was an open-and-shut case, so the solicitor had assured them; plead guilty, come away with a conditional discharge, suspended sentence and a fine. The Offences against the Person Act, 1861, carried with it a maximum penalty of imprisonment for life, but in practice, this rarely happened. Except, once the particulars of the case were dealt with, it was obvious that the prosecutor was out for some sport.

'Knitting needle Nora.' The pompous balding man spoke as if he were treading the boards and was clearly enjoying speaking to such a packed courtroom, drawing out his words like an old pantomime dame.

'Actually,' Nell snapped, 'I don't use knitting needles, slip-pery elm, pennyroyal or any of them dangerous methods. I've very particular about hygiene and cleanliness.' She folded her arms.

'Never had no trouble, never sent no one to hospital.'

'Actually, I was referring to the name as a colloquialism. Isn't that how they refer to women of your ilk?'

Nell's eyes narrowed.

'My ilk? And what might you mean by that?'

'You're very combative, Mrs Gunn.'

'So would you be if you lived down the Shoot.'

He shrugged and leant nonchalantly against the dock. 'I wouldn't know, Mrs Gunn, I'm from Putney.'

And suddenly, he was up and prowling theatrically in front of the judge.

'War is good for business, Mrs Gunn, I should imagine.'

'Is that a question or a statement?' she replied crisply.

'Morality is very elastic at the moment . . .'

'What's he on about?' Renee hissed.

'Ssh, Renee, just listen,' Lily replied.

'I should imagine you are very busy.'

'Look here,' Nell snapped, finally losing her cool, 'it's like how I've said all along. The only women I help are those that have big families and can't afford another mouth to feed. Do you know any men who use preventatives? 'Cause they don't round our way . . .

'And another thing,' she said, rising to her feet and drumming her fingers on the edge of the dock, 'I object to the use of the word "business". I don't take so much as a ha'penny for helping women. Strikes me as there ought to be a law, so that doctors can help in a proper fashion. You know, make it lawful. It'd save so much shame and heartbreak. After all, having a baby ain't a crime.'

Her gaze flickered up to the public gallery.

'Sit down, please, and save us the pontificating, Mrs Gunn,' said the judge wearily, before returning to the prosecutor.

'Let's just get on with it, shall we?'

'I apologise, your honour,' he replied obsequiously, before turning back to Nell.

'If you don't take money then what motivates you to help the women of the Homefront, Mrs Gunn?'

Here she laughed and shook her head derisively.

'With respect, sir, you ain't got a clue what it's like to be a woman round my way, in East London. The Homefront ain't all knitting and queuing.'

A ripple of laughter went round the courtroom, and journalists on the press bench, loving a juicy quote, scribbled away in their notebooks.

'Up West, there are professionals, people in Harley Street so I've heard tell, who'll charge rich women a hundred guineas, and chemists in Soho who flog con tricks. I believe in actually *helping* women who'd more than likely be dead if they birthed another nipper.

'I helped a woman recently with nine kids all under ten. Her husband gave her another baby at the same time as a fractured jaw.'

A horrified hush fell over the courtroom and Mrs Barnett's face immediately flashed into Lily's mind, her mother's flight through the frozen night . . .

'If she had birthed that baby, I doubt very much she'd be here now,' she went on, trying to contain the tremor in her voice. 'I've seen hardship and poverty of the likes you cannot imagine, sir. I've seen good women die from rearing too many children. Bloody useless husbands who spend all the housekeeping on beer and bets. Women's wages'll only spread to so many mouths, you know . . .'

Nell's voice cracked. Recovering herself, she breathed in deeply and jutted out her chin.

'So you ask what motivates me to help other women. Solidarity! That's what keeps women alive round my way.'

'How very noble of you, Mrs Gunn,' the prosecutor replied witheringly, 'except not all are older woman, are they? Prosecution calls to the stand Mrs Rogers.'

An audible intake of breath went round the courtroom as Nan's mum stood up from the bench where she'd been sitting unseen.

Renee stared at Lily, horrified.

'Can you please tell us your connection to the defendant?' he asked.

'I used to be her neighbour. I have nothing against Mrs Gunn, but I do feel when called upon to tell the truth I must,' said Mrs Rogers nervously.

'What was the occasion that required you to seek the services of Mrs Gunn?'

Mrs Rogers, wearing the same taxidermy hat she'd worn to her daughter's wedding, closed her eyes briefly.

'My daughter was fifteen when she got in trouble with a boy. I visited Mrs Gunn to ask for her help, and she obliged.'

'How could you?' Nell yelled from the dock. 'You begged me to save your daughter's name, day after day, you was sobbing on my doorstep, pleading with me until I cracked. I'd have to have had a heart of stone not to help . . .'

'Mrs Gunn, I will not warn you again,' said the judge.

'Please continue,' prompted the prosecutor.

'I didn't know what else to do, where else to go,' Mrs Rogers wept, twisting a handkerchief feverishly between her fingers. 'The boy refused to stand by her. My late husband would've turned her out on the street, so I knocked on Mrs Gunn's door and well, she sorted it. She's well known locally for sorting out problems.'

Still crying, Mrs Rogers stood down and the court was adjourned until the afternoon for sentencing.

Renee turned to Lily, wide-eyed with disbelief.

'That girl in the kitchen, when you interrupted Mum . . . That was Nan, wasn't it?'

Lily nodded. There was little point denying it now Mrs Rogers had just spilled the beans in a court of law.

'I'm assuming it was Jimmy's?'

Lily nodded again.

'After it was all over, he apparently visited Mum, offered

a ten-bob note for her silence. You can imagine where she told him to shove it. Three years later, Jimmy asked Nan back out, would you believe?' She laughed bitterly. 'Trust me, if that pregnancy had gone ahead, you wouldn't have seen him for dust.'

'But why did Nan take him back?' Renee asked.

'Why else? She loved him of course,' Lily sighed. 'Though I must admit, I was surprised when I returned to Stratford and discovered she was actually marrying him.' Lily shook her head and felt an immense wave of anger swamp her. 'He's vermin. The women of Stratford are better off now he's dead.'

Calm yourself, Lily, she told herself, but Renee seemed not to have noticed her uncharacteristic outburst.

'That bastard,' Renee breathed. 'I knew he was a rotten sod, but this . . . How could he do that to Nan?'

Suddenly, so much made sense to Renee. Nan's rage and bitterness, her fury at discovering Jimmy had fathered two illegitimate children after forcing her to abort hers. The man she had loved had betrayed her time and time again.

'Poor Nan,' she sighed. 'She chucked her lot in with the wrong man.'

'It happens,' Lily replied. 'If there was any justice in the world, he'd be in the dock now, not Mum.'

One hour later, Renee and Lily held hands as court resumed for sentencing.

'All rise for His Honour, Judge Montague.'

Lily found herself scarcely breathing as she and the rest of the courtroom stood up.

Once seated, the judge summed up the day's proceedings and thanked the witnesses, before turning to Nell.

'I take into account, Mrs Gunn, your unblemished record, your excellent character references and your guilty plea. I also applaud, to some degree, your desire to see a change in the law. You are not a woman without compassion and I believe you when you say you were motivated by a sense of female solidarity . . .'

Lily felt Renee's fingers tighten round hers and shot her an encouraging smile.

'But the fact remains, we are fighting a war and surely we should be preserving the sanctity of life. The law is not yours simply to take into your own hands. I sentence you to nine months imprisonment and a £50 fine.'

Renee's scream was gut-wrenching as she leapt to her feet.

'You can't lock up my mum!' she cried, her voice echoing throughout the courtroom.

'Sit down, Renee, this isn't helping,' Lily begged, pulling her back down.

Nell's face was a picture of scorn.

'Oh, I get it. It's one law for the rich and another for the poor, ain't it? Bet none of your Harley Street doctors are behind bars. Let's pick on the poor working-class woman and make an example of her, shall we? Well, this is a fine day for justice.'

'You tell him, Auntie!' screamed a voice, as hisses and catcalls rang out.

'Order! Order in court! I must have order in my courtroom!' bellowed the judge. But Nell Gunn wasn't done.

'Men make and break laws, start wars, swing their dicks about and get girls in trouble!' she yelled, jabbing a finger at her chest. 'And it's women like me who mop up the mess. It's always the women what suffer.'

The judge turned puce.

'Take her down!' he bellowed.

'Women are weary with childbirth in this country, your honour, you hear me. They are weary . . .'

Her voice echoed in the shattered silence of the courtroom as she was wrenched from the dock and dragged down to the cells.

The girls got the bus back to Stratford in silence, both stuck in the lonely churn of their own thoughts. They disembarked at the Broadway and walked back to the Shoot. At the door, Lily turned to Renee.

'Oh God. How are we going to break this to Frankie? He'll be back from school by now.'

Renee stumbled back from the doorstep, shaking her head.

'I'm sorry, Lil. I-I can't . . . I need some time to think.' She wheeled round and ran back in the direction they'd just come from.

'Renee, where are you going?' Lily called after her. 'Renee!'

But her sister had disappeared from sight. Lily thought about going after her, but she had more pressing problems to deal with, like how on earth she was going to tell Frankie his mum wasn't coming home for nine months.

Their own home was empty, but Lily thought she could hear faint laughter coming from Julia's.

Without a word, she pushed open the door to the Orwells' and tiptoed up the passage. It was such a happy scene she scarcely wanted to disrupt it, so she watched in silence from the doorway.

Esther was running something up on her mother's Singer sewing machine, a smile playing over her face as she gently teased some white silk under the needle. Walter and Frankie were engrossed in a board game at the table and Julia was at the stove stirring a pot of something warm and spicy-smelling for tea.

Walter sat bolt upright in his seat.

'A-ha! Watch and learn, Frankie my boy, watch and learn!'

he grinned, laying out his Scrabble pieces. 'Rifle. With a double word score, I make that sixteen. Top that.'

Wordlessly, Frankie laid out his letters.

'Syzygy,' Walter read out puzzled, before ruffling his hair. 'Silly boy, that ain't even a word.'

'Syzygy,' repeated Frankie tonelessly. 'An alignment of three celestial bodies. With the Z on a double letter score square and the Y on a triple word, I make that one hundred and five points.'

Walter stared in disbelief, while Julia and Esther exchanged an amused smile.

Esther suddenly caught sight of Lily at the doorway. Her foot flew off the treadle and she stood up.

'Lily! What news?'

Without taking her coat off, Lily sat down next to Frankie.

'Frankie, sweetheart,' Lily began, 'Mum's had to stay in, er, Suffolk for a bit longer.'

His face crumpled.

'Can I visit her?'

'I'm afraid that won't be possible.'

'Why?'

Lily looked to Julia.

'Tell him the truth,' she said softly.

Lily closed her hands over Frankie's.

'Mum's in prison for doing something the police don't like. But she's still your mum, she's not a bad woman.'

The silence spun out and you could almost hear the tick of Frankie's thoughts.

'Mum's appealing her sentence, so there's a chance she'll be home sooner than we think,' Lily added.

Frankie stared at them, his face an opaque mask.

Suddenly he leapt to his feet and, in one swipe, sent the Scrabble board flying.

'What are you talking about?' he yelled as Scrabble pieces

skidded over the lino floor. 'People who go to prison are bad. That's what Mum always says. You're all liars. Who will look after me?'

'Frankie, you've still got me and Renee,' she said softly.

'I don't want you, I only want my mum!'

He ran from the house, slamming the door with a terrific bang.

'Leave him,' urged Julia, catching Lily's sleeve as she made to follow.'

'But what if he runs away again?' Lily protested.

'Trust me, I know Frankie. He needs time to digest this, if you go after him now you'll only make it worse.'

Exhausted, Lily slumped back at the table feeling like a complete failure. The terrible secrets she had carried for so long about Nan's past and her mother's hidden activities were now finally out in the open and their bitter repercussions would be felt down the years. But she wondered if any of them could survive the last and most explosive secret of all.

25

Renee

Renee leant against the wall to Yardley's, out of breath. Since leaving Lily, she had run all the way here before she could change her mind. A tremor of blind fear ran through her at the thought of what she was about to do. With her mum in prison, and her only door to salvation now firmly shut, she really only had one route left open.

She hurried across the yard. The evening air was sticky sweet, laced with the threat of a thunderstorm. It was late. By the time they'd made it back from court, the day shift had already finished and now the night shift was clocking on.

'Blimey, Renee, volunteering for a night shift! You feeling all right, girl?' the security guard joked, holding the back of his hand to her forehead.

'Yeah yeah, Bert, peachy,' she joked.

As she walked up to the offices, she saw the expressions, heard the whispers.

Pausing outside Miss Rayson's door, she drew in a deep breath and knocked.

'Come in.' She'd known the conscientious welfare worker would still be there, working late.

'Renee,' she said, her voice full of gentle concern. 'Sit down, I was going to speak with you tomorrow morning. You beat me to it.'

She came round from her side of the desk, and placed a hand on Renee's shoulder.

'Please tell me how your mother's court case went today. I'm so pleased you decided to go after all . . .'

'She's been jailed for nine months,' Renee blurted, powerless to stop the tears. 'And you were right, I am carrying a baby. Alfie's.'

She was crying so hard now her words came out in between big choking sobs.

'I'm worried if I tell my dad he'll boot me out. Like Betty Maguire's dad did . . . Please help me.'

Silence hung between them, before the older lady removed her spectacles and wearily rubbed her eyes.

'I ain't no tart, Miss Rayson,' Renee wept. 'I loved him.'

Replacing her glasses, the welfare worker looked back with genuine concern in her eyes.

'I know that, Renee,' she sighed, passing her an embroidered handkerchief from her blouse sleeve. 'I know I must look like some dried-up old stick to you girls, but believe me when I say, I know what it's like to be young and in love.'

'Do you, miss?'

'Yes. I lost my sweetheart in the last war. Bill never came home from France.'

'Oh miss, I'm sorry I didn't realise . . .'

Miss Rayson smiled sardonically.

'My dear. It is a universally acknowledged truth that the younger generation imagine that no one older than themselves can possibly have had their heart broken.'

She shook herself: 'None of which, of course, changes the irrefutable facts of your situation.'

Suddenly she was all business again, reaching for the phone on her desk.

'You're not the first Yardley girl to go to this place,' she mouthed as she waited for the operator to connect her, 'and I dare say you shan't be the last.'

Cold hard despair seeped through Renee's veins as Miss Rayson spoke quietly on the phone to her friend who ran St Theresa's Home for Unmarried Mothers in Bexhill.

Twenty minutes later the plans were in place and Renee felt a sense of unreality. There was no turning back now.

'It's one of the better places, Renee. Girls are treated with compassion and discretion. They will arrange everything for the adoption.'

'How long?'

'Three weeks, sooner if possible. I'll need to arrange a petrol voucher for the company car.'

'No, I mean, how long will I have with my baby before he's taken?'

'Six weeks after the birth, give or take,' she replied quietly. 'They will want you to recover from the birth and breast-feed.'

Renee nodded numbly, imagining her baby at her breast, the little life she already loved fiercely, the moment when she would have to hand him over to a stranger.

'Believe me, Renee, this is for the best,' Miss Rayson went on. 'There are many young childless couples who will be able to give your baby the secure home you can't offer.'

Renee nodded, speechless.

'Until then, I think it's best if I transfer you to the box factory on the High Street. I suggest you keep a low profile and tell your sister.'

Renee thanked her, then stumbled from her office, straight into Nan, who was waiting outside to speak with Miss Rayson.

'Nan.'

'Renee.'

They spoke at the same time.

Renee knew she should despise her old friend for helping to lock up her mother, but now she knew the full story, she saw the truth was more nuanced. Poor Nan. She had been forced to give up her own child, and rightly or wrongly, her own mother had had a hand in it.

'I'm so sorry, Nan,' she said.

'So am I, Renee,' she replied coldly. 'Sorry that I ever allowed my mother to talk me into seeing yours . . . Oh yeah, that's right. Turn on the tears now, why don't you? But I'm glad you finally know the truth about your mother. Nell Gunn ain't the saint everyone makes her out to be, she's just a common old knitting needle Nora.'

Renee felt her words like a blow.

'Now, if you'll excuse me, I need to see Miss Rayson.'

Nan paused at the door, her eyes flaming with hatred.

'Oh, and one more thing. Don't think I ain't guessed you've got a dirty little secret of your own. People are already starting to talk. You breathe one word about the fire and I'll make sure *everyone* at Yardley's knows what you're hiding. You'll never be able to show your face in Stratford again.'

'Goodbye, Nan,' Renee replied, walking away with as much dignity as she could muster.

Back at the Shoot, she walked into the darkened kitchen and shut the door softly behind her.

'You're back, thank goodness,' sighed Lily, looking up from her cup of tea. 'Where did you go?'

'There are things I need to explain, Lily. I'm sorry, I've been keeping something from you.'

Lily's face paled. 'Really? Because you don't think this day has been dramatic enough already!'

'Where's Dad?'

'The pub. He's already read me the riot act about how I'm now the woman of the house.'

'Frankie?'

'In bed. He finally came home, thank God.'

'Follow me,' Renee said in a hollow voice.

Inside their shared bedroom, Renee slowly unbuttoned her coat.

'What is it, Renee? You're scaring me.'

Without another word, Renee began undoing the tiny mother of pearl buttons on her dress, her fingers trembling so much she fumbled.

Her dress slithered to the floor with a sigh.

Next she pulled down the elasticated waist of her cami-knickers and unfastened the safety pin securing the bandages she had kept tightly woven around her growing abdomen.

Lily's eyes widened as the bandages unravelled and the truth was revealed.

As they too fell away, Renee stood naked before her sister, and splayed her fingers on the pale flesh of her tummy. Her secret was laid bare and she hadn't even breathed a word. Outside, the thunderstorm that had been brewing all afternoon finally broke. Jagged forks of lightning flashed across the walls, followed by deep rolling thunder.

'Of course, oh why did I not guess?' Lily moaned. 'Give me some time to think—'

'It's all right, Lil. I can't put you in that situation, I never wanted to. I can tell Dad in all honesty you never knew. Miss Rayson's sorting it. She's booked me in to a mother and baby home and is moving me to the box factory until it . . . it's . . .' She closed her eyes, '. . . time.'

Her sister crossed the divide between them and hugged her tightly. So tightly, Renee could feel her heart thudding like a fist, but her words were calm and measured.

'A clean break, sis. Trust me, it's for the best.'

Outside, the heavens opened, the rain overflowing the gutters and splashing onto the cobbles below. Renee felt as if even the sky were weeping for the hopelessness of her situation.

PART THREE

Wednesday, 4th September 1940

26

Esther

Esther had got into the habit of going in to help Lily and Renee every morning before work. Two and a half weeks since their mother was sentenced and the Gunn girls were drowning.

'Morning,' she said breezily, walking into the kitchen to find Lily stirring a pot of porridge with one hand and attempting to clear crumbs from the side with the other. The kettle was whistling so loudly, the lid was close to blowing off.

'How did she do it all?' Lily muttered.

'The hand that rocks the cradle rules the world,' Esther grinned, taking the kettle off the hob and reaching for the teapot. 'My mum reckons that once you have children you develop the ability to do two things at once.'

'I don't know about that,' Lily replied. 'But I do know running a home and working is downright exhausting.' She glanced at her wristwatch. 'Frankie, get down here now and have your breakfast!' she hollered up the stairs. 'You're going to be late for school.'

She turned to Esther.

'I still haven't pressed his school uniform, made my sandwiches to take to work, or sent Snowball out his cup of tea.'

A knock at the door sent Lily one foot closer to the edge.

'Oh, for pity's sake.'

'I'll go,' Renee called, picking her way carefully down the stairs, clutching her tummy.

'For the love of God, Renee, how many times? No!' she bellowed. Seeing Renee's crushed expression, she took a deep breath and started again.

'Sorry, sis, but you heard what Dad said. You're to keep a low profile until you leave. I'll go.'

Esther squeezed Renee's arm as Lily went to get the door.

'Sit down, Renee. I'll bring you a cup of tea.'

'Thanks, Est,' she said gratefully, lowering herself down carefully into the chair.

'Back?' Esther asked sympathetically.

'And lungs and legs. I'm out of breath, my whole body is one big stretch mark and I need to take a flamin' piss every two minutes, but apart from that, Est, I'm tickety-bloody-boo, thanks for asking.'

Esther smiled and massaged her shoulders gently.

'You're going to be just fine,' she soothed.

'I don't know if I can do it, Est,' she blurted. 'The birth, breastfeeding, and then . . .'

'You'll be a smashing mum, Renee,' Esther insisted, kissing the top of her head.

Renee's eyes misted over.

'For six weeks maybe.'

'You don't deserve this,' Esther said, wishing there was something she could do to assuage Renee's pain.

'Oh don't be nice to me, I'm crying every two minutes as it is. But thank you, for actually talking to me about it. Lily hardly dares to bring it up for fear of upsetting me and my Dad's only just come down off the ceiling.'

'It needs to be said, Renee,' Esther insisted. 'What you're doing, well, I think it makes you the bravest person I know.'

Renee squeezed her hand gratefully and Esther ached for her. In four days' time, she was to leave and then her life would never be the same again.

Frankie came down the stairs, just as Lily reappeared in the kitchen.

'It was Mrs Povey seeing if I could cast an eye over the accounts for the butcher's later, apparently Mum's being doing it . . . oh hello, sweetheart, you're up, let me get you some porridge,' Lily smiled.

Frankie said nothing, and when the bowl was placed in front of him, he sat in a sullen silence.

A whistle from the backyard signalled the arrival of Pat, fresh from his ablutions.

'Where's me breakfast, Lil?' he demanded, tossing his wet towel over the back of a chair. Esther realised she wasn't the only one who tensed the moment Pat Gunn walked into the room. Frankie barely moved a muscle, keeping his eyes downcast at all times. Her mother had told her not to judge Pat Gunn, but Esther couldn't help it. He never lifted a finger round the house to help the girls, expected to be fed like a fighting cock and the way he treated Frankie was despicable.

The remains of a black eye were fading from Frankie's face and he'd developed a tic. Every so often, his face twitched involuntarily. The boxing, the cold and muddy runs over the Wanstead flats, being forced to join in with the Bricky Kids' games. His father's ham-fisted method of making a man out of his only son was leaching the life out of him.

Lily set down a plate with the only egg and bacon in the house in front of her father.

He ate greedily, pausing to point his knife at Frankie.

'I'm collecting you from school later and taking you down my club. You're getting in that ring again, boy.'

'But Mum says he's not to box,' Lily protested.

Esther had heard of a boxing ring down the Mile End

Road where boys as young as eight were paid if they drew blood from an opponent. Lily had told her that Nell Gunn, tough as she was, shied from the blooding of young boys.

'I don't give a tinker's toss,' Pat grunted.

'She'll go barmy . . .' Renee warned.

'Just as well she ain't here then.'

And with that, he mopped up the remains of his egg with a bit of fried bread, chewed noisily, before jamming a Woodbine in the corner of his mouth.

'Things are going to change round here and not before time.'

The door slammed behind him and even the house seemed to sigh in relief.

'More tea anyone?' Esther said brightly, reaching for the pot.

'Can you believe I've been back in Stratford exactly one year today?' Lily said, holding her cup out to Esther. 'How about I bring us home some pie and mash this evening on my way back from work?'

'That'd be nice, Lil, thanks,' said Renee with a wan smile, 'it's so boring sitting in on my own day after day. I've read every copy of *Woman's Own* and all your *Vogue*s cover to cover. I'm even looking forward to a game of Frankie's Scrabble, something I never thought I'd hear myself say.'

'That's sorted then. Oh, dash it, I forgot,' Lily groaned, closing her eyes. 'I'm on the fire-watching rota after work, so Lord knows what time I'll be back.'

The Germans had dropped a bomb on the Beckton Road four nights back. It was the first time they had picked out a civilian area, as opposed to RAF targets, shipping and ports. Fearing a taste of things to come, Yardley had doubled fire-watching shifts among their workers.

'Sorry, it's so busy at work,' Lily said weakly. 'You know what it's like, Renee.'

'Actually, how would I?' she snapped. 'I'm a useless mouth now, ain't I?'

A miserable silence drenched the table.

'I actually thought I'd get to spend some time with you, before I get banished to the naughty girls' home,' Renee wept, standing up as quickly as her bump would allow.

'Renee . . . Your breakfast,' Lily called after her sister, but Renee's footsteps were followed by the thud of her bedroom door.

'Leave her,' Esther counselled. 'She needs time to come to terms with what's happening.'

Crestfallen, Lily turned to Frankie, who was locked away in his own world, oblivious to his sister's outburst. When he'd finished systematically picking the last lump out of his porridge, he looked up.

'Please can I go to Julia's after school today?' he asked. He had asked the same question every day since his father had banned contact with her. And every day was the same answer.

'I'm sorry, Frankie, you know Dad doesn't like it. He prefers . . .'

'I know, he prefers me to learn to hit people than read books.'

'I can't go against Dad, you know that,' Lily replied, imploring him to understand, when truth be told, she didn't herself.

His face crumpled, as tears streamed down his pale cheeks.

'I hate school and the teachers hate me. I hate Dad's club, the boys there hurt me.' His face twitched.

'Please, I beg of you, Lily. Let me go to Julia's. I'll be good, I promise.'

Lily heaved a sigh.

'Why not let him?' Esther urged. Anyone could see the poor boy was hanging by the thinnest of threads. He needed to be around a nurturing woman, someone who would feed him nourishing food, allow him to draw and read in peace and safety.

'Very well,' Lily relented. 'I'll tell Julia you're to go to hers after school and I'll make up a cover story for Dad.'

'What'll you say?' he asked worriedly.

'Leave it with me. I'll think of something.'

His eyebrows drew together in a deep furrow and something approaching a smile passed his face.

'You owe me, Little Prof,' she grinned.

'How much?' he asked gravely.

'No, no, I don't mean literally, Frankie.'

'Oh, I see, you were speaking figuratively,' he replied, and gathering his school satchel and cap, he left for school. He left without so much as a goodbye, but Frankie Gunn wasn't one for small talk.

Lily and Esther watched as he crossed the square, waving to Snowball and jumping out of his skin as a pigeon flew down low in front of him.

'He's such a strange little boy,' Lily mused out loud.

'Or maybe,' ventured Esther, 'we're all strange to him?'

'Listen,' she went on, 'let me take out Snowball his breakfast, while you clear up here. There's something I need to give him.'

'Righto,' Lily replied. 'And thanks again, Esther. I honestly don't know how I'd cope without you.'

Snowball was sitting on the steps of the church, hunched over and staring aimlessly at the sky.

'Hello Miss Esther,' he smiled when he saw her approach.

Esther tried her hardest to imagine what this man was like before life got a hold of him. Shell shock from the first war, so folk said, but he had never divulged what had driven him to the streets, and now his homelessness was a fact of life around the Lane.

The state didn't look after him, he was a forgotten man,

but not to the women of the Shoot, who in truth were probably keeping him alive.

'Here's a cup of tea and some bread and marge,' she said, placing down the enamel bowl and cup on the steps next to him. 'And I made you something.'

In her hands she held a drawstring bag, lined with white silk and a pillow, with a white silk pillowcase.

'I got lucky and was given some parachute silk recently, and so I thought I'd make you a bag, to put your bits in and this cushion to make life a bit comfier. I see you sleeping with your head on a bundle of newspaper and well, that can't be very nice.'

He stared long and hard at her and Esther began to feel uncomfortable. Had she insulted him?

A tear broke and tracked down his cheek, washing a runnel through the filth.

'Th-thank you,' he said eventually. 'I must be the only tramp in East London with a silk pillow.'

She heard Lily calling for her from the house.

'I better go to work. Bye.'

'Bless you, my dear,' he called after her, staring in disbelief at his new possessions, tracing his fingers back and forth over the silk pillow.

Esther and Lily walked to work their arms linked, chattering about the day ahead, but Esther couldn't stop thinking about Renee.

'It's so awful, isn't it, Lily? Renee would be the most wonderful mother. Surely there must be something we can do to help her?'

She felt Lily's arm stiffen.

'There really isn't, Esther,' she said. 'I agree, it will be painful, but she needs to put the needs of her child first. Being adopted into a loving and secure family, with a mother *and* a father, will give that little life the best start.'

Esther wasn't so sure, but she knew she'd already over-stepped the line.

'Now, don't forget your special meeting today,' Lily said, swiftly changing the subject.

Mid-morning at the factory, and Esther was thrilled to have been invited into a senior management meeting in the Yardley office boardroom so the bosses could meet and thank the girl who bravely faced down the Luftwaffe pilot.

Sitting opposite Mr Lavender, and the other bigwigs, and between Lily, Nan and Miss Rayson, she felt terrifically nervous.

'Miss Orwell. This is Mr Hesse, head of Export Sales, who's currently in charge of Home Trade Rationing,' announced the Managing Director, gesturing to a suited man to his right, 'and Mr Seager, overall factory foreman, who, like yourself, has kept this factory going with imperturbability and a flair for improvisation.'

'I'm not sure about that,' she flushed.

'You're too modest,' he went on, steepling his fingers together and gazing at her curiously.

'How old are you?'

'Sixteen, sir.'

'Gracious, you're a child.'

'The average age of most of our female employees is now significantly younger than this time last year, sir,' interjected Miss Rayson.

'Well, we are really most grateful to you for your bravery. It's not many who can say they've stared down the barrel of a Jerry shotgun. Your mother and father must be so proud of you.'

'My mother is, sir.'

'Miss Orwell's father died earlier this year from tuberculosis, whilst imprisoned in a ghetto,' Miss Rayson interjected.

His face fell.

'Oh, my dear,' he murmured, looking aghast. 'That is terrible. One wonders where this war will end . . .'

'Indeed,' mused Miss Rayson. 'Miss Orwell has also been one of our most enthusiastic volunteers in the workforce, giving up many hours for factory ARP and fire-watching duties, and has also suggested we start to knit comforters for the troops and a Spitfire Fund.'

'Excellent ideas! Once again, I applaud your selflessness,' the Managing Director nodded.

'It's not really selfless, though, sir,' Esther replied. 'There is much joy to be derived from knowing you are making an important contribution to the lives of others.' Her mind sauntered to Snowball.

'However small.'

'How old did you say you were again?' he murmured.

'Sixteen, sir.'

'Well, it gives *me* great joy to give you these.'

He removed a fancy-looking package from his briefcase and slid it over the table.

'A few little treats, as a token of our thanks from everyone at the Yardley family. I know how you girls all love our Bond Street perfume. We should also like to invite you to our Bond Street salon for a makeover.'

'I'm very grateful to you, to you all, in fact, in my new adopted country, but I cannot accept these gifts,' Esther replied.

'Why ever not?' questioned Miss Rayson.

'I heard the German pilot died later in hospital, from the injuries caused by the crash. Please, sir, I don't feel comfortable taking gifts when a man has died. He was just a boy himself, not much older than me. I don't expect he wanted this war any more than we do.'

Silence fell over the office boardroom.

'From the mouths of babes . . .' murmured the Managing Director, astonished at Esther's refusal of the gifts. 'You're right, of course. But allow me to say this. You, young lady, are just the sort of person Yardley needs. I predict big things for you in this company. That is, of course, should you decide to stay on in your new adopted country once this war is over.'

'Israel is my biological mother, but Britain is now my adopted father,' Esther replied, humbly. 'So yes, I think I shall be staying on, if I'm allowed.'

She didn't dare voice it in this boardroom, but a certain young man may also have had something to do with that decision.

Lily threw Esther a delighted grin and reached over to squeeze her hand.

The Managing Director continued with the day's business, briefing Miss Rayson and Lily about the changes in their marketing strategy towards lipsticks and cosmetics.

'You'll notice that from now on, we shall be launching new marketing slogans, which are already being unrolled in women's periodicals and national press.'

He slid over an advert in *Woman & Beauty* magazine with a large photo of a horrified young woman.

'*What! No Lipstick?*' Lily read the title out loud. 'Is that really an advert?'

'There's no point trying to gloss over the reality,' explained the Managing Director. 'By reminding people that economy in the use of their beauty preparations is just one more sacrifice they must make for our war effort, we will reassure women that we've been dedicated to the service of beauty for many generations through wars and crises. Use carefully those little refinements you can still enjoy, choose well when you must replace, and remember, quality *is* economy. With that in mind, we are bringing in lipstick refills, 1/10 in all shades, and a refill for Yardley Talc, 2/6.'

'Quality is economy,' repeated Miss Rayson. 'That is very clever, sir. We shall ensure the girls all know this slogan as they help to produce and pack these refills.'

'Thank you, now any other business?'

'I've a question, sir,' piped up Nan.

'Go ahead.'

Esther noticed a sly look pass over Nan's face.

'The winner of last December's Miss Homefront competition has left Yardley, so I believe that means there's a vacancy for the crown.'

Lily threw Nan a murderous glare.

'Has she?' asked the Director. 'What, that rather sparky blonde girl in the lipstick room? You didn't tell me that, Miss Rayson?'

Miss Rayson cleared her throat.

'Yes, she is absent, but only temporarily, we hope, sir. She is, um, suffering with her glands, so I've sent her to our convalescence home in Bexhill.'

'That is a relief, please pass on our best wishes, and tell her I do hope she's back in the saddle soon. But Mrs Connor here is right. It's important for morale that we have a Miss Homefront. Why don't we hold a new competition on Saturday afternoon when production's finished?'

'But that's just three days away,' exclaimed Miss Rayson.

'The sooner the better. Invite the *Stratford Express* too, it'll give us a chance to unroll our new slogan in the press.'

With business concluded, management swept from the room, leaving Esther alone with Miss Rayson, Lily and Nan.

'In future, Nan, I'll thank you to leave staff welfare issues to me,' Miss Rayson snapped as she gathered together her papers. Lily was looking at Nan like she wanted to throttle her.

'I'm so sorry, Miss Rayson,' Nan apologised wide-eyed. 'But with Renee now . . .' she paused, 'suffering with her

glands, it hardly seems fair not to give another girl the chance
to be Miss Homefront.'

Nan smiled sweetly as she patted her turban.

'It's funny, isn't it?'

'What is?' Lily demanded.

'The lipstick tallies are all adding up now. Our little lipstick
thief seems to be taking a break too.'

27

Renee

Sitting in just her brassiere and cami-knickers, Renee peered out from the bars of her cell. All right, maybe cell was a slight exaggeration, but the criss-crossed anti-blast tape that covered her bedroom window gave her the distinct feeling *she* was the one locked up, not her mother!

Banished from the box factory after her father discovered she was expecting, and under house arrest until the Yardley works car came for her on Sunday morning, her fate was sealed. The spectre of St Theresa's Home for Unmarried Mothers loomed large.

Grief was the only way she could describe the sensation of her impending loss; the cold, hard panic that slammed into her dreams, wrenching her from sleep as another morning dawned over Stratford, inching her closer to the separation from her child. Her thoughts had begun to crystallise in her mind, always returning to the same point.

This baby – Alfie's flesh and blood – was the only thing she loved purely and unselfishly. She had taken to talking to her bump, apologising to appease her tearing guilt at what she knew lay ahead.

'I can't wait to meet you, little one,' she whispered, laying the flat of her palm on the cool silk of her skin. It was so hot in these late summer days, sitting in her underwear in the privacy of her bedroom was the only way she could get comfortable.

'I'm only allowed to be your mummy for six weeks, so you better be prepared to be kissed lots and lots.'

The skin under her palm twitched and a hand – or was it an elbow or a foot? – protruded and made her whole tummy lurch.

'You heard me!' she said, laughing delightedly.

Heaving up to a sitting position she cradled both hands on her baby bump and, in that moment, missed Alfie more acutely than she had ever done since his death three months previously.

The sense of futility over his premature death sliced deep. She thought of the life cut short that had not flowered and matured into old age. Images too of their final encounter. His fingers threaded through hers. The intensity of their love-making. The silly initials he'd scratched into the wall afterwards. *AB. RG.* Encircled in a heart, scored through with an arrow. Unbreakable. Or so she had thought.

She wondered, too, what kind of parents they would have made. The image of Alfie teaching him or her to ride their bike in Vicky Park burst unbidden into her mind, along with pictures of the two of them together, fumbling through those bewildering early days as they greeted the new life they had made together.

She stuffed her knuckles into her eyes to stop the tears from surfacing. But then she thought of Alfie's family, of what this dreadful war had stolen from them and was power-less to stop them. Before Alfie left to fight, there were so many Buckles, their cosy home could barely contain them. Ordinary, loving and good-hearted people all of them. Now Mrs Buckle had lost both her sons, her only children. Two strong, fine and handsome men who would now never be able to carry on the family name. Just like that, a family tree had been felled. They'd moved away, so Renee had heard tell, to the Lake District, after Mrs Buckle suffered a nervous breakdown.

Searing agony ripped through her heart and she beat her fists against the pillow.

If only her mother hadn't been jailed. If only Mrs Buckle had been well enough to help her. If only Lily were married, she could have passed the child off as hers. *If only. If only. If only.* Renee's brain was broken from trying to find a solution.

The most ridiculous thing, Renee thought, was that now her secret was finally out, she had never looked so well. In fact, the bloom of pregnancy only served to make her looks more exquisite. For seven and a half months now, her body had nurtured the little life growing inside her, swelling gently to accommodate it, and her arms already ached to hold her child. She couldn't wait to meet her baby, and yet she dreaded the first contraction, because this birth didn't mean a new beginning. It meant saying goodbye.

A sharp rap at the door interrupted her thoughts. She ignored it. Lily had virtually bitten her head off when she had gone to answer it that morning.

The knock grew sharper, more insistent.

'All right, all right, keep your wig on, I'm coming,' she huffed and, pulling a voluminous summer smock over her head, she waddled her way down the creaking staircase.

To anyone else, the sight of such a voluptuous young woman in the full bloom of pregnancy would be a beautiful one. But to the starchy, whiskered woman on the doorstep, the only thing that stood out was the missing wedding ring.

'Mrs Clatworthy, Director of Education and head of the Evacuation Scheme in Stratford,' she muttered, glaring pointedly at Renee's finger. 'And this here,' she pointed to a mousy-looking man in tweed, 'is the headmaster of Carpenters Road School. May we speak with Mrs Gunn?'

'Sorry, she ain't in right now,' Renee replied, smiling sweetly and fanning her face in the heat.

'When she will be home?'

Renee shrugged. ''Bout nine months, maybe less with good behaviour.'

Her gallows humour was plainly lost on its audience.

'Young lady, you may not be aware of this, but there is a war on,' bristled Mrs Clatworthy, 'and we are incredibly busy people, so enough of all— Aah, Mr Gunn, I presume.'

Her father had arrived home and Renee's cocky smile slipped.

'Get inside,' he growled, his low voice unmistakably cold.

'Come in,' he said, ushering the pair through the door. 'Renee, put the wood in the hole and make our guests tea.'

Shrugging off his donkey jacket, he sat down heavily and started rolling a cigarette, leaving Renee to close the door.

'Save your rations,' snapped Mrs Clatworthy, 'we shan't be stopping long. I was enquiring as to the whereabouts of your wife. I'm from the school authorities, we last met a year ago when I was trying to persuade her to have your son Frankie evacuated.'

'She's doing a stretch at the moment, so you'll have to deal with me,' he replied as calmly as if his wife had popped to the shops. 'Only make it quick as I have to collect the boy.'

Mrs Clatworthy's jowls trembled.

'By stretch, I take it you mean prison, Mr Gunn?' she exclaimed.

'Well, that explains a lot,' said the headmaster, who had remained silent until now.

'You won't be collecting your son from school, as from this morning he has been permanently suspended.'

Renee turned the kettle off and sat down at the table as he pulled out a thick manila folder. Pat eyed it suspiciously.

'Why?'

'Mr Gunn. Let me be blunt,' said Mrs Clatworthy. Renee doubted she had any other way. 'Frankie Gunn is a deeply troubled child—'

'His pedantic mannerisms and failure to obey the simplest instruction is nothing short of wilful insurrection,' interrupted the headmaster, with a brief twitch of the eye. Renee stared at him intently and wondered how many times her clever younger brother had got the better of this fusty old toad.

'He's too clever by half,' he went on.

'Meaning what exactly?' Renee blurted, exasperated.

'Meaning he's impossible to teach. Take yesterday. He was removed from class after getting into a fight with the teacher. The teacher remarked it was raining cats and dogs. Frankie called him a liar and insisted on wrenching open the window, causing pandemonium in the classroom.'

Renee suppressed a smirk.

'He has a blatant disregard for authority and, in my considered opinion, is verging on delinquency.'

'And can you explain this?' barked Mrs Clatworthy.

She removed a picture from her handbag and slid it across the table.

'The teacher caught him drawing it the other day during Religious Education.'

It took a moment to realise what it was, but when she did, Renee was astonished.

'That's terrific!' she remarked, taking in the trademark fine lines and incredible observation of her brother's drawing.

'I'm not interested in your opinion on the quality of the picture, Miss Gunn, it's what it depicts that I find most disturbing,' said Mrs Clatworthy.

While the police had been attempting to dig up the graveyard, only to find themselves under fire from the entire female population of the Shoot, Frankie had obviously been drawing the entire scene from his upstairs bedroom window.

It was cinematic in its portrayal. The hailstorm of boots and brooms battering the police van, the beleaguered police officers ducking from homemade missiles, the grim faces of the women who had formed a human shield around the graveyard . . . Even the old lady who had emptied her chamber pot out of the window had been captured in her toothless glory.

'If this is a reflection on his disorderly living conditions, then it is little wonder that his behaviour is so unruly.'

As she said the word 'disorderly', Mrs Clatworthy allowed her eyes to linger on Renee's bulging belly a fraction too long.

'Look here. Strikes me, we ain't no more disorderly than any other family,' Renee said hotly.

'That's enough, Renee,' snapped Pat.

'So, what would you have us do?' he sighed, mashing his cigarette out. 'God knows, I've tried disciplining the boy.'

'In my opinion, Frankie's a disturbed child, Mr Gunn, deeply flawed and despite obvious ability, feeble-minded. He needs an institutional education with immediate effect.'

'A naughty boys' home!' Renee screamed, slamming her hands down on the table. 'You can't send him to one of them places, he wouldn't last five minutes.'

Her father stayed silent at his daughter's tirade.

'Dad . . . Dad! Tell 'em no. Frankie's stopping here with his family. Right?'

Pat blew out slowly, puffing his weather-beaten cheeks out, and looked older than his forty-five years.

'I can't deny we're struggling. With my wife in jail, the burden of the family's fallen to me. I'm working double shifts down the docks.'

'It can't be easy,' said the headmaster obsequiously. Renee wanted to scream out that it was Lily who was keeping the family afloat, financially, practically and emotionally, but she knew better than to speak out against her father in front of these strangers.

'And need I remind you that you are in a perilous area?' added Mrs Clatworthy. 'As well as West Ham, there were raids over Stepney and Bethnal Green last week. I have all the paperwork here necessary to arrange Frankie's admittance to a facility in rural Hampshire. In the absence of your wife, all that's required is your signature, Mr Gunn. We can arrange transportation early next week and Frankie can remain there for the duration of the hostilities, longer if required. It really is the safest and most sensible option.'

Pat picked up the proffered pen without making eye contact with Renee.

'Dad . . . Dad, no, please don't do this!' Renee pleaded, feeling hysteria rise up inside her. 'Think what this'll do to Mum, it'll destroy her. You can't send our Frankie away. At least wait until Lily's home so we can discuss it.'

'No choice, girl,' he said gruffly, scrawling his signature on the piece of paper and sliding it into Mrs Clatworthy's outstretched hand. 'It's done.'

28

Lily

There days later, Lily wanted to scream out loud. The hands on the clock were inching closer to her little sister and brother's departure from Stratford and she was judging a beauty competition!

It was a perfect Saturday afternoon, the first in September. The late summer sun was bright, whipping cotton-wool clouds across the seamless blue sky. West Ham were playing at home and the distant roar of the crowd could be heard over the factory rooftops. The sunshine was so unseasonably warm and syrupy that by four p.m., the Director had announced it would be healthier for all if the competition were to be held in the factory yard, instead of the canteen – which of course meant every red-blooded male in the vicinity was peering through the factory gates, hoping to catch a glimpse of a leggy Yardley lovely in her bathers. Even the Bricky Kids had clambered onto the high brick factory walls for a peek.

Mr Hesse was seated to the left of the Director at a long trestle table, with Miss Rayson to his right and Lily next to her.

All the factory girls who hadn't entered the new Miss Homefront had spilled into the yard to spectate. Out of loyalty to Renee, none of the girls in the lipstick room had entered – apart from Nan.

Fat Lou and her team in packing stood watching near the loading bay with Betty, Mavis, Joanie, Joycie and all the Irenes. To Lily's mind, they were a hundred times more stylish and beautiful than the beauty queen hopefuls. She felt a sudden burst of affection for her resourceful tribe of workers. So ebullient, so tenacious . . .

The more privations of war had been thrust upon them, the more the girls had hit back with bold femininity. Elaborate hairstyles had become badges of honour. Elegant pompadours, with hair pinned up at the sides and swept high onto the top of the head in a striking Eugene wave, gleaming victory-rolls, chignons, omelette folds, pin-curls and waves . . . All had been adopted in the lipstick room and used to striking effect.

Off duty, Fat Lou had taken to wearing slacks, despite *Vogue* declaring them 'deplorable', and Lily had to hand it to her, she looked the business. A crisp white shirt was tucked into wide slacks with a deep waistband and side buttons, teamed with a velvet trilby hat and pillar-box red lips. She carried off the new masculine look with great aplomb.

Lily felt a staggering pride as she smiled over at the lipstick girls. As the workload had intensified since Dunkirk, not one of them had grumbled or slacked off. They simply did what the women in their families had done for generations before them. They knuckled down and got on with it. A whip-smart wit and work ethic, honed over centuries of desperate poverty, had shaped these girls into who they were today. Strong. Capable. Magnificent. Unlike her! Lily had returned to Stratford, if she were being brutally honest with herself, looking slightly down her nose at the factory girls, when in truth, they were her superiors.

'How's Renee holding up?' whispered Miss Rayson to Lily as they waited for the competitors to line up. 'I'm going to go over and see her after the competition and just run through

a few of the details for tomorrow. The car will be collecting
her around ten a.m., I've arranged collection for when most
of the neighbours will be at church.'

Lily nodded, grateful for the welfare officer's support and
discretion.

'Thank you,' she murmured. 'She's, well, she's being brave.
She's at home with Frankie packing.'

Miss Rayson nodded. 'Good. St Theresa's is a very respectable place. She'll be with many other girls in the same
predicament as herself. Before you know it, she'll be back
home and in her old job, and she'll be able to forget all about
this unfortunate incident.'

Lily nodded, tears pricking her eyes. Somehow, she doubted
Renee would ever simply be able to brush this under the carpet.

'You're right.'

'That's the ticket,' Miss Rayson smiled, gently squeezing
her forearm.

The girls began their procession round the yard, Nan
leading the way, looking very alluring in a gold lamé rayon
one-piece and a matching headscarf, which glittered in the
afternoon sunshine. A symphony of wolf whistles rang out.

'Let's give a big hand to Nan Connors from the lipstick
room, Edie Tanner in soap, Betsy Myers, canteen assistant,
Winnie Pratchett in dispatch . . .'

'Nan. I can't help but notice your elaborate headscarf,' the
compere remarked.

'Actually, it's called a scarf hat,' she replied, proudly patting
the side of the towering headpiece. 'All the Parisian women
are styling theirs like this. It's in defiance of Nazi occupation.
It's a symbol of solidarity towards my French sisters.'

'Brains, beauty and loyalty. My kind of woman . . .'

Lily rolled her eyes and ignored the compere's voice. She
couldn't concentrate. Her assurances to Miss Rayson shrieked
in her head.

No, actually. No. No. No. None of it was right.

Having the baby of the man you loved was not an *unfortunate incident*. Being forced to give that child away because the father died before he could put a ring on your finger was senseless. Sending a child away to live with strangers because he was a bit different was even more absurd.

Lily tapped her pen on the tabletop. *Think. Think.* What would Nell Gunn do? She wouldn't be judging a flamin' beauty contest; she would be out there, fighting for her family.

Suddenly, she missed her mum more than she ever thought possible, like a deep love-ache in her heart. Nell Gunn was like a bright, colourful thread that wove their family together. Without her, they were all slowly unravelling. She looked over at the lipstick girls larking about at the far end of the yard and realised, she wasn't apart from them. She'd been born and raised in the same streets as them, which meant surely, when push came to shove, she too had it in her to fight. A nasty, dark thought poked her conscience, unleashing a torrent of questions. Had she turned a blind eye to Renee's predicament, because she had also been forced to sacrifice the greatest love of her life? Had she brushed off Esther's concerns, because deep down she knew she was right? The pen dropped from her fingers. Had the last seven years taught her nothing?

'Bugger it,' she announced out loud. They might be a disorderly family. But they were *her* disorderly family. What would her mum do when she got out of prison and found half of them gone?

And then she was standing, drawing on her coat and grabbing her handbag.

'I beg your pardon, Lily?' Miss Rayson looked up at her, squinting against the sun. 'Where are you going, Lily, what's wrong? The competition's only just begun.'

'I know. And I'm sorry, but I'm going to save my family.'

29

Esther

'Lily, where are you going?' Esther shouted as she watched her sprint from the yard.

'I'll explain later,' she called back.

'Strange,' Esther murmured. 'I thought she was supposed to be judging the beauty competition.'

There was no time to think about it, though, as she was due on fire-watching duty. Esther climbed to the roof in silence to relieve the current watch from their post and stumbled straight into an ugly gossiping session.

'I heard she did it behind the Adam and Eve?' whispered Sandra from soap, swatting away a fly from her head.

'She never did!' exclaimed her companion with a dirty cackle. 'Bet she wishes she never tucked into that apple now!'

'They say the bosses have stripped her of her crown, that's how comes they're holding a new Miss Homefront.' Sandra paused to light a cigarette. 'Glands, my arse!'

Her companion sniffed. 'Filthy cow, give herself to a shoe black for thruppence, that one.'

'Her and that Nan always did think they was the dog's doodahs.'

'Careful that waggling tongue of yours doesn't swallow a fly!' Esther interrupted sharply, and the girls jumped.

'Who are you?' Sandra demanded.

'Renee's friend,' she replied.

The girls couldn't get off the roof fast enough.

Esther put down her flask of tea and picked up her binoculars, ready to settle down for her afternoon-into-evening shift. The view from the roof of Yardley's could not be described as pretty, but the sprawling network of canals and railway lines held its own charm. The smouldering September sun burnished the water and metal, so that it shone like hammered silver. Her gaze zigzagged along the tracks and waterways, all snaking off to other mysterious towns in England, places she had only seen in picture books. Smooth rivers, deep woods, bustling harbours. But there was no pull to follow the highways and byways to seek out those corners of her adopted homeland.

These grubby, congested and mean streets were *her* England. Home.

She put down the binoculars and rested against the railings, briefly allowing her eyes to flicker shut. A warm breeze flowed over her bare shins and the sunlight soaked through her eyelids, causing bright bursts of colour within her closed eyes. A feeling of stillness crept over her – it was a peculiar sensation, as if she would forever be stuck in this drowsy early September day in 1940 like a fly in amber. Her breath fell soft and slow.

It was warm and peaceful, sunlight slanting over the concrete, the only sound the ripple of applause coming up from the Miss Homefront contest taking place in the yard and the gentle combing wind humming over the wires anchoring a nearby barrage balloon.

The noises roused her and picking her binoculars back up, she peered through curiously to see Mr Lavender placing a sash over the head of a delighted-looking Nan. Nan was milking her moment in the limelight, as a photographer from the *Stratford Express* stepped forward to take her photograph. Sunshine bounced off the flash of his camera bulb, temporarily blinding Esther.

When her vision cleared, she saw Walter standing beside her.

'You're twice as elegant as her,' he remarked, appraising her with that lopsided grin of his.

'What, even in my battle bowler and dungarees?' she asked, tapping her tin helmet. 'What are you doing here anyway?'

'I bribed Bill to swap shifts with me, so I could spend time with you.'

He pulled her into his arms, and Esther enjoyed the feel of her body against Walter's, his kind brown eyes threaded through with flecks of gold that danced in the late afternoon sunshine.

The pair of them closed their eyes, content to enjoy this shared moment of tranquillity.

From somewhere in the dreamlike darkness, Esther heard the buzzing of a fly. Idly, she swatted it away. The buzzing grew louder, more persistent, gradually drowning out the sound of the compere.

'These flies . . .' she grumbled, but as her eyes opened, her words trailed off. In the distance, the skyline had darkened with a black rash. The swarm of flies grew bigger, louder, until it dawned on her that they weren't insects at all.

'Bloody hell,' murmured Walter, his entire body stiffening as the ominous wail of the siren started up.

'Jerry's come mob-handed!'

Hastily putting his helmet back on, he began to count the planes, wave after wave following the shining curve of the Thames. He gave up when he reached 140.

'Those are bombers,' he said, scarcely able to conceal the quiver in his voice as he pointed a shaky finger at the horizon, 'and those surrounding them are fighters. Hell's teeth! You can't put a pin between 'em.'

To Esther it made no difference, they were all one. *The enemy.*

The deep murmur of approaching engines became a roar, and as they got closer, Esther felt the tremor beneath her feet, like the thundering of a gigantic waterfall. Instinctively she gripped the railing. The bombs began to fall like windfall apples. Thumps followed by sooty clouds of black smoke that stained the blue canvas.

Down below in the yard, the beauty competition had collapsed into chaos as girls ran screaming, clutching at their bathing suits.

'The docks are gonna get it!' Walter yelled as a rain of high explosives whistled down to ground three miles south. In no time at all, the hazy jumble of factories, warehouses and streets were obliterated as the acrid smoke thickened, mushrooming up the narrow streets. The awful thought occurred to them both at the same time. If Goering's Luftwaffe were targeting the docks, then surely industrial Stratford with its sprawling network of freight yards, railways and factories would be just as vulnerable.

'Into the shelter,' boomed Miss Rayson's voice through a loudspeaker in the yard. 'Everyone make your way into the old powder room calmly and without delay.'

'You heard her,' said Walter, turning to Esther. 'I'll help you down, I don't want you slipping on the fire escape.'

Esther tightened the buckle on her helmet strap and reached for the nearest bucket of sand and shovel.

'I'm on duty!' she declared, her knuckles turning white as she gripped the bucket. 'I'm not going anywhere.'

30

Renee

'Come on, Frankie, if we hurry, we can make the late afternoon matinee. Would you like that, sweetheart?' Renee asked, trying her hardest to do up the buttons of her summer mac over her tummy.

'Renee, oughtn't we to stay here? Dad said . . .'

'Come on, let's live dangerously,' Renee said, flashing him a reckless smile. 'I'm bored senseless being cooped up in here. We'll be back before you can say: "Dick's hat band."'

'Who's Dick?' Frankie murmured.

'Never mind,' Renee laughed. Grabbing her handbag, she realised she was a bit over-prepared for a trip to see *Gone With the Wind* at the fleapit on the Broadway. It contained all her essential documents, including ration cards, identity papers, fake Woolies wedding ring, insurance documents and cash, prepared as her father had insisted she be for her journey tomorrow. She had the desperate urge to get out this stifling house and escape to the cool dark fantasy world of Hollywood. One more minute sitting here and she'd go balmy.

'Come on, Little Prof, I'll even treat you to some of them horrible rhubarb and custard sweets you like from Woolies, if they've got any.'

He stared up at her with his delicate chiselled features, those slate-grey eyes so serious, and slid his hand into hers.

'I don't want you to go tomorrow, Renee.'

She looked down and stroked his cheek softly.

'Nor do I, sweetheart, nor do I. Come on, let's go.'

Outside, along Angel Lane Market, she was aware of the whispers as she and Frankie walked hand in hand. Housewives stopped their haggling, costermongers' patter dried up. The market was as packed as she knew it would be – housewives spent a third of their income and a good portion of the day down Angel Lane, especially on a Saturday.

'People are looking at us, Renee,' said Frankie, tugging her hand.

'So let 'em!' She was done with feeling shame.

'Hello, Betty, how you keeping?' She nodded to the elderly shopkeeper as she swept the pavement outside her ladies' outfitters shop where, over the years, Renee had bought many a pair of stockings.

Betty sniffed and, without saying a word, turned her back on her. Renee felt her snub like a blow. It was the same story the length of the Lane. Housewife after housewife turned their back on her.

'Tart,' hissed Maud, the cat's meat seller, spitting at Renee's feet.

With as much dignity as Renee could muster, she stepped over the spittle and carried on walking, pushing back tears of humiliation. She would not give them the satisfaction.

She felt Frankie's warm little hand tighten in hers and she loved him for it.

They continued their walk of shame in silence. Renee had never heard the market so deathly quiet. The whole seething, clannish street of noise and heat stilled. Even Harold Hitch at number 46, purveyor of eels and pies, paused at his stall, knife glinting mid-air, before he brought it down on an eel's head, the only sound the faint slap and wriggle of the trapped eel.

No matter that she had grown up around these people – *her people*. In their eyes, she had committed the ultimate sin. She would for ever more be regarded as the lowest of the low.

Just then, a voice . . .

'Good afternoon, miss, you look lovely, may I escort you?'

She turned, blinking. Snowball! His trousers were held up with string and newspaper poked out of the toe of his boot.

Gallantly, he extended an arm, a filth-encrusted elbow poking out from the hole in the jumper.

Renee gave him her biggest, brightest smile.

'Why, that would be lovely, sir. You may indeed.'

She took his arm like a lady and Frankie giggled.

'We're going to watch *Gone with the Wind* down the flea pit, Snowball. Would you like to come?'

'I would, madam, but I'm expected at the Royal Opera House,' he winked. They both knew he stood a cat in hell's chance of being allowed in the picture house, but he appreciated being asked, almost as much as she adored him for his kindness.

When they reached the Broadway, Renee reached over and kissed him softly on his cheek.

'Thank you,' she mouthed.

Inside the picture house, she manoeuvred her hefty belly down into a chair and exhaled. *Gone with the Wind* was sold out, so she'd plumped for two tickets to see Peggy Moran in *Danger on Wheels*.

It seemed apt. When word reached her father, probably as soon as the West Ham match was finished, she reckoned as how she would probably never be able to show her face in Stratford again. With a wry smile, she realised she'd saved Nan the bother of sharing her news. Besides, she thought, looking at Frankie, who was busy shelling groundnuts into his lap and arranging them into order of size, who cared if your face didn't fit?

The picture flickered into life and Renee tried to lose herself in the film. Motion pictures were her escape from reality, but the baby was kicking like anything and even if it hadn't, she could not have concentrated. The future lay ahead, dark, unformed and impossible.

Thirty minutes in, a great groan went up round the picture house as the screen suddenly flickered and Peggy Moran's face froze.

The manager hastened onto the stage.

'Ladies and gentlemen, there is an air raid in progress and bombs have been dropped in our area.'

An enormous bang sounded overhead sending all the ceiling lamps swaying and the stage trembled. The manager waited a moment before calmly continuing.

'We are closing the cinema, so would you kindly leave in an orderly manner. There is an air-raid shelter outside.'

Renee gripped Frankie's hand, desperately trying not to show her fear.

'Come on, bruv,' she said, hauling herself to her feet. Just then a louder explosion seemed to ripple the floor beneath their feet and she gasped.

Frankie let out a little cry and grabbed her hand. At the same time, her baby kicked out.

'I don't like the noise,' Frankie cried, holding his free hand over his ear. 'Make it STOP!'

A hot prickle of panic ran up her spine as she realised the responsibility for not one, but two lives rested with her. Suddenly she began to regret leaving the Shoot and the comfort and familiarity of her neighbours.

'It's all right, sweetheart,' she said with as much cool as she could muster. 'See, I ain't panicking.'

On Tramway Avenue, no one else was either. The drone of Moaning Minnie was even louder outside as Saturday afternoon shoppers scurried to their nearest shelter. She envied their quiet, calm determination. A policeman cycled past, a piece of cardboard slung round his neck with the words '*AIR RAID TAKE COVER*' chalked on it.

'There's a street shelter up here,' panted Renee, clutching her tummy. She whirled round. 'Or is it this way?'

The policeman blew hard on his whistle.

'Get off the street!' he bellowed in her ear as he flashed past.

The sudden movement and shrill whistle disorientated her and, for a moment, Renee felt faint, stumbling from the pavement into the gutter.

A hand wrenched her back onto the safety of the pavement, just before a fire engine loomed out of the smoke and roared past her in an angry flash of red, bells clanging.

'Are you all right, my dear?' A kindly smartly dressed older man was gazing at her with concern.

'Yes . . . Yes, I'm fine,' she mumbled. 'I'm just trying to work out where's the nearest shelter.'

'Don't worry, we'll get you and your son to safety in a jiffy.'

He smiled and held out his arm.

'Follow me.'

'Oh, Frankie's not my son, he's my—' She didn't finish the sentence, because at that moment, a deafening explosion sounded a few streets away, followed by a vivid flash of orange.

Renee felt the breath sucked from her body as she registered the bang, a whoosh followed by a loud whistling sound.

Instinctively, she ducked down, pulling Frankie with her, covering his head with her coat.

A moment later a plate-glass window was blown out of the draper's shop they were standing in front of, showering the pavement in slithers of glass.

Renee watched in slow motion as an enormous shard of glass propelled through the air towards the elderly gentleman.

A wet-sounding thud and then silence. Renee stared in abject horror. The plate glass had missed her and Frankie, but sliced the man horizontally in two. For a second, he remained upright, but as he fell, the two halves of his body separated and his head rolled into the gutter. Renee heard hysterical screaming. She was surprised to realise it was coming from her.

And then they were half running, half stumbling through a thick cloud of grey brick dust, splintered glass crunching underfoot. On the High Street, a bus slid out of the smoke. Without a moment to register where it was going and in a haze of shock, Renee and Frankie boarded it.

31

Lily

Lily stood in the abandoned Shoot and yelled at the top of her lungs, her voice echoing off the tenement walls. Smoke drifted in greasy ribbons through the deserted square.

'Renee! Frankie!'

Her heart thumped painfully in her chest. She had been halfway home when the sirens had sounded, but by the time she reached the Shoot, Frankie and Renee were nowhere to be seen. She'd checked all the nearest shelters in the vicinity, even ran down the tunnels beneath Stratford station, but no one had seen hide nor hair of them.

Where had they gone? She heard ragged breath, the echo of footsteps coming down Cat's Alley.

'Renee? Is that you?' she called hopefully.

But the face that emerged from the gloom was Julia. Ash-white and trembling, she clutched Lily's arm.

'Esther? Is she all right?' Lily asked.

'God willing, she's at the factory, with Walter,' Julia replied. 'I've just come from there. She's on the roof, putting out incendiary bombs, I can't persuade her to come down. It's Frankie I'm worried about.'

'Me too,' wept Lily. 'I can't find them anywhere. He'll be terrified, poor mite.'

Julia nodded, her face a mask of concern.

'You're right. We must find him. All this noise and confusion, a child like Frankie, he won't be able to cope with it.'

Lily broke down, guilt blazing through her at the knowledge that Julia knew her own flesh and blood better than she did.

'We have to find him. We *must* find him!'

'Calm down, Lily. We will,' Julia replied.

'No, you don't understand, he's—'

She broke off when she spotted Julia staring at something in the graveyard.

'Snowball,' called Julia. 'Is that you?'

They ran to the furthest reaches of the graveyard, and there, huddled under a filthy blanket, was Snowball. He scrambled back against a gravestone when he spotted them, an ancient pain boiling in his eyes.

'It's all right,' said Julia soothingly, crouching down on her haunches. 'We need to get you to safety.'

Instinctively, she understood the vagrant whose past no one knew, only that he was suspected to be a veteran of the Somme, was terrified. Goodness only knew what images of unconscionable brutality he had witnessed during the last war, or what horrors this raid was unleashing in his head.

'Won't you come with us?' she entreated.

He started to shake, clawing at the earth with his fingers as if he was trying to dig his way down to safety.

'Renee and Frankie . . .' he mumbled. 'I was waiting for them. I tried to call out. Stop them. I'm sorry.' He began to rock back and forth, and Lily fought the urge to slap him.

'What do you mean?' she screamed. 'Where were they, Snowball?'

'I was waiting for Miss Renee and the young chap outside the pictures, to escort them home and then this man . . .' he moaned and his head slumped into his hands.

'Which picture house?' Lily babbled. 'What man, explain yourself for God's sake!'

Julia placed a gentle hand on Lily's arm and shot her a warning look.

'Why don't we get you inside, fetch you a nice cup of tea and you can tell us what you saw.'

Just then an explosion tore through the air, spewing earth and debris into the sky.

'Take cover,' screamed Snowball, flattening himself against the gravestone. Some ack-ack guns on Wanstead Flats responded immediately, peppering the skies with shells, and all three watched in disbelief as an enormous barrage balloon drifted by overhead on fire. It was an astonishing sight. Tongues of flame licked the dirty skies, the fierce crimson glow bathing Snowball's face blood red.

'I tried to stop them, but they got on a bus to Canning Town,' he said.

Lily felt a coldness fall over the nape of her neck and drape her whole body.

'But that's in the direction of the docks!'

32

Esther

'Esther . . . ESTHER.' Walter's voice grew more desperate as he groped blindly for Esther's hand in the dark.

'I'm here,' she spluttered, emerging from the thick cloud of smoke that had mushroomed over Yardley's. She felt as if her lungs were being gripped by an iron glove as she staggered towards Walter.

'Thank God,' he cried, gripping her arms to steady her. 'As long as I can see you.'

They clung to one another, breath ragged, hearts thudding as they waited for the ash cloud to clear. Down in the yard, it was all hands to the pump. Miss Rayson, Fat Lou, Nan and all the rest of the girls from the lipstick room had thrown caution to the wind and refused to take shelter, in order to help extinguish incendiary bombs, while Esther and Walter remained on the roof, shaken, but as yet, unharmed. The all-clear had sounded soon after 6.30 p.m. with Dornier and Heinkel bombers escorted by Messerschmitt fighters wheeling back across the Kent countryside to their bases in France, leaving the stench of death and destruction in their wake. There was no relief to be found at their retreat, for the damage had been done.

Incendiary bombs had dropped faster than hands could extinguish them, with service girls working alongside management to keep Yardley's from burning. Thousands of the two-foot-long magnesium-filled cylinders had pinged off the rooftops and streets and unless extinguished immediately with sand or a stirrup pump, they would set off small, potentially deadly blazes.

Pouring with sweat, Esther looked about in dismay as all around her East London burnt. Fire engines streamed to the worst-hit areas of the docks, the light from the fires so bright, you could've read a paper by it. Nineteenth-century wharfs and warehouses burnt fiercely – sugar refineries, oil depots, chemical works and distilleries spewing toxic fumes. Two hundred acres of tall timber stacks blazed out of control in the Surrey Commercial Docks. The rum quay buildings in West India Docks were alight from end to end, an unbroken wall of flame, shooting blazing spirits from warehouse doors, while at Tate & Lyle, sugar barges exploded, the smell of caramel mingling with rubber, tar and paint. An army of rats ran from a burning Silvertown soap works and a short distance along the North Woolwich Road, molten pitch from a tar distillery flooded the road, trapping emergency vehicles.

Further west, the narrow, cobbled streets of Whitechapel were also ablaze. In fact, and for the first time, Esther felt a cold, ghoulish fear creep up at the realisation she was circled by a ring of leaping fire, pure glowing white at its conflagration. Even the Thames was a river of fire, a flotilla of burning craft severed from their moorings, adrift on the water.

London's burning. London's burning . . . The tune played round her head on an infernal loop.

Hitler must have guessed she had paused for a moment's rest for, in that fear-filled moment, the bloodcurdling call of the siren started up again and once more, the sky filled with the drone of hundreds of enemy aircraft flying in tight formation as they came back for a second go. This time, though, they had the light from the fires to guide them along the sinuous loop of the Thames.

'We're in for it now,' murmured Walter, wiping the back of his hand against his mouth. 'And God help anyone stuck in the docks.'

Within minutes, livid flashes lit up the skyline. Esther and Walter stared out at the apocalyptic scene. A great pall of greasy black smoke roiled into the horizon, vast craters pocked the streets and piles of smoking rubble lay everywhere. A broken skyline of buildings stark against the red glow as the earth spewed blood and fire.

'It's like the end of the world,' Esther murmured, as they watched the searchlights swoop from one end of the sky to the other.

Suddenly a tremendous explosion tore through the smoke with a vivid white flash that lit up the factory.

'Get down,' yelled Walter, pushing her to the floor and covering her with his body. Esther felt the compression from the high-explosive blast so powerfully, she felt as if her eyeballs were being sucked clean out their sockets. The ground beneath her chest seemed to ripple. She waited as still as she could as she heard the shrapnel dancing up the cobbles and the soft pitter-patter of debris raining down on her head.

'Esther, are you all right?' Walter croaked as she struggled to her feet. She looked up and realised absurdly the blast had blown his shirt clean off his back. Before she even had a chance to pass comment, there came another ear-shredding explosion. A shower of bricks spewed into the air and a hot wind blew her back.

Crashing to the ground, she huddled amongst the debris and waited for the swirling morass to pass. Esther realised she had been holding her breath and now desperately needed to breathe, but as she lifted her head, her lungs filled with a bitter choking dust and the stench of gas.

In that moment, Esther realised she desperately needed to survive: losing her husband *and* her daughter would destroy her mother. She also realised she was entirely deaf, but as she lifted her head from the ground, saliva spooled from her mouth and her hearing came flooding back.

'Clarnico's has copped it,' shouted a disembodied voice in the smoke.

Walter was tugging her to her feet.

'Esther, we have to take cover. I can smell gas, I think the Beckton gas works has been hit.'

Six feet away from her, an incendiary had rolled into the guttering and was fizzing dangerously. Any second and the blistering canister would go off, showering them in white-hot magnesium.

'I'll get it,' said Walter.

'Don't be daft, you haven't even got your top on!'

Staying flat on her belly, she inched closer to the device over the slate roof.

'Pass me the spade and hold my feet so I don't take a dive over the edge,' she ordered.

'Esther, it's too dangerous!'

'NOW!' she ordered. 'It's going to ignite any second.'

Wordlessly, he passed her a spade and gripped her feet tight as she stretched so that half her body was hanging off the roof. Pouring with sweat, her eyes burning from the stench of gas, she manoeuvred herself over the guttering, and slid the edge of the spade towards the bomb.

With a sudden scraping sound, two spare roof tiles, disturbed by the explosion, slid off the edge and hurtled into the yard, smashing into pieces. The unexpected movement nearly took Esther with them.

'I've got you,' Walter shouted. Esther didn't reply, she had to focus all her energies on getting to the bomb. The lactic acid in her arms was burning and for a dreadful breath she thought she was about to drop the spade.

With an almighty effort, she reached forward and edged the bomb onto the lip of the spade.

'Pull me back,' she ordered. 'Nice and slow.'

When she was back on the flat part of the roof, she edged the incendiary slowly towards the sand bucket and gently slid it nose first into the sand, while Walter covered it with more sand and debris.

They waited and watched. Finally when they were satisfied no smoke was escaping, they showered the rest of the rooftop with water from the stirrup pump, then gingerly made their way down into the yard to check on everyone else.

'Good job,' said Walter as they descended.

Only once they were down did she feel her legs begin to shake.

'All right, who's had me top?' joked Walter, attempting to make light of his shirtless condition. But he wasn't the only one missing attire. Bomb blasts are odd things, Esther realised. The strange compression of the high explosives dropping nearby had sucked off various items of clothing. Miss Rayson's cardigan was draped over the gatepost. Fat Lou's trilby was dangling from a gas lamp out on Carpenters Road, but all eyes were elsewhere.

Standing in the middle of the yard, surrounded by her fellow workers who were staring at her in dismay, was Nan. Her scarf hat had been whipped clean off her head and the ground around her feet was surrounded by tubes of lipstick refills, glinting in the light from the fires. There was even a tube still nestled in the hair of her luxuriant black wave.

Miss Rayson looked from the lipsticks back to Nan. 'I . . . I . . .' Nan stammered, but there really was little else to be said. She had been caught red-handed, or rather red-headed.

'And to think you tried to pin this first on Esther and then Renee,' gasped the welfare worker, grime and despair etched on her features. 'Blacken their names!'

She pointed a shaky finger at Nan. 'We need to get to the shelter, immediately, but you, madam . . . I shall deal with later.'

She turned, muttering furiously under her breath.

'Solidarity to my French sisters . . . Of all the rotten lies . . .'

Nan hung her head and began to sob, a low keening sound like a wounded animal. Then she turned, and still wearing her bathers, covered with a borrowed mac, she turned and fled into the night.

33

Lily

The next morning – a Sunday – after the all-clear sounded, it was a shell-shocked and exhausted group that gathered in the kitchen at number 10 the Shoot. They had awoken to a dark dawn, a dense blanket of acrid smoke still covering everything, the smell of death lingering in their nostrils. Even in an area well used to suffering, this was a new era of terror.

Stratford had taken a battering. As well as Clarnico's sweet factory, the jam factory, Woolies and the Co-op had taken a hit, and half the High Street was on fire. All trains and buses were out of action, as were power and water. Factories by the Cut had been bombed, spewing their noxious contents, breaching the waterways with raw sewage, the smell of human shit pervading everything.

They had washed off the worst of the muck with a quick, cold strip-wash in the backyard, and Julia had managed to find a standpipe in a neighbouring street that was working and had fetched enough water to boil them all a cup of tea. Now it was time to get down to business.

'Snowball couldn't tell me and Julia any more, other than he saw Renee and Frankie board a bus at the Broadway headed for Canning Town shortly after the sirens first sounded, some time after four p.m.,' said Lily to Esther and Walter.

'Then, that's where we must go,' said Esther, standing up
to grab her coat.

'Finish your tea first, and eat these sandwiches I've made,'
ordered Julia. 'It's going to be a long day.'

Lily looked at the older Jewish nurse and thanked God
that without their mum, they at least had her calm, quiet
strength to rely on.

'Julia, would you mind staying here, just in case they come
back?' she asked.

Julia nodded. 'Of course, I'll call on everyone down the
Shoot, in case they can help search.'

'Do you think there'll be more raids later?'

'I think we can count on it,' Walter replied.

'Let's not waste any more time then,' Lily remarked, wearily
standing and draining her tea. 'If needs be, we'll look in every
single shelter in the docks. I'm not coming home without them.'

A turban-clad shadow fell over the lino.

'Not coming home without who?'

Nell's gruff voice filled the kitchen as she stood, arms
crossed, in the doorway.

'Mum!' screamed Lily, throwing herself into her arms and
nearly bowling her clean over.

'W-what, when . . .'

'My barrister finally got me out on appeal, I'd have been
out a lot bloody sooner if it weren't for them bleedin' raids.'

Gently, she pushed Lily back and stared around her domain.

'Now, does someone wanna tell me where the rest of my
kids are?'

Lily opened her mouth, unsure of quite where to start, but
she was interrupted by a knock at the door.

'Yardley's chauffeur,' called a man's voice up the passage.
And it was too. A gleaming black automobile was parked at
the far edge of the Shoot.

'I'm here for Miss Renee Gunn,' said the elderly driver.

'Sorry I'm late, I've had a right to-do getting here, so many roads roped off. It's like crater city out there.' He flicked a look at his wristwatch. 'If we're going to get Miss Gunn to Bexhill before the raids start up again, we really ought to get a move on.'

Nell sat down at the table with a heavy sigh.

'Start talking, Lily. What is going on? Where's Renee and Frankie?'

By the time Lily had explained what little she knew, her mother was up and on her feet.

'I'm sorry for your wasted journey,' Nell said to the Yardley's chauffeur, dipping into an old tea caddy on the kitchen shelf and slipping him enough for a bit of breakfast and a pint. 'But my daughter won't be going to Bexhill, not now or ever.'

She turned to Lily, Esther and Walter. 'Get your coats on,' she ordered. 'And Julia, knock on every door down the Shoot and get word out Frankie and Renee are missing. Oh, and tell 'em Nell Gunn's back.'

Lily thought she'd never been so pleased to see anyone in her entire life.

'Mum, I can't tell you how much I've missed you,' she said, throwing her arms around her.

'Don't get soppy on me, girl, we ain't got time for cuddles. Let's go.'

If they'd thought Stratford was bad, it wasn't a patch on Canning Town. The dockside community had been pulverised and disembowelled.

Nell was absolutely distraught. Not at the destruction they were witnessing, but at the news that Pat had sanctioned Frankie's admittance to a boys' home.

'That crafty bastard,' she murmured in disbelief, as they walked. 'He waited until I was banged up an' all!'

As for Renee's forthcoming spell at St Theresa's Home for

Unmarried Mothers, the blame for that she placed firmly at her own doorstep.

'She came to me in prison. I promised to help her. I've let her down.'

The thought propelled her forwards and Nell Gunn marched through the toppling streets like a woman possessed, in search of her children.

'Where is your father anyhow?' she asked.

Lily shrugged, puffing as she struggled to keep up with her mother.

'I don't know, last I saw he was off to watch West Ham play yesterday dinnertime.'

'Typical! Sneaky sod's probably sitting it out in the basement at the Two Puddings!'

The further they walked into the salty guts of Canning Town, the more harrowing the sights became. The neighbourhood had been nicknamed Draught Board Alley on account of the many white girls who had taken up with foreign sailors. Hundreds of humble, terraced two-up two-down homes, built in the last century to accommodate dockworkers and their families, sat hugger-mugger with the Royal Docks, so close, in fact, you could read the names of the ships. Like Stratford, it was a close-knit community, which existed cheek by jowl with poverty and deprivation.

They paused at the end of one roped-off street. 'Danger – Gas,' murmured Lily, reading out the sign.

Half of the road was smoking rubble. Twenty or so houses wiped off the map by a landmine bomb. It was a frenzy of activity as rescue workers dug furiously at the debris. The stench was unholy. Burnt flesh, and something darker; dust and debris that had lain undisturbed for a hundred years, sucked from the 19th-century fabric of terraced homes and spewed into the atmosphere. Lily knew she'd still be able to conjure that smell until her dying days.

'These old houses are so bloody damp, it's only the wallpaper holding 'em up,' Nell muttered. 'But they was still people's homes. God help whoever's stuck under there.'

She crossed herself and they hurried on, past a double-decker bus slewed half-in, half-out a bomb crater opposite Canning Town station, past a house that looked like it had been sliced down the middle with a giant cheese wire.

Lily stared agog at the half-a-house. She could make out the faded wallpaper, the ripped curtains flapping in the breeze, the dresser still full of unbroken cups and saucers. And incongruously, a foot, still in a high-heel shoe, blasted onto the doorstep.

'Don't stare,' Nell chastised.

As they walked, it dawned on Lily that they were the only people walking *into* Canning Town. Everyone else was hurrying *away*. A convoy of exhausted, filthy refugees stumbling through the streets like zombies, the contents of their homes piled onto coster barrows and perambulators.

'Morning, Doll,' Nell called to one woman she recognised, clutching a small child in one hand and a budgie in a cage in the other. A young sailor was pushing a barrow piled up high behind her. 'Where you going?'

'Where do you bleedin' think, Nell?' she replied. 'Away from here. Jerry'll be back soon and I for one don't plan to be in. I'll camp in Epping Forest if I have to.'

'Ain't you worried about looters?'

She sniffed. 'Nah. 'Sides, not much left to loot. It took a direct hit. Hitler done me a favour. It's a shithole. This is my boy, Danny,' she said, gesturing to the sailor. 'He's home on leave.'

'Cor, not much of a leave for ya,' Nell remarked.

'You ain't wrong there, Auntie,' he laughed. 'I come through Dunkirk three months ago, I didn't realise my mum'd have to go through it too.'

'We're all soldiers now, son,' Dolly replied, before turning around in exasperation.

'Do hurry up, Mother,' she called to an elderly woman in a pink candlewick dressing gown, shuffling up the street behind her, clutching a jam jar containing a set of false teeth.

She rolled her eyes and lowered her voice.

'The mother-in-law. Honestly, Nell, you'd think they was dropping meat pies, not bombs.'

Nell chuckled at the gallows humour. 'Be lucky, Doll.'

'You too, Nell. See you soon. Please God.'

'PG, Doll. Just one thing. You ain't seen my Renee and Frankie?'

'Sorry, love, no. Lot of the schools round here have been set up as rest centres, you could try Frederick Road School, or South Hallsville in Agate Street.'

'Thanks, Doll, I will. Ta-ra.'

'Salt of the earth,' Nell murmured under her breath, as she watched her pal Dolly and her family bravely push their lives away in search of safety.

Snapping out of her reverie, she turned to Esther and Walter. 'You two try Frederick Road, and me and Lily'll go to Agate Street. Then knock on doors, try basements of pubs, picture houses, anywhere that has a white S painted on it, or looks like a shelter. They're here somewhere.'

She paused and for a dreadful moment looked like she might break down. Prison life hadn't suited Nell Gunn, Lily realised. Always a well-covered woman, she'd lost weight, and her face seemed to have folded in on itself. Her voice trembled.

'Find 'em. Bring 'em home.'

Then she was off again, marching to Agate Street.

They took a direct route, only swerving down a side street once when they saw Walter's mother Maureen walking towards them, looking like she was about to give someone a mouthful.

'We'll never get away if we get stuck talking to her,' Nell muttered.

Lily was humbled to see the mobile units of the Salvation Army and the Women's Voluntary Services out in force in the heart of the destruction, offering hot tea, Bovril, sandwiches and clothing.

Finally, they turned into Agate Street and Lily's heart sank. The queue into the rest centre snaked out into the playground as hundreds of homeless people tried desperately to enter the building. Crowds of angry people were surging around the beleaguered ARP workers, volunteers and officials.

Anger and violence were brewing.

'The coaches were supposed to be here by now. Where the fuck are they?' yelled a woman in the queue, trying desperately to keep five kids under control.

'Wash your mouth out!' yelled another woman.

'Well, excuse me for trying to keep my kids alive!'

'My God, didn't I warn about this?' Nell murmured in dismay, gripping the gates to the playground. 'Didn't I say when war first broke out, all them months ago, you can't house East Enders on school floors. Where are the deep shelters? Dear God, are we not human?'

'Never mind that now, Mum, how are we going to get in and look for them?' Lily said despairingly.

Suddenly, Nell spotted a familiar face. A well-known and loved local priest, the Rev W.H. Paton, nicknamed the 'Guv'nor', was hurrying away from the school towards the playground gates.

'Father, have you seen my children in there?' she gushed, gripping his darned cassock.

His face was ashen grey and his eyes filled with tears.

'Sorry, Mrs Gunn, I don't have time to chat, I have to get to the Town Hall and then Whitehall, try and warn the powers that be that we urgently need transport out, but trust me, this is not the place to be in.'

'But I think my Renee and Frankie are in there. I don't want to stay, I just want to get them out safe.'

He paused and blew out slowly.

'Very well, there's an unlocked door, right round the back of the building, but don't tell everyone or else there'll be a rush. And be careful.'

Heeding his warnings, they waited until the ARP warden looked the other way, and crept round the cordon to the sealed-off back of the building.

'Bloody hell,' gasped Nell, as they edged their way past an enormous crater in the playground. A dusty child's hopscotch petered away into a dark pit.

Lily's eyes traced a jagged crack that sliced up two floors of brickwork to the reinforced concrete roof above.

'This building's badly bomb-damaged,' she cried. 'It's not safe! Even if a bomb doesn't drop, it's still an accident waiting to happen!'

Inside was even worse. There must have been six hundred or more displaced East Enders, crammed into every available inch.

Young, old, blind and crippled. Some of society's most vulnerable pressed into a tangle of bodies, some weeping and hysterical, others in a state of profound shock, with nothing but the clothes they stood in.

'Call this a rest centre!' Nell exclaimed, looking about in disbelief. 'Where's the warm blankets, bedding and hot food? These people have lost their homes!'

The volunteers had nothing to offer them but tea. Nell and Lily moved respectfully among them, gently calling out Renee and Frankie's names.

'Have you seen a young blonde woman, she's expecting, with a small boy?' Lily asked, her voice trailing off as the futility of her words sunk in.

The woman, in a state of shock, seemed to stare straight through her as if she didn't exist.

'Shell shock,' Nell whispered. 'Let's try the basement.'

They picked their way through the basement crowd with growing despair. This was humanity stripped down to its most primeval. Treating people like this, it was dehumanising. Inhumane.

'I've searched that side, Mum. I can't see them anywhere, they're not here,' said Lily joining her.

Nell couldn't move, somehow, she was rooted to the spot.

'Come on, Mum. Maybe Esther and Walter have had better luck.'

'I could do with spending a penny.'

'Oh Mum, not here,' Lily pleaded. 'Come on. Let's just go.'

Nell opened her mouth, to rage at the injustice, to scream out her children's names . . .

Perhaps she would have done too, were it not for the distant throbbing of engines. The floor beneath their feet began to vibrate. Teacups on a trolley rattled. They were back.

A woman with singed hair, hugging a dirty brown blanket round her shoulders, broke down, rocking slowly on her haunches.

'Please won't someone tell us. Where are the coaches?' she howled. 'We're sitting ducks!'

'Mum,' Lily murmured urgently, her fingers tight on her mother's arm. 'Please, let's just get out of here. This place gives me the creeps. Something bad's going to happen. I can feel it.'

34

Renee

Where the jiggery hell were they? Renee stared about the room in disbelief, almost as if she couldn't quite work out how she and Frankie had got there, which to be honest, she couldn't really. It felt as if she'd just re-entered her body. Events were hazy. After watching the bloodcurdling sight of that poor man, they had stumbled onto a bus, but as the clouds of smoke had grown denser, the driver had stopped the bus and insisted they all get off.

In the mayhem, she and Frankie had followed streams of others to this rest centre, where they had at last fallen into an exhausted sleep on a spare patch of floor, while they waited out the raid.

Night had given way to dawn and a pale, lemony light filtered down the steps as somewhere up above ARP workers removed the blackouts, sending a shower of dust motes to dance and swirl over the heads of her fellow shelterers. Renee's eyes adjusted. They were in a basement, that much she could see.

A WVS volunteer in green walked past, her eyes flickering down at Renee's tummy in alarm.

'Can I fetch you and your son a nice cup of sweet tea, my love?'

Renee could have wept at the gesture.

'Ooh, yeah, I could murder a cup, thanks,' she said, struggling to sit up, too tired to correct the woman's mistake. Her whole left side was totally numb from lying on the cold concrete floor.

'You're gonna think I've lost me marbles, but where are we?'

'That's all right, my love, think those bombs blasted any sense out of me as well.'

The volunteer smiled and bent down to help Renee into a sitting position. Frankie stirred into life.

'You and this handsome chap are in a primary school that's been converted into a temporary rest centre, South Hallsville, on Agate Street.'

'Canning Town?'

'For our sins,' the woman joked.

As her eyes adjusted, Renee was shocked to see how many other people were stuffed like cattle into the school. There wasn't a spare patch of concrete to be found in the basement, with what looked like huge family groups and neighbourhoods staking out territories.

It was barely contained chaos. Babies grizzling. Old folk weeping. Children quarrelling. So many bombed-out families sitting in just their nightclothes, faces and arms cut to ribbons, blackened feet shoeless and bleeding. One poor woman in nothing but a nightie was perched on a suitcase, caked in blood, her cheeks embedded with slithers of glass, attempting to nurse a tiny newborn baby.

And on their faces was an accumulation of dread, fear and disbelief.

The stench of so many hot, stale bodies crushed together was unholy. The only facilities seemed to be a few latrine buckets, partitioned off behind a blanket. And all the while, a steady stream of people attempted to pick their way down the heaving staircase to find shelter below, just adding to the stew of bodies in the basement.

'Awful, isn't it? It's the same upstairs too,' remarked the WVS lady. 'People have been arriving all night and morning. The hall, classroom and corridors are heaving. But listen, love, it hopefully won't be long. There are coaches scheduled to arrive at three p.m. to take people to the safety zones in Kent.'

Her eyes flickered down to Renee's belly once more.

'You must be ready to pop, you poor thing. Tell you what, let me have a word with officials here and see if we can't make you and your son a priority to get on the first coach out of here.'

She winked conspiratorially.

'My husband's away too. I'm expecting our first, so trust me, I know how tough it is.'

'No. You don't understand, I have to get back to Stratford, I have to . . .' Renee's voice trailed off as she felt tears surface, but something inside her abruptly hardened.

Get a grip, Renee.

She was done with crying. She'd cried enough flaming tears to fill the Thames. She barely recognised herself these days. Tears wouldn't save her baby. Where was the plucky girl who asked for a pay rise, who clung to the back of lorries and dreamed, schemed and charmed her way through life? It was time to find her courage. She glanced at her bag, containing all her documents, the fake Woolies ring on her finger.

In that dark, desperate basement the seed of an idea had planted.

A war widow, with one small boy and a little 'un on the way. There was bound to be sympathy. She could start again, reinvent herself, carve out a new life for her Frankie and in doing so save them both from the fate awaiting them. It would be hard, of course it would, but chaos had provided her with an opportunity. Perhaps the only one she'd get to be a mum.

Doubt swelled at the sheer madness of the idea.

If she chose to run, she would have to accept that it would be a long time, if ever, before she could return to Stratford. She might never see her mum, dad or Lily again. What she was planning weaved such an unparalleled web of lies and deceit that she doubted Nell could ever forgive her. She was about to run away, taking Frankie with her! The ramifications hit home. The police would be called. Nasty words like 'child abduction' floated in front of her eyes.

But what hope did Frankie have if she returned him to the Shoot? His destiny was a correctional institution and hers was a home where she would have to sign away all rights to her baby. *Her baby. No one else's. Hers!*

Renee felt something harden inside her. She would do this. For Frankie, for her baby.

'I say, are you quite well?' persisted the volunteer. 'Do you wish me to see if I can make you and your son a priority?'

Renee jutted out her chin.

'Yes! I don't mind where we go, in fact the further away from here, the better.'

The volunteer studied her face, then Frankie's, curiously and for one awful moment Renee wondered if the lady recognised her, perhaps even knew her mum.

'Right you are, love,' she replied. 'I'll fetch you that cuppa first.'

Renee sagged in relief.

The volunteer stood up and moved off, but was immediately swamped by an angry group of women clamouring for information and reassurance.

When are the coaches arriving? I'm a rate payer, you know! When will we go?

Their desperate voices echoed off the cold basement walls.

'How long are we here for?' Frankie whispered, staring up at her, eyes wide in his grubby face.

'Not long, sweetheart,' Renee replied, stroking his cheek. 'We just have to sit tight and wait.'

A voice rose above the babble.

'It's a disgrace is what it is! It's like the hold of a slave ship. We're all crammed in here like bleedin' sardines. I ain't stopping here.'

Renee recognised the voice as belonging to Walter's mum.

She groaned inwardly. *All I need is to be spotted by her,* she thought. Maureen Smith was known locally as the 'mouth of the south'. If she saw Renee and Frankie, you could be guaranteed it would be all round West Ham by the time the coaches arrived.

Drawing her headscarf further over her face, Renee turned her back and huddled into the growing crowd.

As the minutes bled into hours Frankie grew anxious. Fidgety. She couldn't blame him. Three p.m. had come and gone with no sign of the promised coaches.

'I need the loo.'

'Can't you wait? The coaches are bound to be here soon, then we'll find you somewhere to spend a penny.'

He shook his head.

'Come on then, though goodness only knows how we'll get there.' The makeshift latrines were only the other side of the basement, but a good hundred or so limbs and elbows stood between them and the lav.

'Save our space, will you?' she asked a family next to her.

The smell of ammonia and faeces stung her eyes as they picked their way closer to the 'facilities'. Renee felt the full weight of her baby pushing down on her.

'Don't even think about making an appearance here,' she muttered.

Behind the blanket screen, she waited for Frankie to go to the loo, and covered her mouth with a handkerchief fished from her coat pocket. It smelt of Yardley's English Lavender. Renee felt a powerful pang for Stratford and her cosy home down the Shoot.

Expecting. Sleep-deprived. Hungry (the last thing she'd eaten was some barley sugar at the pictures yesterday afternoon) and awash with tea, she wondered how the hell her life had come to this.

Frankie buttoned up his flies and turned to her.

'I want to go home. I want my mum.'

'I'm sorry,' she cried, touching his cheek. 'Mum's not there. But it's all right, sweetheart, you're with me now. Everything's going to be just fine.' Though, as she cast her eye around the festering toilet, the walls seemed to draw closer together. As Renee and Frankie emerged from the loo the siren went off again. A woman, who'd been rocking back and forth all afternoon, finally lost it, started spouting on about ducks. Hysteria was setting in.

'Quickly, back to our spot,' Renee soothed, ushering Frankie back to their place on the other side of the basement. At the far end of the room, gingerly making her way out of the gloom and back up the staircase was a woman who carried herself just like her mother. A pang of love seared through her, stopping the breath in her throat. What she wouldn't do to be in her mother's arms again. Turn back the clocks. She closed her eyes to stop the tears. As bad as it undoubtedly was here, it can't have been half as wretched as being stuck in a prison during a raid, with no freedom to run. Mentally she shut out the image of her mother, incarcerated behind bars. As painful as that was, it was the only way she would be able to survive. And survive they must. This situation, however squalid and desperate, was her only chance to escape and to keep her baby.

Settling back into their spot, Renee drew Frankie into her arms. As the almighty boom of bombs began once more, his body began to shiver.

An enormous crump and Frankie jumped out of his skin. The ceiling lights flickered, a shower of plaster dust streamed down over their heads. The entire basement took a collective breath in.

'We're going to die,' Frankie whimpered. Then louder. 'I don't want to die.'

'Shut that kid up,' snarled a voice. 'Or we're all done for.'

'For pity's sake, man, he's just a child,' called back a woman. 'You were one once!'

The door opened and three more big family groups entered the school, trailing luggage and bags. They brought the smells of overground with them. Smoke, charred flesh and cordite. Renee's chest tightened in panic: if a bomb dropped now, there would be a stampede.

Fear so primal, she felt it trail its icy fingers up her spine and clamp her heart. 'Please, Frankie, you have to calm down,' Renee begged. 'It's going to be all right . . . The coaches are on their way for us.'

A woman next to her was knitting feverishly. The louder the bombs, the faster her fingers worked the needles.

'Frankie,' Renee blurted, 'did you bring your sketch book?'

He nodded.

'In my satchel.'

Renee pulled it out hurriedly. 'Draw something for me, sweetheart.'

His face screwed up in concentration as he fished out a stubby pencil from the bottom of his satchel and began to draw. Within moments, he was lost in his world.

Renee sagged in relief, leant back and closed her eyes. The diversion tactic had worked. For now.

35

Lily

Monday, 9th September 1940. Day three of the London bombings dawned blacker than the one before. Churchill and his Chief of Staff were in the newspapers, touring East End bombsites, including a shelter under Columbia Market in Bethnal Green, which had taken a direct hit when a bomb had whistled down a chute. But it was the docks that had once more borne the brunt. The bombers had returned, dropping their lethal cargo, reigniting fires that were still smouldering. Twelve conflagrations lit up the river, reported the *Stratford Express*, alongside a grainy photo of a raging inferno in Canning Town. No mention of the woeful conditions of some of the shelters, just photos of 'plucky cockneys taking it'. Lily couldn't stand to read any more propaganda and tossed the paper to one side.

Somewhere in that inferno, Renee and Frankie were hiding.

And there was still absolutely no sign of her father either.

'Where are them sandwiches?' Nell demanded, appearing at the doorstep, fists on hips.

'Sorry, Mum, coming,' Lily yawned, returning to the mountain of bread she was buttering.

'Good, I ain't got long before I need to be back out there.' Then she was off again, tightening the straps on her apron as she walked. Lily shook her head. Where did her mum get her energy from?

She and Julia had organised a feeding station in the centre of the Shoot, staffed by the vicar and the women of the neighbourhood, so that women who had to go to work in the factories could have a bite to eat and a hot cup of tea after a sleepless night. A makeshift crèche had been set up at number 12 with a rota of volunteers to care for those children still left down the Shoot.

She and her mum, along with Esther and Walter, had been forced to abandon their search of Canning Town last night when the bombing got too heavy, and, like the rest of the Shoot, had slept down the tunnels at Stratford Station or in the crypt of St John's on the Broadway. They had emerged, blinking, into the thin dawn light to find a bomb had dropped nearby, blowing out all the windows of the Shoot.

Piling up the rest of the sardine sandwiches, Lily took the plate out to the trestle table in the centre of the square and placed it next to a tea urn and enamel jugs of hot chocolate. At the same time, Mrs Barnett scurried across the square clutching a tray of bread and butter pudding covered with a tea towel.

'The bakers on the Broadway donated this little lot,' she said triumphantly. 'Their roof's half gone. They had a sign out front: *Open as usual, only more so!*'

She cackled with laughter.

'And I went to Cooke's. They're bringing over fifty pie and mash on the house later for tea. It's so good to have you home, Auntie!'

Her face lit up and, bizarrely, Lily thought she'd never seen the usually downtrodden woman look so alive.

'That's the spirit, Mrs B,' Nell replied, before turning to collar the Bricky Kids. 'Oi, you lot, never mind collecting shrapnel, grab some brooms and let's get this mess cleared up or you'll get a clip round the lug holes! And when you're done, go down the council yard and fetch us some disinfectant.'

She turned back to Mrs Barnett.

'Any word from your husband?' she asked under her breath.

'No. Not since the bombs started. And to be frank with you, Auntie, I'm hoping it stays that way.'

Nell nodded as Mrs Barnett returned to the table to serve tea.

'Mum, aren't you worried about Dad?' Lily asked, overhearing the exchange. They'd bumped into the barman at the Two Puddings down the shelter the previous night and he said he'd seen Pat, Mr Barnett and a crowd of other men at the West Ham match on Saturday, right before the sirens went, but hadn't seen him since.

'Your father's big enough and ugly enough to look after himself. It's your brother and sister I'm worried about. Soon as this place is cleared up, me and Julia are heading back to Canning Town.'

'Mum,' said Lily, exasperated, 'we searched every rest centre and checked at every ARP post yesterday. No one's seen them. I think we have to assume they've made it out the East End, they—'

'No!' Nell replied sharply. 'They're in the docks still, I feel it in my bones and I'll comb every bloody inch of every single house and shelter with my bare hands if I have to.'

Her lip began to tremble. 'The Little Prof won't last five minutes out there without me, and Renee in her condition . . .When I find your father I'm gonna kill him!'

Her voice cracked and she gripped the edge of the trestle table until she composed herself.

Lily softened. 'I'm sorry, Mum. Of course . . .

'He did a runner before, don't forget, and we got him back home safe and sound. Like we will this time.'

Julia appeared, buttoning her coat.

'Are you ready, Auntie?'

She nodded.

'Wait, Mum, I'm coming too.'

'No,' said Nell, placing a firm hand on her shoulder.

'It's Monday morning. You're to clock on at Yardley's with Esther. You'll be expected there and the last thing we need is for you two to lose your jobs. Soon as you clock off, you can come and help us search. But like I say, they'll be home safe by then.'

Lily sighed. Winning an argument with her mother was like nailing jelly to the ceiling, impossible.

Besides, a part of her was curious to go to work and see whether that devious tealeaf Nan had the cheek to show her face. The last they'd seen of her was haring into the night on the Saturday.

Suddenly she realised a silence had fallen over the square as the chatter of women and kids dried up.

A policeman was striding up the cobbles towards them, his hat tucked under his arm. In alarm, she realised it was the same one who had arrested her mother. She watched as Nell crossed herself.

Not one soul down the Shoot breathed as they watched, waited, to see who he would stop in front of. It was a peculiar sensation, knowing that someone's life was about to change irrevocably.

He stopped in front of Nell.

'Auntie . . .'

'Spit it out.'

Lily covered her hand with her mouth.

'I'm very sorry to tell you, your husband was one of the bodies recovered from a street surface shelter which took a direct hit from a high explosive in the early hours of this morning.'

She nodded calmly.

'Where is he now?'

'In a makeshift mortuary at Carpenters Road School. We will need you to come and identify his body. I'm afraid the roof came down in one solid sheet and I should warn you, all the shelterers' bodies are . . .'

His voice trailed off.

'I can imagine,' she replied crisply.

Her composure was extraordinary. There was no reaction other than the slightest, almost imperceptible twitch of her eye.

Next he turned to Mrs Barnett.

'I'm sorry to inform you that Mr Barnett was also a casualty.'

A deathly silence descended on the square, only broken by Nell.

'Well, thank you, Billy. We'll be along later to identify the bodies.'

'I'm very sorry to you both for your loss.'

'I dare say,' said Nell smartly.

As he strode off, Lily wept and reached for her mother's hand.

'I'll come with you, Mum.'

'Where?' she replied.

'Why, to the morgue, of course.'

'That'll have to wait, Lil. My concern rests with the living.'

She turned to Julia.

'You ready?'

She nodded, speechless.

'Good. We need to find my children.'

As she walked off, Lily's broken brain spun, but despite her exhaustion, she couldn't take her eyes off Mrs Barnett's face. There was grief, but alongside that emotion, another stronger, purer one shone out. Relief.

36

Esther

Esther guessed it was tiredness-induced hysteria, but she had never seen the girls in the lipstick room so buoyed up.

Not one of them had clocked up more than a few hours' sleep since the bombings began that drowsy Saturday afternoon, just two days ago, but already it felt like a lifetime.

Was it possible to feel positivity amidst such chaos and destruction, and with the spectre of loss at every turn? Maybe positivity wasn't the right word, but Esther felt a purity of purpose that made her feel more alive than she ever had.

She sneaked a furtive glance up from the belt to where Walter was pouring vegetable oil into the lipstick churn, to find him gazing back at her. He had worked tirelessly to keep Yardley's and its occupants safe since the raids had begun, and she hoped it was helping to make him feel more of a man.

Just then, Fat Lou's voice jolted her out of her reverie.

'How about a song to keep us all awake?

'*Hitler has only got one ba*—'

'Lou, not now,' rang out Miss Rayson's voice from the doorway. 'The Managing Director would like to speak with you.'

The machines shut down and they turned to find the big boss on their floor, a rare occurrence.

'Hello, Mr Lavender, you come to join in our sing-song?' said Fat Lou jokingly.

'Lou . . .' scolded the welfare officer.

'Please, Miss Rayson, it's quite all right, I assure you. It's precisely this cock-a-snook attitude of our workers here that will ensure we weather these raids and continue to maintain our excellent reputation for fair play and fast distribution.'

He twisted his hat in his hands.

'I just wanted to say how impressed I am at the actions of every single Lavender Girl here at Yardley's. Especially you, Esther, Walter tells me you risked your life to extinguish an incendiary bomb. Your fortitude knows no limits and I am under no illusions that the reason this factory is still standing, unlike poor Clarnico's, is because of your tremendous bravery.'

He looked around the lipstick room, almost overcome with emotion. A strong stench of burnt sugar hung in the air, a tangible reminder that both the nearby sweet and jam factories, which employed so many Stratford girls, had copped it. Esther felt Yardley's existence owed more to fate than fortitude, but she said nothing.

'I-I'm so proud of you all. Just your being here, the simple act of turning up to work on time, despite the bombs, makes you all everyday heroines in my eyes.

'From today, I'll be closing the factory an hour earlier whilst these raids continue, to allow you the chance to get home safely to your families. You'll still be paid the same.'

'Thanks awfully, Mr Lavender.' Fat Lou glanced at her watch.

'It's five p.m. He's late. Here, you don't think Jerry's got lost, do you?'

'They're German, I shouldn't think so,' said Mr Lavender, with a brave stab at humour.

'And what about that tealeaf Nan, sir? Any sign of her?' Fat Lou asked.

'Not up for discussion,' interjected Miss Rayson hastily.

'Nothing under my turban, I can assure you,' Fat Lou quipped.

A ripple of laughter was drowned out by the siren.

The room was filled with the sound of scraping chairs as the girls filed calmly to the cloakroom to fetch their bags and head down to the factory shelter.

Esther grabbed her tin hat.

'Not tonight, Esther,' said Miss Rayson firmly. 'You were up all night Saturday on the roof, and I know for a fact you were out most of the night last night looking for Renee and her brother. Please, just rest for a while in the factory shelter.'

'But how can I when Renee and Frankie are still missing?'

'Renee is one of the strongest, most resilient girls I have come across,' Miss Rayson insisted. 'Tougher than I think any of us realise.'

'She's right,' Walter said, coming up behind her and sliding an arm around her. 'Let's just sit it out for a while in the shelter here, then when there's a lull, I can walk you and Lily back to the Shoot.'

Sitting down heavily in Yardley's air-raid shelter, Esther had to admit the room, which used to operate as the powder department, was a big improvement on any other shelter she had so far come across.

It was spacious, warm, dry and lined with welcoming bunk beds. It even smelt faintly of the English Lavender talcum powder that used to be packed there. Canteen staff were already brewing up huge urns of tea in the corner and handing out buttered buns.

Like most firms, Yardley's had opened up their shelters to members of the public who lived locally, and half the room was filled with people who lived down Carpenters Road.

She slumped down onto a bunk next to Lily and, within seconds, felt a wave of drowsiness swamp her.

'Just forty winks . . .'

Esther woke with a start, her eyes gritty and her mouth dry as toast. In the distance, the familiar boom and crump of explosions. Lily lay in the bunk next to her, out for the count, poor thing.

Walter was gazing down at her. The gas lamps had been dimmed and all around, people were attempting to sleep.

'How long have I been asleep?' she whispered sleepily.

He checked his watch.

'It's nearly two a.m.'

'Sorry. I must wake Lily, we really must be getting back to the Shoot.

'That's all right. My mum here's been keeping me company.'

'Hello, love.'

Mrs Smith's face appeared out of the gloom.

'Lovely to meet you, darlin',' grinned the woman settled on the bunk opposite. 'My Walter hasn't stopped talking about you. "Esther, this, Esther that . . ." I've hardly seen him since these raids began, so I thought I'd come down here and introduce myself. Meet the girl who my little Walter's so smitten on.'

She grabbed his cheek and squeezed it tight.

'He's a lovely boy, my Walter. Make a fine husband for any lucky girl, so he would,' she said pointedly.

'Leave off, Mum,' he said, blushing.

'Bloody Hitler. What a game, heh? I said this would happen, didn't I say as much, Walter?'

Esther's head swam with tiredness. Walter wasn't wrong about his mum being garrulous. She hadn't managed to get one word in so far. Mind you, this was East London, where as Esther was rapidly learning, everything was rationed, except talk!

'I must say,' Mrs Smith ploughed on, looking about, 'this

is a lovely shelter. Ever so clean. You should see some of 'em. I was down at a school in Canning Town on the first night of the bombings. Caught short visiting my friend, I was.' She raised both hands and sucked in her cheeks. 'Shocking it was. Terrible business. So many people crammed in there. I was surprised to see Renee Gunn and her brother there.'

She leant forward with a knowing smirk. 'Mind you, not as surprised as I was to see she's, you know . . .' Her hand hovered over her tummy. 'Can't say as I'm surprised, mind you.' She sniffed. 'Morals gone out the window and—'

'Hang on, did you say you saw Renee and Frankie?' Esther interrupted, her tiredness vanishing.

'Speak the truth and shame the devil.'

'Which one?'

'South Hallsville, Agate Street . . .'

'Are you quite sure?'

'Course I am. She pretended not to see me, but it was her all right and that funny little brother of hers. I must say, I was surprised to see them there, I assumed Nell was having them evacuated. I said to myself: "That's strange, Maureen."'

But Esther was no longer listening, instead she was frantically shaking Lily awake.

'Lily, wake up, I know where Renee is.'

37

Renee

Renee sneaked a glimpse at her neighbour's wristwatch. Three a.m. Was there ever a more ungodly hour? For some reason, it was important to Renee to keep track of how long she had been in this godforsaken school. Mentally, she tried to calculate how many days and hours they'd been sitting here waiting for transport out.

But try as she might, she could not get her sludge-filled mind to work or sleep. Her brain was catatonic through hunger, dehydration and exhaustion, though she was past eating and sleep was impossible. She gave up and, with a reedy sigh, plucked at her grimy collar. The heat was tropical, the atmosphere so thick you could've put a cup mid-air and it wouldn't have fallen.

Out of the shadows stared hollowed-out, grey faces. Bleak. Despairing.

She stroked her little brother's fine hair as he sketched intently in the dead of night. Renee watched him, spellbound. He seemed separate to the chaos and despair of everyone around him. Maybe this was why he was able to observe and draw them with such astonishing accuracy, his little fingers flying over the sketchpad with a stubby charcoal pencil.

Lonely old men, huge family groups, entire streets of

neighbours, the chatterers and the withdrawn all brought to life on the page.

Even as the day had turned to their third night and the gas lamps had been lit, his drawing had taken on the darkness, the strange waxiness of their faces, the strain of war.

If he had been an adult, no doubt there'd have been an uproar, people rightly protesting at being sketched at their most vulnerable, or worst, accusing him of being a fifth columnist, but as he was a small boy, he was largely invisible.

Guilt sliced through her. She had thought she was doing the right thing, now she was not so sure. With every hour of waiting, hope was slipping away. How much more could he bear? How much more could any of them bear? Renee glanced over at a woman attempting to nurse a tiny fractious baby, yards from her an elderly blind man with badly ulcerated legs was slumped on the floor in obvious pain and distress. It was a bloody disgrace. Some of the neighbourhood's most vulnerable were squashed in here, most of them, like she and Frankie, now into their third night. Too tired, too disabled or injured, old or young to simply walk away from the docklands. And with most of the public transport in and out of Canning Town now out of action, they were effectively trapped, entirely reliant on the authorities for escape.

Somewhere in the soupy darkness, a woman moaned like she was dying. Renee's leg jerked. The baby moved inside her.

'Water,' she gasped, 'I need water.'

Frankie stopped drawing and looked up at her, his grey eyes sad.

The lady next to her stirred. 'They've run out of fresh water down here, love. Try upstairs, if you can get up there, that is.'

Her husband scowled as a high-explosive bomb boomed nearby. It was a noise that seemed to pass through bone and blood and lodge straight in the soul.

'The next one's ours, I'm telling you! Where's the bloody

ack-ack guns? Why aren't we firing back? Where are the coaches? Three flamin' days we've sat here like prize idiots. We're casualties, not casuals!'

'Oh, do shut up, Derek,' groaned his wife, 'you're giving me the right ache. The coaches'll be here. They've said they will, so they will.'

Something inside Renee snapped, and there and then, she knew. The coaches were *never* coming. They had been forgotten, abandoned, or both. A blinding flash of her mother's common sense, so potent she could almost hear her voice in her ear. Renee scrubbed at her face and sat up. My God, what was it Nell had said when the man from the council had tried to bully them into sleeping on the floor of a school hall, exactly one year ago?

'Years this war has been brewing, pal, and now we're facing the filthy terror again. You've had months in which to build decent underground shelters for the families of Stratford and the best you can come up with is a school hall? People are going to die!'

People are going to die! Her mum had been right, was right now, in fact. The authorities didn't know better. There was no fleet of coaches round the corner. And if she and Frankie stayed here, her mum's dark prophecy would come true. The realisation turned the sweat to icy trickles down her back, but then, something galvanised inside her. What would Nell Gunn do? She who questioned everything. There was little point asking the rescue centre volunteers, poor sods didn't seem to know any more than she did. All they could offer was that great British panacea, a cup of tea! As if a tidal wave of tea could hold back the advancing armies! Which left only one option.

'Fuck this for a game of soldiers,' Renee muttered grimly under her breath.

'Come on, sweetie,' she said, gently taking Frankie's sketch-book from him and hauling herself up to standing. 'We're getting out of this hell hole.'

'Where? Home?' he asked hopefully.

'Yes. No. I don't know. Let's just concentrate on getting out of here.'

'You leaving?' asked the man sitting next to them. He was nice enough, Derek, as was his wife, though she suffered terribly – and vocally – with her rheumatism. You learn a lot about your fellow shelterers when you're pressed up against them day and night.

'Yeah,' Renee replied. 'For what it's worth, I don't think them coaches are coming.'

'But what'll you do?' worried his wife, staring at her swollen tummy. 'There's a raid on.'

'I don't care. I've got a pair of legs and a brain. I'm gonna start using 'em. We'll hitchhike out if we have to.'

'Most sensible thing I've heard,' Derek nodded. 'Come on, love, we're out of here too.'

They stared at each other through the gloom, a strange sense of comradeship between them.

'Good luck out there, love,' he remarked, shaking Renee's hand. 'You got more balls than some fellas I know.'

'And good luck to you both,' she replied.

Renee gripped Frankie's hand firmly and they set off. Numbers had mushroomed over the past three days. Twenty minutes it took them, just to navigate through the sea of bodies and edge their way trembling up the densely packed staircase, accusing voices calling over the boom of bombs.

Watch my baby. Mind yourself. Oi, you stepped on my hand.

By the time they reached the top, Renee was exhausted. People talk of fear, of being petrified, but Renee had never felt anything like the panic or claustrophobia in that seething stairway. The dehumanisation of the shelterers had crept up stealthily over the past three days, reducing them to a tangle of elbows, twisted limbs and feet. It was hard to tell where one human being began and another ended. It was like . . .

like . . . a sickening sensation ran the length of Renee's body at the realisation . . . like a charnel house. Death was stalking them, coming closer.

Renee began to tremble, or was it the staircase? In that moment the premonition took full force of her being and she readied herself, for instinctively she knew: you never heard the bomb that killed you.

A sudden violent wash of flame.

'Fucking hell!' screamed a voice.

It was as though time stopped and Renee saw her own death with perfect clarity.

Her and her illegitimate baby, two lives for the price of one.

With a tearing scream, she threw herself over Frankie's body just as the reinforced concrete roof split in two and an avalanche of hot bricks rained down.

Images unspooled like cinema film.

Human hair and flesh falling through hot dust. Limbs twisted at impossible angles. The ground opening beneath her.

She was spinning now. Into the darkness. Separating, her mind and body breaking apart. There was no pain, no noise . . . only . . . 'Alfie?' she whispered.

Her eyes flickered and there he was, Alfie, standing in a snow blizzard in the yard at the paint factory, arms open wide, pockets stuffed with red roses, his face filled with love.

A white mist floated at the periphery of Renee's vision.

Alfie seemed to be welcoming her, beckoning her into the snow and ice. Red petals tumbled from his fingertips. He spread his arms wider still, those ice-blue eyes gently entreating her.

Come on, Renee. Frankie's safe. Come to me.

But it's cold.

Not for long. Come on. You and our baby'll be safe here.

She stepped towards him.

38

Lily

The whole world was on fire! The closer they got to the docks, the more shocking the sights became. The glare of the burning docks rose from behind a shattered skyline, a desolate landscape filled with strange shrouded shapes. The road ahead was blocked off, sealed behind a cordon.

'Mum,' Lily panted, skidding to a halt. 'Maybe we should turn back. Try again in the morning?'

'No!' Nell screamed, whirling round, the glow from the fires reflected in her eyes. 'It'll be too late by then. How did we not find 'em?'

Because they didn't want to be found, Lily wanted to say. If her hunch was correct, Renee had used the opportunity for her and Frankie to escape from their respective institutions, but there was no time to find the words, as Nell was off again, ducking under the cordon and running past a solid wall of fire.

Lily felt the draught of heat suck the breath from her body as she, Julia, Walter and Esther gave chase.

'Mum! Come back!' she screamed. 'They're bound to have been evacuated by now. It's not safe.'

But Nell kept going, running and stumbling over the hose pipes in the direction of Canning Town.

A shimmering shape was silhouetted against the furnace.

The fireman's face was a picture, his sodden tunic steaming in the heat.

'Get to safety!' he bellowed over the roar of water and fire.

But nothing and no one was stopping Nell Gunn. She pushed on, past an unexploded bomb, narrowly avoiding a teenage messenger on a yellow-painted bike, skidding through a tunnel of fire, past a hand sticking out of the rubble like a macabre signpost to the school.

As they turned the corner into Agate Street, a choking pall of pulverised brick dust enveloped them. Lily doubled over, gasping for breath, each red-hot particle burning the back of her throat.

'Mum, I really think we ought—'

Lily never finished her sentence. Because in that moment, a giant cloud of dust mushroomed over everything. The air shuddered. They heard the bomb, but could see nothing.

The night suddenly became electric. Police and fire engine bells. Whistles. Screams. Shouts.

Catastrophic chaos. A woman ran out of the hot dust cloud, the severed stump of her left arm twitching.

Teams of rescue workers in overalls and tin hats were streaming towards the school building, slithering on the rubble.

Lily began to run too, unaware of anything, not even where her mum was.

'Miss, you can't . . .' She tore past the official.

The way forward was blocked by a towering pile of bricks, at least seven foot high. She scrambled up the brickwork, gashing her shins, glittering shards of glass glowing in the darkness.

On the other side, her hand flew to her mouth and she felt acid bile rise up in her mouth.

It looked as if the school had imploded, a vast crater in the middle where the roof had crashed down two floors into the basement. She stared down into the hole. It was the very pit of hell. An enormous smoking crater, covered in a blanket of soft tissue.

Waxy-looking limbs, matted hair and scalps strewn together in a soup of bodies. Monstrous. Forcing herself to breathe, Lily pulled a torch from her bag and tried to gather her wits. She had to find Renee and Frankie.

Up above, she heard a curious creaking sound, then a crack. She swung the torch up, just in time to see the edge of a classroom wall fall, dragging more masonry with it. She leapt out the way just in time, falling and winding herself. For a moment she teetered on the edge of the crater.

A hand reached out, an ARP worker pulled her back.

'Get out of here, miss, now.'

But ignoring him and the stabbing in her side, she ploughed on, skirting the edges of the crater. Swinging her torch about. 'Renee! Frankie!'

Blood seeped from her shins and knuckles. Soft moans and muffled whimpers sounded from under rubble and steel girders.

Lily remembered how many people had been here when they had searched on Sunday. She dreaded to think how many people were entombed beneath the ground.

All about her, rescue workers, wearing masks against plaster dust and smell, were frantically digging under piles of bricks and shifting giant slabs of concrete.

A call went up. 'Silence for rescue!' Everyone fell quiet, listening motionless for signs of life, even for the faintest tapping. Outside a man's voice drifted through the smoke.

'Cancel the coaches, send us morgue vans and ambulances instead.'

Lily watched, transfixed, as a rescue worker abseiled peril-ously into the crater with a rope wrapped round his middle. He swung round 360 degrees, his head torch sweeping a beam of light. And it was in this beam that Lily saw the flash of blonde hair splayed against charred brick.

Falling to her knees by what looked like the top of a staircase, she dug like a dog, flinging aside masonry and rubble.

Bit by bit, her sister's body emerged from the coffin of debris.

Gently, Lily turned her over, Renee's hands still cradling her tummy, and a wash of terror rinsed her from head to toe. There was something about the leaden weight of her. So cold. So limp.

'Hello, you, you gave us quite the run-about,' Lily whispered, taking out her torch and shining it on her sister's face.

No, no, no!

Was it the slick of scarlet that bubbled from the corner of Renee's lips she found the most horrifying? Or the mouth, locked in a silent, never-ending scream? No. It was the look in her eyes that cleaved Lily's heart in two.

Dogged defiance.

'Renee, can you hear me?' Lily wept. She placed her ear close to her mouth, hoping for the exhale of air, anything, a moth's breath even. Nothing. Her blue eyes revealed the truth. The light was gone.

Lily closed her eyes, rocked back on her haunches with Renee's body in her arms and moaned softly. Somewhere in her agony, she wondered how on earth she would find the strength to begin looking for Frankie's corpse. The clamorous stench of death rose up in waves from the crater and Lily fought the urge to be sick.

The scratching noise was followed by a tap. Lily's eyes snapped open.

A plank of wood by Renee's foot shifted. Gently, she laid Renee down and was on her feet in seconds, frantically digging through the debris. First she unearthed a sketchbook, next a dirty brown satchel and then dusty fingers. They twitched.

'Help! Over here! Help me!' She screamed so loud, her voice seemed to split open the fetid air above the crater.

Outside, it took the combined strength of Esther, Walter, Julia and two ARP wardens to hold a hysterical Nell Gunn back behind the cordon. All about was a hive of activity as policemen, firemen, St John's Ambulance and heavy rescue raced into the school, or what was left of it.

A man standing next to them, an official by the looks of him, lifted his head to the heavens.

'My God, my God, this should never have happened!'

The ARP worker holding Nell back, a veteran of the First War, swung round sharply and grabbed him.

'And it never would've if you and your mates hadn't buggered it up.'

'You bastards!' Nell howled, making a lunge for the official.

Esther was beginning to wonder how much longer she could hold on, when they spotted her.

It was a miracle that seemed to defy all the normal laws of life. From the holocaust of smoke and horror emerged Lily, carrying Frankie in her arms.

39

Lily

Eight days later, Renee Gunn and her unborn child were buried under an occluded sky at East London Cemetery in Plaistow with little ceremony.

A capricious wind tugged at scarves and sent hats skittering across the graveyard. Lily smiled. Renee would've liked that. The fleeting moment of levity was quickly replaced with burning grief, alongside a colder, calmer anger.

The 'incident' as the authorities had taken to calling it, was just another bleak brush stroke of death in a picture of absolute carnage. Seventy-three was the official death toll so far. Poppycock! Lily had counted more bodies than that herself on the surface of the crater. God alone knew how many poor souls perished that dark night, but it must've been four hundred. Or more.

This anger was the only thing pushing back the tsunami of sadness. How could she be in a world that Renee was no longer in? Lush, vital Renee with her quick tongue and velvety smile?

Lily moaned and covered her eyes.

My beguiled and broken heart.

It was hard to comprehend that she wouldn't look across the lipstick belt and see Renee yakking away, blue eyes sparkling with mischief under her white turban, five foot nothing of cockney sass. Harder still to comprehend what had actually killed her. The Luftwaffe bomb had finished her off, of course, but what about West Ham Council's grievous dereliction of duty, bungling officials who might or might not have sent the coaches to Camden Town instead of Canning Town. It was that rumour above all that had nearly done for Lily. Camden Town was nine miles north and in completely the wrong borough! Had her sister died because someone hadn't bothered to spell out an address? Others were claiming that the leader of the convoy of coaches, ordered to rendezvous at the George, a well-known local pub, went to a pub of the same name in another borough. No one knew for sure and now that a news blackout had been imposed and a security cordon placed around the school, Lily knew the authorities would do their utmost to suppress the truth.

But it wasn't just the needlessness of all those deaths as a direct result of such shabby organisation. It was also the judgmental society Renee and Frankie were running from when they found themselves in the abysmal rest centre in the first place, and the utter lack of decency and humanity on the part of the authorities. Those too had been nails in her coffin as surely as that bomb had been.

The King and Queen had visited the site, three days after the bomb had hit, and on the same day their own palace had been bombed apparently. They had talked with the rescue parties, offered comfort and solace to the survivors. Being a staunch royalist herself, Renee would have had the right needle to have missed them, Lily thought with a hollow laugh. She wondered whether Their Majesties had been told how long the refugees had been sitting in that school waiting for transport when the inevitable bomb had found its mark. Or whether they, like her, had tried to visualise Renee's final hours. She couldn't imagine the mounting panic her sister must've felt, or the conditions in that squalid school as the days had crawled by. But she didn't need to. Frankie's vivid sketches had revealed all. The horror had leapt off the pages . . . The amorphous huddle of festering people left to die. The sketchbook had been confiscated at the hospital by someone in a suit. An official?

'Important evidence . . . Public morale . . . Order of the War Cabinet . . .' the words had tripped smoothly off his tongue.

In their haze of grief, they had scarcely thought to ask, but Lily had managed to retrieve one sketch, at least. Torn in haste before it had been taken away.

It was the last picture of her sister alive, and it was as close to a photograph as possible. Unbeknownst to Renee, Frankie had sketched her in the school. Her eyes were closed, a tendril of blonde hair damp with sweat curled over her temple, her hands resting lightly on her unborn child.

Even in the squash of people, it was a moment of extraordinary intimacy. Like there had been no one else there but she and her baby. She had never looked so beautiful.

Lily had wanted to keep it, but Nell had other ideas.

'You and your baby can sleep tight now with your Alfie, darling girl,' she whispered. Gently, she kissed the picture and bending down, placed it on Renee's coffin.

The thud of earth covered it. Lily closed her eyes and images flew at her in the darkness.

The jigsaw of body parts laid out on tin trays on the cold chipped floor of Romford Road Swimming Baths, which had been drained and set up as an emergency mortuary. The luggage tag attached to Renee's big toe. Undertakers in bowler hats from T. Cribb & Sons picking their way through the bodies.

These thoughts came fast and without warning, roaring through her head, and suddenly she found herself back in the rank darkness of that school, wading through corpses and eviscerated bodies. But she had to free her mind from the haunting fear of that night. She must, for that way madness lay. Lily moved her head from side to side, as if to physically shake out the horror trapped inside. Frankie's drawing was the only way she wanted to remember her little sister.

As the space above the coffin was filled in and mourners stepped forward to place their wreaths, Lily reached out and gripped her mother's hand.

The lipstick room was there in force – all except Nan, who still hadn't been seen. The general consensus was that she never would be now and good riddance.

The Yardley girls were determined that Renee would go off with the glamour she craved in her short life.

'I thought about nicking it, but I know you'd only come and haunt me,' joked Fat Lou, placing Renee's treasured signed studio portrait of Rita Hayworth next to her small headstone.

Lily could see she and the rest of the girls were trying desperately to keep their composure, but it was too much.

'I wanted you to rest with someone as bright and pretty as you,' she said, her voice finally cracking. 'Th-thank you, Renee, for kissing the back end of a horse.'

And then, under her breath: 'You'd have made a smashing mum.'

Lily felt a searing stab of pain at Lou's words. She was right. Renee had died without experiencing the absolute joy of cradling her baby in her arms. Renee had died without knowing so many things, in fact.

Lily's impossible secret, the one she had kept hidden from Renee, shuddered inside her and Lily wanted to scream out the truth across the freshly dug grave. Maybe it was better Renee had never known the real reason why her big sister had fled Stratford, for she would only think Lily a coward.

Nell stared, stony-faced, across to the far side of the grave-yard.

'I suppose in some ways we're the lucky ones,' she murmured. 'Least we got a decent body to bury.'

A long line of black moved across the graveyard. With a jolt, Lily realised it was mourners for the public burial. It seemed as if there was no end to this slow dark line, as a tide of people came to mourn the dead. A veil of darkness had swept its way over war-torn East London and Lily wondered if they would ever see the light again. Churchill had spoken to the nation recently with one of his rousing speeches, talked of the need to 'stand together and hold firm', to 'not flinch or weary of the struggle'. He was right, but Lily was already so bloody weary.

'Can you believe they're still digging bodies out of that crater?' Nell said under her breath. 'When will the authorities admit they made a mistake?'

There was no answer to that. Lily, like everyone else in Canning Town, was numbed by the injustice and neglect. The tide was turning in the East End, though. Three nights ago, a group from Stepney had stormed the Savoy Hotel's swanky underground shelter in protest at the closure of the Tubes to shelterers and further east, a huge crowd had kicked down the locked door to Bethnal Green Underground. People were claiming their right to safety and Lily felt sure that soon the government would be forced to acquiesce. Simple, humbling courage displayed by ordinary working Londoners. Even if it was too late for Renee.

A flash of red caught Lily's eye. In the breeze, a handful of blood red petals skittered and tumbled over the freshly dug earth of Renee's grave. Lily looked about. Strange. No one there was carrying any wreaths lavish enough to contain roses. She turned back to her mother as the brief ceremony came to a close.

'Do you want to wait a bit?' Lily asked her mother as the mourners moved off to toast the short life of Renee Gunn down the Carpenters Arms. 'Say a private prayer with the vicar?'

'No, I'm afraid I don't believe in Him any more. I just want to get back to Frankie at the hospital.'

Lily looked at her mother, stunned at her renouncement of the faith she had always cherished.

'Mum, we buried Dad yesterday and Renee today. Don't you think maybe you ought to go home and rest? You've been at Frankie's bedside for eight days solid.'

'Well, I ain't there now, am I?' she snapped. 'Who's coming?'

She turned, and Lily caught Julia's eye.

'Come on,' she said softly. 'Let's follow your mother to the hospital.'

Julia and Esther took an arm each and, with Lily moving painfully between them, they followed Nell slowly from the graveyard.

'How you feeling, Lily?' Esther asked.

'Lucky to have come away with nothing but a couple of broken ribs and some bruised shins,' she replied.

'I haven't said it to you yet,' Julia said as they walked. 'But you were incredibly brave to have gone in and found your brother and sister. Reckless, but brave.'

Lily smiled ruefully.

'Not sure about that. Do you think Frankie will be all right?'

'The early signs are good, Lily,' Julia replied. 'There are a lot of broken bones, but no serious damage, or so it would appear, to his internal organs.'

'So why does he look so ill? He's not said a word yet.'

'The doctors are deliberately keeping him sedated to allow his body a chance to heal and get over the shock. He'll get there. He's stronger than you might think.'

She squeezed Lily's arm.

'It's you and your mother I worry about.'

Nell was waiting for them at the entrance to the cemetery and just as they reached her, the howling banshee siren started up.

'Let us bury our dead in peace, you dirty bastards!' Nell wailed, her clenched fist held aloft against the sky.

'Come on, Mum,' said Lily, gently picking a stray rose petal that had caught in her mother's hair. 'We need to hurry if we're to see Frankie.'

40

Esther

Frankie was in the basement of St Mary's Hospital in Plaistow, now only taking and treating casualties of the raids. A bomb had fallen on the hospital the day before the bomb had hit the school in Canning Town, and many of the wards were now lit by candlelight while the staff calmly worked on with battery-powered nightlights. How those brave doctors and nurses carried on, Esther had no idea.

Frankie hadn't moved a muscle since they left for the funeral. He lay like a perfect white marble statue of himself, the flickering candlelight casting shadows over his face. Not even the distant thunder of bombs roused him from wherever he was.

Nell fussed about, smoothing down his sheets, gently plumping his pillow, before plopping into a chair next to him with a deep sigh.

'You back, Mrs Gunn?' joked an exhausted-looking nurse pushing a trolley of glass medicine bottles. 'Don't you have a home to go to?'

A shuddering explosion overhead rattled the bottles on the trolley and everyone took a breath in.

'Probably not,' Nell joked weakly.

'The doctor will be around later to speak with you, but Frankie's going to be evacuated to a hospital in Surrey. He's out of immediate danger and he needs to be able to recuperate somewhere quiet and safe.'

As she moved off, all eyes were on Nell.

'Will you go too, Mum?' Lily asked.

For the first time, Nell Gunn looked hesitant, the thought of leaving her beloved Shoot presenting her with a dilemma.

'Mum, you're not betraying anyone by leaving Stratford,' said Lily. 'Frankie needs you.'

A sudden roar of anti-aircraft guns let rip overhead with a deafening barrage as London finally began to bare its teeth and fight back.

'He deserves better than me,' Nell said quietly when the noise subsided. She scrubbed wearily at her face. 'I have to face facts, I'm a terrible mum.'

'No, you're not,' Julia protested. 'Besides, show me a mother who doesn't think that, and I'll show you a liar.'

Nell's head jerked up, her eyes haunted in the candlelight.

'Except I *actually* am! Where was I when Renee needed me? Prison is where! It's my fault she's dead!'

A tear broke and slid down her cheek.

'I'm tired, Julia, so tired. I've been fighting all my life. A bad first husband, the depression, rent strikes, the war, prison. Now I've lost another husband, a daughter *and* a grandchild. Lord, I'm as old as time . . .'

'You're not,' Julia replied.

'But I feels it. I'm done with it, with this life and this history.' Her voice was laden down, a penetrating sorrow to her words.

Esther stared transfixed at Nell. In the candlelight, her hair was the colour of dust.

'I think . . .' Nell struggled to compose herself. 'I think, Frankie's better off without me.'

'My dear, you are so wrong. He needs you more now than ever. Frankie is . . .' Julia hesitated, wringing her hands. 'How can I say, he's not like other children, he's not cut from the same cloth.'

'Exactly,' Nell protested, 'and I don't know him. God knows I love the boy, but I don't understand him. What kind of mother does that make me? Baffled by her own child?'

'Actually, given the nature of Frankie's condition, it's a miracle you've managed this long.'

Nell looked up, confused.

'What do you mean, his condition?' she asked sharply.

'Mum,' said Esther suddenly, 'you have to tell her your suspicions. Now.'

'Yes, you're right, Esther,' Julia replied, folding her hands on her lap as if to ready herself.

'Nell, I'm not sure how to say this, where to start . . .'

'From the beginning,' Nell said warily.

'Very well. In Vienna, I worked as a nurse at the children's clinic on a ward at a prestigious hospital housed in the University of Vienna. I worked there under the tuition of a wonderful man by the name of Hans Asperger, a paediatrician.' She smiled, suddenly enraptured by the memory.

'He was as remarkable as the children we treated. Softly spoken, little round glasses, he looked like a boy himself, but I was never fooled by this. He had a formidable brain.'

She turned to look at Frankie in his hospital bed and instinctively lowered her voice.

'The clinic took in the children other people had written off as problematic, those who were gifted, sensitive, cast out by their peers . . .

'Instead of seeing children in their care as flawed or sick, they saw them as suffering from neglect by a society that was failing to provide them with thoughtful teaching methods.

'A lot of the children in their care were dismissed as feeble-minded, but the clinic never saw them as problem children to be shut away in cold, loveless institutions.'

Her smile grew wider, peeling the years off her.

'Hans was – *is* – a very gentle, intuitive man. He and his colleagues at the clinic wanted to help all children have the best possible chance of finding their potential. Each one is a future chef, scientist, poet, musician, farmer, professor . . .' She glanced at Frankie. 'Or artist.'

'What's this got to do with our Frankie?' Nell asked.

'Because I strongly suspect that Frankie has what Hans Asperger has described as a condition named Autismus, or as displaying what he called autistic psychopathy.'

'And with your permission, when this dreadful war is over, I'd like us to go to Vienna, introduce Frankie to Hans Asperger and the other children in the clinic. Help him to discover his potential.'

Nell stared at her, thunderstruck, trying to absorb it all.

'What goes on in this clinic?' Lily asked, intrigued.

'Oh, it was a wonderful place, Lily. We all had a voice and a role, even women,' she glanced at Esther, who was listening, rapt. 'Especially women. After the First War, people were starving, so the clinic promoted ward maids and transformed hospital kitchens, which enabled thousands of starving children to be fed.

'Between the wars, I helped to observe the children. Mornings began with exercise classes in the fresh air, then we taught them music, literature, nature study, arithmetic and history. Afternoons were devoted to rest and play. At weekends, after church, we taught them plays and we performed concerts . . .'

She laughed wryly.

'I say we taught them. In many cases, these children taught us. Some children with Autismus have unique gifts, you see, like Frankie's gift for drawing. It's just a matter of discovering them. They can be highly intelligent, despite a lack of so-called common sense, which men like your father pride, Lily.'

Lily nodded slowly.

'They might not be able to make small talk, relate with understanding or compassion, which of course marks them out as different. But trust me when I tell you, *they* are the teachers, not us.'

Nell's tears flowed hard and fast as she absorbed what Julia was saying.

'Are you quite sure this is what Frankie has?' Lily asked, reaching for her mother's hand over the hospital bed.

'Not a hundred per cent, no. I would need the clinic to assess him, but instinct and experience tells me. Have you noticed how literal Frankie is? How the slightest change in routine throws him? How difficult it is to read his facial expressions?'

Nell nodded, remembering how he got into a terrible rage at school when art was swapped for arithmetic, all the times she watched the Bricky Kids aping about, pulling silly faces, only to see Frankie watching them from the sidelines with a face like stone.

'Repetition, symmetry, building huge collections are traits common to many children with Autismus. They like to create order out of the chaos.'

Nell thought of Frankie's collection of hundreds of match-boxes and felt a slow light of understanding kindle inside her.

'He is a stranger to the world around him, yet the world around *him* is strange,' Julia said. 'Do you see?'

'And you say there are other children, like Frankie?' Lily asked and Julia nodded. 'Hundreds, maybe thousands, the world over, and it crosses a broad cross section of people, though mainly, it must be said, boys and men. Before I was forced to flee Vienna, Hans confided to me that he thought his work so far had only revealed the tip of the iceberg, that this condition is perhaps not so rare, when—'

She broke off and Esther looked at her fearfully.

'—when the Nazis took over the hospital.'

She shook the cloud of fear and foreboding from her face.

'When we win this war and they have gone, you must all come with me to this wonderful place, a place that humanises children like Frankie.

'You see, this war makes me realise why we must fight harder than ever. Nazis want to murder anyone who is different, who does not fit their idea of Aryan perfection. Not just Jewish people, but the Roma people, disabled, homo-sexuals, political opponents. Anyone they deem to be inferior. So for children like Frankie, we must fight for humanity, for civilisation.'

'What's become of this man and his clinic full of children like Frankie?' Lily asked, and Julia's gaze fell to the hospital floor.

'Hans professed to me his commitment to speak out for these children and protect them, but in doing so, he puts himself in grave danger. To the Nazis, they are "undesirables" and therefore not worthy of life. The Gestapo were beginning to take notice of these children when I left.'

She shook her head, 'I fear for them all. But please, let us talk only of Frankie and as we are speaking so candidly, I say what I say in the spirit of honesty and reconciliation.'

She paused.

'Your son has great potential, but of course, he's not your biological son, is he, Nell?'

Nell and Lily exchanged a look that Esther would never forget as long as she lived. A deep silence smothered the room, broken eventually by Nell.

'Did you tell her?'

Lily shook her head.

'She must've guessed.'

'Working at the clinic taught me to look at life with open

eyes,' Julia said gently, 'and when you start to do this, it's amazing what you notice.'

It was as if a curtain lifted so vividly, Esther actually wanted to laugh.

'Of course, you're Frankie's real mother,' she whispered, staring at Lily. 'That's why you left, all those years ago, when he was a baby.'

Lily nodded, white-faced with shock.

'So you can imagine how I felt when I saw history repeating itself with Renee.'

'Who is his father?' Esther blurted the question before she could stop herself.

'A silly teenage crush and certainly not one who wanted to stick around and save my reputation,' she snorted. 'Isn't that right, Mum?'

Nell sighed and sagged further back in her chair.

'You mightn't be able to say his name, but I can. Jimmy bloody Connor. The lowest toerag to have walked the streets of Stratford.'

'Jimmy! As in Nan's Jimmy?' Esther exclaimed, unable to reconcile an image of smart, sensible Lily with a man as sleazy as Jimmy.

'I was sixteen, Esther,' Lily mumbled, looking mortified. 'My God, when I think back to how naive I was. He used to wait for me outside the factory every day, told me how special I was.' She laughed bitterly.

'I fell for it mind, hook, line and sinker. That's probably why he goes for the younger ones, easier to get in the sack.'

A repulsive image of Jimmy slobbering over her in the cloakroom at his own wedding, when she'd been just fifteen, flashed unnervingly through Esther's mind, shortly followed by Lily's warning to stay away from him. No wonder! Suddenly it all made perfect sense.

'It was me who first realised she was carrying,' Nell

continued. 'Me who came up with the idea to pass Frankie off as mine to save the scandal of his illegitimacy, and Pat and I raised him as our own. Believe me, we're not the only ones to live such a lie.'

An exhausted tear trickled down Nell's cheek.

'Mum's right,' Lily agreed, passing her mum a handkerchief. 'Though I didn't see it at the time.'

Lily shook her head, haunted by the memory and turned to face her mother. 'When you told me I was having a baby, I was so scared. I was just a kid myself really. Back then I couldn't find the words to tell you how dirty and ashamed I felt.

'You had no reason to feel ashamed,' Nell wept, anger building in her. 'It was all that bast—'

'But I did, Mum,' Lily said, cutting her off. 'And when Jimmy told me he didn't believe the baby was his, I wanted to die. I'd only ever been with him. I-I thought I loved him.'

Her voice trailed off as she stared at the floor. In the distance they heard a bomb find its mark, followed by the screaming of a fire engine. Bedlam was unleashing outside, but Esther doubted Lily and her mum were even aware.

'I think we better leave you both to talk,' said Esther tactfully, standing up.

'*No*,' said Lily, her head snapping up, 'please stay. This is the first time we've ever talked about this, isn't that right, Mum? Having you and Julia here helps.'

Nell nodded.

'Please stay.'

Esther sank back onto her chair.

Lily drew in a deep breath, summoning up the courage to continue her story.

'We went away for a spell, made up an excuse about visiting an old aunt in the countryside, and when we came home, Mum had a new son and I had a . . . a brother. Not sure how many people down the Shoot fell for it, mind, but who's going to dare question Nell Gunn? Those days when we arrived home, Mum, watching you care for Frankie, were pure torture.'

Nell rested her hand on Lily's.

'I'm so sorry, Lily, but there was no other way to save your reputation.'

'My *reputation*,' Lily snorted, rolling the word around her mouth like it was a phial of poison.

'Jimmy's reputation certainly didn't seem to suffer,' she spat. 'In fact, while I'd been away, giving birth to his child, he'd fixed his sights on Nan and got her in the same predicament. Poor girl was even younger than me, just fifteen,' said Lily despairingly. 'Jimmy hit a new low when he threw her over after the abortion, only to ask her back out a few years later.'

'How could she have married him?' Esther asked.

'Love, I suppose,' Lily shrugged. 'Jimmy was very persuasive. I bet he did the dirty on her. In fact, I dread to think how many other women and girls there are out there he's fathered children with.'

'If he couldn't keep it zipped, he ought to have it chopped off,' Nell snapped.

A silence seeped over the bedside as the implications of all that was being revealed sunk in.

'When I walked in on the aftermath of Nan's abortion, I just wanted to get away,' Lily whispered, hugging her arms about herself. 'It was a total mess, an impossible situation. I'm sure plenty of girls have been able to live alongside their child and pretend he's a brother or sister, but not me. It was too hard, aching to hold my baby in my arms, but seeing him reach for you, Mum, instead.'

Nell's green eyes were fathomless in the dim light of the ward.

'I did what I had to do, love,' she repeated like a mantra.

'I know, but back then I couldn't live that lie, I had to get away.' Lily hesitated, stumbling over her words. 'S-seeing as we're being so honest, I-I've written letters to Frankie, Mum. Dozens of them over the years, to explain why I left. I came back with the intention of showing them to him one day, but now I see,' and here she turned to Julia. 'It's never going to be that straightforward, is it?'

'Not to a child like Frankie, I'm afraid, Lily,' Julia replied. 'His brain is wired a little differently to yours and mine. What this boy needs now is consistency and stability. He's already lost a father and a sister. He cannot lose his mother's identity as well.'

'Which is why things *must* continue as before,' Lily urged her mum. 'Despite what you say, Mum, you've done a smashing job with Frankie and I'm so grateful. That little boy adores you, and you adore him. Your lives are braided together, which makes *you* his true mother. Not me.'

'Lily's right,' Julia said, gently entreating Nell to understand. 'A mother is the one who the child looks to for guidance and security. You gave him the home life Lily never could. That's the ultimate gift of love, surely?'

'Maybe,' Nell replied, 'but I won't stand in your way, Lily. If you want to go to Surrey with Frankie and tell him the truth, I'll support you. With your father and Renee gone, nothing feels normal any more, whatever normal is, heh, Julia?'

Julia raised one eyebrow. 'You're learning! But please remember this. Never ever lose faith in Frankie or belief in your own strength as a mother. Carry that love like a fire cupped in your hands.' She reached over, touched Nell's cheek with her fingertips. 'In Yiddish we call people like you, Nell, a *mensch,* a person of integrity and honour. You see life for how it is, not how you would like it to be.'

Lily nodded.

'What Julia's saying makes sense. I won't be going to Surrey with Frankie, Mum, but you must. *You must.* He's your son, not mine.' Lily's gaze flickered to the slim little body in the hospital bed. 'Being back in Stratford has made me realise why it's time to lay the past to rest and stop clinging to an impossible dream.' She spoke cautiously, sounding the words out carefully. 'Maybe, in letting go of Frankie, I'm not making a sacrifice, but giving him the ultimate gift of love, because surely true love doesn't come in neatly packaged titles? This way he has a mother *and* a sister who love him very much.'

Esther wanted to cry for her brave friend and the impossible secrets she had shouldered throughout her young life.

Instead, she hugged her. 'You'll always be a part of his story,' she whispered in Lily's ear.

The all-clear wailed loudly, breaking the loaded atmosphere round the hospital bed and the noise seemed to stir something in Frankie.

'Hush, he's waking up,' said Julia, gripping Nell's hand.

Frankie's face twitched and he opened his grey eyes groggily, as if awaking from a long, deep sleep.

He stared with that grave and serious look around the people gathered at his bedside, until his gaze settled on Nell.

Pure love and relief kindled.

'Mum, you're back!'

Afterword

July 14th 1941, ten months later . . .

The world we fight for might not be a brave new world,
but it will be a new world for the brave

Vogue, January 1941

Lily

Monday morning and by the look of the blousy clouds loafing across the blue skies, it was going to blossom into a perfect summer's day over East London. Lily stepped outside number 10 and breathed in a big lungful of air, before choking and making a grab for her handkerchief.

'Good grief,' she spluttered, eyes smarting from the sulphurous stench. Not yet eight a.m. and already Berk Spencer Acids over the Cut were brewing up something tremendously ripe. Half the women of the Shoot were whipping their washing off the communal line. Judging by the gentle south-easterly blowing, it would only be a matter of time before the sheets flapping on the line would end up with tiny holes from airborne droplets of acid.

Lily was going to miss a lot of things about Stratford – except the air.

She shook her head in disbelief – could it really be her last day? The job offer had come so fast and out of the blue, she'd barely had time to consider whether she was doing the right thing, but maybe that in itself was a good thing. Gut instinct told her she would not regret the move.

Hurrying across the square, Lily's gaze was snagged by some activity on the outer edges of the graveyard. Snowball and his small team of helpers, including Mrs Barnett, were already out and hard at work despite the hour.

'A bit of elbow grease, that's what I like to see,' Lily called as she surveyed the fledgling beginnings of the small Dig for Victory allotment that was forming.

'Well, this garden won't dig itself,' Snowball grinned, plunging his spade into the soil and pausing to mop his brow.

A smile blossomed over Lily's face at the change in the vagrant. Since his involvement in the feeding station, founded in the darkest days of the Blitz, he was a man as transformed as Stratford itself. Somehow, he had found purity of purpose in volunteering to help prepare hot soup, tea and sandwiches for those battling through endless nights of bombings. No more shuffling among the rotten cabbages in the market, he had a use for his hands and a place to go each day where people needed him. The gap between Snowball and the residents of Stratford had closed as so many had found themselves in the same predicament as he: homeless! The bombs had proved to be a great leveller in more ways than one.

After eight relentless months of bombings, they had gone ten weeks now without a bad raid in Stratford and were breathing an exhausted sigh of relief. Hitler had shifted his attentions elsewhere, to invading the Soviet Union, and cautious optimism prevailed. Since that fateful 'Black Saturday' as the start of the Blitz had come to be known, there had been no invasion. No surrender. No negotiation. Just a dogged British will to survive. Hitler might have razed their homes and streets, but he had not succeeded in crushing their spirits. And in Snowball's case, he was now positively thriving. The government had put the call out for civilians to become more self-sufficient and start digging their own allotments to help feed families now that rationing was biting. It had taken off in East London in a big way and now every square inch of green, every windowsill, school playground, park and railway siding was being cultivated and turned over to food production. Where old houses had been blasted away, allotments of all shapes and sizes had been hastily constructed, the greenery incongruous amongst the rubble.

But Lily doubted that any garden held as much poignancy as the Shoot's.

In long rows, where once the perimeter railings stood, root vegetables with stately names like Home Guard potatoes had been sown, along with other so-called 'vegetables of national importance' like beetroot, carrots and cabbages, flanked by fat blackcurrant and gooseberry bushes, which come the hard winter months would hopefully bear food for the hungry families of the Shoot. Scraps of white silk fluttered from the bushes to ward off the birds – though Lily wondered where on earth he'd managed to lay his hands on silk . . .

'The pillowcase Miss Esther made me,' Snowball explained when he saw her looking. 'Thought the fruit bushes needed 'em more than me.' Lily laughed out loud. Only the Shoot could have bird deterrents made from an enemy parachute. There was a wonderful irreverence to it.

Lily's eyes roamed the bucolic scene, both content and intrigued, for Snowball was nothing if not resourceful. He'd scattered old eggshells in the soil to deter slugs, and glistening bands of copper round the herbs to stop the snails in their tracks.

'Is that a cup of beer in the ground?' she queried.

'Slops tray from the Two Puddings . . . slugs don't like it,' he explained, seeing her confused expression.

All at once, the sulphurous air closed around her.

'W-what are you planting over there?' she asked carefully, her eyes travelling to where Mrs Barnett was crouched in the furthest reaches of the graveyard, gently patting down the earth in quiet solitude.

Snowball saw where she was looking and his smile vanished, his mood suddenly as sombre as hers, for they both knew what lay beneath the soil at the back of the churchyard.

'It's going to be a garden, Miss Lily,' he replied thoughtfully. 'A memorial garden, with sweet peas, lavender and roses. I-I hope your mum approves.' He looked up at her worriedly, his rheumy eyes scanning hers.

'It's a smashing idea, Snowball,' Lily enthused, sliding her arm around his shoulder. 'I think she'll be very touched.'

Their thoughts travelled to that chaotic morning, only eleven months ago, when the police had tried to dig up the ground there. They had come looking for evidence, but the Shoot had served them up people's justice, alongside decent working-class values of solidarity. No one knew for sure how many foetuses there still were folded in the shadows, how many shameful secrets buried deep beneath the soil. Only her mother knew that, Lily supposed, and she was a keeper of every woman's secret. It didn't really matter, though. What mattered was that women should never be forced to suffer and make such impossible choices, nor be treated like criminals for seeking control over their bodies and lives. For women like Mrs Barnett, that time was a long way off, but until then it seemed fitting that fresh green shoots and sweet-smelling flowers should grow from a place of such darkness and despair.

With time and care, the memorial garden would grow into a magical green oasis, nestled in the industrial heart of East London. No one could ever guess at what lay beneath the lavender and rose bushes. But it was more than flowers and shrubs, it was a chance to make sense of their pain and mark their private losses.

Lily experienced a ripple of sympathy towards Mrs Barnett for the first time. For hadn't they both lost a child? Granted, Frankie was still walking this earth, but he would never be a son to Lily. She saw that now. Since Julia's revelation about Frankie in the hospital, Lily had thought of little else. There was no denying that the pain of giving up a child – her unique son – would never leave her. The loss was almost a physical part of who she was now.

The simple fact was, she could never be the mother that Frankie deserved. He needed security, stability and continuity. Distancing herself from him was the only way that made sense, at least for now. She thought of the many letters she had written to Frankie, love letters really, born out of a silly fantasy that she could escape to a society where being his mother was possible. But this was real life, not Hollywood. After they had left the hospital, Lily had given the letters to her mum, entrusting her with the decision over whether to reveal the truth to Frankie, if she felt the time was right. But for now, Frankie had enough on his plate making sense of this baffling life, without one more bewildering truth to comprehend. One thing at least was simple. Lily's love for that beautiful boy. His happiness and peace of mind, not hers, were all that mattered.

'Them unmarked graves matter, don't they?' Snowball's tentative voice cut into her thoughts.

She smiled gently and nodded. 'I believe so.'

Her mother's voice drifted through her mind. *Down the Shoot, everyone is somebody. We all count.*

Looking now at Snowball and the new life he was breathing into the Shoot, Lily suddenly understood with perfect clarity. Lily looked up past the taped-up windows, up further still, over the jumble of bomb-shattered chimneystacks to the slither of blue sky beyond. When she'd first arrived back in Stratford, nearly two years ago, forced to confront her past, the Shoot had felt oppressive, claustrophobic even. Today, the view of the sky was still narrow, but crucially *she* had a broader view of the world, thanks to her mum and Julia. She had returned an outsider, but she was leaving a cockney, and despite the distance, she knew now her roots would always be firmly planted in East London soil. She belonged.

'You better be going, miss,' Snowball grinned, reaching for his spade. 'It's your last day, ain't it, and you don't want to be late.'

Somewhere in the distance, she heard Yardley's steam hooter sound over the rooftops.

'Oh blimey, is that the time?' she gabbled. 'The bosses'll have my guts for a laundry line.'

'You sounded just like Miss Renee then,' Snowball chuckled.

Lily stilled. 'Did I?' she breathed. 'Did I really sound like her?'

'Oh, I didn't mean to offend, Miss Lily . . .' Snowball replied hastily.

On impulse, Lily reached down and planted a kiss on the old man's cheek, leaving behind a scarlet cupid's bow.

'You didn't, Snowball,' Lily replied. 'In fact, it's the biggest compliment you could've paid me.'

'Oh, that's a relief,' he replied, his apprehension melting to pleasure. In the last ten years, he'd only been kissed twice. Once from Renee and now her big sister.

'Snowball, one last thing before I go. Could you do me a great favour?'

'Anything, Miss Lily,' he said, puffing out his chest.

'I've asked my mum, Esther and all the girls to write to me with memories of Renee, the silly things she said, the way she used to strut about the place like she owned it, so I can remember her, *really* remember her as she was, not as I found her. She had too much spirit and gumption to be thought of as a victim. Would you maybe write to me too? Renee was so fond of you.'

Snowball's smile softened, the dirt of the soil creased deep into the fissures of his face.

'It would be an honour, Miss Lily. I've so many happy memories of Renee, she was quite a girl! I'll send them across the sea to you.'

At such kind words, a tear broke and slid down Lily's cheek.

'Gosh, across the sea, sounds so far away, doesn't it?'

'I've been on longer sea voyages,' Snowball shrugged, revealing a tantalising glimpse of his past. ''Sides, you'll always belong in the Shoot.'

'Yes,' she replied. 'I think you're right. I never really believed that, until now.'

Snowball watched as young Miss Lily Gunn turned on her heel and ran down Cat's Alley, with what looked to be a spring in her step for the first time in a long time.

Esther

As it was Lily's last day at Yardley's, the girls in the lipstick room had done their best to give her a surprise send-off party despite their meagre rations.

By six p.m., Esther, along with Fat Lou, Betty, Joanie, Joycie, little Irene, Mavis and Miss Rayson had decorated the canteen with homemade bunting, and Yardley's chef had even managed to pool enough rations to bake a fruit cake and scones. Arguably there was little in the way of actual fruit in the cake and the scones had a wafer-thin scraping of marge, no butter or jam, but no one cared. They were alive and not much else mattered.

No one in East London would forget the Blitz, for it had irrevocably altered not just the streetscape, but each of them in ways no one could have predicted.

Esther gazed round the canteen. For herself and the girls, had come a strength they never knew existed as they saved the factory from ruin night after night. For Walter, acceptance. For Mrs Barnett, who had gathered round the buffet table with her mother and the rest of their neighbours from the Shoot, the Blitz had brought freedom from a personal hell, and for Nell, understanding.

Setting aside the exhaustion, there was an enormous collective sense of pride in their individual responses to the onslaught. Only shamed Nan had emerged with little dignity. No one had laid eyes on her since she had hared off into the night after being exposed as the lipstick thief. Miss Rayson had visited her mother in East Ham, only to discover Nan had joined the WAAF and been posted to Portsmouth for training. Fat Lou and the girls had been all for going down there and causing trouble for her with her new bosses, but Miss Rayson had cautioned against it and Esther agreed. Nan was a troubled soul. As long as she lived, Esther would never forget the bile and rage on Nan's face when she had tried to attack the German pilot. Jimmy's twisted betrayal had cast long shadows in Nan's soul. Pursuing her would only stir up a hornet's nest, Esther was sure of it. Besides which, Miss Rayson reckoned she wouldn't dare show her face at Yardley again.

But the girls were all united in one thing – their grief over the loss of Renee. There was a huge hole in their hearts over the senseless waste of Yardley's brightest spark and her unborn child. After twelve days of digging, the authorities had finally ordered that the crater be sprinkled with quicklime and concreted over, entombing generations of families forever.

Seven Gunns, distant relations possibly, six Lees, six Glitzes and so many, many more. Seventeen families from one street alone, Martindale Road. Two babies no more than five days old. All dead. Pulled out and buried or concreted over.

What hope?

For many in the tight-knit community of Canning Town, the horrific memory would never be so neatly covered over.

But they had to look forward, and stoically keep putting one foot in front of the other with as much endurance and resilience as they could muster, for what other way would they win the war?

'Ssh, she's coming,' whispered Betty, poking her head out of the canteen door.

Fat Lou put her fingers in her mouth and issued such an ear-splitting whistle, everyone fell silent.

Miss Rayson had entered into the subterfuge and lured Lily into her office on the pretence of a meeting. Now she opened the canteen door.

Blind Eric hit the ivories and a gale of song filled the room.

'For she's a jolly good fellow . . .'

'You swines!' Lily screamed, clutching her heart. 'You told me you couldn't come for a drink, as you were mopping the floor,' she laughed, pointing at Esther, Fat Lou and the girls.

'What can I say, we lied!' Esther shrugged with an impish grin.

Then they descended, and in time-honoured Yardley's fashion, covered her tunic with bows and bright paper flowers. Even her elegant chignon contained in a crocheted snood was woven through with bright little ribbons.

'I don't expect they'll do this in New York, will they, Lily?' remarked Miss Rayson with a small smile.

'Gracious no, I shouldn't think so,' Lily chuckled.

A silence fell as Mr Lavender tapped the side of his glass with a spoon.

'I shan't take up too much of the celebration,' he said, 'though personally I don't feel like losing such a valuable member of the Yardley family to our American cousins is much to celebrate . . . I'm jesting of course, Miss Gunn goes with our blessing and we wish her luck as she steps into this bold new world. She has displayed remarkable bravery, as has every single one of you. Yardley is making an important contribution to the nation's needs at a vital time now we are producing components for aircraft alongside cosmetics.' He paused.

'I feel I should make special mention of one particular girl who, though not born and raised on these streets, is a part of the lifeblood of this firm. Esther Orwell will you please step forward.'

Esther's eyes widened and she shook her head.

'Oh no . . . this is Lily's . . .'

'Oh, stop being so modest,' Lily laughed, dragging her over to where the Managing Director was standing with Miss Rayson.

'I once made the mistake of trying to reward this young lady with a gift, I shan't make that mistake again, but I can't let her selflessness go unmentioned.'

He turned to her, visibly moved.

'Miss Orwell. I thought I knew all there was to know about business. I was wrong. You once said to me: "There is joy to be derived from knowing you are making an important contribution to the lives of others."

'I see now that in order to function, all firms have a duty to give back. Thank you for teaching me that. With that in mind, we are setting up a bursary, to help get a young woman into employment at Yardley's, one seeking safety from the war and the ravages of the Third Reich.'

Esther nodded as she looked up at the older man.

'We'll need to discuss the details further and get your input into how we best go about achieving this, but in the first instance, we would like to call this the Esther Orwell Bursary. What do you think?'

He gazed at Esther expectantly.

'I think that's a wonderful idea, sir,' she replied thoughtfully, 'and I have many ideas how we can go about helping vulnerable young girls, but I must insist on one thing . . .'

'Which is?'

'That we change the name to the Renee Gunn Bursary.'

An expectant hush fell over the room as Esther looked to Nell.

'If her mother has no objections, of course.'

Nell shook her head.

'You see, sir, to me, Renee's life personified real courage. She always fought for the underdog, so it would be fitting, don't you think, to give a girl the opportunity and the chances not afforded to Renee? She was the bravest and kindest girl there ever was.'

For a brief moment, Esther panicked. Had she over-reached herself, insulted the bosses and Renee's memory, but then Mr Lavender drew himself up.

'A remarkable idea. A toast to Lily and her sister, the namesake of our new bursary.'

After the chinking of glasses and applause had died down, Esther and Lily joined their mothers by the buffet table.

'So much wisdom for one so young,' Nell remarked, taking Esther's hand in hers. 'Thank you, darlin'. I'm so touched. Renee's name will live on because of you.'

Esther shrugged, glowing under the older matriarch's praise.

'You're so welcome, Auntie. I think we were all a bit in love with Renee.'

For a moment they all seemed lost in their memories of Renee, and was it Esther's imagination, or did a whisper of lavender drift through the canteen?

'So this move,' said Nell, turning to Lily. 'Are you sure this is what you really want, love? America's a bloomin' long way from East London.'

Lily sighed.

'I know, Mum, and trust me, I've thought of nothing else since Olive asked me to be her right-hand woman, but working as a beauty representative at the new Yardley salon on Fifth Avenue, well, it's something I've dreamt of for years. I can't turn my back on an opportunity such as this, but I promise you, Mum, this time I'm not running away.'

'Of course you must go,' urged Julia.

'But I do worry about you, Mum,' Lily went on. 'I hate to leave you on your own.'

Nell and Frankie had only returned to the Shoot recently. Nell had been champing at the bit to get home and as soon as there had been a break in the bombs, she'd hightailed it out of Surrey and back to her beloved Shoot. In Nell's absence, Julia had been working her socks off at the Shoot's feeding station and the small trestle table of sandwiches at the outbreak of the Blitz had now developed into a communal cost-price restaurant in the church with hot soups and stews, staffed by herself and Snowball. Hope, it seemed, lay not with the authorities, but in practical everyday responses dreamt up by resourceful neighbourhoods. Esther suspected Nell Gunn was itching to get involved.

'What you worried about me for?' she exclaimed, 'I can look after meself, can't I?'

'You know what I mean,' Lily laughed. 'Anyway, you needn't worry about money, every penny I make I'm going to send back to you and Frankie.'

Nell sighed and touched Lily's cheek. 'I don't want your money, love. None of it will bring back the ones we love, will it?'

Pat might have been a tough man, with little understanding towards the boy he had been forced to father, but it didn't mean that Nell didn't mourn him alongside Renee or love him any the less.

'Life goes on, it has to. 'Sides, I got that one to keep on the straight and narrow, ain't I?'

She nodded to where Frankie was sitting next to Blind Eric at the piano, tracing his fingers over the keys, wearing his usual grave expression as Eric taught him to play.

'And another thing, I ain't alone, am I?' Nell remarked, touching the gold cross on a chain, which was now back at her throat. 'Julia and Esther are moving into your old room and Julia'll be teaching me how to cope with Frankie, you know, how to bring out the best of him. She's even got him enrolled in some art club ain'cha, Julia.'

'That's right,' Julia replied, 'he's joined the East London Group. They meet regularly at the Bethnal Green Men's Institute and I think Frankie might well be their youngest member. They're really gaining a reputation for producing some remarkable realist paintings, so Frankie's talents can finally start to be nurtured.'

Lily looked at Julia admiringly.

'Thank you for what you're doing for him. Perhaps if you do take Frankie to meet this Hans Asperger one day in Vienna, you might make it as far as New York so you can both visit me?'

'I think you can count on it,' Julia smiled.

Lily smiled back and for the first time since she had met her, Esther realised she looked unburdened somehow. It must be a relief to Lily to know she and her mum were moving in. Frankie needed a strong collective of women around him who understood his special needs. Physically he had made a full recovery, but who knew what trauma he was hiding, from surviving such a gruesome tragedy? At least he had the right women around him to rebuild his life and help him to make sense of it.

'We'll look after him, Lily, I promise,' Esther vowed, squeezing her hand. She knew accepting this job offer hadn't been an easy decision for her friend and one she had wrestled with. She also knew Lily's love for Frankie was at the heart of everything she did.

'I suppose we're just one more unconventional wartime family, ain't we?' shrugged Nell.

'Talking of families,' said Walter, sidling up to the group looking hot and flustered.

Fumbling in his pocket, the stain of red spread further up his chest as he pulled out a velvet-covered box.

'Walter . . . what . . . ?' Esther began as he sunk to one knee.

'Please, Esther, let me explain . . .'

A hush fell over the canteen at the sight of a man on his knee. Walter nodded at Blind Eric and he began to play a familiar tune. Johann Strauss's *Blue Danube* waltz filled the canteen. Esther laughed out loud. Clear as day, she saw her father in her mind's eye, sitting at his piano, filling up her life with music and love. Gone, but never forgotten.

'I used to think of myself as a bit of a nobody,' Walter said, his voice trembling as he gazed up at her. 'Then I met you, Esther, and for some reason you seem to care about me the way I do you, which makes me just about the most fortunate man this side of the Stink House Bridge. Would you do me the very great honour of being my wife?'

Esther grinned down at him, as the intoxicating scent of lavender filled her nostrils, dizzying her senses, so much so that she swore she saw red petals drifting past the window.

'Get off your knees, you silly goose,' she laughed, hauling him to his feet. 'Of course I will!'

She kissed him and the entire factory broke out into a deafening chorus of whistles and applause. Esther and Walter were painting on their brightest faces and getting on with the business of living. Despite everything, life in East London's biggest beauty factory was continuing.

Churchill was right. Beauty was a duty, but so too was love. Outside, one of Stratford's famous seven airs gusted gently along the Cut.

AUTHOR'S NOTE:

Secrets of the Yardley Girls

'Come along and meet Eileen,' I said to Ann. 'You never know, you may have worked together.' It was a long shot, but when I found two ex-Yardley workers from Stratford, East London, to interview as research for this book, I thought I'd take a punt and interview them together.

You see, research is so much more fun when you can actually *meet* with people who inhabited the world you're writing about. Archives are all well and good, but what about speaking to the women who lived through the war and listening to their first-hand memories? What of the colour, the vibrancy and the voices that bring a place to life?

I'm passionate about documenting the lives of working-class women born into poverty, but also steeped in rich and vibrant communities; women from whose social histories we can learn so much. Women such as these leave no paper trail, so it's important to shine a light on the richness and complexity of their lives.

Women like Ann Roper, 86, and Eileen McKay, 90, who both worked at the famous Yardley factory along Carpenters Road in 'Stinky Stratford', along with over one thousand other young women.

'I don't mind,' shrugged Ann, as she parked her shopping

trolley next to the table in the café in Morrison's in Stratford. 'I'm an East Ender, I'll chat with anyone.'

In walks ebullient Eileen, ninety years old but with sparkling brown eyes and soft skin that make her look a good decade younger.

'It's you, isn't it?' gasped Ann.

'Oh, my days!' exclaimed Eileen, instinctively reaching across the Formica tabletop and clutching Ann's outstretched hands.

Turns out, not only did they work together, they were close pals who both worked on the same conveyor belt packing Yardley's famous creams. They'd lost touch after Ann left the factory to get married in 1950 and hadn't seen each other for sixty-eight years, until now.

Stranger still, *both* of them had brought the same photograph by sheer coincidence of the two of them aged fifteen and eighteen, two ravishingly beautiful, spirited young girls, enjoying a moment of fun on a tea break, larking about with Eileen's arm slung round Ann's neck.

We had a Davina McCall *Long Lost* moment, as tears of nostalgia filled their eyes and the years melted away.

'You look just the same,' marvelled Eileen, shaking her head. 'I always thought about you.'

Our interview quickly turned into a lively reminiscing session, with a couple on the next table coming over to say that they couldn't help overhearing and how touched they were to see Ann and Eileen's reunion. We even recreated the photo they took as carefree young girls taking a break from the conveyor belt. The hair might be a little greyer, but look at those faces! Still oozing spirit and mischief!

Eileen and Ann were two cogs in an enormous production machine. During the Second World War, Churchill declared that 'beauty was a duty' and Britain's oldest cosmetics firm, Yardley, rose to the challenge, rivalling the big American companies like Max Factor. A memo from the Ministry of Supply pointed out that make-up was as important to women as tobacco was to men. Women who wore red lipstick went from being regarded as risqué to patriotic.

A Limitation of Supplies Order cut production of perfume and soap but, paradoxically, production of those goods that were permitted meant sales of lipstick, creams and powders increased by many hundred per cent overnight. And because men and older single women were drafted into the war effort, it meant the factory was entirely staffed by older men and younger girls . . . girls who found themselves catapulted into a dangerous – and in some cases, thrilling – new life.

By the time this book was set, in the 1940s, the House of Yardley was already an established brand, famous for its lavender water, soaps, talcum powders and complexion creams, sold in Bond Street and all the best department stores. The factory was somewhat less glamorous. Situated downwind of the West End, in an East London backwater known as 'Stink Bomb Alley', it was a huge employer of local women, who were known locally as the Lavender Girls. Their fragrant name masked the unsavoury reality of work in the canal-side factory, sandwiched between a paint firm, a fishmeal factory (crawling with maggots in the gutter outside) and an abattoir.

'Do you remember the smell?' laughed Ann.

'Cor, not many,' Eileen laughed. 'There were seven different types of air down Carpenters Road, depending on whether the factory was distilling lavender, or boiling up animal bones for the soap. We always smelt lovely, though.'

The rivalry among surrounding firms was as potent as the atmosphere.

Within a half-mile of each other in Stinky Stratford there was the Oxo factory, Clarnico's sweet factory (which sadly was badly bombed as I described in the chapters on the Blitz), Spratt's the dog food firm, Berk Spencer Acids and, on the other side of the bridge in Bow, the Bryant & May match girls. When the clocking-off hooter blasted over the canal – or as it was known to many, 'the Cut' – the doors to all the factories flew open and out came a stream of apron-

and turban-clad factory girls. But it was Yardley who came to define the industrial heritage of Stratford.

'All the girls wanted a job at Yardley's,' Ann confides.

This was because Yardley had the best staff welfare around, perhaps only rivalled by East End sugar manufacturer Tate & Lyle in neighbouring Silvertown, offering good wages, bonuses and perks a-plenty. As well as a monthly sale in the canteen, where the girls could get their favourite Yardley lipstick or perfume at cost price, they had an annual black-tie dinner dance at Stratford Town Hall, a beano to Margate in the obligatory 'Kiss me Quick' hat, and the Yardley Social and Sports club, which allowed girls to compete in netball, hockey, whist drives and swimming. Or for those not sports-inclined, you could try out for the Yardley Follies dance troupe, where the girls performed at the legendary Theatre Royal in Stratford.

'They even performed in the chorus behind a young Cliff Richard,' a lady called Kathleen who worked on the brillian-tine belt revealed.

On their 180th anniversary in 1950, Yardley took all their staff to the Grosvenor House hotel in the West End of London for a posh dinner and dancing. 'I'll never forget it,' a lady called Rene from the powder room said. 'I wore a green cocktail dress and I felt like a film star.'

The family firm took a paternalist approach to staff welfare, encouraging the girls to save by helping to set them up with savings accounts. If you had the sniffles or the 'curse', you were ushered in to see the welfare officer for a gargle or a lie-down with a hot-water bottle. For more serious afflictions, Yardley's sent their girls to a convalescent home in Bexhill by the Sussex coast for a fortnight's paid leave. Yardley's even paid for all workers to have an annual chest X-ray, with a machine that was wheeled into the factory.

As an extra incentive, girls in the various departments got

the chance to win the shield for best housekeeping and most productive/tidy belt. The lucky winners would be sent to the deliciously named Bond Street Beauty School for a makeover.

'For all the good it did me,' joked Kathleen. 'Soon as I got home looking all lovely, me mum said: "Go and wash that muck off yer face!"'

With such perks, it was little wonder Yardley's was a coveted job and people didn't leave until they married. For those that chose not to become a Mrs, they could look forward to joining the Yardley '20' club, where two decades of service would be rewarded with an engraved gold watch. That said, I suspect it would be hard to remain single. Yardley's was known locally as the 'Marriage Bureau'.

A glance through the Yardley News in 1954 reveals in one month alone, Alfie Pedgrift from dispatch married Rose Callow from soap, Walter Scales in the wages department got spliced to Betty Cardew in the powder department, and Arthur Rogers in dispatch made an honest woman of the fragrant Millicent from perfumery.

As well as being all done up like a decorated wedding car, the newlyweds would get a chit from local department store Boardman's so they could stock up on tea sets and linen, as well as a copy of *The Art of Homemaking*.

With so many young women crammed into one place, it was inevitable that booze and boys would play a prominent role.

'Oh, we used to talk about boys all the time,' chuckled Barbara, who worked in the powder room from 1962–68. 'There was a fella who used to come in to service the machines. He had an unfortunate tic and used to blow raspberries. Being young, we thought this was hilarious and used to fall about. Another lad used to wheel in barrels of goods and we'd call out: "Nice bum!" We were shameless.'

Carol in box-making, who also worked there in the 1960s, confesses to a couple of cheeky gins on a Friday dinnertime.

'We'd all leg it back, terrified of being late. We had some larks. Used to get some of the blokes who worked there in the empty barrels and roll 'em around the firm.'

'We talked about sex mainly,' states Joan, who worked on a belt gluing boxes in the 1960s. 'I was the youngest, so I got well-educated. I'll never forget one morning tea break on Christmas Eve. We're sitting round drinking our tea and wondering why it tasted so funny. Someone had put a load of whisky in the tea urn! We were slaughtered and it was only ten a.m. There was no more work to be done after that!'

Molly, who worked in the soap room as a fourteen-year-old, trimming lavender soap by hand with a knife, insists she only went to Yardley because she liked nice smells.

'I used to take my letters in there; they smelt gorgeous so when I sent a letter it was all perfumed. I worked there with me mum and my sister. Used to thumb a lift home on the lorries as the buses were full of factory girls. You can imagine the laughs we had.'

Bosses turned a blind eye to the high jinks, provided the work got done. What golden days for British industry! This fair family firm really did care about their employees and, as such, was held in high regard locally, with people believing it belonged to the area and its people. John Lewis, eat your heart out.

'They really did look after us like family. I used to earn twenty-five shillings, given to me every Friday in a brown paper packet. It would go straight to my mum, who'd give me back five,' says Ann.

Eileen agreed. 'We felt proud to work there and be a Yardley girl. Such smashing-looking girls worked there too. We all used to walk down Carpenters Road at clocking-off time, and all the boys from the surrounding firms would shout: "Aye aye! Up the Yardley Girls!" trying to carry our bags and wolf-whistling.

'We were a tight-knit community at Yardley's, all the girls were friendly and looked after one another, supported one another through life's trials. Say if someone's mum died, we'd all rally round.

'We shared everything, because we were all in the same boat, you see. We were all poor. I remember growing up in Bethnal Green, by the mouldy cabbage leaves in the markets.

'I remember saying to my dad: "Daddy, can I have a dress like Shirley Temple?" He replied: "But Tin-Ribs (his nickname for me), we haven't got Shirley Temple money." But we were lucky because at least we were never in debt and could answer our door, unlike some who were too scared to in case the tallyman was knocking. I went to work to help my mum and I was proud to.

'When I married my husband, Ernest, nicknamed Curly, in 1958, my supervisor, a woman called Ivy Lack tried to talk me out of leaving. "What do you want to get married for?" she asked.

'But I was a young woman who was in love. They did me proud when I left. Gifting me a beautiful pink-and-gold dressing-table stool, which I still have, as well as a set of silver cutlery. I'll never forget my Yardley days and the enormous camaraderie. It's funny looking back. We had no money, but we had everything of true value. Family. Love. Laughter.'

Like so many other firms, in 1966 Yardley moved out of East London to the burgeoning suburbs of Essex to a new modern factory. And so ended a way of life in Stratford.

Today, Yardley, Stink Bomb Alley and Angel Lane Market are sadly long gone, buried beneath the sprawling Olympic Park and a landslide of gentrification. What times. What joy. What women! We shall never see their like again. I only hope my fictional characters do justice to the real-life Yardley girls.

I decide it's time to take my leave of Ann and Eileen, allow them to continue their reunion in peace. But just as I'm leaving, a man walks past our table, bashing into the back of Eileen's chair. He walks off without so much as an apology or a backwards glance.

'What you have to understand, Kate,' says Eileen despairingly, 'when you're eighty you're invisible, when you're ninety you might as well be dead. People don't see you. History's going out the back door.'

Eileen's right. That's why readers like *you* are so important. It's your interest in books like this that keeps the past alive.

Up the Yardley Girls!

With thanks to Eileen, Ann, John, Irene and Barbara, whom I interviewed, and Eastside Community Heritage for allowing me to listen to their oral history interviews with former Yardley workers for the *Only a Yard to Yardley* project.

https://www.hidden-histories.org

Wartime Tips from Britain's Beauty Bibles

As the Yardley girls experienced, make-up and cosmetics became extremely scarce during the Second World War, but there was no end of thrifty advice on offer from women's magazines and even from the government in a booklet, *101 Ways to Save Money in Wartime*. I spent many a happy hour reading through back copies of magazines like *Woman & Beauty*, *Vogue* and *Good Housekeeping* to bring you the best of the bunch. If you try any, please let me know how you get on. I think they'd work just as well in 2019 as they did in 1939!

Your hands are what you make them. Neglect them now and you may well be war-marked for ever. After any dirty job, massage with cold cream or any grease, before washing.

Vogue, 1943

For dry skin, add rose water to half a cup of bran and enough honey to make a cream. Substitute milk for rose water for wrinkled skin.

Woman & Beauty, 1943

To tone up tired skin, beat the white of fresh egg to a stiff froth, then add half a teaspoonful of fresh lemon juice. Apply to skin and neck for 20 minutes.

Groom your eyebrows nightly with castor oil for soft, lustrous and thick eyebrows.

Home Notes, 1942

If you're short of cleansing cream, use a teaspoonful of liquid starch in water, a cupful of chamomile tea, or a spoonful of the water in which rice has boiled.

Vogue, 1943

If you're stuck for rouge (blusher) why not use your lipstick? It does the job.

Home Companion, January 1943

For a stimulating bath, mix bath salts, or sea salts from the chemist, or simply add ordinary mustard to give a tingle to your skin. Get out and give yourself a sponge down as cold as you can take it, and a brisk rub all over with a rough towel.

Woman & Beauty, November 1939

To stop a shiny face, use an astringent liberally in the morning (witch hazel will do) splashing it all over your face.

Woman, October 1941

A little intelligent attention every day to hair, face, feet, figure; combined, of course, with a few obvious health rules that include daily bathing, a fair quota of exercise, fresh air, sound sleep, and a well-balanced diet. Letting up now will let you down later; a woman past caring, may soon find herself past repairing.

Vogue, 1941

Before using a new pack of cotton wool, unroll it and place it in front of the fire (not too near). The heat will cause it to swell to twice the size and it will last longer.

Carrot juice is excellent for the complexion and helps to correct any tendency to corpulence, while cucumber juice is one of the finest slimming cures.

. . . powdered bicarbonate of soda is a reasonably effective deodorant.

101 Ways to Save Money in Wartime

You can easily shampoo and set your hair yourself should you find yourself marooned miles from a hairdresser. Opinions vary as to how often you should wash your hair, but every ten days for greasy heads, every three weeks for dry ones, seems to be a fair average.

Vogue, 1941

Let's do some vigorous massage. Slap your cheeks with alternate hands, giving your cheeks a gentle upwards push at the end of each slap. Put the bottom of each palm under each eyebrow bone and push upwards to lift the flesh which forms furrows between the eyes. Tap the skin under your eyes with butterfly lightness . . .

Mother, May 1944

If you put cleansing cream or tonic onto dry cotton wool, half of it soaks into the wool and is lost. You can make one bottle last practically as long as two by remembering to wring your pad of cotton wool out in cold water before applying the tonic.

Woman & Beauty, 1943

Brace up. There may be a slump in our world affairs but there must be no slump in our personal appearance. Poise is a lovely thing, lift your head and straighten your shoulders, and everything seems different. Worries cannot lie on a straight back. They fall off.

Woman's Journal, 1943

Hair gets shorter. Legs go barer and browner ... Cherish your make-up, it's a last desperately defended luxury.

Vogue, 1941

The 1940s Look by Mike Brown (Sabrestorm Publishing 2006) is bursting with fascinating information on the fashion, hairstyles and make-up of the Second World War.

Sources and Further Reading

For more information on Dunkirk, I read the excellent *Dunkirk: The History Behind the Major Motion Picture*, by Joshua Levine (Harper Collins, 2017). I also interviewed remarkable 100-year-old Dunkirk veteran Dennis Brock.

To help understand the concept of shelter drawings and visualise what Frankie would have seen and drawn in those underground shelters, I read *London's War: The Shelter Drawings of Henry Moore*, by Julian Andrews (Lund Humphries, 2002).

For the Blitz and the disaster at South Hallsville Primary School in Canning Town, I read the following:

The Blitz: The British Under Attack, Juliet Gardiner (HarperPress, 2010) – this contains a very vivid and moving passage on the bomb that hit the school.

The Secret History of the Blitz, Joshua Levine, in partnership with the Imperial War Museum (Simon & Schuster UK, 2015)

Living Through the Blitz, Tom Harrisson (Penguin Books, 1978)

London's East End Survivors: Voices of the Blitz Generation, Andrew Bissell (Centenar, 2010)

The Lesson of London, Ritchie Calder (Searchlight book No.3, Secker & Warburg), held at the British Library

Noonday, Pat Barker (Penguin 2015)

An East End Farewell, Yvette Venables. Simon & Schuster (2015)

But it was interviewing Blitz survivor Stan Moore that really opened my eyes to the horror of Britain's biggest wartime civilian tragedy.

I visited three excellent and free archives:

For more information on Yardley's and the war in Stratford, I visited Newham Archives and Local Studies Library in Stratford, who hold a collection of back copies of the beautiful old *Yardley News* as well as back copies of the *Stratford Express*, all of which were invaluable and authentic sources on wartime life in Stratford and the Carpenters Road factory.

I also read *The House of Yardley 1770–1953* by E. Wynne Thomas, Sylvan Press; (1953).

For more information on the war in East London, I visited Tower Hamlets Local History Library & Archives.

For more information on beauty and fashion in wartime, I paid a visit to the treasure trove that is the archives of the Fashion Museum in Bath and spent many a happy hour browsing through back copies of *Vogue, Woman's Journal* and *Woman & Beauty.*

For further information on fashion and beauty in wartime, I read:

Fashion on the Ration, Julie Summers (Profile Books in partnership with the Imperial War Museum, 2015)

Style Me Vintage, 1940s, Liz Tregenza (Pavilion, 2015)

The 1940s Look: Recreating the Fashions, Hairstyles and Make-up of the Second World War, Mike Brown (Sabrestorm Publishing, 2006)

And finally, *Neurotribes. The Legacy of Autism and How to Think Smarter about People Who Think Differently* by Steve Silberman (Allen & Unwin, 2015) This book is astonishing. To parents, or anyone affected by autism, I thoroughly recommend it.

A note to readers: Hans Asperger was a pioneer in the field of child psychiatry and paediatrics, particularly for his contribution to the understanding of autism. However, in 2018 a study was released by a medical historian which states that Asperger was an active participant in the Nazi regime, assisting in the Third Reich's so called 'Euthanasia Program'. This has provoked debate within the autistic community. The National Autistic Society address his problematic history on their website and say, "we are listening closely to the response to this news so we can continue to make sure the language we use to describe autism reflects the preferences of autistic people and their families". For more information, please visit: www.autism.org.uk

Acknowledgements

Huge thanks to Karen Cullen, Head of Marketing for Yardley of London for allowing me to delve through the cupboards of their archives in Windsor, which I was delighted to see groaning with the most beautiful old Yardley perfume and make-up bottles and pots. The evocative smell of Yardley's English Lavender these empty bottles still contained after more than fifty years did more to transport me to the Carpenters Road factory than any time machine could have. Reading *The House of Yardley 1770–1953* certainly helped too, though.

Enormous thanks to Judith Garfield, MBE, Director of Eastside Community Heritage, who is a passionate supporter of collecting and preserving the people's history of the East London. I am indebted to you for allowing me to listen to all the powerful oral histories you and your colleagues have collected for your project – Only a Yard to Yardley. It was listening to these vivid stories (held at the University of East London), which piqued my interest for setting a novel at Yardley.

To the original Yardley Lavender Girls – Barbara, Joan, Linda, Irene, Eileen and Ann. What a joy for me and my research assistant, Sarah Richards, to have met you all and heard about what it was like to work at Yardley's in the glory days. Your joy and pride at working in the Carpenters Road factory was infectious and helped me to understand the place this factory held – and continues to hold – in all your hearts.

To John Moore – the original Bricky Kid – thanks for showing me round your manor and where you bunked into the Gaff!

To Stan Moore, for sharing his memories of growing up in Canning Town and witnessing the aftermath of the bomb that hit South Hallsville School. It was a pleasure to meet you.

To my pal Trisha from Stepney, whose mother was the inspiration for Nell Gunn's character, you're a legend.

To dear Henry Glanz, I thank you for sharing your remarkable life story with me. Henry was on the last Kindertransport evacuation – which brought ten thousand Jewish children out of Hitler's Germany to Britain when war began – when he was fifteen, leaving behind his parents and brother, who died in the camps of Occupied Europe. Esther's character is very much inspired by Henry and his extraordinary bravery, and the story of how she faced down the German pilot is based on a true story that Henry told me. I feel so blessed to have met you, Henry.

To my dear writer pals, Dani Atkins, Sasha Wagstaff, Faith Bleasdale, Fiona Ford and Jean Fullerton. What a very dull world it would be had I not met you all.

To two of the most passionate, driven and dynamic women in the business, my agent Kate Burke and editor Kimberley Atkins, who are both just superb at what they do. Thank you for your support and guidance always.

Huge thanks to my sidekick Sarah Richards for helping transcribe interviews and generally making my life easier with such effortless skill and ease.

Book bloggers, where would we be without you, so many brilliant bloggers out there, but Beverley Ann Hopper and

Kaisha Holloway stand out for their total devotion and passion to reading and promoting authors. Thank you, ladies!

And saving the best to last, my dear and very inspiring readers, who offer me such wholehearted support, in the form of letters, emails, treasured family stories and drawings (thank you Sue and Val in particular). What a difference it makes to know you are out there reading this.

Please do get in touch. I'd love to hear from you.
www.katethompsonmedia.co.uk
www.facebook.com/KateThompsonAuthor/
@katethompson380
katharinethompson82@gmail.com
Instagram: @kate.thompson1974

Secrets of the Lavender Girls

Coming 2020

Nell Gunn, Snowball and Esther will be back, along with more characters from Britain's biggest beauty factory, as they battle the twists and turns of war in Stratford. Will Nell find lasting love? Will Snowball reveal what forced him onto the streets? And will Esther be able to tame the wild child she takes under her wing as part of her new bursary? As flowers and vegetables blossom in the Shoot's new Dig for Victory allotment, can the inhabitants really bury their pasts?